Frances Frederica Montrésor

At the Cross-Roads

Second Edition

Frances Frederica Montrésor

At the Cross-Roads
Second Edition

ISBN/EAN: 9783744730372

Printed in Europe, USA, Canada, Australia, Japan

Cover: Foto ©Andreas Hilbeck / pixelio.de

More available books at **www.hansebooks.com**

AT THE
CROSS-ROADS

BY

F. F. MONTRÉSOR

AUTHOR OF

"INTO THE HIGHWAYS AND HEDGES," "FALSE COIN OR TRUE,"
"THE ONE WHO LOOKED ON," "WORTH WHILE"

SECOND EDITION

LONDON

HUTCHINSON & CO

34, PATERNOSTER ROW

1898

TO

"D A I S Y"

PREFACE.

I HAVE called this story "At the Cross-Roads," because in it I have tried to describe how first the man, and afterwards the woman, stood where two ways met, where each was bound to make that choice which is "Life's business."

They are (at least so it seems to me) everlastingly together and yet everlastingly alone. Together, because it is impossible for either to choose good without blessing, or evil without cursing, the other; alone, because choice is of necessity individual and lonely, and because we cannot take our neighbour's place, even though we may pay "shame for shame" and "sin for sin" and "love for love."

F. F .M.

CONTENTS

Part I

CHAPTER I

Contents

Part II

Part III

Part I.

she moved and made the tea, and even the way in which she ate, reminded the man of the adoration of his youth. How he had worshipped this girl six years ago! But one can't put Time's clock back. There was the prison life, and all it had taken away of youth and hope between them. There was an ugly fact besides, which he never cared to think about over much.

He watched her with a curious, regretful look in his eyes, but she met his glance with one that was overflowing with love pure and simple.

Gillian had often been accounted hard, and she was certainly far from perfect in her relations to her own family; yet where Jack Cardew was concerned, I think that she knew how to give good measure, without stint, and running over. She was at her best to-night, and she was happy.

To be loving and giving is the natural prerogative of all Mother Eve's daughters, I suppose, whether they be Friday's bairns or Saturday's. They are stinted of their birthright sometimes, poor souls, and Gillian at any rate had had arid seasons in her life; seasons which had left deep traces on her. There was, however, this difference between the man and the woman. He, who by natural temperament had been the more impulsive of the two, now remembered the past, and thought about the future; but she, who had been noted for practical wisdom, who in the old days he had laughingly called "worldly-wise," flung all care from her, and revelled in this hour that brought him to her, drinking deep, deep of joy, to the forgetting of all else.

She waited on him with an evident delight that was purely womanly. She noted several things while she did so. The roughness of his hands, for example, of which the nails were broken; the way in which sun and wind had tanned his face and neck, and even his hair (his hair had once been golden red, but it was duller than heretofore, and it had become white on the temples); also the rareness of his smile, and the curiously watchful expression of his eyes—eyes that had been so frank and often merry, but that had somehow acquired the look of one who lives amongst enemies.

The changes she noticed sent momentary stabs of sympathy and pain through Gillian, but she was not critical where Jack was concerned, though on every one else her judgments were shrewd and swift. One must hold at arm's length in order to criticise—Gillian generally held people so—but *he* lay at her heart of hearts, too close for judgment.

Presently the bell rang again, and Gillian, going to the door, admitted a tall, thin old man, who followed her into the room awkwardly, and sat down opposite to Jack Cardew without speaking. His big, ugly mouth worked nervously, and he crossed and uncrossed his legs and drew his thick eyebrows together, looking earnestly the while at Gillian's visitor. He had been very fond of Cardew years ago; he had obstinately believed in him, even in despite of judge and jury, but he was of an unready tongue; moreover, he could not recognise the boy he had liked so well, in this rough stranger.

Jack made no remark, but waited rather defiantly for whatever greeting Mr. Molyneux might choose to bestow on him. He had not, he told himself, expected any welcome from Gillian's relatives. He was certainly not going to make advances.

Jack had had a charming filial manner to the old man—once.

"I am glad that you are a free man again," said Mr. Molyneux slowly, and held out his hand.

Jack nodded curtly. He did not accept the overture, and his watchful blue eyes rested on his quondam friend with a scrutiny that the next moment changed to amusement. "Are you, sir? Well, that's almost more than I expected," said he.

Mr. Molyneux contorted his face and crossed his legs

afresh, but before he was ready to speak Gillian took up the word.

" Uncle Stephen has been good to me during all these years that you have been away."

Her voice was a contralto, and very soft and full in tone. Jack laid down his knife and fork when she spoke. It was strange to hear those familiar tones again.

" He is the only one among my relatives who has stood by me," she remarked. " But I think that my step-father would have forgiven me for going my own way if only I had proved incapable. He can't quite swallow this small amount of success ! It's such a bad moral, you see."

Jack glanced round the room while she spoke. Its shabbiness was partly hidden by the flowers and the firelight, but it struck him that the success must have been only comparative.

" Do you mean to say that you are quite on your own hook, and that Mr. Clovis allows you nothing ?" he asked.

" Oh, he behaved very well," said Gillian, " though naturally he thought that I was mad. He hoped that I should be starved into a right way of thinking ; and if I had come home, he would, I am sure, have killed the fatted calf at a moment's notice. He was quite prepared to play the good father to my prodigal."

" Why did not you let him do so ? "

Gillian coloured. " There are occasionally reasons for preferring husks," said she. " But I have no complaint against Mr. Cloves."

" And your mother ? " said the man.

" Mammy has just put my little step-brother into velveteen knickerbockers. He is much prettier than I was at seven years old, and I think that he more than makes up for my shortcomings," said Gillian.

She smiled, but there was a touch of unconscious sadness in her tone. The man remembered that Gillian's remarks had often been shrewd, but the sadness was new to him. No doubt she too had had a hard time of it.

His ideas as to what he meant to say to her were undergoing a transformation.

The two men were silent for a space. Mr. Molyneux had come to countenance his niece, but he did not think it necessary to talk. Jack had fallen into a habit of appearing stolidly impassive.

He had broadened since Gillian had last seen him; she was sure that he must measure a good deal more across the chest. She felt half inclined to laugh at the way in which he sat composedly eating, while her uncle was so much more evidently touched by this reunion.

She alone chattered, feeling all the while that it would take very little to make her cry.

Gillian had a good deal of self-command as a rule, and was rather by way of despising emotional women; but, as she remarked, "It isn't every day that one's dream of six years comes true."

Jack Cardew pushed away his plate when she said that, and got up suddenly, and came round to where she was sitting, and put his hand on her shoulder.

"Gillian, how soon will you marry me?"

Gillian looked up at him, at the face that time and sorrow and bitterness had written strange things on. For a moment a mist swam before her eyes.

"Just as soon as ever you like," she said simply. "We have waited long enough, Jack."

Mr. Molyneux rose from his seat with a sigh. His long lean figure, his good, ugly face, were not without dignity, in spite of his grotesque awkwardness.

"I hope that you are worth it, lad," he said.

"You're sanguine if you hope as much as that," said the man. "No fellow in this world is worth what Gillian has given. Six years! Good Lord, six years!"

not worth while—I suppose, though, that I must have been
rather off my head when I tried to escape." He paused,
and glanced sharply at her. "You heard about that
unlucky attempt?"

"I heard. Of course I knew that you were not to
blame."

"The warder died. I lengthened my sentence by two
years, as you know. It was rather a heavy price to pay
for three minutes' enjoyment. I got a cut over the eye—
the scar is there now—and luckily that finished me for the
time. I did not know any more till I woke in the infirmary
ward again, and heard the doctor say I was dying. I did
not want to die then. It was queer, for I was quite willing
to before; I shouldn't have shirked it fighting, but somehow
I could not bear to slip out of the world through that
d——d infirmary bed—not even though three years of
hell was before me if I lived. Well, I told you that my
youthful pluck, such as it was, had been knocked out of
me; but I got a second wind after that illness, and that
lasted. I gave up the Eternal Justice, and that sort of
fable, and I had no more hopes of a reprieve, but I learnt
a few dodges which made things rub less, and I—oh, well,
I worked through, and came out of it sane and well, as
you see. After all, I am only thirty-one now, and I may
live long enough to have a pretty good time of it yet.
There is nothing like starvation for giving one an appetite."

Gillian looked straight at him, with an infinity of pity and
understanding in her eyes. She, too, had been a-hungered
though not quite in the sense he meant. She, too, knew
what it was to grow bitter with a hope deferred.

"Oh yes, I know," she murmured.

"No, my dear, I hope you don't," said he, with an odd,
unexpected touch of gentleness.

"After I got my release I worked my way out to
South Africa."

"Oh, Jack! But that was very obstinate of you, when I sent you the money for the passage."

"It was wonderfully good of *you*, Gillian," he said gratefully. "I was awfully surprised. I could not have spent your present on first-class accommodation! I really couldn't. I kept it, and it brought me luck. Yet if I had taken in the fact that it was money that you had *earned*, I——"

"Well, dear?"

"I should have sent it back to you," he said, reddening. "The Lord knows I am not much to boast of, but I have not fallen so low as to be willing to eat up what a woman has slaved for."

"But it comforted me to work for you," she cried. "It was just the only comfort I had."

And that was true enough. The fruit of her labour had been given gladly. Yet no one save the One who knows all secrets, ay, even the secrets of women's hearts, guessed how much it had cost Gillian to speed Jack on his way. How she had longed to bid him come home to her *first!* and yet had understood, in spite of that weary longing, that it must be better for the man's self-respect that he should go, and rid himself of the prison taint, before he should come to claim her.

A more eager expression came into Cardew's face and he put his hand on Gillian's. "What I am now going to tell you is the most extraordinary part of the whole story, and if it had not happened I should not be here. Gill, I told you that your present brought me luck! I bought shares in a gold mine with it, and to begin with they were a good speculation, and within the year my capital was doubled."

"It was time that the luck changed," said Gillian; but she drew back a little, and a shadow came over her joy.

"The fellow who persuaded me to take the shares was

a rum sort of chap, but I've seen worse," said Jack. "I
went on an expedition up country with him. He had a
wife up in the mountains, a big negress, and he had
a whole swarm of children! Most of them were as black
as my boots, and some of them were brown, but one was
as fair as you are!"

"This *is* an extraordinary story!" Gill ejaculated
softly.

"The old chap was fond of the fair one—he was quite
silly over him, and so was the negress. When the child
got lost I thought both father and mother would go out of
their minds! I couldn't stand the row about it and so I—
I went to look for the little fellow."

"Did you find him?"

"I found his body," said Jack, frowning. "He must
have fallen into a stream at the back of the hut, and he
had been washed miles down between the mountains. I
carried him home as best I could. It wasn't easy, but
I knew that they would want to bury him. The stream
was quite shallow; I climbed up its bed. The water was
never above my waist. I was pretty sick though, before
I got through with the job! It was the toughest thing I've
done!"

"It was good of you," said Gillian. "Were they
grateful?"

"The mother *howled*. It was like a wild animal!" said
Jack. "And the father swore once—when he took it from
me—afterwards he didn't say anything. I'd not like to see
that again. It's queer that people should get set like that
on a child."

He relapsed into gloomy silence, forgetting the point
of the narrative till Gillian reminded him of it with a
question.

"You said 'the luck changed,' but this is not a cheerful
tale, is it, Jack?"

He laughed then. "Oh yes, it is, but I have left out the cheerful part. I was toiling up that stream with the poor little chap's body when—I hit upon diamonds. It was by the veriest chance! I wasn't hunting for them, I wasn't thinking of them; I couldn't believe in what I'd found. I just stuffed the specimens in my pocket to show Bransome (that's the name of the man I stayed with), but I forgot to show them, till I brought them out by chance one day. Bransome pounced on them with a yell! I think if I'd been any other chap I'd hardly have got out of that place alive, but he played the game squarely with me —and he told me what to do. He is my partner, and he manages the concern out there! It's a pretty big concern. As far as money goes I'm very rich."

"But if it had not happened you would not have come back," the woman repeated slowly.

She was a woman who liked what money can buy, but at that moment she thought only of that which can neither be bought nor sold.

"You would never have come back. And during all these years I have believed that you were sure to come!"

"I wouldn't have come to you poor," he said doggedly. "I was in two minds about it, as it was. I am a disgraced man, and poverty and disgrace together are too strong a couple of devils for any woman to tackle; but I— I did not forget you, Gillian."

Neither of them spoke for a minute. Gillian sat staring into the fire, with compressed lips. Jack Cardew remained stolidly quiescent. He felt that he cut a poor figure beside this woman, whose faith fairly startled him. Yet he knew that according to his lights he would have been right not to come near her again, had this wonderful fortune not befallen him.

"You see," he said awkwardly, "I used to be a gentleman, and there are some things a man (even if he has been a convict) can't drag a woman into."

Gillian turned round at that, and drew her hand gently away from his. "Jack, I think I understand," she said. "And I shall never blame you, but answer me this honestly. Do you *want* me to be your wife or not? If not, say so now, and go, for the sake of our—seven years of waiting."

She wore a little turquoise ring on her left hand, and she put the fingers of her right hand over it while she spoke.

"I am not going to boast about constancy," she said. "That's just a matter of temperament. I know that many women, who are infinitely better than I am, can love first one man, and then, if he dies or fails them, another. I know that I only care and only shall care about you. But that is because I am made in that way. I can't help it. I"—with a faint smile—"don't think I should have chosen such an inconvenient characteristic, if I had been allowed any say in the matter. But one thing I can choose, and I will. I hate getting on stilts, you know, but I must say this strongly. I would rather be dead, and I loathe the thought of death, than married to you if you don't love me. I could not stand it. You owe me nothing else, but you owe me so much honesty, Jack."

Then the defiant look on the man's face melted, and his manhood rose up. He caught her in his arms and pressed her close to him.

"Before God, I am not such a cur as to lie to you," he cried. "I had come here meaning to say you had better for your own sake give me up, because I am not the man I was, and you won't like me when you know me—I can't say it now, for I love you—I swear I love you, Gillian, I am not a quarter good enough now, but at least i love you."

"Then that is all I want," said Gillian.

CHAPTER II.

"*A PITY BEYOND ALL TELLING.*"

"A pity beyond all telling
Is hid in the heart of love."

W. B. YEATS.

IT is strange to realise in what different worlds the denizens of the same street live. The place, for example, where Gillian met her lover was lifted more than its actual five stories above the work-a-day life. It was hallowed for evermore for the woman who had welcomed love there. Gillian was almost sorry to bid it farewell; she thought whimsically of the old Bible story of Jacob, who set up a pillar in the place where he had wrestled and prevailed. Not that she had much conscious religion, or that her pillar would have borne any grateful inscription.

Gillian rather prided herself on being essentially of this world, though she had never scoffed at spirituality in others since she had counted Jane Ogland as her friend.

On the Sunday after Jack Cardew's return Lady Jane sat alone in her small, bare room, enjoying the luxury of solitude. She greatly liked to be alone, though in her busy life she reserved little time, as well as little of everything else, for herself.

It was six o'clock in the evening. Jane had lit her lamp, and now sat quite still in an old-fashioned wooden armchair, that was furnished with linen-covered cushions. Jane always rested on Sunday. "The Imitation of Christ," that book that appeals to so many souls of all sects, lay on her knee; she read it in the Latin edition, for the stateliness of the old language pleased her. Like her namesake of long ago she possessed scholarly tastes, though few people guessed as much.

Lady Jane was a very small woman, with delicate, finely cut features and pencilled eyebrows. She had been rather pretty when she was young, though some people had considered her too colourless; now that she was middle-aged her beautiful soul had had time to impress its character unmistakably on her face. She wore white cambric frills in her sleeves and round her throat. They relieved the extreme severity of her black gown. Her hair, which was flaxen in hue, and very fine and soft, was parted in the middle and brushed plainly on either side of her white forehead. Despite the extreme simplicity of her attire, and the scantiness of her furniture, there was a certain quality of dainty freshness about her person, and of distinction about her room. Lady Jane was a very dignified lady, and the singularly muddy places she had walked in from her early girlhood had apparently left no stain on her. Yet she had been very sad in her youth, and the peace that rested on her now had been bought with a heavy price.

A square table with carved legs was placed by her chair, and a bunch of violets in a cut glass stood on it. An old-fashioned chiffonnier, and a stool comprised the rest of her furniture. The walls were distempered blue. With the exception of the glass full of violets there were no ornaments in the room; yet it was a pleasant place, and one that sometimes suggested a reminiscence of some far-away French convent cell.

Jane read on quite undisturbed by all the noises in the street. At one period of her life, the sound of a crying child, or of a scolding woman, or of a drunken man, would have

2

so distressed her that she would have laid aside her silver-clasped book, and would have told herself anxiously that while these sad things happened *she* had no right to peace. But that phase was long over now. Her deep sympathy had found its vent, and was no longer morbid or restless.

Indeed, it was her restfulness that had first attracted Gillian Molyneux. "It's so extraordinary to meet a woman who is satisfied," that young woman once remarked. "Most people take to good works when other things fail them. They feel lonely and dull, and have to fill up their lives somehow, poor things, so they try to pretend that they have got what they want, or, at any rate, that they are doing good. I should hate them all if I were a poor person! But Lady Jane is different. She is as different as a piece of real sixteenth-century tapestry is to my mother's new 'antique embroidery.' I like Lady Jane."

Lady Jane had liked Gillian too, and had felt, at first sight, a strong instinctive tenderness that was almost pity, for the girl.

Mr. Molyneux was an old friend of Jane's, but Gillian had never seen her great-uncle before the day when she came to stay with him in London. She was then just one and twenty, and in the heyday of youth and prosperity.

Jane soon discovered that old Mr. Molyneux was rather overwhelmed by the very modern niece who was of so different a type to the women he had been acquainted with in his youth. The girl's freedom of speech and high spirits had startled him, while the punctilious politeness with which he had treated her had rather oppressed Gillian.

"I am not at all the sort of woman Uncle Stephen has been accustomed to," she had confided to Lady Jane. "He tries to be kind, you know, but I can feel that he doesn't approve me. I can't act up to being something between

a Madonna in a shrine and a Queen of Sheba on a visit!
I was not brought up on those lines. You see I've had
a very liberal education."

And Jane, who had also had a "very liberal education,"
and who, moreover, remembered having met Gillian's
mother before the fortunate advent of Mr. Clovis, had
suddenly understood Gillian, even better than Gillian
guessed.

She had rejoiced heartily when the engagement to Jack
Cardew was announced.

Jack Cardew was the lion of that season; he had made
a great literary hit, and Gillian, who liked lions to roar
softly at her pretty feet, had begun by being laughingly
amused by his preference, and had ended by (immensely
to her own surprise) falling in love with him. She had
fully intended to make a rich marriage; she was almost
comically discomforted at her own backsliding. It was
really a shock to her to find that her "worldliness" was
apparently only skin deep, but Jane, who had always
suspected her of hiding a heart, was gently triumphant.

"She has never had love enough to ripen in. It's the
best thing that could possibly happen to her," Jane
declared.

At fifteen Gillian had been distinctly original; at one
and twenty she was fascinating, though there were always
diverse opinions as to her claim to beauty. Her eyes were
curiously two-coloured, red-brown near the pupil, and
almost blue-grey near the outer edge of the iris; they
often laughed when her lips were grave.

Gillian attracted more attention than many a prettier
girl during the season that preceded her engagement. She
was a very amusing and wonderfully self-possessed young
woman, and she was sometimes accused of being an arrant
flirt. Flirtation, however, implies at least a touch of sentiment, and her warmest admirers seldom ventured so far

as a lowered voice or tender glance; for her sense of humour was keen, and her amusement disconcerting. Her abounding health and vitality showed itself in every movement. It was a pleasure to see her dance or run or play cricket; she never tired, and was never out of temper.

Gillian's complexion in those days was not pink and white like her mother's, but sun-kissed and clear like a boy's; her bright rippling hair was the only beauty she had inherited from Mrs. Clovis, whose refined and delicate features were far more regular than the daughter's. Gillian's mouth was large, and her chin very round and full. The lower part of her face was perhaps too massive, though it showed character. Mrs. Clovis liked to dabble in soft emotions, while Gillian (till the day she met Jack) scoffed at, and shunned them; yet Gillian in reality was passionate, where her mother was sentimental.

The course of love had run pretty smoothly at first. Lady Jane had gone to see Gillian's trousseau (or at least such portions of it as were visible at the Métropole, where Mr. and Mrs. Clovis had taken rooms) and she had renewed acquaintaince with Gillian's mother. Lady Jane frequently took herself to task for the strong antipathies that none would have guessed lay beneath her gently composed manner. In spite of her best endeavours she disliked Mrs. Clovis.

Jane had worked a dainty set of handkerchiefs for the bride, rising earlier than usual to embroider delicate flowing G's. She delighted in giving, and Gillian had been very pleased.

Then, most unexpectedly, the crash had come. One fine morning, when the wedding day was supposed to be drawing quite near, Jane heard that Jack Cardew, that promising genius, for whose writings publishers and editors contended, had lately sued the Planet Insurance Company, which had refused to pay the insurance money on the burnt MS. of a political novel.

Jane remembered, as if it were yesterday, how scornfully Gillian had laughed at the whole affair.

"What fools they must be!" the girl had cried. "Well, Jack will bring a second action for libel and get heavy damages, and that will be rather a blessing, for he is awfully in debt. I tell him *I* shall be both mercenary and revengeful enough to be pleased at that."

A faint uneasiness had touched Jane at the words, though she had been far from guessing what would be the result of the trial.

Gillian had been rather fond of declaring herself mercenary. Her mother was a woman who always expressed the most delicate and unworldly sentiments in the choicest language, but who, if given an inch, was apt, in the most lady-like manner possible, to take an ell. The girl suffered slightly from reaction. She inherited a love of luxury, but no one could accuse her of veiling her inclinations in fine words.

Cardew's story, to which he adhered steadily throughout the trial, was simple in the extreme. The novel had been very heavily insured. It was to be published serially in a leading magazine (beginning to run with the New Year) but it was not to come out in book form till the following autumn. He had (he said) taken up his manuscript in order to look through it. He had been interrupted by a friend, in whose company he had gone out of the house, leaving his novel on the writing-table, with a lighted candle beside it. He had left his door open. On his return he found that the candle had been blown over on to his papers, and the novel had been reduced to ashes. He consequently claimed the insurance money. The company refused to meet their policy on the ground that the loss was not accidental.

Cardew lost his case, and on leaving the court was arrested by the public prosecutor for attempting to obtain money under false pretences. All the evidence that had been given on the defendant's side in the previous trial was sifted again in the criminal court. It was shown that Cardew was heavily in debt. It was further shown that the story of the accident was untenable. The writing-table stood close to an open window, but the muslin curtains that shaded the window were unsinged. The sheets of paper had been piled about twelve inches high; it was impossible that they should have been so entirely consumed unless they had been wilfully destroyed. A paper almanac that stood on the table was uninjured, and the table-cloth had not so much as a hole in it.

The most curious feature in the whole business was that Cardew should have invented so lame a tale.

The girl who was housemaid at the time swore that no one had entered the house during Mr. Cardew's absence; there was no ground for supposing that the novel had been maliciously destroyed by any one but the author. There was one motive which might have actuated him. It was proved that he was in very pressing need of ready money. He was, at the time of the trial, engaged to be married to the step-daughter of a rich man. It was probable that he was anxious to realise enough to stave off an impending bill of sale on his furniture.

Lady Jane had not followed the course of the first trial with much attention, but she read the daily summaries of the second, in which Mr. Cardew was prisoner instead of plaintiff, with growing fear. She did not believe him guilty, but her heart ached for Gillian. How terrible all these disclosures must be to the girl to whom he was engaged! How awful it was that all a man's sins and extravagances should be dragged into such a piercing light, and sifted publicly! It was difficult to realise that publicity was but a small evil compared to that which was approaching.

Jack Cardew was found guilty and sentenced to four years' penal servitude. It was the maximum sentence, but as he grimly remarked, he was always unlucky.

He had done his best to release Gillian from her engagement, but Gillian had refused to be released. She had bidden him good-bye tearlessly, but with white lips.

"Do not waste time in talking nonsense, Jack," she had said. "You cannot break with me, because you are part of me. You'll find me waiting for you when you have lived through this. You must live through it, for my sake."

He had broken down when she touched him, but she had been determined not to cry.

"There will be time enough to be sorry—afterwards," she had said.

Jack was hotly in love with her at that time, yet it flashed across him that he had never known this woman before.

"Gill—I—I have done such idiotic things—I thought when you heard all they said at the trial (and lots of it was true) that you would hate me," he cried.

He had been boyish still, in spite of his twenty-four years. He had looked at her through unshed tears that he tried to wink away, that he was horribly ashamed of.

"But I am not a scoundrel, though they have proved me one," he added, with an attempt at a smile.

Gillian had laughed, with a short, scornful laugh that had startled them both. "Was it necessary to tell *me* that?" she had cried. Then a protecting tenderness shone in her eyes. Some day Jack's children would see that look. It brought the blood to his cheek, and he carried the memory of it away with him. "Was it necessary? Why, Jack, I love you!" And so they had parted.

It had surprised every one but Jane that Miss Molyneux had insisted on holding to her engagement to Mr. Cardew in spite of his conviction and of the opposition of her relatives. Gillian detested poverty, but a certain sturdy self-respect and sense of justice made it impossible to her to accept support from her step-father while she was strenuously resisting his authority.

She had that genuine faculty for business that so many French, and so few English women possess, she was enterprising and industrious, and she very quickly discovered her own worth.

"If you were not as a rule so uncommonly sensible, I should say you were stark, staring mad," her step-father had declared when Gillian had first announced her intentions of accepting a post as accountant to the "Co-operative Cooking and Housekeeping Association," which was then only just starting on its highly fashionable career. "Post? What should my step-daughter want with a post? A post means working her fingers to the bone for a mere pittance (and precious fortunate if she can get that) where a woman's concerned."

But Mr. Clovis had proved wrong. Gillian made a good deal more than a pittance, and though her carpet was threadbare, and her gloves were carefully mended, it by no means followed that her purse was empty. She had succeeded beyond expectation, and she had known how to take advantage of good fortune.

Indeed, Gillian usually got what she set her heart on, and did what she meant to do. One had only to look at her, to see that she possessed in herself some of the elements of success.

Lady Jane had felt deeply for the girl's loneliness when she had heard of the step Gillian had taken. She had even, in spite of an almost morbid horror of interfering, offered to find rooms for her friend under the roof that

sheltered herself. But Gillian had refused the offer, after
a moment's consideration.

"It would not do," she had said. "You see, Lady Jane,
you and I like each other rather, don't we? and you know
so much more about me than other people know. You
are too sorry for me. I could not live with so much
sympathy, it would unstring me. I can and I will get
through these years of waiting, but they will be hard, and
I can only get through them in my own way. I feel a
brute, but I can't help it. Dear Jane, I am very grateful,
but I must harden my heart and set my teeth—and you
would make me soft, and I could not bear it."

And since that day she had talked no more of Jack, and
had faced the hard days bravely, in her own way. And
behold now they were over! That fact had been conveyed
to Jane by a telegram on Saturday night; it was no
wonder that she was haunted by the thought of Gillian
even while she read her Thomas à Kempis.

Jane thought of the girl who had undertaken to work
and wait for a disgraced man; she thought of the woman
whose whole mind had apparently become absorbed in
business, and who had shown herself so uncommonly
capable of managing both men and money.

Jane had a large capacity for loving faith, but even she
had sometimes wondered if Gillian still cared at all for
anything unconnected with her work. Miss Molyneux had
been the making, and had become the manager, of the
company for "Baking other people's pies." She was
always immensely amusing on the subject of her experiences, and her anecdotes betrayed a shrewd and serviceable
knowledge of human nature. She was an apparently frank
companion, but there is no reserve so impassible as the
reserve that wears apparent frankness like an armour.

Jane was still meditating on these things when the
subject of her meditations came to see her.

Gillian greeted her very quietly, and made some trifling remark about the weather and the price of coals, unbuttoning her gloves the while with rather needless slowness and precision.

London had robbed her of her colour, and there was a little upright line between her eyebrows that told of care and responsibility. Yet to-day she looked younger and softer and altogether unlike her usual self. She glanced up suddenly.

"You know, don't you, Jane?" she said.

"Yes, I know that he has come back, and I am very glad," said Jane.

Gillian laid aside her hat and jacket, and sat down by the fire. "Sit down in your own chair, please. It rests me to look at you. Your room is like a Quakers' meeting. I feel as if it was a great deal better for me than going to church."

Jane complied and waited for further revelations. Presently Gillian laughed, with the tears standing in her eyes.

"Glad? And what do you think I must be?" she said. "Oh, Jane, I have no words fit to say in it. 'Very glad' sounds so inadequate. One is 'very glad' when one does a good stroke of business, or when one comes into an unexpected fortune (which, by the way, has happened to Jack). I was 'very glad' when he first made love to me, when I was a girl. But now—— Ah, when you have waited six years, and when every day of all that time you have felt so sore for him that you had to tell yourself not to think,— and when you have longed for him so that it was iike something fierce locked up in a secret place, and you knew you simply *dared* not unlock the longing, lest it should be too strong, dared not, except sometimes when every one else was asleep, why then——"

"Oh, my dear," said Jane softly, and laid her hand on Gillian's half shyly. At the touch Gillian suddenly put her head down on Jane's knee, and sobbed.

"I must cry," she said. "Oh, Jane, it does not in the least matter how silly I am now, does it? He has come back, he has come back. And sometimes I thought he would die first, but I never told myself I thought so, for fear that—oh, Jane, I want to hear some one say the words to me. Say it please! Say, 'Yes, he has really come back, and all the long years are over, and you have got your heart's desire.' I can hardly believe it, but if it was not true I should not be crying for joy in this absurd way, should I? Jane, say it to me."

"Jack Cardew has really come back. And all the long years are over, Gillian. And you have got your heart's desire," said Jane, in the gently decided accents that always carried conviction with them. Even her voice shook a little as she added, "And, thank God, it is quite true."

She was a little awestruck at this breakdown of Gillian's reserve. Presently Gillian lifted her head, and pressed her hands to her flushed cheeks.

"Dear saint!" she cried, smiling. "What funny things we poor mortals do when we get into your palace of truth! Truth is very demoralising. I was very wise not to come too often while Jack was away. But I can afford to be a fool to-day.

"I am glad of that," said Jane. "For I think it is high time that you should be a little foolish, my dear, and I am more thankful than I can well express that he has been brought back."

Gillian sat upright, and shook her head, the pucker between her brows deepening. "You are the only saint I love," she remarked. "And I don't feel good at all! Jack brought himself, and Providence has not been particularly kind to him. *I* have stuck to him because I am a woman, and could not help doing so, but I do not see that he has much to thank God for."

"It seems to me," said Jane tenderly, "that *you* are no small gift."

"I am like part of himself, and you do not say 'thank you' for part of yourself," said Gillian. Presently she added reflectively, "But we've changed sides, you know."

Jane waited expectantly. "You see," said Gillian, staring intently into the fire—"You see, Jack was rather up in the clouds when I first knew him. He was chock full of theories. He was a poet, and he had a great many illusions. Of course he had had a rough time of it before his book was taken, and yet I believe that I had really seen more of the mean side of life than he had. Jack was always getting into scrapes, because he was so extravagant, and so awfully sorry for 'any poor chap in a hole,' but I always knew that I was not half so good as he was (in spite of the scrapes). Why, I became ashamed of lots of things, after I knew him, that I had never thought twice about before! Mammy and I were so very poor before we met Mr. Clovis. Poverty is uncommonly bad for a girl's morals, I think! Well, Jack is *not* up in the clouds any longer, and I am sure that I don't wonder at that!" A fierce light came into Gillian's expressive eyes. "He has been abominably used," she declared. "Small blame to him if he is rather bitter, and if he wants to make up for the bad time. All you good people may be shocked at the change in him, but I am not, no, not in the least!"

"But you must not be bitter too," said Jane, "for, dear Gill, you are so fortunate. So few of us who want *much* get the thing we have passionately longed for."

Gillian drew Jane's face down to hers and kissed her. "Then I won't be bitter," she said, "and, indeed, on the whole I am not. The only person I bear malice against is the parson who did not believe in Jack, when he turned to him in his worst hour."

"It was a shame, but he did not know," said Jane. "I

sometimes think that when knowledge comes to us, that in itself will be both reward and punishment enough."

Gillian made a funny little grimace. "Enough for saints, perhaps! But I must say I hope that chaplain will be punished in a less purely spiritual manner! I may be wronging the poor dear gentleman, but I can't help a suspicion that he would feel a less refined retribution more! There, what a blessing it is that you can laugh."

Jane shook her head. She had never harboured a desire for revenge on any one, but some inexplicable affinity made her always quick to understand Gillian.

"But I have once or twice felt more inclined to cry, Gill," she said.

Gillian got up from the floor, and began to put on her hat. "Some day I shall give this room a looking-glass, for my own benefit. Did you hear me tell you that Jack has made a fortune? Or did you think that the fact was not worth your consideration? He struck on diamonds somewhere or other in South Africa. We shall be very rich."

"I am glad. You will not have to think so much about money then, and you will like having it very much, will you not?"

"Certainly, and other people will like it too, and we very much hope that some will have reason not to like it. Had Jack come back poor, we should have started for Australia, and I would have set to work to cook and wash and sew for him—that is, if he would have let me. Now I must set to work, after quite another fashion, to re-establish him in society. I shall like that even better than the other plan, for it requires especial talent, whereas any one can cook and sew."

Lady Jane's delicate cheek flushed. "I should imagine that those who hold that Mr. Cardew was wrongly sentenced will be proud to stand by him, and in your place I should welcome them gladly. The others you would surely not wish to meet."

Gillian looked at her with a twinkle of amusement. "Yes, that is how you would behave. You would hold your chin right up in the air, and you would not condescend to notice the unbelieving majority. You would only say quite gently, 'Poor creatures. They know no better!' Oh, I know you, my friend. You are much prouder than I am! But that is not the way to make the majority veer round. You don't care about having the world on your side, so long as you have Heaven, do you? *I* do. I have always a preference for the bird in hand."

"I am not in the least proud," said Lady Jane. "But there can be no doubt that the people who are likely to be influenced by the fact of Mr. Cardew's having money are people whose opinions are not worth our consideration."

"Individually they are not worth a snap," said Gillian. "But collectively they count. Public opinion does matter, to every man who is not mad or an enthusiast. Do you think I do not see how much it has embittered Jack to have it against him? He says he does not care. But he does."

She put her hands before her eyes, for a moment, with rather a weary gesture. She knew that with Jack's arms round her she could forget all else, but, alas! her arms, though she clung very close to him, could never shut out care.

"Men are not like us. They are so much more— sensible," she said. "Now, Jane, if we were poor, do you suppose that after what has happened there would be a chance for us in this country? You may say that there is not much chance now. But you wait and see." Her face dimpled with a mischievous smile. "You see if I don't make friends with the world, and the flesh, and the—— Oh, I beg your pardon, dear."

"Very well," said Jane, laughing in spite of herself. "But they are none of them worth it!"

CHAPTER III.

"THE LADY DOTH PROTEST."

"The lady doth protest too much, methinks."

"OAKLANDS PARK" was the name of the brand new "place" that Gillian's step-father had perched on the summit of a Devonshire hill.

Mr. Clovis had an ornate taste in architecture, and his bride had secretly shuddered when first introduced to the aggressive mansion, that was large without being dignified, and pretentious without being comfortable.

Oaklands Park possessed nine towers and a drawbridge; but its windows were of modern shape, and it was fitted throughout with electric light. In the fond eyes of its owner it combined all the beauties of an old castle with all the conveniences of a modern hotel. Mr. Clovis was nearly as proud of his house as he was of his wife—and that is saying a great deal.

Mr. Clovis had become acquainted with Mrs. Molyneux and her daughter when he was taking a holiday at Boulogne. The pretty and elegant widow, in her simple black dress, had seemed to him a singularly touching and pathetic figure.

Mrs. Molyneux was gentle, and he admired gentleness; she was fond of church-going, and easily distressed at the least approach to un-orthodoxy; the soap-boiler secretly had a deep reverence for piety in women.

Mrs. Molyneux was slight—far slighter than Gillian—and very fair, with small, regular features, and a marvellous

31,

and quite genuine complexion. When she and her daughter walked together people often exclaimed that it was impossible to believe that "that great girl" was the little widow's child. The great girl was always being bidden to "take care of her dear mother." Indeed, Gillian undertook the office of caretaker at a very early age, and the post was no sinecure, for Mrs. Molyneux was one of those people who require, and usually get, a good deal of attention.

Mr. Clovis was then a man of about fifty. He was short and square. He had rather protuberant eyes, and scanty grey whiskers. He wore a large diamond on his little finger, and a large pearl in his tie. He was extremely careful about his aspirates. He had been successful in business, and was a shrewd judge of character where men were concerned, but during the process of building up a fortune he had had little time to study women.

Mr. Clovis told Mrs. Molyneux all about Oaklands Park, which was then being built, and about a scheme for "improving" a little Devonshire fishing village into "quite a smart watering place." She, in return, confided to him the sad story of her poverty and her debts, of her devotion to her fatherless child, and of the hard struggle that her "perhaps foolish" pride of birth led her to hide from a rough world.

A delicate compliment was implied. Mr. Clovis, in spite of those too careful "h's," was not put on a level with the vulgar herd, for to him she revealed herself. He certainly proved worthy of the confidence. His final advice, for they had many consultations, was simple and practical. There was an easy way out of the monetary difficulties that so beset her. The rough world would be pretty considerably smoother in its manners when she was in a position to tip it freely. The fatherless child should get as good a father as she had lost (he felt that this was putting it modestly, for the late Mr. Molyneux had not, apparently, done well for wife and daughter); as for the unkind relatives-in-law, she might, if she so pleased, snap her fingers at them all, and start with a fresh set!

Mrs. Molyneux had bravely suppressed a shudder. She hardly looked forward with joy to her introduction to the Clovis family. "But for one's child one can do anything," she said to herself. When she did not quite come up to the high standard demanded by her "pride of birth" she generally assured her conscience that she sacrificed her feelings to Gillian's welfare. Some uncomfortable natures cannot let a lie pass, and must needs rub the gilt off the gingerbread before they will swallow it, but Gillian's mother was never one of those. "He will be another father to you, my precious," she had said to Gillian, who was then a sturdy girl of fourteen; but Gillian had shaken her head.

"One can't have *two* fathers, mammy," she remarked, "and I have not forgotten mine.

Mr. Clovis stayed to lunch the day after the engagement was announced. He took the bottom of the table, and Gillian stared frankly at him. Mr. Clovis had never had much to do with young girls, and was more abashed than she was. He became pompous when he was not at ease; he used very long words, and flourished his dinner-napkin. By the time the second course was served Mrs. Molyneux *almost* wished that she had not accepted him.

Then he grew a trifle bolder and made jokes, and Gill's eyes brightened. She always saw a joke, and she never giggled, but threw her head back and laughed outright, with a ringing peal of laughter that disconcerted her mother.

"My *dear* love!" Mrs. Molyneux murmured, in the soft voice that yet had a touch of acidity in it.

But Mr. Clovis smiled benignantly. He stretched out his be-ringed hand and patted Gillian's head. "We are going to be great friends, and I h-hope you will be h-happy in your new home, and like your new papa, my dear," he said.

"People can't have two papas, and I've had mine, you know," Gillian replied frankly. She was a young woman who could stick to her point. "But," she added after a moment's reflection, "I am very glad when you come to see us, it makes lunch so much more amusing, and then I am allowed to put cloves in the apple-pie."

Mrs. Molyneux looked nervous, for the worst of Gill was that she was occasionally possessed by a spirit of mischief, and at such moments there was no knowing what she would say.

"And how is that?" asked the would-be papa.

"I roll the pastry, for I have a lighter hand than mammy, and I like cooking ever so much better than lessons," explained Gill. "But mammy does not like cloves—in tarts, you know. She says that they taste too strong. *I* have got a vulgar taste. I like them very much. They make the apples more interesting, I think."

"I hope that Miss Gillian will continue to like Cloves," said the guest. He could never refrain from a pun.

"Oh yes," said Gillian, her face dimpling with laughter. "And, if you please, may I call you 'Mr. Cloves' when you marry mammy? It would be so much nicer than 'papa.' Papa would be such a silly name for you, and Mr. Cloves sounds quite right, and really means something, because——"

"My darling girl!" interpolated her mother warningly; but Gillian was determined to get out her sentence.

"Because you *are* like the cloves in the tart, you see. You are strong, and dark, and——"

"And I give a masculine flavour to the feast, eh?" he cried. He shouted with laughter. "Miss Gillian knows what's what. She likes the masculine flavour. She is a sensible little girl!"

"Then I need never call you 'papa,' or 'father'; and I may call you 'Mr. Cloves'?" said Gillian triumphantly And "Mr. Cloves" he was from that day.

The incident had been characteristic of Gillian, who was both good-tempered and self-willed. She took up her own position, but she met the inevitable step-father pleasantly. Indeed, she did more than that; she helped to make his home bright, for she had a light hand for other things than pastry. She had positive genius for keeping house in the broadest sense of the term. She loved to make every one thoroughly comfortable; she also loved to be thoroughly comfortable herself.

"Mr. Cloves," for his part, had been a kind step-father to her, and her distinct appreciation of all the luxuries he gave her amused and pleased him.

Mrs. Clovis had been Mrs. Clovis six years when a son and heir was born. In the spring following Gillian became engaged, and in the succeeding autumn she left home.

It was against all her principles to be the cause of daily jars. "I had rather be bad, or mad, or both together, than a bone of contention," she had declared. "You can't help railing at Jack and I can't help standing up for him, so I had better go."

Mr. Clovis had comforted his wife somewhat grimly. Miss Gillian would stick to her convict just as long as her funds held out, he opined; she would be glad enough to return to the lap of luxury when poverty began to pinch.

But seven years had passed, and Gillian had not returned.

During that time her mother had heard pretty constantly from her, and had even, on one occasion, visited her in London. There was no vulgar quarrel between them.

"I miss my dear love constantly," Mrs. Clovis often averred. "But I do not think it is the mother's part to stand in the way of her daughter's best happiness. If my darling girl feels that she has a vocation, why should I withhold her from a wider sphere of usefulness ? "

It was inferred that the vocation lay in the direction of "Co-operative Housekeeping," and Jack Cardew was never mentioned. Mrs. Clovis had a way of ignoring inconvenient facts, and "Gillian's convict" was decidedly inconvenient. Mrs. Clovis preferred not to think about him—for more reasons than one.

The mistress of the house lay on her sofa, with a letter from her daughter open on her lap. The sofa was heaped with cushions and drawn up to the fire, for she loved warmth and softness.

The big drawing-room that the soap-boiler had never (by his unaided efforts) managed to make home-like, was very cosy and cheerful now. The coldness of the state apartment had thawed under feminine influence.

The hard, gilded chairs, and the alabaster figures, that Mr. Clovis had admired, but never felt at ease with, had been gently banished one by one. The symmetrically arranged poets, that had once rested in calf-bound glory on an inlaid table, had given way to magazines and novels from Mudie's. Bits of needlework lay about. A big basket of toys stood in the bay-window. Mrs. Clovis herself gave the finishing touch to the air of refined comfort that pervaded the room.

Her fair hair was still untouched by time, and there were only a few fine lines about the corners of her mouth and eyes. Her fur-trimmed tea-gown suited her slim figure. Mr. Clovis liked to see her attired in soft clinging raiment, and she liked his admiration.

Gillian's father had had an unpleasant habit of turning everything inside out, and examining the wrong side, but Mr. Clovis took the angelic qualities of his wife for granted, and she was aware that her lines had fallen in pleasant places.

Nevertheless there was an anxious expression on her pretty face to-day.

"MY DEAR MOTHER" (wrote Gillian), "Jack has come home at last. You and I have not spoken of him of late years, for it seemed that there was no use in repeating the same arguments over and over again, but you know that I have always (since the day that we were engaged) considered myself bound to him. I have never, for a moment, wished to be free, and, as I explained when I left home, I made myself independent of my step-father's bounty solely in order that I might marry Jack whenever he should come to claim me. We were married yesterday at St. Clement's. Uncle Stephen and Lady Jane were present.

"Jack has come back rich, which of course will make everything easier. I knew that it would be impossible, after all that has been said against Jack, for you or Mr. Clovis to approve my marriage, but I have hopes, now that the thing is done, that you will let me come to see you both. I do not think that Mr. Clovis will abuse my husband to my face.

"We are going to Paris, but shall be in England again in a fortnight's time. Then we shall take rooms at the White Hart, and I shall walk in one day and pay you a morning call.

"I know that Mr. Clovis will be angry, but I don't think that he will set the dogs at me. Tell him so from me, please.

"Your affectionate daughter,
"GILLIAN CARDEW.

"I believe in my husband with all my heart, and with my brains as well! I am absolutely convinced that the world will come round to him yet."

Mrs. Clovis read the letter for the third time, and sighed

so heavily that her husband, entering the room at that moment, asked what was the matter. She stretched out her hand to him without rising.

"Dear George," she said, "I am terribly shocked and distressed about my poor unhappy child."

"What? Miss Gill?" he asked cheerfully. "Come now, don't you worry over that young woman. She is precious well able to look after herself! I heard only yesterday that that Co-operative business of hers is doing remarkably well. More than she deserves, I say!" He spoke with some chagrin.

"I do not imagine that she is thinking much about the business at present, George."

Mr. Clovis's face brightened; he sat down by his wife's sofa, and patted her hand kindly.

"I suppose then that she wants to return to the paternal roof? I am glad of it. She's got tired of slaving for idle women who can't manage their own households, or roast their own legs of mutton, eh? Well, well, I always told her she would sicken of it! And mind you, I don't forget I promised to be a father to the girl. I sha'n't be hard on her, my dear. Let her come home. The only condition I make is that we have no more of the convict business."

"But he is in England again," said Mrs. Clovis faintly. "And—oh, George, it is too terrible—she—she—has married him."

Mr. Clovis bounced out of his chair with an oath. His face grew quite red with indignation and distress. "The scoundrel!" he cried.

Mrs. Clovis put her handkerchief to her eyes. "It has been a fearful shock to me," she repeated. "To think that my own girl should have shown so little confidence in me! It has hurt my deepest feelings."

Mr. Clovis was excitedly walking up and down the room.

"Married! Is it actually done? Give me the letter, Eva." He caught it out of her hand. His prominent eyes started with eagerness while he read it. Mrs. Clovis sobbed softly. She was aggrieved at the way in which he took the news. He hardly realised her trouble sufficiently. "Dear George" was sometimes wanting in delicate perception.

"A mother's heart yearns over her lost child. I know that my darling girl has no thought of the pain she gives me. Gillian can never even understand——"

"Yes, she has evidently been and gone and done it," interrupted Mr. Clovis. "Too late to interfere now! The fat's in the fire, and no mistake! I would have given a hundred pounds to have stopped this, I would indeed."

His voice sounded quite husky with emotion.

"Poor girl! poor girl! Married to that d——d blackguard. We ought never to have let her go away. But that was my fault! Why did I not keep a still tongue in my head? She could not bear to hear her thief rated at! But that was natural enough. 'I believe in my husband with all my heart, and with my brains as well.' The deuce she does! Poor thing, poor thing! No, I sha'n't set the dogs on her. What would be the use of that? But I'd like to duck the convict in the pond, and give him a roll in the pig-stye after, if I could get the chance. 'Pon my word I would!"

Mrs. Clovis shivered. Her husband was terribly unrefined.

"Gillian says that he is very rich," she said presently. "That of course can make no difference to the way in which I regard the matter, but the world has a respect for wealth."

"Respect? Of course it has! And a precious ass it would be if it had not," said Mr. Clovis explosively. "But it don't follow that it has no sense of decency. Why, Cardew has been convicted of fraud, he is *worse* than a common thief. That pill will want a good deal of gilding if people are to swallow it. I don't think somehow that Miss Gillian will ever get 'em to take it down. In spite of his riches—which we've only his word for—I should think it would make most honest folk ——"

"Don't talk in that way, dearest, if you please," cried Mrs. Clovis, a trifle fretfully. "I can hardly bear to think of it."

Mr. Clovis pulled himself up, and looked at the fair woman on the sofa with compunction and tenderness. He was often called vulgar, and his wife's large circle of acquaintance wondered how she could have married him ; he sometimes wondered at it himself.

"She is your daughter, my dear," he said, with a gentleness that was not without dignity. "And I was fond of Miss Gill, for her own sake too. Tell her that she may come when she likes. To my thinking she's been a great fool, but she ain't the only woman that has been taken in by a rogue, and it ain't for me to shut the door on your girl. But I won't have her convict here, and that's flat. I am sorry for Gillian, I am sorrier than I can say about it, and I don't feel as if I had done my duty by her, but I won't have Jack Cardew contaminate *your* drawing-room ! "

Mrs. Clovis flushed nervously, and put a white diamond be-ringed hand on her husband's arm.

"Dearest George, I know how much you think of poor me," she said gently, "but I feel that I ought to say that I am sure you make a mistake, and that Jack Cardew never committed a fraud in his life."

"Pooh !" said her husband, frowning. "What do you know about it ? " Sure ? Why, how can you possibly be sure ? Did you steal up to town on a broomstick, missus, and fly

down Mr. Jack's chimney and burn his precious book for
him, while I thought you were asleep by my side?" He
laughed himself into good humour again. "That was it, no
doubt," said he.

Gill's humour was not inherited from her mother: Mrs.
Clovis wept instead of smiling.

"I could never have done such a wicked thing as to
destroy his manuscript," she cried seriously. "But please
remember, George, that I have always, always told you
that he was innocent."

There was an anxious eagerness about this asseveration
that might have seemed ridiculous to some men, but Mr.
Clovis was always tender to his wife's ways.

"Lord bless you! The convict ain't worth your crying
about, my dear!" he said with cheerful common sense.
"You are a deal too soft-hearted—though that is the right
fault for women, after all—and there ain't no use in your
taking on so."

He patted her delicate fingers with the palm of his
broad brown hand. "You are too good," he repeated.

"No, no," she protested. "I am not so good as all that.
But I have told you that I know he was innocent. I—I
have done all I could do. I—I could not do any more."

"Why, of course not," said Mr. Clovis soothingly.

Eva was very foolish at times, but he liked her
foolishness.

CHAPTER IV.

"WHITHER THOU GOEST, I WILL GO."

"Whither thou goest, I will go ; and where thou lodgest, I will lodge : thy people shall be my people, and thy God my God."

GILLIAN had been married in the last week in February.

It was in April that the newly married couple returned to Devonshire. The day after her arrival was soft and balmy, the warm touch of spring was already in the air.

Jack and Gillian walked through the lanes that smelt of wet moss and rich mould. There were primroses in the banks, and the branches above their heads were covered with ruddy buds and with tiny curly leaves, creased still from their tight packing. The sun had had no time to kiss the deeper colour into these wee baby things, they were as yet more silver grey than green and full of the tender freshness of infancy.

Gillian Cardew stretched up her arms, and broke off the crisp, juicy twigs while she walked. In her face was the joy of living, but not the unconscious joy of early youth. She knew that she was happy, she was tasting every moment.

"The sap is rising everywhere. I think that it we were to hold our breath, and keep silent, we might *hear* the stir of life and growth," she said. "Oh, Jack, why did I never know before that spring was so wonderful, so very wonderful ? "

"It promises well," said he. "But one never can tell what the year will be. All those poor little beggars that have been in such a hurry to come out will get nipped by a hard frost, as likely as not, or"—with a glance at her bunch of sprigs—"they will be broken off by a cruel fate before they have had time to unfold."

"Oh, that won't matter in the least, if they help to make your room bright!" said Gillian.

She smiled while she spoke, but the jesting words held truth. To bring brightness into his life was indeed what she was trying to do, and it was probable that she would not stick at a trifle, with that end before her.

Gillian had a warm heart—for one person—and her love was too absolute to be ashamed.

Her companion drew a long breath, and looked at her with the odd, wondering look that always made Gill laugh with a lump in her throat. Nothing, not even the finding of the gold, had astounded Jack so much as the unlimited welcome he had received from this woman; but he could not rid himself of the impression that he was in a fool's paradise. The iron had so entered into his soul that it was hard for him to trust in happiness.

Presently they came to a gap in the hedge, and a stile, on which they sat, Gillian at the top and Jack on the step. The stile led into a field, and a red bullock was munching hard by. Gillian, who loved all four-footed creatures, tried to coax him to come nearer still, but he only stared at her, with the wise, soft eyes whose placidity had never been troubled by the loves and hates of poor humanity, and returned comfortably to his meal. Beyond the field was a copse of firs, and through their dark branches one could catch a glimpse of blue sea.

Gillian rested her ungloved hand on Jack's shoulder, and began to sing softly for pure pleasure in the fresh sweetness of the country :—

> "In Scarlet towne, where I was born,
>   There was a fair maid dwelling
> Made every youth cry, 'Well-a-daye!'
>   Her name was Barbara Allen.
>
> "All in the merry month of May,
>   When green buds they were swelling,
> Young Jemmy Grove on his death-bed lay
>   For love of Barbara Allen."

Her voice was a full and very sweet contralto. Jack was struck by its richness.

"Why do you stop?" he said, when she paused at the end of the second verse.

"I like the singing of the birds better," she said. "There is nothing sad in their chirruping, but a woman's voice is bound to have a pathetic tone in it."

"Yours has," he said.

He reflected silently for a time. Gill gave him plenty of food for reflection.

"Look here," he began presently, "we've made no plans yet. Where do you want to live, and what do you want to do? You shall always do just whatever you like, Gill."

"Am I to have my own way *always*?" she laughed. "What an excellent and much-to-be-applauded arrangement! But"—with a merry glance at him—"I don't quite believe in it." Her eyes rested on the mouth that fell into rather sullen lines when he was silent, on the blue eyes that encountered the world somewhat defiantly. "You don't look as if you were a very yielding character, do you know!

"I should be an ungrateful brute if I did not give you all that is in my power," he said. "That means all that I can buy, my dear. There are some little trifles, such as a good name, that can't be bought for love or money."

"I am not so sure of that," said she. "Well, Jack, I should like a house in Park Lane."

"Good! we'll have it. But"—with some surprise—"I should have thought you had had enough of London!"

"Enough? We've not begun the siege. I want a country house as well, with plenty of room in it. We will ask the world to shoot (you are a good shot, are you not?), and the world's wife shall come too, and act in amateur charades."

Jack frowned. "I don't think that you understand, in spite of all my explanations, that men won't want to shoot with me—that is, the respectable sort won't. As for the other kind—well, I am not such a blackguard as to let you know the other kind."

"You just see whether they'll come or no! But we must whistle the right tune. I am thinking what it had better be." She rounded her lips to a whistle, and began piping scraps of tunes, some merry, some mournful Presently she broke off short.

"Philanthropy, in a new form, will really be the safest card to play. The new form must be sure to hit the public taste, though. The scheme shall have something to do with children. How would it do to start free play-rooms all over London? The children might trot in and out of the streets and play in them. There should be a rocking-horse and battledores and shuttlecocks in each room. Yes, and on cold days we will have a fire burning. There shall be a girl in charge, who shall wear a scarlet skirt and a white apron. 'The Children's Room' shall be painted on the door, and no one over twelve years old shall be admitted. Have you money enough to do all that, Jack?"

"I believe so," he said. "And it is a pretty enough idea."

"It is picturesque, and I fancy it would be popular," she said thoughtfully. "And," as an afterthought, "it really would not be at all bad for the children. But it must be done on a big scale, and the rooms must all be thrown open at once. It will propitiate the East End parson!"

"Now that I am free I don't want to propitiate him"—Jack's voice took the rather sullen tone that Gillian was beginning to know—"and I thought you hated the species, Gill."

"Oh, to be sure, so I do," cried Gillian cheerfully. "But we can't afford to despise any body of people yet. It does not do to be too fastidious at first. We'll be more particular later on ; but "—with a twinkle in her eyes—" if we mean to make friends with the world, we must have the Church on our side."

The man laughed rather scornfully. "Do as you choose," he said.

Gillian slid off the top rail, and stood beside him. Her face wore momentarily a tenderer and graver expression. "I only want whatever you want," she said earnestly. "Where you go I must go, the people who believe in you I love, and your enemies are mine. Oh, good gracious! that sounds like a bit out of the Bible, but I said it out of my own heart. Did some Jewish woman say it before me?"

"'Whither thou goest, I will go ; and where thou lodgest, I will lodge : thy people shall be my people, and thy God, my God,'" Jack quoted slowly. Then he laughed aloud. "To think of you and me, of all people, taking to quoting Scripture! How remarkably pious! The last part of the vow does not mean much to us, does it? Moreover, darling, that Jewish girl made that promise to a good old woman, unless my memory is quite at fault, not to a disgraced man."

"She made it to the person she liked best in all the world, I suppose," said Gillian. "And so do I."

They climbed the stile, and went on across the field, she with her hand on his arm. There had been a heavy dew, and the butter-cups held tiny drops in their golden cups, and the thistle's spiky leaves glistened with moisture.

"It is almost dazzlingly bright, after London," said Gillian. "I think that a sun bath is very good for you and me. Jack, tell me, please, where would you have gone, and what would you have done with all this wonderful fortune, if I had not been waiting for you?"

He glanced sidelong at her, and shrugged his shoulders. "Hardly worth inquiring into. It is not a pretty subject, perhaps. What would *you* have done if I had died in gaol, eh?"

"The best of me would have died with you," she said. "And the other part would have grown fat and prospered. Perhaps it would have married some one else—I don't know. I am not a Lady Jane. That is not a pretty subject either, for I should not have made a good wife to any one but you."

"Upon my word, I am glad the other chap did not have a chance of trying you!" he cried wrathfully.

They reached the fir plantation now, and were confronted with a huge board, with "Trespassers will be prosecuted" on it. Gillian got over the fence.

"It is my step-father's property," she said, "and Mr. Clovis won't prosecute me. I will go on up the hill, and show mammy my wedding-ring. I think"—hesitatingly—"I think that for just this once I had better go alone."

"I should imagine that they would certainly prefer that you should," said Jack grimly.

Gillian was standing under the shadow of the firs now, and he on the other side of the fence.

"When you say that, I feel inclined to clamber back again," she exclaimed. "I don't care a fig what any one but you prefers. There! I am glad I've made you smile. Good-bye!"

She turned away, and began to walk quickly up the
winding brown path, singing again as she went. Jack
Cardew stretched himself at full length on the grass, with
his hands under his head and his straw hat tilted over his
eyes. The sunshine soaked through the brim, just as
Gillian's warm, passionate love pierced through the crust
that misery and injustice had formed round him.

"It's wonderful!" he muttered. And his heart added,
in defiance of his scepticism, and really because there is no
other way of expressing a benediction, "God bless her!"

Gillian walked a little slower when she found herself,
once more, in the familiar garden that had been the joy
of her early girlhood. It was true that she had very little
sentiment for any one but Jack, yet this return to her old
home touched her more than she had expected.

The whole place was less aggressively new than it had
been. Nature works quickly in Devonshire; and the brick
walls were clothed with creepers now, while the lawn was
soft as velvet, and the heart-shaped flower-beds, that were
dotted about on it, were full of hyacinths and crocuses.

A chubby little boy, in an inappropriately smart suit of
clothes, was digging up bulbs with such energy that he did
not hear Gillian's step till she was quite close to him.

"Why are you pulling up those poor flowers?" she asked.

The small boy turned round to stare at her with the
frank stare of childhood. Then he rubbed his earthy
hands on his knees, and smiled, a friendly, broad smile.

"There isn't room for them all," he said. "Look here,"
producing a paper bag from the pocket of his knickerbockers. "These are what I've bought with my own
money. I must find a place for them, so I had to dig
up the wrong ones."

"Oh!" said Gillian. "Why are yours more 'right'
than the others, I wonder? And are you allowed to
revolutionise the beds?"

"Father lets me," said he. "Are you a visitor? The visitors' door is round the other side. Mother is in the drawing-room. I'll show you the way if you like."

"I know my way, thank you," said Gillian.

It amused her that this little innovation should offer to take her to her own mother. "So you are my step-brother? How you have grown!"

"I am George Algernon Clovis," he replied, with some pride. "But I am called George. Father has got one Christian name, but I have got more than him, because——" He paused and rubbed the back of his head, with a gesture that reminded Gillian of Mr. Clovis. "I can't remember because why, but father knows. There he is! Hallo! Hallo, father!"

He waved his spade above his head, and ran to meet Mr. Clovis. Gillian, with a smile, watched the two coming towards her.

The child had been a pretty baby in short frocks on the last occasion on which she had seen him; he was not in the least pretty now, except in the eyes of his proud parents. His broad, good-tempered face, his comically round little figure made Gillian laugh.

"It is really a pity that both mammy's children should have taken after their respective fathers in looks," she remarked to herself.

"How do you do, Mr. Clovis? How well George seems, and how did you ever persuade mammy to consent to the cutting off of his curls?" she said.

She was anxious to avoid anything like a scene, and was apparently much less embarrassed than her step-father. But Mr. Clovis refused to take the situation so lightly.

"Well, Miss Gill," he said, "your mother has carried a heavy heart on your account for the last six years. And now I hear that you've married against her will. I used

4

to think better of you when you were a little girl, I did indeed. I ain't going to continue the subject, because the thing is done. In fact, I hadn't intended to have spoken my mind at all. But I am not going to pretend that nothin' has happened, and that we can just say 'Good-morning' and 'How well little George looks' as if it was yesterday you left us!"

Gillian gasped. She was taken by surprise. She did not for a moment believe that her mother had ever "carried a heavy heart" on any one's account for the space of six years. Yet her step-father's rebuke actually made her blush.

"You think that I am a horribly hard and light-minded young woman, don't you?" she said. "Well, so I was— till I liked Jack; and so I am, I daresay, where he is not concerned."

George had returned gaily to his work of destruction. Gillian and her step-father walked across the sunny lawn, and up the steps to the terrace where the peacocks were spreading their tails in the sun.

When they reached the French drawing-room windows Mr. Clovis paused.

"Your mother is in there," he said, pointing with his thumb. "You had better go in by yourself." He looked across the lawn at his son, who was throwing spadefuls of earth on to the trim grass. "I make no doubt that if you had had a father alive he would have prevented all this. I am sorry if I was hard on you, Gillian."

"Oh," she answered, with an odd mixture of levity and earnestness, "no number of irate fathers would have prevented me from marrying Jack, so do not reproach yourself on that score. I don't think you were exactly hard on me, Mr. Cloves. But you see some circum-stances" (she could not quite say, "You see my mother") "differently." Something in the expression of his face

moved her to add with apparent irrelevance, " But, all the
same, George is a lucky boy."

The window was ajar, she opened it, and walked into
the pretty room. Her mother rose from the sofa to meet
her.

" So at last you have remembered your poor mother,
dear love," she cried.

" Why, mammy, you look even younger than you did
when I saw you in London. I declare you look younger
than I do now ! " said Gillian. " And how nice and 'comfy'
everything is. The whole place is immensely improved
since last I was in it."

She bestowed on her mother a brisk and unemotional
kiss, and unbuttoned her jacket. " May I stay to lunch ?
I've encountered Mr. Cloves, and he has lectured and
forgiven me, so it will be all right. Look ! "—holding up
her hand—"Look with what a very thick ring Jack has
wedded me ! I tell him that it is vulgarly ostentatious.
Is it not a blessing that the wedding is over ? I am not
nervous, as you know, but I was so dreadfully afraid that
something would happen at the last moment ; I nearly
shouted for joy when we were pronounced man and wife.
Oh dear ! please don't cry, mammy. It really is so much
the best possible end to the story. And "—in a gentler
tone—" I think I've had my share of weary waiting."

" You wrote such a cold, such a heartless letter, dear
Gillian," said her mother reproachfully.

" Did I ? I am very sorry," said Gillian. " But you
know I can't write tender letters." She blushed slightly,
with a sudden recollection of a letter she had once written
to Jack in prison. " The fact is, that if one is in love
with such an unlucky person as Jack, one's whole supply
of the milk of human kindness gets used up," said she.
" There has been such a demand on my sympathy on his
account, that I've had none over for the rest of the world.

You wait till you have been in love with a convict, mammy, and then see if you can't make excuses for me. But "— rather shyly—" I will try to be nicer now."

"I am ready to forget and forgive," said Mrs. Clovis. "But I cannot bear that light way of speaking of serious things. I do not think that a newly married woman should jest about love. To me it is quite a sacred sub- ject."

"To be sure, so it is. I forgot that," said Gillian gravely. She never bandied words with her mother. In the days when they had lived together she had generally let all Mrs. Clovis's fine sentiments pass unchallenged. They had left as much impression as water leaves on a duck's back. Their intercourse had been peaceful as a rule, and her mother had only accused Gillian of undue levity on the rare occasions when the girl had spoken from her heart.

Mrs. Clovis leant back on her sofa; she was easily appeased by acquiescence. "It is a great joy to me to see you again, dear love. Now tell me all about yourself," she said.

Gillian sat down on an easy chair, with her foot on the fender-stool, and proceeded to enlarge on her plans. She never despised her mother's opinion on any subject that required worldly wisdom in the solving. Mrs. Clovis listened with interest. She was by no means devoid of natural affection. She was fond of Gillian; and though, when their interests clashed, she was incapable of putting her own last, she was nevertheless genuinely eager for her daughter's welfare.

They were discussing affairs very amicably, when they were interrupted by an early visitor.

Lady Hammerton was announced, and trotted into the room close on the footman's heels, her bright, mobile old face shining with intelligent interest at sight of Gillian, her worn, silver-clasped bag hanging over her arm. The old lady's eyes were as alert as those of a hungry robin on the look out for crumbs. Her cheeks had still a pretty touch of pink in them. Her hair was silvery white. In her youth she had been the toast of the county, and as popular as she was pretty.

Mrs. Clovis greeted her with effusion.

"Dear me! Why, here is the prodigal daughter!" cried the old lady. "And what have you been doing all this time, eh, Gillian?"

Gillian had been a great favourite with her, and though she had heard all about the dear girl's "vocation" and the mother's "self-sacrifice," she tenaciously, and somewhat unfairly, clung to the opinion that Mrs. Clovis told "tally-diddles," and that Gillian had been harshly treated.

"I have been making and saving money for a man who, after all, does not need it," Gillian unexpectedly replied. "And, quite lately, I have been engaged in marrying and honey-mooning with him."

"Come, that is a very interesting reply," said Lady Hammerton approvingly. "You were always original, my dear—especially in the excellent and business-like way in which you kept the accounts of my society. I have had a series of incapables since you left, and we are terribly in arrears. Well," opening her bag, "I daresay that you can guess what I have come for, at this early hour."

"Yes, to get subscriptions for 'The Home of Rest for worn-out Race-Horses,'" said Gillian promptly.

She looked on with amusement while Lady Hammerton "collected" from her mother. The sprack old lady, so intent on business, Mrs. Clovis with her many little airs and graces, seemed to her to be playing exactly the same comedy, even to the saying of just the same things to each other, as they had played years ago when she had lived at home. Only she herself was changed; changed by the whole breadth and depth of the love that was the most vivid part of her life.

"Now what will you give me?" said Lady Hammerton, turning round to Gillian with the bag still gaping open-mouthed. "I remember that you would never subscribe, my dear, but seeing that 'the man does not need it' it really seems a pity——"

"The man is Jack Cardew," said Gillian. "And I think that he would probably subscribe if you were to ask him."

"I asked *you*, Gillian," said the old lady briskly.

"I keep my purse in my husband's pocket," Gillian replied unblushingly. "We are staying at the White Hart at present; but we are thinking of taking a house in the neighbourhood. If you will come to tea or luncheon with us one day, we will see if we can't get something"— she smiled, the dimples showing bewitchingly in her cheek and chin—"something handsome out of Jack."

Lady Hammerton shut her bag with a doubtful little shake of the head. She was both parsimonious and generous. She lived in a rambling under-servanted house, that had been in her family for generations, and she openly screwed down the very necessaries of life, for the sake of her rather eccentric charities. Yet she was greatly respected in the neighbourhood. Her opinion carried weight. No one could fail to be impressed by a woman who was so absolutely without fear of what people might say. At the present moment she was perfectly well aware that Mrs. Cardew was offering her a direct bribe.

Lady Hammerton habitually rode her hobbies insanely hard, consequently she wanted the money badly. Yet if she had no fear of man, she had an old-fashioned fear of God before her eyes, and an equally old-fashioned sense of her responsibilities as a great lady.

Gillian saw the struggle between conscience and desire.
" I should not ask you to come," she said, "if I did not
know that my husband is absolutely innocent of the thing
with which he was charged. I am very proud of Jack."

The old lady held out a slim little hand, encased in
a threadbare black cotton glove. " Then he ought to make
a good fight for your sake," said she, "and I hope he will.
I'll take your word for him, my dear, in spite of judge and
jury. I have always had a respect for your excellent good
sense, Gillian. I do not think that you would be easily
hood-winked. When I remember how beautifully you
kept the accounts of my society, I hope that my confidence
is justified."

" Thank you," said Gillian, with the light of victory in
her eyes. " It *will* be justified."

Lady Hammerton took her leave with a sympathy for
Mrs. Cardew warming her heart. She was old, but she
had plenty of spirit left. She had no patience with the
pessimistic fashion of the day. She was a little hard on
the softness that complains of the sadness of life. But
Gill had always attracted her. The ring in the younger
woman's voice brought an answering fire to her eyes.
Yes, she would certainly call on the Cardews, and, what
was more, she should tell every one of her intention.
After all, what was a trial by jury? Why should she
take the opinion of twelve ignorant men against one of
her own class? She had known Jack Cardew both as boy
and youth. He was a gentleman, and a cousin of her
own.

Gillian having escorted her champion to the hall door,
returned laughing to the drawing-room.

" Isn't that splendid, mammy?" she cried. " And you
see there is no doubt about Jack's character, because *I* kept
that stupid old society's accounts so well ! "

She lunched with excellent appetite after that small

success. She coaxed her step-father into good humour, and made friends with her step-brother. Every one was sorry when she declared it time for her to depart.

"I asked father, and he says I've got twice his number of names 'cos I have got to be just twice the man he is," the son and heir said to her, when she bid him good-bye. "I shall have to be awfully big, if I am twice as big as father," he added rather doubtfully.

"George will probably go into the Horse Guards," said Mr. Clovis, eyeing the little dumpling of a boy with a kind of prospective pride. "I don't say it is a paying profession, mind you. But *he* won't have to trouble his head about that. He'll begin where his father left off."

George, who was fortunately a very simple little fellow, looked puzzled and rather bored at this conversation about himself.

"Never mind," said Gillian, "I should not try to be twice as big as Mr. Cloves if I were you. I think"—with a friendly glance at her step-father—"I think that if you do as well you'll be all right." And she meant what she said, for Gillian had a genuine respect for Mr. Clovis.

She started on her homeward walk in good spirits, and at a round pace. She hated to be long parted from Jack, because (though this was a weakness that she never confessed) she was apt to be haunted by a purely unreasonable terror lest he should have vanished—back again to that prison where it seemed to her at times that she too had laboured and despaired.

Had there ever been an evening when the remembrance of him had not been present with her while she walked from her office to her room in the Strand? Had there ever been a morning when she had not known on waking that his day's toil had begun?

While she made her way through these deep winding lanes, looking up at the dappled sky through interlacing branches, she thought of her many journeys to and fro in London.

"How many weary women are there in England, who are working and waiting, and trying not to feel too much?" she wondered idly, then noticed a very evidently "weary woman" sitting at a little distance from her, at the foot of the hill that had to be ascended before the village was reached.

The woman was holding a baby, slung in a shawl, the ends of which were tied round her own neck. The baby was a puling delicate little mite, and the mother too was sickly. She had seated herself on a stone at the bottom of the hill in order to suckle her child. Presently she rose and toiled on, pausing often to regain her breath.

Gillian always averred that she was not philanthropic. She had none of Lady Jane's craze for saving and helping every poor and miserable creature that she came across; yet when her vigorous walk brought her alongside of the wayfarers, the sight of the baby made her pause.

"You are fagged out," she said. "Shall I carry the child up this hill for you?"

The woman stood still, and gazed dully at the lady. Knees and arms were shaking, and she was so physically over-strained that she was incapable of mental effort.

Gillian put one hand under the child, and with the other loosened the knot of the shawl.

"Why, it is no weight at all!" she cried, taking possession of the small burden. The baby was wailing, a weak, fretful little wail.

"She is hungry," said the woman. "I have been poorly, and I have not got milk enough for her. There ain't no use in her carrying on like that. I can't give her what I haven't got. I can't help it!"

"No, I don't suppose you can," said Gillian. In her heart she considered that it was very hard on the baby

that so incapable a " poor thing " should have the responsibilities of motherhood. " I should think that you had
never been able to help anything," she added.

She drew the folds of her own cloak round the child,
that it might be sheltered from the dust that the warm
south wind was blowing in their faces. When she reached
the top of the hill she sat down on a strip of grass to wait
for the woman. The baby felt more comfortable in her
strong young arms, and stopped crying. Gillian laid her
cheek against its head and felt the pulses beating underneath the soft down. She had never imagined herself to
be fond of children, but she coloured and laughed with
pleasure when the little aimless fingers clutched at her
hair. She made cooing, coaxing noises to the baby, she
talked to it in a wonderfully tender voice. Gillian had a
voice that could be sweet as honey—Jack knew that well
enough. She had never in her life before spoken so softly
to any one save him. And the odd part of it all was that
this particular baby was nothing in the world to her. She
could not imagine why to hold it in her arms seemed to
bring her into closer kinship with the whole beauty of that
spring day—she who was never a poet like Jack.

When the mother came up to her, she relinquished the
child with some secret unwillingness, but asked no
questions, and offered no farther aid.

Gillian had lived long enough in London to be chary of
promiscuous alms-giving ; moreover, she had hardened her
heart on principle, for she had needed all her savings for Jack.

The mother nodded her thanks sullenly, and so they
parted.

Gillian gave her husband a highly coloured and amusing
account of all that had happened to her since she had left
him in the morning. They dined *tête-à-tête*, and both
laughed over her story of Lady Hammerton and the sub-
scription. Gillian was triumphant when she succeeded in

making Jack laugh. She took great pains to amuse him, and she always dressed beautifully for his benefit.

"Well, I daresay that you'll succeed in buying some votes for me," he said. "But do you really think it is worth your while to take this trouble?"

"Ah, that is what Jane said," said Gillian.

She pushed her chair back, and, walking across to the window, stood looking out at the night to hide her momentary disappointment. Trouble? She would have counted nothing a trouble that was done for Jack. It is to be feared indeed that at this stage in her life Gillian would very cheerfully have sacrificed every and any one's happiness for the sake of saving him a finger-ache. Yet, and alas! even now she felt the working of that inexorable law—not even her love could step between him and mortal suffering.

"What is it that you want most—most in all the world?" she asked wistfully. "Once upon a time it was to write beautiful poems, and to make a great name."

"I made a name with a vengeance, didn't I?" said Jack. "Oh, I am not ambitious now, my dear, and I could not write any more. The person who wrote 'beautiful poems' does not exist. He got knocked on the head in gaol. What do I want? To be thoroughly lazy and comfortable, unless——" he hesitated for a moment.

"Well?" she said eagerly.

"——Unless I could see a chance of finding out who was my enemy, and making him swallow his lies first, and be punished for them afterwards," he said slowly.

"Ah, then you want to punish him, even more than you want justice," she cried.

In the days when she had first known Jack he had been hot-tempered and thin-skinned. She had been wont to laughingly assure her lover that she could see that he had a very red-haired temper. Yet she had known him to be generous, and if he gave offence thoughtlessly, he at least never bore malice. Something in the slow bitterness of his tone now made her hotly indignant, not with him, but with the hardness of the fate that had so changed him.

She had suffered for and with Jack, as only a woman can suffer for some one else. But it was in the daily contact of their married life that she realised most fully all the evil that adversity had worked.

Gillian had never railed against destiny, because she was an essentially practical person, to whom prayers and curses seemed as a rule equally beside the point. She had set herself to do what she could for Jack, finding some salve for her painful sympathy in the hard work that enabled her to lay by money for him. It was characteristic of her that she no sooner felt sad than she began to make a plan to relieve her feelings.

"Let us set to work to find out,' she said.

But the eagerness had died out of the man's face. "What is the use? The evidence was all thoroughly threshed at the trial. No reasonable person could have had any doubts about it. If I wasn't guilty I ought to have been, and we shall never find out any more. We won't waste our time in hopeless races after justice. We've done with shadows."

"But the truth must be somewhere," she said.

"When we are all dead some one may possibly fish it up," he answered. "If I saw a real chance of getting at it I'd take it, Gill, but I'm not going in for wild goose chases. Let's enjoy ourselves now. We'll eat and drink, my darling, for to-morrow—it won't matter to us how the world wags. Another set of poor beggars will be shifted up and down instead of us; and those at the top will have excellent reasons for believing in Providence, and those at the bottom will perhaps believe in the devil. It is all the same in the end, but in the meantime one may as well take what one can get. Why do you stand at that window? Come over here, Gill."

She came quickly, and sitting on his knee, hid her face on his shoulder.

"Jack, Jack, I cannot bear to think of the end," she whispered. "How can *we* ever be parted? Hold me fast. That's right. Oh, I wish we could drink the water that made people forget. What was it called? You wrote a poem about it once. Lethe? Yes, that was it. I want so to forget all the misery that is over, and all the blankness that waits for us at the bottom of the hill."

He comforted her tenderly enough, though rather awkwardly. He was surprised, for Gillian was supposed to have no nerves. "Why, you never used to trouble your head about anything but the present," he said. "It is all that confounded time alone in London that has tried your nerve."

Gillian looked up with a smile.

"I am sure I was meant to be a most comfortable, stolid sort of person. If I did not care about you, I should never worry about anything. It is you who wake up the soul in me—even now."

That night a sudden idea came to her, just as she was dropping to sleep.

"Was there ever any woman who had reason to hate you?" she asked.

"No. And no woman would have seen a man sentenced, and held her tongue," he said. "Women are not so cruel."

"It might have been for some one else," said Gillian. "She would not have thought about the cruelty then. One might do anything in the world for some one else."

CHAPTER V.

THE DEEP UNREST.

"Oh passionate wail, that is not sound alone,
   Nor only man's, O Nature, but thy breast
   Unveiling, doth proclaim the deep unrest,
   Thy dole and ours, that maketh us as one."

THE big new house that Jack Cardew had built in
Park Lane was lit up and garnished. The window-
boxes were filled with flowers, and more than one of
the passers-by had paused to feast his eyes on the blaze
of colour—the brave show of pinks and crimsons and
blues.

The season was at its height, and the discussion about
the Cardews, which had raged so hotly at one period of it,
was practically at an end. Some few people refused to
have anything to say to them, but on the whole Mrs.
Cardew was well supported. A wonderfully large number
among her acquaintance took a highly charitable view of
the case; Mr. Cardew was very liberal, and was consequently, in some quarters, liberally judged.

Moreover, there were elements in the story that hit
the public fancy. Gillian was decidedly fascinating,
and some men thought her beautiful. It must be owned
that she got on better with men than with women, but
she was careful not to make enemies, and prosperity
suited her.

We all like to hear about love on a grand scale. Jack

and Gillian were a really refreshing example of it.   One
lady averred that a man who had it in him to be faithful
for six years could not have done all the dreadful things
that Mr. Cardew was accused of.   Gillian laughed over
that speech, but she knew perfectly well that it represented
what many felt.

"I refrained from telling her that I simply threw myself
into your arms, Jack," she said.   "Really you had not much
chance of flirting in gaol, had you?"

The hot summer day had worn to its close, and the
scent of the flowers was heavy on the evening air, when
a girl who had been walking up and down in front of the
new house, paused, and leaned wearily against the area
railing, and looked up at the dining-room windows.

"I shall always hate the scent of pelargoniums!" she
said to herself.

Then she walked on, and returned again, and at last ran
quickly up the steps of the house and put her hand on
the door bell.   Apparently the handle burned her, for
she withdrew her fingers, with a hasty glance round,
and once more took up her troubled pacing up and down,
up and down.   A policeman stared suspiciously at her.
This was the fourth time that he had seen her run up those
same steps and make a futile attempt to ring that bell.
Was she mad, or up to no good?

"What are you about that you can't leave that there bell
alone?" he asked.

The girl started, looked at him with frightened eyes
and hurried away without answering.   She took a longer
walk this time, but came back again, as if the house were
a magnet, drawing her in spite of herself.   This time she
did not ascend the steps, but stood at the bottom and
scolded herself.

"Oh, you coward, you horrid little thing!   You came
here on purpose.   Why can't you find the pluck to ask for

him ? Here you stand with your ridiculous feelings, and let Geoffrey die, just because you are such a pitiful idiot ! I wish that I could beat you."

She bit her lips, and clenched her small hands hard. She really would do it this time. Then the hall door opened, and the master of the house came out.

It was years since the girl had last met him, and his face was a little turned from her, but she knew by his size and by the colour of his hair that he was Mr. Cardew. She was blushing, a burning shamed blush that seemed to tingle all over her. She made a step forward, and tried to arrest him.

He passed on without paying any heed to her. The words she had meant to say stuck in her throat. She was physically incapable of bringing them out.

A wave of despair came over her. She put her hands before her face, and choked back a sob.

"I can't do it!" she cried. Her weak flesh occasionally appealed, in vain, for pity, to her stern spirit.

Mr. Cardew stopped, and turned round. "I beg your pardon. Did you speak to me?" he said.

He supposed that she was begging. She looked like a lady, but beggars of every kind and description assailed the house in Park Lane. He did not, as a rule, believe their tales, but he frequently gave, all the same. He was the despair of the "Charity Organisation." He was terribly given to encouraging the undeserving.

"No—I mean yes," said the girl breathlessly. "I am afraid you don't remember me at at all, Mr. Cardew. I am Bertram's and Geoffrey's sister."

He repeated the words wonderingly, then he remembered. "Oh—yes, we saw a great deal of each other once. That was before anything happened."

He was not pleased. The girl saw and felt that. She turned as if to flee. When Jack had been poor he had been very generous, now that he was absurdly and fabulously wealthy, he probably suspected and resented attempts on his pocket, thought she. Every one knows that the poor give more willingly than the rich. Never again would she dream of asking a rich person for help.

As a matter of fact, Jack hated to be confronted with ghosts from the other side of that gulf that lay between his youth and his manhood. But the sight of her distressed face made him endeavour to put aside his rather morbid dislike.

"How curious it is that we should meet," he said, trying to speak easily, "and how clever of you to recognise me after all these years!"

"It wasn't very curious," the girl blurted out. "And it wasn't clever. I don't think I should have known you if we had met in Oxford Street. But I heard that you had built this house, and I have been walking about outside."

She had carefully rehearsed all that she had intended to say to Mr. Cardew. Her little speech was to have been dignified and straightforward.

"You were my brother's great friend, and my father always trusted you, and so I have ventured to come to you for advice "—that was how she had meant to have opened the conversation. Behold she had forgotten every word that she had prepared. She blundered painfully and naturally.

Jack was surprised, even dismayed. "You waited outside? But why on earth, since you were so kind as to wish to see me, did you not ring the bell and come in?" Then at last a faint suspicion that she was in some trouble dawned on Jack.

"Will you come in now? I want to hear all about my old friends. Why, Enid "—he had always called her by her Christian name when she was a child—" Why, Enid, it

5

is uncommonly nice of you to have thought of looking me up." He held the hand he had taken in his, and led her straight into the hall. He saw when the light fell on her face that she was very white and tired, and after one glance at her he took her into the dining-room and deposited her in an armchair.

"Sit still. I am going to give you some wine," he said.

"Oh, nonsense!" in answer to a faint remonstrance. "It is not the first time by a good many that we've had supper together. Do you suppose that I am going to let you drop down dead on the way home?"

"I shouldn't do that. I always look a great deal more delicate than I am," said she.

She was a slight girl and she was most unbecomingly dressed. Her face was full of expression, and very bright when she was amused. Life had been hard on her, but she could still laugh and she was easily interested. Her hair was uncompromisingly scraped off her broad forehead, and plaited in tight plaits. It was a soft light brown, but it never had a chance of looking pretty. Her eyes were dark blue, but the lids were red, for she was apt to work at all hours. Enid liked pretty things on other people, but she was absolutely regardless of her own personal appearance, having long ago given herself up as a bad job.

"No complexion, and no features. Only bones!" she had once severely remarked, on a rare occasion when she had looked in the glass.

But the glass was unfair! Only an extraordinarily dull person could have talked five minutes to her without seeing anything but her physical defects.

She had the charm of a wonderfully quick sympathy, and her devotion to the people she loved was unstinted and singularly unconscious.

Enid had gone through agonies of anticipation, and had crucified an inherent sense of independence on her way to Park Lane. But while she looked at her old friend, she forgot all about herself; even, momentarily, forgot her reasons for coming. Jack Cardew had been immensely admired by the Haubert family. Enid thought ruefully, "How sad it would have made father to see him now!"

Enid had been a little girl when Jack had first become intimate with her brother; she had shared in the family pride and delight in the recognition of his genius. The Hauberts were exceedingly literary and artistic, and though Mr. Cardew was originally "Bertram's friend" they all took the deepest interest in him. Enid had been just seventeen at the time of the trial.

Gillian herself was not more absolutely certain of Jack's innocence than were the Hauberts; but they had their own heavy troubles just then. It seemed to Enid that up to this moment she had never fully realised what a crushing thing it was that had befallen this man. His whole expression was changed, even the way in which he walked was different. She noticed too that his manner of speech was slower and more deliberate. When he was a young man he had talked quickly and impulsively; sometimes brilliantly.

"You did not wait outside just in order to welcome me back to London. What is it that you wish to say?" he asked, when she had finished drinking the wine which he had poured out. He had made an evident effort to be friendly, to set her at ease, to bridge the years that lay between their old friendship and the present moment. Enid felt the effort, and wished that she had never come. She did not know *this* Jack Cardew, this grave, middle-aged, bronzed person.

"I made a mistake," she cried.

At that his effort relaxed and he laughed outright. Her

last words did really carry him back to the past. Enid had always been the most rash member of a rash and improvident family.

"But you are in for it now," he said.

He recollected a funny scrape that he had helped her out of when she was a child. Bertram had got her into it, but it was always Enid who bore the brunt of a mishap. Jack had taken people very much at their own valuation when he was a boy, yet he had liked Enid the best. Some instinct had told him, even then, that the little quixotic sister had finer stuff in her than had the brother she worshipped.

"I hope that Geoffrey is taking care of you," he said. "I am sure that you are wearing yourself out, for you were always the hardworking member of the family."

"Ah, then you do not know," she cried. "Geoff was dreadfully hurt when he was playing in a football match at school. We did not think that it mattered much at first, and doctors are so expensive, you know. We let him go on till"—her voice broke a little—"till it was too late. He was badly kicked here,"—putting her hand to her back. "It was by an accident, of course. He did not even know who did it—that is, if he did know he would not tell us. But—he has not been able to sit upright for the last five years. It happened just six months after the other."

Jack guessed that by "the other" she meant Bertram's death. Bertram had been killed by an accident on the very same unlucky day that had seen the beginning of all Jack's own troubles.

Jack recollected that he had been very shocked at the time. Later, his overwhelming sense of the injustice that had overtaken himself had swamped his pity for his friends. Death in life had seemed to him a harder fate than death.

Enid stood upright. His silence hurt her. "I do not think you care in the least about Geoff now," she said. "I was quite wrong to trouble you. Good-bye."

She was a quaint little figure, indignant and disappointed. She had thought that she could ask him for help, but she could not when it came to the point. Enid was always embarking in inadequate cockle-shells on rough seas. She had immense spirit, but, unlike Gillian, she was not born to succeed. Her temperament and her soul were unequally yoked.

"No, you were quite right, but you don't give me any time to take in all this information about you," said Jack. His smile was still kind. "Poor chap! So *he* is a prisoner And without hope of release, eh?"

Enid shook her head. "The doctor at the hospital said that there is no hope of complete recovery, but he may live as long as any one else."

"He is a weight on your hands, then, I suppose, for Mr. Haubert never managed to bring much grist to the mill."

"Geoff isn't a weight, he is what makes everything worth doing," she cried. "And my father is dead."

"I am sorry," said Jack.

It sounded curt, but he really meant it. Somehow the remembrance of the gentle drawing-master, who had had a great deal of talent, and no idea whatever of teaching, who had been full of ideas, that other men reaped, who was always a failure, but always sweet-natured, softened him. The Hauberts were all so fond of each other. This poor girl must have suffered a great deal.

"Mr. Haubert was such a very good sort," he said gently. "Of course you know that better than I do, but I wish I could have seen him again. So you and Geoff are left all alone. I would come and look him up if he would like to see me. But perhaps he wouldn't. Is there anything that I may do for you?"

"If you would help me to find work," she said breath-lessly. "I was at a type-writing office, but they have just turned me off. It wasn't my fault. I worked very hard. They have taken somebody else instead. She lives with her father and mother, and does not have to pay for her board, so she can come for less money than I can. She does not want it half so much. She only buys new clothes with her salary," Enid cried, with tears in her voice. "And Geoff and I lived on what I earned. I've got nothing else."

"Poor little girl! It is horribly unjust," said Jack. "But most things are. Yes, I can find you something to do. Gillian has all sorts of schemes on hand. Ah, you have heard about them," for she nodded brightly, the smile coming back to her face. "Well she is sure to find room for you in one of them. You shall turn out some one else this time, to make it even, if you like."

"No, I wouldn't like, unless it is some one with a hundred a year, and even then I had rather not. Isn't there"—wistfully—"Isn't there any fair place for me anywhere?"

Mr. Cardew smiled. "I think I may safely swear that there is. And, I say, the salary is always paid in advance in Gillian's schemes." He drew out his pocket-book shyly.

"I don't see how Mrs. Cardew can always do that," said Enid bluntly. "I would not take it if I had anything left. I'll work it out, every penny. Oh no, not all that."

"Why," he exclaimed, with a sudden inspiration, "this isn't an advance, Enid. It is what I actually owe you. We used not to be so proud about borrowing from each other! I got ten pounds from poor Bertram on the evening of that awful accident. It ought to have been repaid to you long ago, but my own affairs put everything else out of my head. This is yours, and with the interest—"

"Oh, never mind the interest. I am not a Jew," she

cried happily. "But is it truly Bertram's? I thought that it was *you* who generally lent to him."

"Yes, but I was in a hole just before the smash up," he answered, with so gloomy a face that she perforce believed him. "Did you not see in the trial how it came out that I had been borrowing money?"

"We all knew that the evidence at the trial was false, because they found the wrong verdict," she said. "And now I am going home to Geoff. I can't tell you how thankful I am. You won't ever know, I am afraid."

She was in such a transparent hurry to be off now, with the precious note in her hand, that he kept her no longer. He only insisted on the reckless extravagance of a cab.

"For if you walk, you will be robbed to a dead certainty," he said; "you were always unlucky."

"Not to-day! How kind you have been. And this,"— with a glance at her tightly clenched hand, in which the note was screwed up—"this is like a present from dear Bertie."

Jack smiled to himself. "But I thought that it was *you* who generally gave him presents!"

He walked on towards the Embankment after that, instinctively making his way river-wards. There is something in the flow of water that is fascinating to a troubled spirit. Jack was becoming restless; luxury was already beginning to pall on him. If it were not for Gillian he would have stepped on board a steamer and gone off somewhere. He had sworn that the only aim of his life was to be lazy and comfortable, but then that ideal is not altogether easy of attainment. How could he be comfortable when every one was bent on confronting him with the ghost of his former self?

It was refreshing to get away from the fashionable quarter of the town. He was glad that Gill was enjoying this plunge into society, and that she knew better than to bother him to share all these gaieties with her. It was only fair that she should have a merry time now. She was quite right, and he wished he could follow her example. Somehow the spring of enjoyment was broken in him.

He leaned over the stonework of Blackfriars Bridge, and watched the flow of the tide. The expression of his face was so melancholy that it awakened the suspicions of a Salvationist "captain" on the prowl for "souls to be saved."

"You will not find any help in the river, my friend," said the captain.

Jack not unnaturally resented both the interference and the assumption of friendship. He was unfortunately reminded of the gaol parson. "I am afraid I shall not," he retorted, "seeing that in this benighted country one is not allowed to give impertinence the ducking it deserves."

He stood upright to look at the man who had disturbed him, then half repented of his reply. The "captain" was very small and puny, with the sunken narrow chest and round shoulders of the city bred. Jack could have picked him up with one hand, and when he saw him wince at the rough words he felt as if he had struck a girl.

"I only saw your face, sir," said the Salvationist apologetically. "I did not notice that you were not a poor man. Some one jumped off there the night before last, and I was just too late to stop him. He was starving, and it has been on my mind since."

"And since we are on the subject, what earthly right had you to suppose that he didn't know his own business best?" asked Jack. "And why the d——, if you *are* to interfere, should my broadcloth be more protection than his rags?"

The captain coloured. He was a fair-skinned, almost boyish-looking person, with the luminous eyes that are so often seen in consumptive subjects.

"It should not make any difference," he said; "but," he added with a simplicity that amused Jack, "I find it hard to act on that. I am naturally a shy man, sir, and the flesh is weak."

He coughed at the end of the sentence, and the handkerchief he put to his lips had dull red stains on it.

Now Mr. Cardew had started in life with a heart that was unusually soft where other people's physical pain or weakness was concerned. Experience had hardened him (if he had not felt so keenly it would have hardened him less), but to this day a sort of fierce sympathy often lay at the root of his bitterness.

"I have no mission of interference," he remarked, "but I should imagine that you are killing yourself at this work just as surely as if you jumped into the river."

"I sha'n't live many months, anyhow," said the Salvationist eagerly. "So I may as well make the most of the time. If I could only persuade you ——"

"But you can't," said Jack, this time good-naturedly. "And what is more, you don't even know that I am in any need of persuasion. I am not your friend any more than you are mine. Why have not I every bit as good a right to go my way as you have to go to Heaven?"

The captain stared dumbly at his interlocutor. A thought was evidently struggling for expression, but he could not not manage to express it. He was not a man of a ready tongue. He took refuge in a cant phrase and walked off with a hot sense of failure and shame at his heart. It seemed to him that the stranger's blue eyes pierced straight through the evasion, their momentary friendliness changing to a rather scornful amusement. The captain had an ingrained respect for the upper classes, he recognised with self-reproach that a most unworthy bashfulness had prevented his "testifying" truly. Bashfulness is perhaps not the fault to which the disciples of the gospel of noise are most prone, but this especial soldier was always haunted by a miserable conviction of his own weakness.

Jack leaned again over the balustrade, and watched a handful of straws stick for a second against the bridge, and then whirl under it, carried away by the current. "Like straws on a river," "Like straws on a river," he repeated to himself aloud, and then quite unexpectedly the old surging craving for expression began to rise up. He was like one who has been half frozen, and who begins anew to feel life tingling painfully in all his veins.

He had fancied that that desire to clothe his sensations in words, to make manifest had died for ever. He was wrong. It was not dead, but sleeping, and One passing by had awakened it.

Quicker and quicker images thronged by him. His own broken life was but one among a million. From every corner of the city the voices of victims went up. The taint of the smoke of the sacrifice was on everything.

He thought of Geoffrey Haubert bound by a life sentence of imprisonment. He thought of the hundreds to whom existence is a foregone failure. It seems to him that the profound immorality of the whole scheme of creation shouted aloud to—to what? To any man with a spark of justice in his soul?

He had always realised that the evils he himself had suffered were not the fault of those who had convicted him, but rather of an overruling fate that so disposed events that no jury could have found him otherwise than guilty. Gillian was inclined to be bitter against men, but Jack, in his cooler moments, acquitted them. He had been the companion of thieves, and deep in his heart he cherished, not scorn, but indignation for the outcasts of humanity.

"We breed criminals and then we build prisons for them," he had once remarked to the chaplain. "It seems illogical to the lay intelligence. But we only follow the example of the power that creates everything. That does the same thing on a much larger scale." That was before the time when he had ceased to argue with and contradict his spiritual pastor, and had fallen in with the custom by which the rubbing of the burden was eased. Now, while he stood a free man again on the city bridge, he thought of those first months in the prison—months that had been followed by a merciful deadening. It was borne in on him that he was awake once more, and that for him to live by his senses only was impossible.

He might have done it. He might have made a brute of himself, but he had married Gillian, and he was never a man who could take a middle course. Yet there had been moments when he had almost regretted the compulsion that saved him. He must needs swim strongly who swims against the tide, and Jack was aweary of trouble. Shall the unjustly treated be just? Shall man be better than the gods?

"Nay, but Gill had waited." The answer came not from his brain but from his heart. "She and I must always stick together, whatever happens," he said aloud. That " must " had already kept out a good many devils.

It was nearly twelve o'clock when he reached home. The drawing-room door was ajar, and he went in wondering that Gillian should still be up, and, to his dismay, stumbled upon guests. It seemed to Jack that his house was never free of them. Gillian was everlastingly entertaining. Then he remembered that she had told him that it was a " debate " night, and that that was the reason why they had had dinner early, and why he had gone out.

The pretty room was lit by a number of pink wax candles, and about twenty men and as many ladies in evening dress were comfortably disposed on low chairs and sofas. Gillian always declared that to make people thoroughly comfortable was the first step towards a successful entertainment.

There was a moment's hush when the master of the house came in. He looked curiously unlike the other men who were present; he seemed to bring quite a different atmosphere into the room. It appeared to him that every one was rather startled; a little doubtful what to say to him. He derived a grim amusement from the scene. He avoided this sort of social gathering as a rule, but he was not exactly shy.

Gillian had been making her guests laugh. Her remarks sometimes inclined to the audacious, but no debate that she took part in was ever dull. She looked her best at night, for her bare neck and arms were beautiful, and her odd, two-coloured eyes shone like stars.

When she caught sight of Jack standing in the doorway her expression changed, and she was momentarily silent. Then she laughed merrily. "My husband is always too much in earnest to debate," she said. "You have come in by accident, haven't you, Jack? But now that you are here, do please stay and support my side."

Jack walked across the room, and stood facing them all, with his back to the fireplace.

"What is it about?" he asked. A thrill of pleasure made Gillian's eyes sparkle more brightly than ever. Among all these people, Jack was the only one who seemed to her worth looking at. She loved the tones of his voice, the very way in which he stood. No other man had ever so much as caused her pulses to quicken. She always agreed with Lady Jane that she was a lucky woman, in that, having been born with the sort of temperament that made it impossible to her to give of her best to more than one person, she had actually become that person's wife. The lady who was sitting next her had observed the graver expression that had softened her bright face, and secretly pitied her. " Mrs. Cardew carries it off well, but of course she must feel the awkwardness of the situation. And he really *was* a convict, though no doubt he was very unfortunate," she said to herself.

"The question is, ' Is the sense of justice innate or acquired ?'" Gill replied, in answer to his question. There was a touch of mockery in her voice. Mrs. Cardew went in for debates because they were the fashion of the year, but her practical mind secretly revolted at the futility of discussing the unalterable.

"Innate," said Jack. "We are born just. That is why the nobler among us wear themselves out in hopeless rebellion. The majority grow less just as they get older and weaker. The power that turns the world round is too strong for us in the end. We succumb to the inevitable, and invent pretty fictions to prove that the inevitable is inevitably good. We fall in with the fallacy that priests have——"

"But, my dear Jack, you are arguing on the wrong side," cried Gillian. "I maintained that justice is not innate, but acquired."

CHAPTER VI.

"YOUR WORLDLY WIFE."

GEOFFREY and Enid Haubert lived in what Geoffrey called "a room and a cupboard," in the attics of the Middlesex Buildings, a huge block of houses in the neighbourhood of King's Cross. Geoffrey slept in the room which was also their sitting-room; Enid had the tiny chamber that was made her own private property by a wooden partition.

Enid was fond of her home. The ascent to it was toilsome, but when you had once reached it you had a really wonderful view over chimney-pots. The wooden partition gave character to the "whole place," she declared· The "whole place" was not very spacious if you judged it by its actual dimensions, but then there are so many things that cannot fairly be measured by a carpenter's rule.

The partition was stained to a walnut shade (Enid had stained it), and little unframed sketches, chiefly of London, were pinned up all over it. The walls were of a faded salmon pink, and the ceiling sloped towards the fireplace. Geoffrey's sofa stood by the window in summer, and by the fire in winter. A square deal table was by his side.

The brother and sister had taken possession of their quaint eyrie with great delight. They had moved into it after their father's death, when it became clearly impossible to afford the rent for the house he had lived in.

In spite of Geoffrey's misfortune, in spite of the recent

78

bereavement that was so tender a grief to them, they had both enjoyed the move. The Hauberts all possessed a great capability for finding fun and pleasure in small things. It was a quality that perhaps counterbalanced their general uuluckiness. They had made very merry over the furnishing of that attic. It was so delightfully cheap that Enid blithely declared that she should always have a margin over to spend on extras. They were, considering all things, pathetically courageous. Geoffrey was carried up the long flights of stairs by two kindly medical students who had made friends with him in the hospital. It did not strike him that the room was a prison; on the contrary, he shared with Enid a proud sense of ownership.

That was two years ago, and alas! since then "the beautiful, cheap, airy place" had been the scene of a struggle that came very near to tragedy.

Hardly any one knew how poor the couple on the top floor really were. They hid their difficulties bravely. An injudiciousiy kind lady had once come to see them, and had offered to send "the poor cripple" to a Home for incurable patients. From that day Geoffrey and Enid, though by nature sociable, had fought shy of genteel visitors.

It is needless to say that the margin that Enid had counted on was invariably used up in advance. "Extras" were out of the question. She lay awake at night planning how to provide Geoff with necessaries. She earned a somewhat uncertain livelihood by illustrating for cheap magazines. She had a good deal of talent, but she had never been properly trained. Indeed, it may fairly be said that she had never been trained at all. She had picked up hints from her father, who had delighted in her bright fancy, but who, with characteristic want of forethought, had never considered the desirableness of giving her a profession at her fingers' ends. Geoffrey, who on the whole had always been the least artistic of the family, had yet the delicacy of touch that distinguished every member of it. He had learnt to mount specimens for the micro-scope, and only grieved that there was so small a demand for his one accomplishment. Geoffrey and Enid both loved their handicrafts and would have been very happy had it not been that they unfortunately found themselves nearer starving than living.

They held on as long as possible, but at last Enid announced one day, with would-be cheerfulness, that she had taken a place in a type-writing office, where she hoped eventually to earn sixteen shillings a week. "A good, steady income." The hours in the office were long, and it was a great wrench to her to give up the employment that she enjoyed (even though she had grown thin over it) for a mechanical work that wearied and bored her. It was sad too to leave poor Geoffrey without the companion-ship he needed; yet with the wolf half-way in at the door she was bound to take whatever she could get.

Enid, in common with her father and Bertram, had always loathed monotony. She was easily made happy, and she could work enthusiastically hard, but she liked her freedom. When she woke up on Monday morning her spirits sank at the consciousness that every minute of the week's work was cut out for her. Nothing but the near view she had had of starvation, and the bug-bear raised by the philanthropic lady, would have induced her to persevere. She did persevere, and grew less childish and less light-hearted in the effort. At nineteen she had taken on herself the responsibility of breadwinner without a qualm; but at three-and-twenty she was an anxious-minded little woman.

It was late by the time that Enid reached home after her expedition to the West End. The shops in Cromer Street were still open, for working people do their shopping

in the evening. She made a variety of purchases on the
way. Jack Cardew had paid the cabman. She trembled
to think what that long, long drive must have cost! She
turned the last curl of the spiral staircase breathlessly.
She had run all the way up the stone steps. Her feet had
hastened to carry good news to Geoff.

"It's all right," she cried on entering the room. "Oh,
Geoff, he is quite sure he can find something for me to do,
and I have brought back all sorts of things for supper, and
I paid the rent before I came up, and he was very kind,
only so altered, and I am dreadfully late because I waited
so long outside the door."

Geoff, who had been lying with his face to the window,
gave a funny little grunt, and turned towards her.

"I say, I had made up my mind that you had been run
over," he said. "You do give a fellow shocks, you know."

Geoff had a comical face, that had once been very round
and freckled. He had been distinctly an out-of-door boy.
Bertram had been very handsome, but Geoff had never
had any pretensions to good looks. His nose turned up,
and his mouth was too wide, albeit pleasant in expression.
His brown eyes were candid, and good to meet.

Enid sat on the floor by his sofa, while she poured forth
her story in a disjointed and somewhat confused fashion.
Enid told Geoffrey a good many things, especially a good
many amusing things. She had a habit of treasuring up
any small episode that she might make a story of it when
she got home. The boy looked at the outside world
through the girl's eyes. Yet he thought for himself too,
and his reflective powers were fast developing in this
unboyish life that had been forced on him.

Presently Enid drew down the blinds and prepared
supper. She had bought candles on the way home, and
she recklessly lit three. "Let us pretend we are rich, just
for to-night," she said. "It will do us so much good!"

6

She wheeled Geoffrey up to the table, and stood blushing deeply.

"What is the matter, Judy?" the boy asked. (No one knew why Enid had always been called Judy by her brothers.)

"*For what we are going to receive the Lord make us truly thankful,*" said Enid.

She rushed through the grace at an almost unintelligible rate. It was a reminiscence of nursery days. It did not sound very reverent, yet it meant a good deal. Enid had had a hard time, and had carried through it a very childlike quality of religious belief.

"Don't laugh, Geoff. I *am* so thankful," she said.

"All right. I don't mind," said Geoffrey. "I am sure I am precious glad too."

They enjoyed their supper thoroughly. It reminded Enid of the first meal they had eaten in their own room—but with a difference. The wolf was driven away, for the time being, but he is a visitor whom it is difficult to forget. Enid could still be merry, but her old careless light-heartedness was dead.

She revelled in doing nothing after supper. From talking of Mr. Cardew, the brother and sister turned to memories of the old days when their father had been alive, and when Bertram had been Enid's pride and hope. It was not often that they talked of the past, they were both too young and too interested in the present to indulge in much retrospect, but this was an especial occasion. On especial occasions Enid's thoughts always turned lovingly to the father and brother in the next world.

"Bert would have been pretty well astonished if he could know all that has happened to his friend," said Geoffrey. "Poor Bert! How sold he was when his manuscript was returned to him. You've got it still, haven't you?"

"It is in the old play-box in my room. I put it away with his cigar case and his photograph album, and those pictures of the ballet-dancer that he would hang up in the parlour. It is tied up just as he left it." Enid sighed heavily. "I wish that the publishers had not been so stupid!" she said.

Her faithful heart still grieved that Bertram had been disappointed. She had renounced her own ambitions with less pain than she had felt over his failures.

"I wonder —— " began Geoffrey, and then stopped short.

He had been on the point of wondering whether Bertram's book had been worth printing, but a sense of loyalty prevented the remark. Moreover, though Enid had a good temper on the whole, she invariably lost it if she heard any one she was fond of disparaged, whether justly or unjustly. He was disinclined to tease her to-night.

"Do you know what I've been thinking?" he said presently. "I've been thinking that I ought not to have let you go to Mr. Cardew. He used to be a good chap, I know, and of course we never believed a word of what they said about him, but all the same there are some things a man should not have his sister do."

Enid opened her eyes wide with astonishment. To think of Geoffrey—Geoffrey, who had always been her charge, and who was five years and a half younger than she was—holding forth on what a man should not let his sister do! She was amused, and yet very tenderly amused. She was an exceedingly womanly little woman, and his assumption of protection gave her a secret thrill of pleasure.

"How ridiculous of you!" she cried, laughing.

"Well, I don't see that," said Geoffrey sturdily. "Of course if I was like other fellows I should provide for you." He so seldom referred to his own incapacity that Enid was quite startled at the allusion to it, and began to wonder uneasily whether he felt worse. "But I am not, and I suppose I never shall be now. I've only earned ten and sixpence during this last month, and I cost you a lot more than that. You see, Judy, when it comes to your going—— "

"Oh, don't," she cried, interrupting in dismay. "Geoff, dear, don't say that you believe that it is your duty to follow the advice of that dreadful woman in the frightful beaded jacket, who wanted to take you away from me."

To Geoffrey's utter dismay she began to cry. She was worn out by the over-strain and under-feeding of the last few weeks, she was unstrung by the excitement of the day, and Geoffrey's alarmed scolding had no effect, till the moment when he impatiently wished the philanthropic lady at the bottom of the sea. Then indeed Enid sat upright, and dashed away her tears, declaring in a rather shaky voice that she had only been laughing all the time.

"But it was a stupid joke," she said wistfully.

Geoffrey looked away from her thin, eager little face. "All the same one ought not to live on one's sister—when it is all she can do to keep herself," he said.

Geoffrey had been slower of development than the rest of his family, but he was also more pertinacious. Enid had more than once been impressed by certain qualities in him that had struck her as unfamiliar, unlike the ways of the two men she had known best. She got up, and moved restlessly about the room till he called to her not to fidget. Then she turned round sharply.

"Geoff," she said, "I think it would be awful to live alone! I could not do it. Some girls don't mind it, but I should just feel that there was no more reason for doing anything if I had only myself to work for. I simply could not stand it. I believe I should let myself starve. You see if there was no one to come home to, nothing would be worth bothering about, it would all be so pointless and so horribly blank. It frightens me even to fancy it. I've always pitied the poor things who have no one belonging to them. When you have got some one, why, of course you are anxious, I don't deny that—but then you are not all by yourself in the crowd. You see I think about this room when I am at work, but I should never live in it without you, because without you it would be like a tomb. The streets give me a sort of queer feeling sometimes, they are so full of people who pass without caring or knowing anything about each other; but then I know they have most of them got their own belongings somewhere, just as I have got you. If you were not here the crowd would—would scare me. There would be nothing to hold on to."

Geoffrey's face flushed. "All right, Judy. I had not seen it like that. I don't want to go into one of their beastly homes. I should hate it. It was only that I thought that you would have a better chance without me. I suppose that it is because you are a girl that you feel such odd things."

"I suppose so," said Enid, with a quick smile.

"We'll stick together then," said he. "And I say, we won't talk such rot any more." Whereupon they both cheered up, and were merry enough for the rest of the evening.

Yet—for the doors that divide one phase of our lives from the next hang on wondrous small hinges—yet from that evening the sister recognised that Geoff had grown up, and that their relations to each other had changed. Accident had made the lad physically dependent on his sister; but character, which is stronger than anything that touches us from the outside, was fast tending to make her seek and find moral support in him.

"Geoff is growing into a man," thought she, then

sighed to think of the limitations of that manhood, remembering with a little stab of pain what Jack Cardew had said—"a prisoner without hope of release." Happily Geoffrey never took life bitterly, nor added to pain by forestalling it.

Two days later a letter arrived from Mrs. Cardew, who never let the grass grow under her feet, and who fixed a day and hour of meeting, and begged that Enid would bring her samples of anything that she could do, and any certificates that she might possess. Gillian wrote in a very business-like manner. Whatever might be the ulterior object of her philanthropy, she always set to work with a will, and on a basis of excellent common sense.

"But I haven't a certificate to my name," poor Enid cried hopelessly.

"Take your drawings. Drawing is the thing you do best, and I will write a character for you," cried Geoffrey—which he did in terms that made them both laugh.

"I know that Mrs. Cardew will be capable, and cheerful and managing, and I shall loathe myself for being so ungrateful as to hate her," Enid declared. "It's so depressing to feel that one ought to like a person when one doesn't. When I am rich I will never be kind, I think! At least, if I am, I will never let any one know it. I will give every one what they want anonymously."

"You might stick oranges full of sovereigns, and throw them in at windows," suggested Geoffrey. "I say, what a lark that would be! But in the meantime do unpin those sketches that are stuck up on the partition and put them together; and oh, Judy, can't you do something to your boots to make them appear decent?

"I *have* inked the white places on my gloves, and I can't bother about my clothes any more," said Enid. "It really does not matter what I look like; I am not going in for an ornamental situation. Oh dear me, I wish I did not feel so shy of Mrs. Cardew. I wish she were not such a very fashionable person."

"How do you know that she is?" asked Geoffrey.

"I have heard a great deal about her," said Enid with a sigh. "The girl who sat next me at the office is a niece of Mrs. Cardew's dressmaker. There are columns about Mrs. Cardew's dresses in the fashion papers. She has as many clothes as Queen Elizabeth, and her ball was the biggest entertainment of the season. The flowers were all roses, and they grew the whole way up the staircase, and cost hundreds of pounds. She goes in for all kinds of charitable schemes, but she says quite openly that that is because her husband wishes to spend his money generously, and that she does not care about poor people herself. At the Fancy Fair her stall was crowded, and they say that she is the most beautiful woman in London."

"Then you will like her," observed Geoffrey. "For you fall in love with any one who is beautiful. You take after father and Bertie in that respect."

And Geoffrey was right, for Enid returned from the dreaded interview Gillian's warm admirer.

She told her brother all that had happened in the detailed manner that Geoff was accustomed too. "Mrs. Cardew is not a bit the sort of person I had fancied she would be," she said. "That picture of her in the *Queen* is not in the least like her. There is a great deal of character in her face. It is so strong. Do you know, I think that she is a very fashionable lady only on the surface, and that underneath she is—oh, I don't know how to explain it to you—she is more of a primitive woman than most of us. But I admired her. Do you remember how well the peasant women walked at that funny place in the mountains where they all carried their goods to market on their heads? Mrs. Cardew walks just as they do, and she holds her head up as if she were wear-

ing a crown, and were proud of it. She has lovely eyes
that are set wide apart, under very straight eyebrows.
The curve of her lips is very full, and her chin very
round, and her throat like a column. How I should love
to take her portrait! I was shown into the library. It
is a large room, with carved oak book-cases; presently
she came in. She shook hands with me. Her hands
are well shaped and strong, not narrow and small as mine
are. Then she said, 'I am glad to meet any old friend
of my husband's. He has been telling me that he once
saw a great deal of you.' Her voice is deep for a woman's,
with a great deal of tone in it. I believe that Mr. Cardew
must have asked her to be very nice to me, and I think
that she likes him very much—more," added Enid quaintly,
"more than most people like their husbands. I said, 'Yes
indeed, we were all fond of Mr. Cardew years ago,' and
she was interested, and would have me tell her all about
that time when we were in North Crescent, and when
Jack and Bertram were so often together. I could see,
though, that it was not about us that she really cared to
hear, but about her husband. She listened with great
attention. I fancy that she hopes that she may some
day get some clue to that mystery that led to the trial."

"Well, she tried to make use of you, it seems to me!"
cried Geoffrey. "I don't know that I admire your beautiful lady."

"Oh, but you would if you could see her," said the
girl quickly, "and if I were a man, she is the kind of
woman that I should want to marry. When she had
heard all that I could possibly remember about the Jack
Cardew we used to be so fond of, she made a funny little
face, and said, 'And now for business.' She asked direct
questions, and in less than a quarter of an hour she found
out just what I can, and just what I can't do. Every now
and then her eyes laughed. She was sure that I had

better not attempt to be any one's secretary, or to keep accounts, or to teach. She looked at my sketches, and said, ' What a pity that your drawing is weak, when your colour is so good and you have so much imagination! But this is what you enjoy doing, is it not? I am convinced that it is a great mistake to waste your time over anything that you don't like.' I said, ' Yes, but I must take what I can get, and one can always make oneself do the sort of work one hates.' The she gave a little decided nod. ' Oh yes, it is possible to cut a round peg into a square one, and *vice versa ;* but it is a painful process, and the bother of it is that you are bound to lose so much material in whittling. I don't approve of waste. Let's try to find a tolerably fitting hole.' "

" And has she found it ? " asked Geoffrey.

" She is going to," said Enid. (Gillian had evidently inspired her with confidence.) " I am sure that she will. I mean to strengthen my drawing, Geoff. I am going to the free classes that Mr. Cardew has started in the East End. Mrs. Cardew is to lend me the money for bus fares till I am earning something. I would not let her give it to me ; and she said that was quite right. She says she was rather poor once, and that it was very bad for her morals and did her a lot of harm. She never agrees with the people who say that poverty is good for girls. She is not even certain that it is good for boys ! "

" Hear, hear ! What an immoral lady ! " said Geoffrey. " She does not seem to have said any of the things benevolent people generally say. I think that she must be rather nice after all."

Gillian's account of the interview was shorter. It had been no great affair to her. She had not looked forward to it with dread, nor gone away elated. It had been but one small episode in her busy day.

" I have seen your friend, Miss Haubert," she said to

Jack, while she poured out his coffee the next morning.
"She is a good little soul, and I fancy cleverish in her way.
Her sketches are full of spirit and fancy, and her eyes were
taking me in all the time ; but she is not the sort of girl to
get on in the world."

"The 'getting on' instinct is not in her family," said
Jack. "But do what you can for her. You can make
some work for her somehow, and pay her well for it, can't
you ?"

"Yes, I could easily do that," said Gillian, frowning
thoughtfully. "But it would be such bad economy. One
makes jobs for the incapable, whose name is legion ; but
Miss Haubert really has some talent. I hate to do a thing
in a wasteful way."

Jack laughed. "You are a born manager ! You started
all these schemes in order to woo the world on my account,
but I believe that now you are bitten by philanthropy."

She shook her head. "Oh no, philanthropists seem to me
to attack symptoms ; they are quacks, each advertising his
own especial nostrum. I never for a moment flatter myself
that I do the least permanent good to mankind at large.
One man is enough for my ambition to work for, dear !
See, what a pile of invitations. Three are to Scotch
moors and two to Yorkshire, and one to yacht in the
Mediterranean."

Jack looked at her with rather lazy admiration. "Yes,
you have conquered London society," he said. "How
much longer is this whirl going to last ? Even you are
fagged, Gill ; and, except at this hour in the morning, you
never have a spare moment. Do you really enjoy this
sort of thing ? It seems to me that we are in rather a
stifling atmosphere, and that there is not room to stretch in."

Gillian, who was watching him, read the expression on
his face aright. "You are longing to be off, alone, somewhere," said she.

"No, no, I don't want to leave you," he answered, with some compunction, and a passing wonder as to how Gill knew. "It is only that I have an idiotic fancy that I could get my bearings better if I were to go to the North Pole, or the top of a mountain, or the middle of a desert, or—anywhere out of reach of humanity, where there would be boundless space, and leisure to turn things over. I felt a bit dazed with the turn of the wheel at first, and now I want to get far enough away to see things. I don't know that I can explain. It's only a fancy."

Gillian played with her untasted breakfast for a while; then did the very hardest thing that she had yet done, even for his dear sake.

"Do go," she said. "I shall be all right."

He got up, and paced the room with long, energetic strides. He was longing to go, yet he was fond of Gillian, fonder possibly than he knew.

"What will you do?" he said.

"I will go on wooing the world on your account," said she. "It is a most amusing occupation, Jack—and it is useful too! I do not need solitude and boundless space, for *I* don't puzzle my head over Life, with a big L, dear. Who was the clever person who remarked that women do not see the wood for the trees, nor men the trees for the wood? I am a woman. I do not care about general views."

Jack smiled. "There is no doubt that you are very much a woman. So I am to start off, eh? Are you sure that you won't be dull?"

He did not often smile and—perhaps this also was because she was a woman—the smile strengthened her resolution.

"Oh, I should be ashamed to be that," cried she. "If I feel so, no one shall guess it. Have it all out with yourself under the stars, but come back to me in time for——"

"For what, Gill?"

"For Christmas Day," she said, in a low voice.

He looked puzzled. "But I thought you did not care about that sort of thing?"

Gill laughed, and blushed, and turned her head away. "Oh, my stupid Jack!" she said. "Are all geniuses so slow in the uptake? Of course I am a thoroughly worldly woman, but the world is full of babies, you know! I do not understand prayers and meditations, but I understand that."

"Oh, I say!" he exclaimed, startled.

"You need not say anything," said Gillian, "but come back in time—won't you—to your worldly wife?"

CHAPTER VII.

THE GHOSTS OF BYGONE YEARS.

GILLIAN was not whimsical. She was a young woman who had usually a very distinct reason for whatever she did. She was not subject, as Jack was, to sudden cravings for either solitude or travel ; when therefore she refused all gayer invitations in order to bury herself at Drayton Court with old Lady Hammerton, she had, as she frankly confessed, an end in view.

Lady Hammerton was third cousin to Sir Edward Bevan, with whom Jack had contended lustily during the whole time of his legal infancy. Sir Edward had, most unfortunately, been constituted Cardew's guardian. Unfortunately, because never was a man, good in his way, more unfitted for the charge of boys.

The old knight was not in truth very popular with any one. He was a low Churchman ot an almost extinct type, and a renowned temperance lecturer. He was also a millionaire. He spent thousand of pounds in a somewhat belligerent form of philanthropy. He both bribed and drove unwilling sheep into the path that was presumably of salvation. In his own family he was cordially disliked and feared. Yet he had fine qualities, and, to the best of his belief, his life exemplified his preaching. His integrity was absolute, and that he was an unpleasing example was perhaps not entirely his own fault.

Sir Edward was a stern and aggressive ascetic. He

93

did not fast because he would have considered such a practice papistical; but the monkish spirit that sees evil in all that gives pleasure to the senses was his, in large measure. His son was fourteen years Jack's senior; he had been a man when Jack at twelve years old had been delivered to Sir Edward's injudicious mercies. Cyril Bevan had been preached to from his earliest infancy, and familiarity had bred in him a contempt of a good many things that most of us hold sacred. It was tragic enough that the son of so scrupulous a father should be a profligate and, when it suited his purpose, a hypocrite; but there are some lessons that mother nature teaches with a heavy and unsparing hand.

Jack had been an incorruptibly honest boy, with clean and wholesome instincts, and warm affections. Sir Edward ruined his temper, but Jack somehow managed to preserve his honesty intact, which, considering all things, was a good deal to his credit. He hated Cyril Bevan heartily and his guardian boyishly. He would probably have done exceedingly well at a public school; but Sir Edward regarded public schools as sinks of iniquity, and kept the lad, so far as it was possible, under his own eye.

The painstaking stupidity of the conscientious seems at times to bear more bitter fruit than the carelessness of worse men. Jack was a real grief to his guardian, who, though he certainly never spared the rod, had at moments a dim idea that the child was spoilt. The boy became more insubordinate as he grew older and began to feel his strength. There came a day when the time-honoured practice of Solomon's advice became an impossibility for a very simple reason. After a highly undignified scuffle, such as only a very stupid man would have provoked, Jack broke both the rod and the last remnant of authority that his guardian had possessed, and went out of the house never to return to it.

It was after this lamentable occurrence that Lady Hammerton had chanced to meet the lad, and had persuaded him to take refuge with her at Draycott Court. She had hoped to patch up a reconciliation between guardian and ward, but gave up the attempt when she discovered how far matters had gone.

Lady Hammerton was one of the few people who understood Sir Edward, but she had the deepest pity for Sir Edward's ward. She had in her youth refused an offer of marriage from her third cousin, and had since congratulated herself on her wisdom, but she liked him none the less for that.

Now that she was an old woman and Sir Edward was an old man, they were still friends, and Sir Edward was expected at Draycott Court on the occasion of Mrs. Cardew's visit.

Draycott Court is an old timbered house, built with wings at right angles, that shelter the rose-garden. The timber is black with age, and the roses have bloomed against it for Heaven knows how many summers.

Gillian had no great love of old buildings ; she preferred everything that was new, but even she was impressed by the dignified pathos of the place.

Beyond the rose-garden, that Lady Hammerton herself kept in order, and which seemed to hold in its heart the very sweetness and charm of bygone days, was the outer garden, and that, alas ! was neglected and overgrown. A blush would sometimes rise to Lady Hammerton's cheek when she walked in it. The grass paths that needed clipping, the sweet tangle of flowers, the delicate garden ladies half choked and crowded out by their hardier cousins, the wild wreaths of convolvulus that barred her way, all seemed to breathe reproach upon her—a reproach that was insistent and silent !

What would her forefathers have said ? Would clean

kennels for homeless curs, and fields where worn-out cart-horses might rest their weary legs, appease those angry ghosts?

" But I am perfectly justified," the old lady would reply to these accusing thoughts. "I inherited debts, and I have paid them off. That is something. As to the rest, I have no child, and why should I spend money for the benefit of Cyril Bevan? Sir Edward is as old as I am, and my life is the better of the two. It is his son who will come after me. What is the use of bolstering up the old place for such as him?" and she continued to save and scrape that she might give with both hands to her fads.

Lady Hammerton was not in the habit of having visitors to stay with her. They cost too much. But she always made an exception to her rule for her cousin, and on this occasion she broke through it for the Cardews.

Hammertons, Cardews, Bevans—these were all riders of hobbies. They had intermarried for generations; they were cranky and ill to live with. They carped at each other's madness; they quarrelled bitterly and often, and forgave seldom. Yet when an outsider attacked one of them, the others were all absolutely certain that that outsider was wrong.

Mr. Cardew had contributed handsomely to the old lady's charities, but it is probable that she would have stood by him in any case. She was sorry that Gillian came alone.

Gillian arrived one fine summer evening, and seemed to bring with her an atmosphere of present-day energy and bustle, that was foreign to the quiet old house.

In the hot weather the hall door at Draycott Court stood wide open all day. Lady Hammerton came down to the hall to welcome her guest. She had put on her best dress to do Gillian honour; it was of that peculiar blue that is only seen in very old silks, and that is just the colour of columbines; the pink in her cheeks reminded Gillian of a faded blush-rose. She greeted her friend very kindly, but with old-fashioned ceremony. Gillian smiled to think what a different flavour her welcome here had to the reception she would have met with at any of the other houses to which she might have gone. Not that she would not have been gladly received anywhere, for Gillian was a much sought after person nowadays, but here she instinctively felt that her visit was a really important event.

There is an especial charm about the hospitality, as there is about the friendship, that is extended to a few only.

"We have been considering where you would prefer to drink your tea, my dear," said Lady Hammerton, "and I think that you will like best to have it on the terrace. Londoners like to see green trees. But I will take you to your room first."

The oak-panelled raftered hall seemed silent and vast as some dark old church. The evening light fell through a stained window on to the broad, shallow staircase and on to the young woman and the old woman as they mounted the polished black steps.

"The carpet has worn out," said Lady Hammerton. "But the oak looks handsome enough without it, and there are no children to clatter up and down. The maids go by the back way, and the ghost makes no noise."

"Have you seen the ghost?" asked Gillian.

"Oh yes," said the old lady simply. "Many and many a time; but he does me no harm, and I do not think that he even notices me. We come and go, but he stays on. When I am dead he will still be here; and Cyril Bevan will be afraid of him."

"*You* are not afraid?"

"Dear me, no!" said Lady Hammerton. "But I come of gentle blood on both sides, my love—not that that is

7

anything to boast of, for the Almighty puts us in our places—and good blood is not cowardly. Poor Cyril's mother was a nobody. You can see that by the way Cyril tells lies. Not that I have met him since he was twenty-four, but he told me a fib then, and I have never forgotten it."

"I do not like Mr. Bevan either," said Gillian. "Mammy and I saw rather too much of him once. All the same, when you come to consider that he must now be nearly fifty, it seems rather hard to remember a fib that he fibbed at twenty-four. Oh, good gracious!" cried Gill, stopping short suddenly, and regarding the old lady with laughter-filled eyes. "I've told heaps of white lies in the course of my life, and I would tell a jet-black one, any minute, in order to save Jack from any harm! I am sure that I would. Now, do you think, after this, that you want to have me to stay with you?"

"There are fibs and fibs," said Lady Hammerton sturdily. "I have always respected you, my dear, and I am very pleased to have you here. Look, this is to be your room."

Gillian glanced round eagerly as they entered. The walls of the chamber were hung with tapestry, and over the fireplace was an extraordinary old picture, in a black frame.

"It is not at all a proper subject, but it is one that the old masters were unaccountably fond of," said Lady Hammerton. "The replica of that picture hangs in the National Gallery. When your husband was a boy, and stayed in this very room, I turned it with its face to the wall."

"Susannah and the Elders!" cried Mrs. Cardew triumphantly. "Oh, I am so glad that I have got Jack's old room. He once told me all about it."

Lady Hammerton shook her head. "I am afraid that

Jack must have peeped," she said regretfully. "And I have always assured Sir Edward that he was really a nice-minded boy."

"So he was," said Gillian quickly. "He was always the most generous and honourable——Oh, I forgot that I did not know him then!"

She laughed and blushed, but Lady Hammerton saw nothing to laugh at.

"You must talk to Sir Edward," she said. "I have often endeavoured to persuade him that he does not understand boys. He is too suspicious. You will see him to-morrow, and I hope that you will support me."

Gillian had a curious sensation for a moment. She felt as if, in this queer old room, she had seen the man with the hour-glass pushed back. The old lady was not childish or dreamy; she understood, when it was put before her, that Mr. Cardew was no longer a boy, but a man verging on middle age, and a man who had been the victim of a most terrible misfortune. She knew that Sir Edward had long ceased to be Jack's guardian. Yet the old miserable quarrels were still fresher to her mind than the later tragedy, and the poor lad more vivid to her than the man.

"I want to talk to Sir Edward Bevan about Jack," said Gillian. Indeed, truth to say, that was her first object in coming. Yet she had had another reason too. She had had a fancy to see the house that had sheltered her husband when he was a boy, and a desire to give pleasure to the woman who had befriended him.

Lady Hammerton found her young friend greatly improved by matrimony. Gillian, whom she had once fancied a trifle too hard, was now both gentle and merry. She never interrupted a long story nor showed the least weariness of the ways of old age. She was sympathetic as well as amusing. She waited on the old lady like a daughter, and was respectful as she had never been before. Lady Hammerton was charmed, and Gillian took infinite pains to be charming.

Gillian slept in the tapestried chamber where an angry, sore boy had found sanctuary, and her gratitude took shapes that were pretty as the grey doves that flew over the roses and cooed in the elms. She could not do enough for her hostess. She was an essentially practical person, and to do was always her instinct. When she was a girl Gillian had not cared about the society of old people, but it never occurred to Lady Hammerton that all this tender, willing service was given for Jack's sake. It is not always that good deeds, like curses, come home to roost in recognisable form.

"I never before wished for a daughter, but I should really like to have you for my constant companion," the old lady said one day. "I feared that you might find it dull here, for you were so fond of gaiety, but you seem quite content."

And Gillian, although she had no desire to be the constant companion of any one save Jack, to whom her thoughts flew like homing birds, and though she could not have borne to have lived in this haunted, old-world place, turned her bright face to Lady Hammerton with a smile that was as warm as summer sunshine.

"I am very content to be with you," she said.

The two ladies sat at tea on the terrace on the evening of the day on which Sir Edward was expected.

"I am delighted that my cousin will meet you," Lady Hammerton remarked, with a pretty little air of triumph, "for I am sure that he would never have given poor Jack credit for so good a choice."

Gillian looked straight before her under her level brows. Lady Hammerton little guessed how hot an indignation some of her old stories aroused.

"I mean Sir Edward to like me," she said, "because I

believe that it will be good for Jack's reputation that he should say publicly that he has never believed that judgment just. In London people live so fast! they have pretty well forgotten what the trial was all about, but here in Jack's own county it is different."

"But my cousin Edward had never much faith in any one's goodness," said Lady Hammerton; "I noticed that when I was young. I felt that I could not marry a man who had not got it in him to thoroughly trust another person."

"I think that you were wise," said Gillian. "But Sir Edward does know that Jack never tried to get money on false pretences. If he did not believe that I would not shake hands with him to-day. As it is——" She set her small square teeth hard together, and left the sentence unfinished. As is was, she found it difficult to forgive the tyranny that had shadowed Jack's youth.

"But it is silly to take matters tragically," she remarked. "It is a kind of cutting off one's nose to spite one's face. Do you know that when Jack was in prison Sir Edward wrote to him? There was a great deal of—preach" (Gill had been about to say of cant, but changed the word in deference to Sir Edward's cousin) "and of moralising in the letter. The writer seemed to imagine that all Jack's misfortunes were a judgment on gambling and racing and going to plays. It irritated me! But Jack was surprised that Sir Edward should actually have been sure that he was innocent."

There was a tone in Gillian's deep voice that made her companion look at her with quickened interest.

"Think of that! he was immensely surprised. One learns to be thankful for small mercies!" said Jack's wife.

And at that moment a spare, grey-complexioned man came round the left wing of the house and walked towards them between the bushes.

Lady Hammerton greeted the new comer with just a tiny flutter of excitement. Thirty years ago Sir Edward had proposed to marry her, here in this very rose-garden. Since then he had divorced his wife, and had quarrelled with his only son, and had taken to lecturing on temperance, and to protesting against papistical tendencies in the Church. Since then Lady Hammerton had grown old and a trifle eccentric, but the rose-garden was the same as ever, and the ghosts of roses long dead haunted the old couple still, and sweetened their intercourse. Sir Edward had never a hard word for his cousin Anne, and Lady Hammerton was the one person in the world who was disinterestedly glad to see him.

Gillian's keen sight was softened by no kindly mist of bygone years. She thought Sir Edward a sour and peevish old man. He had a high, narrow forehead, and a scanty fringe of grey beard grew under his long chin. The lines that ran from his nostrils to the corners of his thin lips were very deep. The cut of his coat gave him the look of a Dissenting minister.

Nevertheless Mrs. Cardew smiled brightly when he was introduced to her; and the clasp of her firm hand, the abundant health and strength that seemed to emanate from her, gave the visitor a sense of warmth and comfort. He was a constitutionally chilly person, apt to shiver on the warmest day.

Gillian, at her friend's request, presided over the tea-table, and she made the centre of a picture pretty enough to cheer even an old man's heart. Sir Edward had expected to see a smartly-dressed and bepowdered town lady. Mrs. Cardew, in her loose cambric blouse, with her glossy hair brushed back in waves from her forehead, with her straight glance and stately bearing, took him by surprise. He approved the simplicity of her dress, not guessing that fresh simplicity, though becoming, is by no means cheap.

It appeared to him that, in respect to marriage, Cardew must have had better luck than he deserved. Then he reflected that beauty is but skin deep, and very deceitful; but the reflection halted. It was difficult to think of the mortality of mortals while watching Gillian. Gillian was so very much alive.

They lingered over tea till the sun began to cast long shadows; then Mrs. Cardew wandered off to read the old dial and to feed the pigeons, and presently betook herself to the house to write to Jack. Lady Hammerton's bright old eyes followed the younger woman's movements with approving pleasure.

"Mrs. Cardew has grown a notable person," said she. "I do not know another, of the present generation, who can walk across a lawn as she does. I always say that it takes brains as well as health to walk well."

"She has a most independent carriage," said Sir Edward. He could not help admiring Mrs. Cardew, but he did not think so much independence befitting in so young a woman.

"Well, cousin," said Lady Hamerton briskly, "I must say that it is lucky sometimes when girls have got wills of their own. I do not know what would become of some of the Jacks if all the Jills were of the gentle and yielding kind."

Sir Edward relaxed into a grim smile. "Jack has a will, and a temper too," he remarked, "though I ought to have broken it."

"Now, there I am convinced you were mistaken," Cousin Anne replied, with an emphatic nod of her head. And they plunged into the old, old dispute, that had lost its bitterness through age, and argued quite amicably, with blunted weapons that gave no wounds.

Gillian, standing by her window, watched the old couple for a minute, then turned away with a smile, and began to write to Jack.

"Dearest"—she wrote—"Sir Edward Bevan and Lady

Hammerton are carrying on the ghost of a flirtation in the rose-garden, and they do not want me, who am no ghost, but quite vulgarly alive, and of to-day. The atmosphere is full of the past; it almost makes me sad. I wish for you every moment of the day, but I am glad that you are miles away, and that I had strength of mind enough not to go too. I am so properly behaved here, that you would hardly recognise me. I visit poor people, and go to see my mother (who is looking worn and nervous), and retire to bed at ten every night, and hardly ever shock my dear old lady. I do not think that I can stand Sir Edward Bevan long. I tingle with rage when I consider how bad he must have been for you when you were a boy. No wonder that you have such a red-haired temper, and are altogether such a bad lot. I think that his religion is heavy enough to drag him down to—— where do you suppose, darling? But I daresay that the recording angel will remember that he wrote to you in prison, and that that may pull the other way. I will try to remember that fact too. I hope that the desert is doing you good! I am manfully, no, womanfully, endeavouring not to be jealous of it. Men are jealous of other men only; it is women who are jealous of the interests they can't share. But do write books again, Jack. I do so want you to take your place in the world once more. You must not be wasted because that awful unjust thing happened. I know that it would have spoilt most men's lives, but you are not like most men; you are my Jack, whose little finger is worth more than all the world to me. My dear, my dear, I sometimes could wish that I were a good woman such as Jane is, because then I might be more of an inspiration to you; but perhaps if I had been religious I should not have loved you quite so well. You would not have got it *all*.

"Now do not go in for a black wife in the desert, because if you do she will be sure to follow you to England. It takes all my civilisation to prevent me from trotting off to

Africa, and the happy Blackamoor (or will she be brown ?) won't be hampered by petticoats or scruples. Mammy would be so shocked ! Do not get a sun-stroke, because I should mind that more than a regiment of black wives. I am all right as usual—except that I ache to see you.

" Yours (quite and entirely),

" GILLIAN."

She folded her letter with a shrug of her shoulders. It seemed feeble and inadequate. It was impossible to express to Jack the half of what she felt and hoped for him. Then she put on her hat and went out again, calling cheerily to her hostess as she passed through the garden,—

" I have been writing a line to my husband, to tell him how well we do without him. It does not do to let him grow conceited ! "

CHAPTER VIII.

"*SHE IS LAYING UP NO CROWNS OF GLORY.*"

THE village post-office was but a quarter of a mile from the Court, and Gillian, having posted her letter, was loth to turn back. The atmosphere of Draycott Court seemed to her to be mentally as well as morally stifling. The importance given to the smaller details of life, the routine of minor duties, worried her to-day. Even her amusement at the pretty philandering of the old cousins was tinged with impatience.

Stress and passion were all over for the kind old lady who pursued her fads with an aftermath of energy. Mrs. Cardew was too much a woman of the world and had too much self-control to allow herself to appear bored, but there were moments when the fundamental difference between youth and age made her impatient, when she felt as if she were a giantess bound by cobwebs.

She had got half-way to Oaklands Park when, at a turn of the winding lane, she met a funeral. She squeezed into the hedge to let it go by, averting her eyes with a qualm of sick disgust. Gillian was no coward, and would have faced any danger with decision and presence of mind, but she hated to come in contact with death. The sight of a dead beast filled her with just the same sort of horrified revolt as did the sight of a dead man. She had an almost Oriental shrinking from a corpse.

The procession was very simple. A cart with a village-made coffin on it was followed by four mourners, who tramped along with business-like gravity, but who were by no means overcome by grief. One of the men touched his hat to Mrs. Cardew.

"We are after buryin' Liza Pocock, ma'am," said he.

"Oh, poor thing!" cried Gillian with a shudder.

Then they tramped steadily on their way, and Gillian hurried on, scoffing at herself because her heart beat faster, as if in protest against that which would one day still it.

Gillian had lately learnt that Liza Pocock was the name of the woman whom she had once met carrying a baby up the Drum Hill. Liza had been in service in London, but had returned to her native village to die. Her husband had not accompanied her. He was an old man, and reputed a miser. It was said that he grudged the journey money, and had let her kill herself by tramping. Gill had heard this gossip from Lady Hammerton, who always took a keen interest in the affairs of the village, and who dealt out blankets, beef-tea, and advice, with sprightly beneficence. Mrs. Cardew said to herself, with the humour that often tinged her reflections, that Liza, who had always offended by her sullen reserve, had now put the last stone on the heap of her delinquencies, by slipping out of the world without giving due warning.

What had become of the baby? Gillian wondered if the poor mite had survived its mother. She turned a few steps out of the road, in order to knock at the door of the cottage where lived Liza's "granny."

Mrs. Adams was sitting by the fireplace, rocking a wooden cradle with her foot, and reading from a Bible that rested on the table in front of her. She considered it right and proper to read her Bible while her grand-daughter was being buried, but her eyes were tired, and she was not sorry to be interrupted.

Mrs. Cardew seemed to bring a wave of fresh air into the stuffy room. "I have come to ask how baby is. May I peep at her?" said she. She knelt down by the cradle, and gently lifted a corner of the sheet. "She is dreadfully thin, and her arms are like sticks! Do you think that you are giving her the right food?"

"There isn't no manner of use, to my mind, in pampering her up with first one thing and then another," replied Mrs. Adams. "That child ain't meaning to live whatever is done. She dwindles every day. Have you heard that Liza was took three nights ago?"

"Yes," replied Gillian shortly. She was anxious to avoid hearing details about Liza's last hours, and her usual *savoir-faire* deserted her. Gillian always owned that she had no talent whatever for visiting the poor.

"She had a great fancy to see you, ma'am, just on the last evening about eight o'clock, but I didn't see what call you had to come through all that thunder-storm, and so I told her. "'Tisn't likely I should ask such a thing of Mrs. Cardew,'" says I. "'But I'll send for the vicar if you wishes it, Liza, for that is a different matter altogether, and it is what he is for, and it is only fitting, and high time too, that you should begin to think about your soul.' For indeed, ma'am, I knew by her breathing that the end was not far off, and Liza was always a terrible heathen. But she wouldn't 'ave the vicar, not even though I told her plain that it was her bounden duty to turn her thoughts that way. It was you she kept wantin' to talk to."

"Me!" cried Gillian. "But what possible good could I have done to her?"

"That is what I said, ma'am—meaning no offence. 'Mrs. Cardew is young,' I says—'though not so very young now. And though she may 'ave got religion, she don't appear as if she 'ad. She'll leave without a word of sacred things, or so much as offering to read the Bible, and she don't speak as I've always been accustomed to 'ear ladies speak.' (You'll excuse my outspokenness, ma'am, for I am meaning no disrespect.) 'I can't feel sure,' says I, 'that she will even pray by your dying bed.' That is what I said to poor Liza, ma'am—I would not make so bold as to rebuke my betters, for I know my place."

There was a stern gleam in the old woman's light blue eyes, that brightened into anger when the corners of Mrs. Cardew's lips twitched with a suppressed smile.

"You were perfectly right," said Gillian. "I am sure that it would never have occurred to me to pray by Liza's bed; but no one who knows me would ever expect that sort of thing from me. What could she have wanted?"

"I could not say for certain, I'm sure, ma'am," said Mrs. Adams. Then she added unwillingly, for her conscience pricked her for disregarding her grand-daughter's last wishes, "It had to do with something she'd said in a witness box at a trial, but as I says to her, she had no time to go worriting over that, when she had so soon to stand before the Judgment Seat."

Mrs. Cardew sprang to her feet with an exclamation of dismay. But the moment before she had congratulated herself that she had not been summoned; now she would have given pounds to have been in time to have heard Liza's belated confession.

"Oh, why did you not send for me?" she cried.

Mrs. Adams pursed her lips, and looked askance at her visitor. She had never approved of Mrs. Cardew. She resented the jokes that Gillian made, the way in which she laughed, the strain of originality that ran through her character. She was a conservative old woman, and she also, though secretly, resented the fact of a self-made man rebuilding Oaklands Park. Mr. Clovis was a kind land-lord, and she never dreamed of refusing to take advantage of his kindness, but in her own mind she did not put either him, or his wife, or his step-daughter, on a level with the " real gentry."

" I hadn't no thought that it might be a convenience to *you* to send up to the Court," said she. " My mind was took up with Liza's dying."

Gillian stood silent for a moment. She was not a child to let her anger master her sense of the expedient. There would be no use, but rather hindrance, in expressing indignation.

" Of course you could not possibly know that I should be interested," said she. " But please try now to remember exactly what Liza said to you."

She put her hand in her pocket, and held half-a-crown between her finger and thumb. Gillian never gave gold where silver would do as well. Cardew was extravagant ; but his wife, albeit she could spend lavishly, was apt to get her money's worth.

After all there was not much information to be gathered. Liza Pocock had been parlour-maid in the house where Jack had lodged in his bachelor days. It had been her business to answer the front-door bell. She had sworn at the trial that she had let no one into his rooms between the hours of five and seven. It appeared that she had sworn falsely. She had said to her grandmother, "I did not mean to do Mr. Cardew any harm, but now I think I did injure him without wishing to. I would like to tell her, before I go. I fancied I might get *him* into trouble if I let on that he had gone into Mr. Cardew's room. He told me not to tell of it. I did not know then that he was dead. No one guessed that he was anything to me. How should they ? I did not hear of the accident till a month later, and then by chance. By that time I could not go back on what I had sworn, and I didn't take in that Mr. Cardew could be punished. I was mazed with my ow... troubles. I didn't understand till quite the last."

It was a confused statement at the best, and Gillian

found it hard to disentangle the pronouns, and to detach what Liza had said from the grandmother's comments and guesses.

She questioned and cross-questioned, till the old woman grew huffy and tacitly refused to answer any more. Then she put the half-crown down on the table.

"If I had been sent for I might have got on the track of the truth," she said. "But even then Liza's confession would have been too late. Nothing can ever undo what been has done. Nothing."

She spoke with a sternness that made Mrs. Adams momentarily uncomfortable.

"I did not get at the rights of all that Liza was telling," she said, "It did seem more befitting that she should turn her mind to solemn things, ma'am. But if she had done Mr. Cardew a wrong, no doubt she wanted to ask you to pardon it, he being in foreign parts."

Mrs. Cardew paused on the threshold of the door.

"I should certainly not have forgiven her—if she swore against my husband. Perhaps it is as well for her that I did not come," she said briefly. "Well, Mrs. Adams, I will ask Mr. Clovis if he will let you have the milk for the baby from that cow that has just lost her calf. Good-evening."

Mrs. Adams shook her head. "*She* ain't laying by any crowns of glory for herself," said she.

Gillian went on her way with a grave face. She felt excited, but at the same time baffled. She was a brave woman, but there were moments when the sense of the inevitable subdued and almost terrified her. Through good report and ill she had clung to Jack. She knew in her heart that, though she was no saint like Jane, she had yet fought in her own fashion with devils of despair and recklessness, that had all but pulled her lover down. She knew too that the struggle had been none the less grim because she had never spoken of it, or posed as a saviour.

She had a confidence in herself that was not vanity but
was founded on experience. She was a woman who held
very strong natural weapons, and who knew how to use
them ; but no natural weapon can force Death to relinquish
that which he has set his seal on. He alone hears no
argument, and has absolutely no price. Gillian felt that
he had shut a door in her face, and that her warm hands
might beat against it in vain. The thought depressed her.
She had ceased to enjoy her walk, and the very beauty of
the evening jarred on her. She said to herself that she
disliked pathos, and that there was always something
unavoidably pathetic in the going down of the sun.

She found Mrs. Clovis in the garden, entertaining a bevy
of ladies. They were all discoursing on the iniquities of
Miss Nina Tyrell, a black though pretty sheep from whom
whiter and better folded lambs were carefully guarded.

" I have told Alice and Ethel that I really will not have
them speak to Nina," a stout, motherly looking lady was
saying when Mrs. Cardew joined them on the lawn. " Of
course we must bow when we meet her, for I always say
that there is no need to be rude to any one, and her father
is a gentleman, though he *has* married his cook. But after
her behaviour at the hunt ball I should not like my girls
to be seen talking with her. I wish that she did not sit
next us in church ! "

Mrs. Cardew smiled. She reflected that Mrs. Lacy's
girls must be thirty if they were a day, and that Nina
must be now nearly nineteen.

" It certainly would be dreadful if little Nina were to
have a dangerous influence over the Miss Lacys," said she.
" How does she get on with her step-mother ? "

But no one could answer that question, for the new Mrs.
Tyrell was not visited.

" She goes to all the dances at the barracks unchaperoned,"
said the vicar's wife. " She let Mr. Dagmar drive her

home in his dog-cart, and they both smoked all the way."

"If it were only Mr. Dagmar, but there is Captain Hartfield too, and he is a married man," said Mrs. Lacy.

"We are giving a little carpet dance next week, and I have been wondering whether there would be any harm in inviting her," said a very gentle little lady timidly. "I should not wish to do anything that could give offence, but——"

"I should not ask her," said Mrs. Lacy decidedly ; "one ought to consider one's own children first."

"I was quite willing to have her to the school feast," said the vicar's wife. "She might have helped to cut the bread and butter, and a school feast is always more or less of a public entertainment—one asks every one. But I would not go beyond that, and I should have kept Rose and Ernest at the other table. Ernest always wants to be too friendly."

"She did not go to cut the bread and butter, did she?" said Gillian.

"No, she did not. I thought her note most ungrateful," said Mrs. Dawson ; "but Nina Tyrell has no nice feeling."

"That is exactly what mammy used to say about me when I annoyed her," cried Mrs. Cardew, laughing. "I was always such an unfeeling girl, was I not, mammy? Poor Nina! I wonder whether it would amuse her to come to stay with me in London. We might manage to crowd the ineligible Mr. Dagmar and the old married flirt out of her head."

Mrs. Lacy grew red with eagerness. "Amuse her! You are almost too good-natured, Mrs. Cardew," she said. "Why, I am sure that there are many really nice girls who would dance for joy at the chance. It does seem almost a pity——"

She broke off short, for Mrs. Cardew was looking at her

8

with rather a disconcerting twinkle in her eyes. Some of the matrons agreed afterwards that the poor lady's evident eagerness was rather ridiculous, and yet there was no doubt that since Mrs. Cardew was so hospitably inclined it did certainly seem almost a pity——

Gillian lingered till they had all gone, and then sat down in a garden chair by her mother.

"I am not at all fond of girls, and it will be a great nuisance to have to look after Nina," she remarked, " but I was determined to make Mrs. Brown and Mrs. Dawson envy her! I think I succeeded."

"But really, dear love," said Mrs. Clovis languidly, " Mrs. Brown has every right to take care of her own daughters, and a vicar's wife is so bound to be particular."

" Is she ? " said Gillian. "She belongs to a society that professes to rescue girls out of the streets, does not she? Yes, I know that she does, for she bothered me to collect subscriptions on a horrid little card, no longer ago than yesterday. Well, mammy, if she sets a dozen poor creatures who have come to grief at a dozen washtubs, do you suppose that that will be a set-off against having given one girl of her own class a good shove on the road down ? "

Mrs. Clovis evaded the question. "I do not like to hear you jeer at a religious work," she said gently.

"But if Nina is really in danger of going too far," persisted Gillian, " is it not absurd that these extra-pious people should devote all their energies to amusing and enlightening Whitechapel when they have got a subject close at hand ? and if she is only rather silly, then why do they draw their skirts away ? Naturally she flirts with men who are bad style, when all the respectable mothers keep their children at the other side of the table. Any one can see that it is her nature to flirt with *some one.*"

"I am glad that you did not say all this to Mrs. Dawson, dearest," said Mrs. Clovis with genuine thankfulness.

"Oh, well, what Mrs. Dawson ought to do, in order to be consistent, is not, after all, my business," said Gillian. "Neither for the matter of that is what becomes of Nina Tyrell. I do not profess to interfere with any one's soul. In fact, I have been reproved on that score this very afternoon, by old Mrs. Adams. Do you know that Liza bore false witness at the trial?"

Mrs. Clovis gave a little jump. She had always been a nervous woman, and her present easy life seemed to have increased her delicacy in this respect.

"How you startle me!" she cried. "You introduce painful subjects so violently. Surely, dear Gillian, it is better to forget that miserable business entirely. It is all over, and nothing that we can do or say can make any difference now. Jack cannot be tried again in any case; and I for one always felt certain that he was innocent."

Gillian could have replied that her mother had taken an odd way of showing her confidence, but she refrained, having seldom any desire to quarrel.

"It is easy to talk of forgetting," she said, with a smile that was unconsciously sad. "I think that forgetfulness and forgiveness are both constitutional, and have very little to do with one's will. Of course it is more comfortable to forget, but if one has been pretty deeply marked, why then the scars won't ever quite rub out. I should never wish to forgive a person who had deliberately done harm to Jack. I should be ashamed of myself if I could. Why, what is the matter, mammy?"

Mrs. Clovis had uttered a sharp exclamation of genuine horror, and pressed her lace handkerchief to her face. She was really moved, and her voice trembled.

"You speak so—so profanely," she said, "sometimes you quite frighten me! I know that, if I say to you that that is not what the Church teaches us we should feel to our enemies, you will laugh at me, for you always laugh at sacred things. Perhaps that is my fault, Gillian (though I must say that I have always been a good church-woman), for I know that before my second marriage I was sometimes driven to—to pursue a course of action that I should not countenance now. But I was never profane, never. It hurts me to hear you declare that you would actually be ashamed to forgive—that is Jack's influence."

"No," said Gillian gravely, "Jack is softer than I am." But the sight of her mother's distress surprised and filled her with compunction. She put her cool strong hand on Mrs. Clovis's small delicate one, with an unusual demonstration of affection.

" I am a brute," she said. "I did not in the least mean to shock you. I am sorry I aired my heathenish sentiments! But I do think that you are dreadfully easily upset to-day. I suppose that is because there is thunder in the air. You never can stand thunder, and I am like a cart-horse! No change of climate affects me in the least. Look here, do you think that Liza's baby might be supplied with milk from the farm? I do not know whether she is insured, but I am quite sure that she is not properly fed at present."

Mrs. Clovis brightened up at the suggestion. She was always kind to poor people, and she was very glad to put that other subject aside. There was no doubt in her mind that she would always have been a scrupulously honourable woman had she started with plenty of money. Since she had married Mr. Clovis she had played the *rôle* that he had expected her to play *con amore*. She had not been in love with "dearest George" on her wedding day, and his vulgarities had then been very obvious to her, but now she was surprisingly fond of her good husband. He had lifted her suddenly from overwhelming difficulties into an atmosphere of admiration and luxury. To do her justice, it was not the luxury that touched what heart she possessed.

She did not wish to be reminded that she had ever been a
little less angelic than he thought her, and perhaps that
feeling was not entirely to be condemned.   Mrs. Clovis
loved her son too; he was dearer to her than her daughter
had ever been.   Gillian had faced angry duns, and had
been consulted on all kinds of unchildish subjects before
she was fourteen, but the boy had seen no ugly side of
life, he simply adored his pretty mother.   Mrs. Clovis had
leaned heavily on Gill, but had yet been secretly sore at
the girl's want of respect.   She was an illogical woman,
who was apt to consider it hard that she could never have
her cake after she had eaten it.

Mr. Clovis joined the ladies on the lawn presently, and
took a rather fussy interest in the consultation about Liza's
baby.

He enjoyed doing village-benefactor, and his step-
daughter's keen sense of humour was often tickled by him.

"When are you coming to stay with us, Miss Gill?
What?   Oh, to be sure, I should have said Mrs. Gill, but
the other comes pat to me," he said when she took her
leave.

"When you invite my husband," answered Gillian, with
the directness that sometimes disconcerted people.   "Certainly not before."

Mr. Clovis shook his head ruefully as he subsided into
the chair that Gillian had vacated.

"She is very fond of her convict," he remarked.   "It is
a sad pity, a sad pity!   She is a loyal wife.   But that she
could not fail to be, considering whose daughter she is, eh,
my dear?"

CHAPTER IX.

THIS KIND GOETH NOT OUT.

"This can come forth by nothing but by prayer and fasting."

GILLIAN hurried along the road on her way back, fearing lest she should be late for dinner; but she was destined to meet with one more interruption. She had reached the turn of the lane where she had encountered the funeral, when she came upon another unexpected sight.

A girl, in a pink cotton dress, and a short fair man were loitering side by side, he with his arm round his companion's waist. The girl slid from his embrace when she saw Mrs. Cardew, and lifting a pair of very beautiful dark eyes, stared defiantly, but the man raised his hat.

"Why, I believe we are quite old friends. Won't you remember me?" he said, holding out his hand to Gillian.

He had a winning smile, and his light-coloured eyes had a twinkle of fun in them. One hardly noticed at first that they were rather shifty and difficult to meet. He appeared younger than his years, till a close inspection showed the tell-tale crow's feet. He had a singularly pleasant and melodious voice, and was indeed a most easy-tempered rascal.

Gillian evaded the hand, but answered him civilly. "Dear me, yes! I remember that we met at Monte Carlo," she said. "It must be fifteen years since I last saw you, Mr. Bevan, but I never forget a face—even of the most casual acquaintance."

The recollection amused her. She had once been afraid lest her mother should marry the "horrid little man." She had had an instinctive girlish distrust of him. He could do her no harm now, and though she was by no means inclined to grant friendship, it was not her way to make enemies. Cyril Bevan was not worth her enmity.

Mr. Bevan glanced up at her with his head on one side. He possessed unbounded assurance, and though he was quick-witted, he was apparently impervious to a snub.

"You were in short petticoats, with your hair in a pig-tail," said he. "It is immensely clever of me to recognise you!"

He thoroughly appreciated the improvement that years had worked. The sturdy, independent school-girl, who had frequently stood in his way at Monte Carlo, had turned into an unusually distinguished woman. She was not so pretty as her mother had been, but she had more *aplomb*, and more character.

Mrs. Cardew smiled in a politely perfunctory manner. "Immensely," she assented. "I must leave you to that comfortable reflection." She turned to the girl. "I am lucky to have met you, Nina. I have been wishing to talk to you. Will you walk a little way with me? for I shall be late for dinner if I stop."

Nina Tyrell hesitated. She was surprised, and she was rather curious to know what Mrs. Cardew could possibly have to say to her.

The girl had noted the change of manner when Gillian addressed her. Mrs. Cardew had then spoken in a friendly way, but she had held Mr. Bevan at arm's length. Nina was accustomed to being ostracised, and was morbidly conscious of shades of expression.

While she debated, Gillian settled the question. "You must forgive me for robbing you of your companion. Good-evening—so amusing to have met again," she said to Cyril

Bevan, with a slight bow of dismissal, and somehow Nina found herself walking on.

"You don't mind hurrying, do you? My old lady will be so put out if I am unpunctual," said Gillian. "Every-thing goes by clock-work at the Court. I could not live that kind of life, but it is a refreshing change for a time. There is no sense in staying with the same kind of people one is accustomed to seeing at home. We talk about change of air, but it is change of mental atmosphere that we want. Don't you think so?"

"I don't know. I don't often think," said the girl defiantly.

She was pouting, and she was a trifle sulky. She was habitually on the defensive when she was in the society of women, and a sudden suspicion that Mrs. Cardew was about to improve the occasion had assailed her. She turned carelessly away from Gillian, and plunged her hand into the hedge to pick a wild rose. Her own clear pink colour was as pure and transparent as that of the newly plucked flower that she stuck in her belt. The light brown hair on her forehead curled in a way that called to mind the tendrils of a vine.

"At least she will be no trouble to launch," thought Gillian.

"I hoped that you would agree with me," Mrs. Cardew said pleasantly.

"It does not matter whether I agree or no," replied Nina. "I am nobody."

Gillian smiled, but with a keen perception of the soreness that underlay that last speech. "My remark was not dis-interested," she said. "I wanted you to agree, because I wish to persuade you to come to London with me when I return there. Come and find out how you like the atmo-sphere of town, Nina. For my part I enjoy the winter season more than the summer."

"Oh!" said Nina, standing still. It was such a big, surprised "Oh," that they both laughed, and the girl's distrust melted a little.

"Well?" said Gill.

Nina pulled her flower to pieces, and blushed. "Why, of course I should like it," she said. "But I am sure I can't think why you should invite me. I don't suppose you would if you knew all about us. My father has married Polly—she was our cook, you know—and no one calls. Not that I care about that. We are much better without visitors. I don't want the stupid old cats to come and pity me—and I am fond of Polly."

"Are you? That is right," said Gillian. "I found a step-parent not half bad myself."

"Ah, that was different," said Nina wistfully. "Every one respects Mr. Clovis, and you have a mother."

"Will you come in November?" said Gillian.

"It would be great fun," the girl answered, wavering. She reflected rapidly that she had no dresses fit to wear, and that she hated to be patronised; but her youth jumped at the idea of change and pleasure. "It is very kind of you, but I get along all right with Polly, you know. If you are asking me just because you are sorry for me, I must tell you that I much prefer my step-mother to any of the ladies I've ever met. I could not have stayed in the house with Mrs. Dawson or Mrs. Brown, or any of them! I don't need to be pitied a bit."

Gillian's eyes flashed understanding. "Oh dear! I was not attempting to pity you," she said. "That is not my line. I am dull while Jack's away, so do come, Nina."

"Thanks awfully," said Nina shortly, and so it was settled.

"Am I really bitten by philanthropy?" Gillian asked herself mockingly while she hurried on. "No! It must have been the spirit of contradiction that made me invite that little goose ! Mrs. Dawson always irritated me. Yet being married to Jack is having an extraordinary effect on me ! I am getting appallingly soft-hearted. I really don't know what I shall come to if this goes on."

The clock in the gateway was chiming the hour when Gillian entered the quadrangle ; but Lady Hammerton was still out in the rose-garden.

"You would be late, my dear, had I not put dinner off for half an hour," said the old lady. "I did that on account of Sir Edward. He has been much perturbed this afternoon. I did not think that it would be wise for him to dine while he was so excited. Young Edward has been here. Young Edward is slippery and plausible like his mother. I sometimes fear that he purposely enrages his father when he has failed to get his way. Sir Edward suffers greatly from liver. It is very bad for him to be angered."

The little old lady looked very bright. Perhaps she unconsciously enjoyed a stirring up of the waters. Real sorrow no longer came nigh her—that was a thing of the past.

"Young Edward !" cried Gillian, laughing. "Why, he is quite elderly ! He used to philander with mammy at Monte Carlo ! Luckily Mr. Clovis came to the rescue, like the good old dear he is. It was funny to meet Mr. Bevan again. He reminded me of uncomfortable times in bad lodgings."

Gillian had had rather an exciting afternoon too, and though *her* liver was not affected, the thought of Liza Pocock's funeral would have haunted her, had she not valiantly exerted herself to amuse the old people.

She made the poor old father forget his bad son while he listened to her merry talk, and after dinner she sang love-songs, to his mingled pleasure and dismay.

Gillian sang with verve. She sent the fire and glory of

youth thrilling through the old drawing-room. The pathos and longing of years of waiting were in her voice, the passion of pity that had been poured out as precious ointment for one man, the triumphant joy that was pathetic too, seeing that keenest pleasure touches pain, and grief alone comes unalloyed.

Lady Hammerton nodded over her knitting, and murmured, " Very pretty. Very pretty indeed, my love," at the conclusion of each song ; but Sir Edward moved uneasily, and shook his head. He understood better than his cousin Anne did.

Because in his day he too had loved hotly, he could not help but be moved by the tones of this woman's voice ; because he had learnt to count all violent emotion as impure, because he believed that to please Heaven one must become more or less than human, he was shocked and distrustful.

He got up at last and went to the piano. Gillian's curious eyes welcomed him with a smile.

" I can see that you like music," she said.

" I like her only when she acts as the hand-maiden of religion," answered the old knight, who, whatever his faults might be, always stuck to his guns.

" Oh, but I cannot sing spiritual psalms," said Gillian. " There is no use in trying to convey a sentiment that one does not in the least comprehend. Do you wish me to shut the piano ? "

Sir Edward struggled for a moment with what he considered his unregenerate self. " Yes," he said.

Gillian promptly did so. " It is always a comfort when people know their own minds," she remarked good-humouredly.

Sir Edward looked at her with a fanatical light in his eyes. " When I was young I went to many concerts and plays. I saw and heard much that is calculated to appeal to and foster the emotions, but I do not think that I have anywhere heard a more beautiful voice than yours. I am old now, so perhaps you will let me say that it seems to me sad and deplorable that your great gifts should be devoted to the service of the world."

"They are generally devoted to Jack," said Gillian calmly. "Jack is my religion. I had none before I met him. I am glad to have this opportunity of talking to you about him. I have been wishing to tell you that your belief in his innocence greatly astonished and gratified him."

"Was he astonished?" said Sir Edward; somehow the phrase seemed to hurt him. "Jack gave me a great deal of trouble when he was a lad, but I never knew him steal or lie. His faults were exceedingly grave, but they were not of that kind. Was he astonished?"

"Of course he was," said Jack's wife, with the candour that could be unsparing on occasion. "He had imagined that you had always been of the opinion that he was thoroughly bad. He had fancied that you would, if you felt anything on the subject, have been pleased when your view of him was so confirmed."

Sir Edward winced. "We are all bad," he said at last. "The best among us are full of wickedness. Jack was an unruly lad, and from what I have heard since, I fear that he is an ungodly man."

"Did you read his book?" asked Gill.

"I read but one book," replied the old knight. "That teaches me all I need to know—it shows me my own great sinfulness, and the efficacy of the one and only sacrifice."

"I see. But for people who do care about something besides their own souls, Jack's book was wonderfully interesting," said Gillian. "It was so alive and burning with sympathy! It actually impressed even me, who am not at all the sort of person that he was when he wrote that. You see, I am naturally callous. I don't care a button about 'humanity' so long as I am comfortable. Now don't you think that a man who could make a thoroughly selfish young woman almost ashamed must have had some godliness in him? That is, if godliness means goodness."

"My dear lady, I can hardly doubt that the young woman was, and is, biassed by her partiality for the writer," said Sir Edward. "And if I might venture so far I would earnestly warn her against that too intense love of the creature that leads astray." He spoke with real feeling, and Gillian's reply came quick and warm from her very heart.

"It's not intensity that leads astray," she cried. "If I were a preacher how I would preach on that! When you don't care enough, when the fire is a flash in the pan that is fed by the worst, not the best of you, *then* you may be overcome by your feelings. Oh, of course there is that kind too—need we call it love? There is another name for it, I think. Do you know what I would preach? I would say, try if you possibly can to find some one you like better than your own body and soul. It makes a wonderful difference when you do! It gives you self-control (for you are no earthly use to the some one if you have not that). It occasionally keeps you straight. It obliges you to patience. It forces you to courage. Is that leading astray?"

The old man sighed heavily. "No human affection is perfectly pure," he said. "You trust too much to it, though you speak persuasively." Yet he looked at her with interest. This woman, who was Jack's wife, had fine possibilities in her: he would willingly have converted her.

"I spoke warmly," Gillian answered, with a touch of dignity, "but few of us can bear to hear our religion blasphemed." Then she held out her hand to Sir Edward, with a very frank and stately friendliness. "We have been outspoken! Will you be equally so in declaring your conviction of Jack's integrity? Here, in your, and his, own county your opinion carries weight."

Sir Edward smiled, a slow, stiff smile, for he was out of practice in that line.

"I imagine that you seldom lose sight of the end that you have in view. Yes, I will do as you ask," he said. "And I only hope that Cardew is grateful to you." And Gillian went to bed that night well pleased.

A few weeks later she returned to town in quite a triumphant frame of mind. There was no doubt that her plans carried well, and that her tactics seldom failed. She missed Jack sadly, but at least she could work on his behalf with good assurance of success. The torturing knowledge of a misery that might be driving him to madness was a thing of the past now. That is, it was so far past, that Gillian could rejoice in the certainty that he was free and that she was his wife. In one sense, indeed, nothing that cuts deep is ever "done with."

Gillian carried Nina Tyrell back to London with her, and here it must be owned that for once she was nonplussed. Nina was even easier to float than had been imagined. Nina's manners improved with marvellous rapidity, and she took to society as a duck to water. She had more than beauty, she had charm, that indefinite quality which, like charity, can cover a multitude of sins. The defiance, which had been so evident in her manner, was driven back into some dim recess of her soul from whence it peeped only at rare intervals. Yet Mrs. Cardew possessed enough penetration to be aware that she did not thoroughly understand her guest.

"Nina is like a little cat," Gill said once. "She is so graceful and quick, and to a certain point she is friendly, but at the bottom of her nature there is something that eludes one. I believe that it is something untameable."

Mrs. Cardew would have gladly done a little match-making on Nina's behalf; but Nina, while more than ready to flirt, had no intention of being bound. Gillian's kind intentions were frustrated, a fact that rather piqued her, for she had counted merrily on success. She remonstrated with the girl one day, being moved partly by a shrewd suspicion of the difficulties that surrounded Nina at home.

"You had much better marry, little Ninon," she said. "I don't think that you are cut out for single blessedness. You will be very dull when you grow old! Do not let all the chances go by."

Nina was sitting on the fender-stool, playing with her rings. She lifted her slim hand and dropped the trinkets into her lap one by one.

"There goes the fat major," she said; "but none of my rings are heavy enough to represent him adequately. There is Mr. Dagmar (one of the stones has come out, but you know his reputation is rather damaged). There is Mr. Wilmot (that is the ring you gave me, and it is much the best that I have). Oh, Mr. Wilmot, you should not roll away and hide under the coal-scuttle when I am praising you. It is not polite to do that."

Gillian laughed. "It is not at all polite, but I agree with you that that is the best you have," she said significantly. And at that, the untameable demon peeped at her from between Nina's heavily fringed eyelids.

"It is very kind of you to take any trouble about me. I cannot think why you should care," said Nina.

"And upon my word no more can I!" cried Gill. But after a minute's reflection, she apparently found the reason. "The whole fact of the matter is this. I have a naturally economical spirit," she said. "It strikes me as such terrible waste when a girl makes a mess of life, and joins the depressing army of more or less unhappy women. I might have done it myself if I had not married Jack. Not that I should have moped or have made a fool of myself, for I am not that kind, but I believe I should have become rather bad. It is not good for any one to fight solely for her own hand; if she is self-dependent it makes her hard, and if she isn't it makes her melancholy."

"Oh," said Nina, with an odd little grimace, "I wonder why married people aren't nicer, if matrimony has such an effect on their characters? Will any man do, please, Mrs. Cardew?"

Mrs. Cardew preserved a discreet silence.

Nina arranged all her rings on the palm of her small, pink hand, and considered them with mock gravity.

"Keep one, and throw the others away," said Gillian.

"But I should be certain to get so awfully tired of one," cried Nina lightly.

The discussion dropped there, for Gillian was too sensible to preach long to an unimpressionable hearer. This pretty little enigma must buy her experience. Probably Mrs. Cardew's attempts to advise would have ended at that point had not an officious acquaintance induced her to warn the girl once more.

The officious acquaintance had met Miss Tyrell in the Lowther Arcade, walking with Mr. Cyril Bevan, who at one time had been a well-known figure in London society.

"Dear me! how very funny," Mrs. Cardew had replied, when, to her secret annoyance, she was presented with this bit of information. "How very funny! This is the second time that Nina's step-brother has been taken for that scamp. I see the likeness myself—it struck me to-day when Mr. Wood came to fetch the child. But Mr. Bevan is much the better looking of the two! Between ourselves, I wish Nina were clear of her step-relatives. Her father married beneath him, but Nina is curiously loyal, and won't hear a word against her step-mother. She will be so amused when I tell her what you fancied. You had rather I did not mention it? Oh, but it is too good a joke to be lost. If you only knew Mr. Wood! If you could only talk to the excellent dull man! I have to shovel up his dropped 'h's' when he has been calling here. He is rather a trial to me, but he is attached to Nina, and he is unsophisticated beyond belief! Directly he opens his lips that odd likeness vanishes. I am convinced that he fancied the Lowther Arcade was quite the right place to take Nina to. I am bound to own that the rascal is much the more amusing of the two."

They both smiled at that, but Gillian's face grew grave when the visitor had left. She had invented "Mr. Wood" on the spur of the moment. It must be allowed that on the few occasions when she did tell lies, she did it, as she did most things, with spirit and freedom, and for a very distinct purpose.

"But I doubt whether Nina Tyrell is worth it," she said to herself.

Gillian felt that it was as well to stand by a girl, for girls have often a pretty bad time of it, and are frequently such little fools. The motherly element in her inclined her to the protection of anything that was weaker and younger than herself. Yet when Nina made her appearance, Gillian addressed her with decision and vigour.

"You should not force your hostess to invent stories on your behalf," she said. "Mr. Bevan is an altogether impossible person. Of course, if you choose to know him, that is your affair, but you must not make appointments with him while you are staying in this house—for that is my business."

Nina blushed under the sudden attack. She was looking unusually pretty in the black velvet hat that Gillian had given her, and when she pouted, her red lips were more fascinating than at any other time.

"Oh, I know that all the respectable people turn up their noses at Mr. Bevan," she said. "Well, they turn them up at me, too! He and I, we are in the same boat. He always says so."

"You and he! Good heavens, you baby!" cried Mrs. Cardew.

She broke off short, and looked at Nina with an expression in her beautiful eyes that the girl did not in the least comprehend. "I hope to goodness that mine will be a boy, for I don't think that boys are quite so ridiculously silly," Gillian murmured *sotto voce*. Then she took Nina by the shoulders and forced her into an armchair.

"If I were a crying woman I declare I should cry to hear you talking about things that you don't in the slightest degree understand!" she said. "Cyril Bevan ought to be gently chloroformed out of existence—I will not wish him a painful death, because he is not worth hating—for daring to put himself on a level with you. To begin with he is certainly old enough to be your father. How old are you, Nina? nineteen?"

"I shall be twenty in January," said Nina. "But I am not a baby. I know perfectly well what I am about." She drew off her gloves deliberately, and held up her left hand, on which a ruby glowed.

"Yes, I see. Very pretty," said Gillian drily. "Mr. Bevan has lately been through the bankruptcy court. Does he intend to marry you on his debts?"

"We do not intend to marry till Sir Edward dies," said Nina coolly. "Cyril will be rich then—that is, if he only holds out, and with me to back him I think that he will."

She nodded her head with an amount of determination that was certainly not childish. In spite of the round infantine curve of Nina's cheek, and the pout of the pretty lips, she was by no means softly sentimental.

"Sir Edward is trying to bribe Cyril to join with him in cutting off the entail," she explained. "But Cyril shall not give in! No, not if I have anything to do with him. Sir Edward must surely die soon. Only fancy what a horrid shame it would be, if, after waiting for years for the estate, poor Cyril were to be cheated in the end. It shall not happen!"

"I am almost sorry for Jack's old guardian," said Gillian.

"I am glad to hear you say so. It sounds as though you thought we should win," Nina exclaimed triumphantly. "We simply must, you know. Why, Mrs. Cardew, you ought to be on my side, for you waited too."

"I? I waited for Jack. That was an entirely different matter," said Gillian. While she spoke a wave of pity filled her heart.

Yes, she had waited for the man who had certainly touched whatever was finest in her. Her love for him had constantly given the lie to certain elements of cynicism and hardness that were also in her character.

"There was no question of dead men's shoes. I saved every penny I could because I fancied that, for a time at any rate, we should be poor."

"Did you?" said Nina, in *naïve* surprise. "Oh, I should never have supposed——"

"That I should have married a poor man," said Gillian. "Oh well, if it had been any other poor man I should not have done it. A cottage never seemed to me the most delightful place for love's abode. I infinitely prefer a big house. But you are setting your affections on such a very distant and shadowy palace. I doubt whether you'll find its glories satisfying. I sincerely trust that you won't get there."

"Why, that isn't a bit kind!" Nina declared. And

Gillian wondered whether the occasionally childish manner was consciously assumed, or whether the girl was less calculating than she appeared.

Gillian had known the evils of genteel poverty herself, and was not as shocked as many women might have been at Nina's eagerness to possess Sir Edward's money.

"It is not unkind, Ninon," she said. "It only means that I think that you are too good to be sold to Mr. Bevan, even supposing that he were likely to pay the price. As a matter of fact, I believe that he has seldom been known to pay any debt."

"I told you that I know all that!" said Nina. "I do not imagine that Cyril Bevan is what people call 'nice.' No more am I. I do not think there is any one at Churton Regis, excepting you, who would ask me inside her drawing-room. Cyril is good company, anyhow, which good people generally are not. He is kind, too, and he is the one person I know who never wearies me and is never shocked. He comes to see me when I am at home. Do you think that I would let any of the others do that? He never laughs at poor dear Polly, or thinks her 'awful'! When I marry him I may see as much of her as ever I like, and have her to stay, and give her a thoroughly happy time. He won't mind a scrap. Fancy having Polly to stay in Mr. Wilmot's house! Now, could I?"

Gillian had a vague recollection of having seen "Polly" blowsy, red, utterly unpresentable, and not too sober. At the recollection, her heart warmed again to Nina. "No, you could not. It would be most unwise," she said. "But is Mrs. Tyrell indispensable?"

"Yes, she is—there!" For one second the black eyelashes glistened with moisture. "She is. I like Polly. You do not know how she has stood by me. I would rather die," cried Nina with a flash of pride—"I would rather die than that all the old gossips at Churton Regis should know what my home has been. But since Polly has married my father I have had a better time. A lady could not manage him as she does. It was dreadful before. I won't break with her. I won't marry a man who would despise her and me."

" There is no reason why he should," said Gillian.

" But he would, if he was Mr. Wilmot and I was irrevocably married to him," said Nina. " And the moment he began to disapprove I should want to be free of him ! I hate disapproving people ! They make me wickeder than I naturally am. I know quite well that I should have to stand on tiptoe to get anywhere near him, and standing on tiptoe bores me. I like to sit in a cosy low chair, and to be amused by a good-tempered person who does not expect too much. I believe I could make quite a good sort of wife to that kind."

She twisted her ring round so that it might catch the light. " You see, Mrs. Cardew, I believe I do really like Mr. Bevan," she said. " Of course I know he is oldish, and a funny, unromantic little man, isn't he ? But I was not meant for grand experiences. I can't bear men who expect me to feel a great deal. It would be charming if we came in for the property together ! How I should laugh. What a sell for Churton Regis if I were to end by being quite prosperous."

" Yes, I agree that that would be delightful," assented Gillian. She reflected for a minute ; then, " If my husband says that a man is a bad lot, that man must be pretty far gone," she said. " Jack has a soft side for rogues and vagabonds."

" Mr. Cardew is the one person in the world for whom Cyril has a *bona-fide* dislike. I have no doubt the dislike is mutual," Nina answered calmly. And again Gillian laughed, with an odd sense of sadness underlying her amusement.

That Nina should be really fond of that slippery, shameless rogue ; that, though she was but nineteen, she should have no ideal of what a lover should be, but should be content to marry on a basis of mutual toleration, did strike Mrs. Cardew as somewhat melancholy. She decided silently that she would write to her husband, and that she would ask him to tell her exactly what he knew to Mr. Bevan's discredit. Facts were evidently the only efficient arguments, and if Nina refused to alter her course for them, she must e'en go her own way.

Jack's reply was decisive enough. The story he told was put as briefly as possible. It was neither pretty nor edifying, and need not be given here. Gillian handed the letter to Nina without comment. Most women would have refrained from showing it to a girl, but Gillian never went in for half measures.

Nina turned rather white on reading it, and put it into the fire when read. She did not, alas ! doubt the truth of the accusation. "I did not ever suppose that Cyril Bevan was exactly good," she said at last.

Gillian Cardew held out her hands to the girl. "Ninon, forget all about him," she cried. "You are so young and so pretty, and you have never really been in love with any one. There are dozens of honest men in the world, and you shall see plenty of them here. Marry one of them ! "

Nina was still pale—perhaps it was her pallor that made her look older and harder. She stared into the fire for a minute, then raised her eyes to Mrs. Cardew's. Once more the reckless demon looked out of them, and almost startled Gillian.

"That is a nasty story. It is almost too bad, even for me," she said. "But, do you know, I've had about enough of honest and good people. They are generally cruel, I think. It is amusing to imagine how the honest and good

man would look if he were to see my father in the state I've
seen him in. And I can picture the excellent gentleman's
disgust when he first realises how his wife is regarded at
Churton Regis ! But thank you very much for the trouble
you have taken. You are always so sensible, and I have
no doubt that you are quite right." And with that Nina
quitted the room, and left Mrs. Cardew to her own
reflections, which, on the whole, were hardly pleasant.

Gillian *had* been sensible, and to the best of her belief
she had been kind, and common sense and kindliness go a
very long way. "But Jane would have done much better,"
Gillian said to herself. At that moment she vaguely felt
that there are evils that turn the edge of any such
weapons as she held, and the thought depressed her. She
shivered, just as she always shivered when she met a
funeral.

" I believe that women really need a religion to keep them
straight," she said to herself. "And poor little Ninon has
nothing. I at least have Jack." And with that her lips
parted in a smile that was so sweet that it seemed a pity
Jack was not by to see it.

Part II.

CHAPTER X.

THIS TIME I FELT LIKE MARY.

"This time I felt like Mary, had my babe
    Lying a little on my breast like hers."

"The night was darker than ever before
    (So dark is sin)
When the Great Love came to the stable door
    And entered in,
And laid Himself in the breath of kine
    And the warmth of hay,
And whispered to the star to shine
    And to break, the day."

"COME back for Christmas," Gillian had said. It was actually on Christmas Day itself, that Jack stood by his wife's bedside, and looked with an odd mixture of satisfaction and amusement at the child she had given him.

It was early morning. The nurse had just put out the lamp and let the daylight into the room. Some children were singing carols in the street.

"Noel, Noel, Noel, Noel!
This is the salutation of the Angel Gabriel."

The little lads stamped and beat their arms to keep themselves warm. They sang with cheerful lack of expression, but with great decision.

"When Mary had swaddled her young Son so sweet,
Within an ox manger she laid Him to sleep,"

they shouted in their shrill, boyish voices.

139

Jack laughed as the sounds reached him. It could hardly be said that he believed in that old story, yet the sight of Gill's happy face made him realise with unusual tenderness the picture that the quaint words called up. Heavenly hosts and angelic choirs were not "in his line," but the tiny head on Gillian's breast seemed somehow connected with the Christmas carol, with that other Baby who lay in the warm hay of the manger.

"Our child? Is it really? It is very small and red and ugly, isn't it?" said he.

He gave a quick glance round to make sure that they were alone, then knelt down by Gillian and kissed her. In his secret soul he had been afraid, more afraid than he would have cared to own. Misfortune had so hounded him that he was inclined to reckon on the jade as his most probable companion. He was the son of a gambler, and a deep-seated belief in luck was in his very blood. On this occasion Gill's star had evidently been in the ascendant. His heart throbbed with relief.

"You are all right, are you not?" he asked. "And you've got your own way, eh, Gill?"

Gillian smiled, with a soft, tender triumph in her eyes. She was rather pale, but the round curve of her cheek was as perfect as ever. Already she had forgotten pain in the joy of having brought a man-child into the world.

"I was sure that I should give you a boy, darling," she whispered, "and you know that I am always successful. Take him. I want to see him in your arms, Jack."

Jack put his hands under the little creature, and lifted it very gingerly.

"It is so ridiculously tiny and soft!" he said, biting his under lip, which quivered oddly.

"Do you know that I—love him?" she murmured, in a half-laughing, half-wondering whisper. "I never before really loved any one but you in this sort of hot, silly way. Now there are three of us."

" Three of us against the world," he said. " I only wish it had a luckier father."

"You must not call him ' it.' He is a person. He has got a brand new soul, in a brand new body ! He is immensely important !" She laughed again, but with happy tears in her eyes. "Oh, Jack, it is so wonderful !" she said ; and the words made him think of the spring day in Devonshire, when she had cried the same thing while they had walked together under the budding trees.

" It is very funny. I never in my life saw such an indecently helpless and absurd little object as this," said Jack "Are they always so ridiculous ? "

The nurse coming in at that moment exclaimed indignantly. " It is a most remarkably fine boy, sir !" she said, in an aggrieved tone. " I never before saw one so big nor yet so strong. But three hours old, and see how he lifts his little head already ! But indeed, sir, you ought not to be talking in here at all. The lady would have you sent for, but she ought to be asleep, and it is not to be expected that you should understand anything about the blessed child." She eyed him with great disfavour. "Absurd little object !" she repeated under her breath. " And he the father of as beautiful a boy as ever was."

Jack laughed outright, and laid the baby down on Gillian's arm. " Go to sleep, Gill," he said. " Good-bye, Goliath, I shall have quite enough of you by-and-by."

He smiled again while he ran down the stairs, amused at the nurse's ready partisanship. " Three hours old, and he has found a champion already," thought the new-made father. " What a queer fuss women make about babies."

He sat at his writing-table, with his pen in his hand and a sheet of foolscap before him. He had taken to writing again of late. He stared straight before him, but wrote never a word. Presently his head sank on to his hands. "Us three! and I might have been one alone," he said.

Us three! It surprised the master of the house to find how large and important a place the third member of the coalition took. He had known no family life in his own boyhood; he was amused at the elaborate nursery arrangements, at the amount of time Gillian spent over her baby.

He was very tender to his wife in the early days of her convalescence. He was secretly proud that she would let no one but himself carry her. Weakness always appealed strongly to him.

As for Gillian—Lady Jane, for whom she had sent a week before the child was born, felt that the change in her was as beautiful as the miracle that yearly clothes the branches with tender green. Mrs. Cardew with a baby in her arms was another woman. Or rather, perhaps, that other woman that had always existed in her was freed, and crowned, and allowed to have full sway for a short season.

"I should like you to come to me, Jane," she had written. "I have not many superstitions, but I think it will be good for my baby to be in your arms. I want to see you in my nursery. You must be my boy's patron saint. Mammy can come later. Mr. Clovis is still obstinate about meeting Jack, but he has a very soft side, and I don't think he will hold out much longer. We shall have the house full for the christening; but just at first I shall keep the outer door shut, and I want you alone. When the world and the etceteras arrive on the scene I know that you will depart."

And Lady Jane went to her, for she loved Gillian very well, the world and the etceteras notwithstanding.

"But do you not think that we should be prepared for the possibility that the child may be a girl?" she had gently suggested during the first moments of her visit.

Jane was conscientious and sympathetic. The "we" showed her sympathy, and the question her conscience.

Gillian's face dimpled with laughter. "No, my friend," she said, "I refuse to prepare for misfortunes. That is a waste of power, for when they happen no preparation makes the least difference. I may have a girl, and I may die, you know, but I don't mean to! The boy will arrive all safe." And so he did.

Lady Jane had seldom been happier in the course of her quiet life than she was during those weeks, when Gillian was getting stronger every day, and when Gillian's child lay often on her knee. She had befriended many people, but yet had known few personal and equal friendships. She enjoyed Gillian's society greatly. There was a strength of character in Mrs. Cardew that was akin to something in Jane's own personality. The two women understood each other's silences, as well as each other's speech.

"Mammy is coming next Thursday," Gillian said with a sigh, when her baby was a month old. "She is rather piqued because I had you in the house when the boy was born, but I know that she cannot bear any one but herself to be invalidish. She will enjoy her visit much more now than she would have when I was upstairs. I know how to make mammy comfortable."

"You are very clever at making every one comfortable," said Jane. "I must be leaving you to-morrow, if you please."

"Exit the saint, and enter the world!" said Gill. "I can always see that you do not like my mother, Jane, in spite of your polite endeavours to hide the fact. Jack does not like her, either. But he is not so conscientious, and never takes any trouble to dissemble. He infinitely prefers my step-father. Yet mammy has been quite polite to him, and Mr. Clovis is quite the contrary! The perverseness of man is unaccountable! Well, I have got my way, and she is coming. I am determined that I will not quarrel with her. It looks much better that Jack should be on good terms with my people. Besides," with a glance at the child in her arms, "she is my mother, after all." And that last reason had more weight than might have been inferred from Gillian's tone.

"I think that you always get your own way," said Lady Jane, with a smile.

Gillian shook her head wisely. "No, not always, but I seem to because I know better than to mention my defeats. There is wisdom in that, Jane!" Jane smiled over the characteristic reply. "But I sometimes break my rules for you," said Gill (it was no wonder that she fascinated Jane). "I will tell you of a defeat now. I wanted him," laying her cheek against her child, "to be called Jack, after his father. I like no other name so well. But Jack will not allow it. He says the little chap shall not be named after an unlucky person. I have been obliged to give way, and to retire gracefully to a second choice."

"And what is that?"

"Stephen Hope," she replied. "Stephen was my father's name, and I was fond of him. I like my uncle Stephen too, though he does not approve of me. I shall ask him to be baby's godfather. That will be an excellent move, for it will bring Jack and him together once more."

"And why Hope?"

An odd, wistful look softened Gillian's expression. "Oh, I don't know. Jack is melancholy, but baby is going to be the antidote to all that. His wee fingers may be stronger than mine," she said.

"Ah, yes," said Lady Jane dreamily. "It was a baby in a manger that was the Hope of all the world."

"I am not religious, you know," Gill hastened to asseverate. She would have laughed had any one save Jane ventured on such a remark in her presence, but there was

an absolute simplicity about the little lady that made it
impossible for an honest person to distrust her. Jane's
soul, like flame, leaped up instinctively, and all that she felt
and saw fed the fire.

"I do not know whether I am, either," she answered
simply. "But I am the better for being here. You and
the child have shown me many things."

"I? My goodness! (but I really require a much stronger
expression.) My good friend, your charity is wide, but
do not let it dress me up as an angel, please. White never
suited me, and I can't play the part of moral teacher!"

"I do not fancy," said Jane, with the slow thoughtfulness
that rather quaintly emphasised her remarks—"I do not
fancy that an angel would be able to teach one much.
It is birth and death and love and hate that teach one.
But I have seen motherhood only through other women's
eyes."

Gillian nodded. "But you have seen the other three
through your own," she said to herself. And how she
knew that I cannot explain, though it is a knowledge that
women recognise in each other.

Lady Jane pursued her own thought. "It is not yet
the time for angels. They wait. They are always there,
like the still peace that is always on the tops of the
mountains. They hold a secret in their hands, but they
are in no hurry, because they see eternity."

"Some people climb up to the tops of the mountains
in hopes of getting a glimpse of that secret," said Gillian.

"I know that they do," said Lady Jane. "I daresay
that they are right, but——"

"But what, Jane?"

Tears stood in Jane's eyes. "I have not found it there,"
she said. "But sometimes I have caught a glimpse of it
among men and women down below,—among those we
call bad, as well as among those we call good. Even a

glimpse is enough to save one from breaking one's heart over the misery that one cannot help."

"There are some people who do not possess such uncomfortable possessions as hearts," said Gillian. "And perhaps they are the best off, after all."

"Are there?" said Lady Jane. "But I have never met with any such."

Gillian wrote to Mr. Molyneux that same day, and invited him to be one of the godfathers. She meant to persuade Mr. Clovis to be the other.

Lady Jane, and Mr. Clovis, and her uncle Stephen were the three people she respected most in the world, putting her husband, who was on a different level altogether, out of the question. She never consciously considered how much she respected Jack, hardly even how much she loved him. One does not stop to analyse the way in which one draws one's breath.

Old Stephen Molyneux, whose life had never been so closely bound up with any one's that he could not consider, reflected long over Gillian's request. He had not seen the notice of the child's birth that was in the *Times*, for he never read the newspapers. He forgot all about his breakfast, and let his coffee cool while he chewed the cud of this piece of news.

His maid Elizabeth came in presently with a tray in her hands, and looked with disfavour at the untouched meal. Elizabeth was a comfortable, fresh-complexioned woman of a strangely old-fashioned type. Gillian called her "the prehistoric survival." To a certain extent she ruled in the master's house, but there were limits to her power. She managed his household, but not him.

Mr. Molyneux had a chivalrous and rather distant respect for women, but no one woman had ever had great influence over him. So far, at least, as any one knew. One would have said that he was born to be a bachelor, except for the rather contradictory fact that he had a great and pathetic love for little children.

"Shall I make some fresh coffee and boil another egg?" asked Elizabeth, with as much reproach as she dared throw into her voice.

"Eh? Why, it is eight o'clock. Time to have done breakfast. You can clear away," said her master.

"And he not so much as tasted bite or sup!" the poor woman cried indignantly when she got outside the door. "A baby of three days old has more sense of whether he is full or empty! The master is that unnoticing that if I was not here to bring him up his meals he would die of forgetting to eat, and would never find out what he was dying of till after he was in his coffin."

For all that she did not venture to remonstrate, and the old man pursued his reverie undisturbed.

So Jack had got a son! It was not an improbable occurrence, but it surprised Mr. Molyneux, who had never thought of that likelihood. Gillian's uncle was much fonder of Jack than he was of his niece, whose worldliness repelled and shocked him. Yet he had respected the girl for sticking to her lover through such adverse circumstances. He had been greatly astonished at her steadfastness. He could not comprehend how a young woman who talked so cynically and lightly could yet have a capability for faithful attachment. He owned to himself that he had not done Gillian justice. He was too old to understand so new-fashioned a lady; but he had liked Jack Cardew at first sight.

Mr. Molyneux was a collector; his rooms were full of all sorts of curious hoards. He followed his own fancy, and collected only what struck him as beautiful, valuing nis treasures in proportion to the pleasure they gave him, and caring not at all for the conventional standard of worth. What friends he had he had chosen equally arbitrarily.

He had missed the spark of genius—he was only eccentric. He had artistic taste of all kinds, but the power to turn it to account was lacking. He saw that power in the younger man, and he hailed it with rare delight.

Jack's pride had been very much on the alert in those early days before the book succeeded, but Mr. Molyneux was so curiously simple-minded in some respects that the most wrong-headed and touchy genius could hardly have suspected him of offensive patronage, and the young man was warm-hearted as well as warm-tempered.

If Jack built castles in the air, they were quite out-topped by his friend's. In his secret soul Mr. Molyneux was sure that this boy would be the greatest writer of his century, that he would stand a giant among men. He had no qualms of doubt, he was absolutely convinced of Jack's genius.

The success of the book had made no difference in his estimation of it. Had it failed to win popular approval, that would have made no difference either, it would scarcely even have disappointed him. Mr. Molyneux, though kindly, was out of touch with his fellows; though humble-minded as to his own deserts, he was incapable of taking the standard of the majority. Jack Cardew was more human, consequently he was a more vulnerable, yet in some respects a stronger man.

Possibly Stephen Molyneux's life had held few bitterer moments than those when he sat dumbly watching the Cardew who had come out of prison, changed, hardened beyond his recognition, though not beyond Gillian's.

Mr. Molyneux had heard of the attempt to break bonds that had resulted in the death of the warder. Jack had got more than half through his time when he had lengthened his sentence by that mad, hopeless outbreak. It had seemed to the older man that—if only for the sake of the woman who waited—Jack ought to have forborne. Perhaps constant intercourse with books, that appealed rather to the brain than to the emotions, had not fitted the old recluse to understand so passionate and unphilosophic a nature as Cardew's. He had not meant to be hard on the "poor lad," but the bitterness of his disappointment had an element of sternness in it.

He had endeavoured to be kind to Gillian while she was alone in London, but her bid for popularity had appeared to him frankly vulgar. The sort of thing to be expected of her mother's daughter! He had not gone near the grand new house, he had not desired to visit Jack and Gillian again.

Yet now he was conscious of an inconsistent wish to talk to Jack once more. He would like, too, to see the child. Children were so easy to get on with, they did not mind ungainliness, they took every one naturally and simply. He found them pretty—prettier than anything in his collection. He stretched his long, thin legs, and shambled out. He walked with long, uneven strides. He was a person with whom it was impossible to keep in step, either metaphorically or literally, but he got over the ground fast. In less than an hour he was in Park Lane.

The man-servant stared with some surprise at the tall, shabby old gentleman, who had apparently no idea that nine o'clock was an odd hour for a call. "I don't know whether Mr. Cardew is up yet, sir," he said doubtfully.

"I have got a book in my pocket, so I can wait," said the old gentleman, and forthwith produced a small, calf-bound volume and sat down on the chair nearest to him. He curled one leg round the other, and became at once absorbed, bending his long back over his book, happily unconscious of his surroundings, rejoicing in that treasure that does not wax corrupt, and that age has but mellowed like old wine. Every now and then he read aloud, the stately Greek sounding strangely in that modern hall.

"Since, my friend, there are two models in the nature of things, one divine and most happy, and the other ungodly and most miserable, they, not perceiving that this is the case, through stupidity and extreme folly unknown to themselves, become similar to the one by unjust actions, and dissimilar to the other. Wherefore they are punished by leading a life suited to that to which they are assimilated." He paused, nodded in assent, as if the old philosopher were present, and repeated the passage : "Wherefore they are punished by leading a life suited to that to which they are assimilated."

"Oh, dearest Uncle Stephen, I am so distressed that you should be left sitting in the hall ! I heard your voice as I ran down the stairs, and I knew it could only be you who would quote Greek at this hour, and in such an uncomfortable chair ! But how charming of you to come to see my darling child. Dear Gill will be so touched ! "

Mr. Molyneux hastily slipped his book into his pocket, and turned to confront Mrs. Clovis. It went against his instinct to be rude to a lady, therefore he was obliged to take the hand she held out to him ; but he had never trusted "Eva," and his distrust was plainly to be seen in the expression of his face. It was many years since Mrs. Clovis had last met her first husband's uncle, and their relations to each other had not been of the pleasantest, but she glided over rough places with wonderful facility.

"You have always been so good to my girl," she murmured. "And I can think of nothing but her just now."

Mr. Molyneux stammered violently, and twisted his lips in such an extraordinary fashion that Mrs. Clovis hastily looked away from him. Her uncle's uncouth ways were always repulsive to her. She shrank from any form of material ugliness, and, oddly enough, rather prided herself on this trait. Moral and physical fastidiousness are not at all the same thing, but it pleased her to fancy them allied, and her husband encouraged her by being honestly proud of his wife's " delicate fancies."

" My dear Gill is so strong," she went on, finding that Mr. Molyneux could not bring himself to the point of coherent speech. " She was always so healthy when she was a child. I could have found it in my heart to envy her, if a mother's heart could envy."

" I came to see Cardew," said Mr. Molyneux, getting out the words at last. He stood looking down at the pretty lady with a total disregard of her charms that would have piqued her had she not always considered that Uncle Stephen was decidedly " wanting "—almost idiotic, in fact, in some respects—in spite of his reputation for learning. He did not notice how soft and fair she looked in her dove-coloured dress, with the bit of fine baby-work in her hand, nor how young she was to be a grandmother, nor how her fresh white apron became her (and these were all things that most people would have seen) ; but at the moment he mentioned Jack's name he distinctly apprehended something that would have eluded nine men out of ten. He knew, by one of those flashes of intuition that occasionally startled those who took his absence of mind for granted, that Mrs. Clovis was afraid of Jack Cardew.

" Poor dear fellow ! " she murmured softly, and at that moment Jack made his appearance.

" I am glad to hear this news," said the old man, "and I have come to congratulate you."

Jack held out his hand with one of the rather rare smiles that made him look like his old self. When their fingers met the friendship that had once been leaped between them.

" He is the ugliest little chap ! " said Jack, " and she is as well and jolly as possible. She has set her heart on your being godfather."

" I should rather like to see your boy, Jack," said Mr. Molyneux shyly, and drawing Jack aside.

The father stared in amazement. He had never before happened to stumble on this trait in his friend's character.

Mrs. Clovis laughed; her gentle laugh always set the bachelor's nerves on edge.

"How charming of you to want to see baby! Will you come up to the nursery with me? Dearest Gillian will be quite delighted."

But Jack came to the rescue. "No. I will fetch Goliath down to the library," he said. "Masculine society will do the fellow good after so much petticoat worship."

Mrs. Clovis fluttered upstairs after him. She was proud of her grandson, and hoped that Gillian would know better than to trust him to Jack's want of tenderness. Her own sentiment being a good deal on the surface, she was jarred and repelled by surface roughness. But Gillian was pleased when Jack demanded his son.

"I should like to see you and Uncle Stephen and baby conversing together," said she; "but I am sure that Uncle Stephen does not want me. Don't let him give baby the ink to suck, please; he is capable of any atrocity when he has got an absent fit on, and baby puts everything into his mouth."

"Dear Jack is so rough. I do hope that he will take care of the darling," Mrs. Clovis whispered somewhat reproachfully. A remark that brought a smile to the lips of Jack's wife.

Gill would have laughed outright could she have peeped at the scene in the library where Jack had cleared the oak table and had piled together the sofa cushions, flanked with big books, and had laid his son and heir down in the middle of the impromtu cradle.

"He hits out well, doesn't he?" said Jack, and the two men stared down at the little atom of humanity with quaint gravity.

"He is born with a silver spoon in his mouth," said

Mr. Molyneux, "but I don't know that that is much advantage."

The younger man shrugged his broad shoulders. "Oh, you are a philosopher, sir," said he.

"He is like you already."

Jack frowned. "So Gillian says. I had rather that he was not."

Mr. Molyneux stammered painfully, and shook his head. "With a son to come after you, and so devoted a wife," he said (but mention of the wife was evidently an after-thought), "you—you have no business to despond."

"I know that. I mean to play again now," said Jack. There was a decision in his voice, and a purpose in his blue eyes that rejoiced his friend.

"This chap would not be at the table at all if it were not for Gill and me," he remarked. "The cards are queerly dealt! I had almost come to the conclusion that it is not worth while to take any trouble about the game. The odds are generally against the players! But one can't be such a sneak as not to do what one can for the child one is responsible for. I won't repeat history." He glanced, in speaking, though hardly knowing that he did so, at a water-colour sketch that hung on the wall.

"Is that your father?" asked Mr. Molyneux. "Yes, I see that it is. It is like you. The face is more oval, though, and handsomer. The mouth is weaker, but better-tempered, and the forehead is higher, and not so broad. He died young, did not he?"

"He won an immense sum at Monte Carlo and the morning after he was found dead, shot through the heart."

"Murdered?"

"No, he killed himself," said Jack. "He found that the game was not worth winning, I suppose. But it was a bit hard on my mother and on me, eh, Goliath?"

"Goliath" roared lustily in reply. His father picked

him up with awkward gentleness. Already the child liked to feel himself in those strong arms.

Mr. Molyneux looked from the portrait to the man before him. Jack had a stronger grip on life than his father had had. *His* throwing up of the cards would have been moral rather than physical. The old man wrestled silently with many unaccustomed thoughts. It was perhaps as well that there had been a woman in this case. He could not have done much for Jack. He did not consider Gillian a high-principled lady, but there is a saving power in love itself that lies below all principles.

"Give my kindest regards to Gillian, if you please, and tell her that I shall esteem it a great honour to be her son's godfather," he said, with old-fashioned politeness.

CHAPTER XI.

"THEY ARE NOT SO VERY HAPPY."

"And withal we are conscious of evil
 And good—of the spirit and the clod;
Of the power in our hearts of a devil,
 Of the power in our souls of a God
Whose commandments are graven in no cipher,
 But clear as His sun—from our youth
One at least we have cherished—
 'An eye for an eye and a tooth for a tooth.'"

THE christening of Stephen Hope was a very grand affair. It took place in a highly fashionable church, and the pomps and vanities that were to be vicariously renounced were very well represented.

"One would think it was his wedding instead of his christening, by the look of the carriages, and the red cloth, and the beautiful dresses," the nurse had remarked gleefully.

The little speech was repeated among the guests, and there was a soft ripple of laughter, subdued out of respect to the church, but bearing witness to the spirit with which any entertainment in which Mrs. Cardew played hostess was carried out.

I say "entertainment" advisedly, for Gillian did not greatly trouble her head about the religious aspect of the ceremony. She was very happy; she was enjoying her social success; she did not attempt to disguise the fact that she was a proud woman when she walked up the aisle

155

with her boy in her arms. She could not refrain from shooting a merry glance from under her eyelids at Lady Jane, when that little lady renounced the devil and all his works, with the glory of the world and the carnal desires of the flesh, in the name of Stephen Hope. It struck Gillian that Jane was really taking a good deal on herself—considering whose son the baby was.

Stephen roared lustily when the drops of water woke him to a consciousness of being in strange hands; his mother gathered him into her arms, laughing under her breath.

" Baby is like his father and mother. He does not approve of parsons," she whispered in Lady Jane's ear.

Jack Cardew was not present. " He could not," he said, " stand so much tom-foolery." To tell the truth, the whole business struck him as unpleasantly profane, and he had no taste for profanity.

" I do not see why the boy should be baptised at all," he had said. " But if you wish it done, why not let the clergyman and the godparents carry it through between them, without all this fuss? Lady Jane will mean every word that she says, and I daresay that if you set about searching carefully, you might find such a thing as an honest parson, eh? Still, do as you choose, Gill. A baby is chiefly its mother's affair, I suppose. I will come and support you if you really want me to."

" I never want you to do anything that you do not like," she had answered, " but I think that baby must be properly christened, dear. It is all very well for you, who are a genius, to despise conventionalities, but I should feel that we had not given the boy—who may turn out to be quite a matter-of-fact and ordinary person, like his mamma—a fair start in the world, if we were to omit the opening ceremony."

So " the opening ceremony " was as elaborate as it could

well be made, and the font was wreathed in white flowers, and the most exquisite choir in London sang the hymns.

Mr. Clovis was not present. Lord Brancaster took the place that Gillian had hoped that her step-father would have been cajoled into filling. Lord Brancaster would doubtless be useful to his godson hereafter; he had influence in the diplomatic service. Gillian had considered that point; yet she was sorry, no one guessed how sorry, that her kindly obstinate "Mr. Cloves" still refused to countenance her marriage.

Cardew leaned against the churchyard railings, and waited for the christening party to come out.

His stature always gave him an advantage in a crowd, and he was amused to see that quite a large number of idlers had been attracted by the smart carriages and the red cloth.

Jack despised parade of any kind, but he was aware that Gillian rather enjoyed it, as a sign of success. He laughed at this trait in his wife, but he never laughed bitterly at her, for if Gillian liked pomps and vanities, he had very good reason to know that she loved him incomparably better. There was a wide gap between her love and her liking.

Cardew thought a good deal about his boy while he waited. He was making more vigorous efforts than had hitherto seemed to him worth while, to dive to the bottom of that miserable mystery that had so nearly wrecked his whole life. Nearly? Once he would have said "quite," but the woman and the child between them had forbidden the luxury of despair. For Stephen's sake he would endeavour to clear his name, so far as it was possible to do so. There was one stain that no explanation could wash away, that his son would one day know of and pass judgment on.

Cardew took no lenient view of himself, and since he

had struggled out of the slough of apathy into which he had sunk, he had despised himself for sinking, with a severity that it was to be hoped that Stephen would never emulate.

To struggle up is a painful process; most painful because no outside criticism touches us so keenly as the censure of our higher self on the self that fell. That, indeed, is the very judgment of God, before which every soul stands ashamed, and beside which the blame and praise of the world is nothing and of no account. Indeed, the opinion of his fellows was becoming of curiously little moment to this man, whose ambitions and plans were weaving themselves daily more tightly round the boy. He had sworn he would do his best for the chap, and Cardew's best meant a good deal. He was bound to make his son respect him if he could; he knew by his own experience that a shattered faith in the goodness of fatherhood is a sorry gift to give one's child.

Well, his boy would not believe him guilty of a crime which he denied. Jack knew that his son and Gillian's could never make that mistake. Yet Stephen would one day see the blood on his father's hands. Jack would not deny that, nor even make excuses for it.

"Poor little chap, will he take it to heart when he knows? I took it to heart when my father shot himself and deserted my mother and me," thought Jack. Which, he wondered, was the blacker crime—that a man should kill himself and so betray the two who trusted him, or that in a blind fight for his freedom he should inadvertently send some one else to his death? Inadvertently, for Cardew had not meant to kill, he had only meant to get out. That inner judge at least acquitted him of malice.

Jack had laughed when he heard the medical evidence which proved that that particular gaoler had suffered from a weak heart. The laugh had been taken as a sign of his callous brutality. The doctor alone, who had oddly enough conceived a liking for him, had understood that the jeer was at persistent, dogging ill-luck, and that No. 48 was more mad than callous. He would probably actually have lost his wits if his captivity had lasted another year. His mind reverted too often to his prison experiences, they were vividly present to him while he waited in the crowd ; he was still dwelling on them when he felt a touch on his arm, and, turning sharply, confronted one of his clerks.

"I beg your pardon, sir," said the man. "Your butler told me that I should find you here."

"Anything wrong at the office ?" asked Jack.

"No, sir. It is only that a boy has been caught in the act of stealing from the till. Mr. Whiteman said I was to tell you that he would have sent for the police at once, but that he did not wish to act without your orders."

"Where is the boy ?"

"In your room, sir. Mr. Whiteman turned the key on him."

"Very well. Say that I will come in the course of an hour," said Cardew. "The lad may cool his heels and repent for a bit."

The office was in the Strand. Cardew and Bransome had formed a company for the working of the mine. Gillian took the keenest pleasure in every detail of the business, and possession had apparently awakened new capabilities in Jack. In his younger days, his talents had seemed to lie in the direction of spending rather than of making money, but he was not lacking in power, and he worked hard in the endeavour to master the intricacies of business. It was significant that the manager knew that it was necessary to suspend judgment till Mr. Cardew had been consulted about the delinquent.

Jack waited till the christening party came out of church ; then he put his wife into the carriage—looking somewhat amused at his son's lusty roar. "The chap does not at all like being made a Christian of," he remarked.

"It is lucky for the baby to cry. He is a lucky boy," said the mother. "Oh, Jack, are you not even going to eat his christening cake?"

"I have to pass judgment on some one else's boy who is not lucky," said Cardew, turning away.

He took a hansom to the city with the sound of "Goliath's" healthy voice still ringing in his ears. He was silently proud that the child was so vigorous and fine. He felt singularly disinclined for the errand on which he was bound. Boys had become interesting to him of late, and though not much given to false sentiment, he hated being the means of sending any one to prison. Perhaps there was some mistake. At any rate the lad should have the benefit of any shade of doubt.

On reaching the office, Cardew listened to the story that was told him, with that impassive expression that he had acquired in gaol and that he was apt to put on in an unpleasant emergency. He asked one or two questions, and then held out his hand for the key of his room. "I will see the boy alone," he said.

The boy heard the master's heavy tread on the passage, and sat upright with brightening eyes. He was a thin scarecrow of a creature, and at that moment he was so painfully hungry that he found it difficult to think connectedly of anything but his bodily sensations. He wished to collect his scattered wits, but his brain seemed to be working so fast and excitedly, that it was impossible to frame a coherent sentence.

When Mr. Cardew, having shut the door carefully behind him, came up to the table by which the boy sat, the boy stared up at him with a fierce, intent stare like a trapped rat, but was quite speechless. Cardew's large and substantial figure loomed bigger, and wavered in a mist, in a very remarkable manner, and his voice seemed to come from some miles away. The boy could not quite grasp what was being said to him. Then he felt a hand on his shoulder, shaking him slightly.

"Wake up, I am asking you when you last had anything to eat. Are you hungry?" said Jack.

The boy made a violent effort to get a mental hold on the situation. This was not a policeman, it was Mr. Cardew. He was not in a street, he was in a room. He felt better when Cardew opened a window, and when a plate of bread and meat was put before him; he grabbed at it in a way that unmistakably answered Jack's last question.

"I don't want you to give me anything," he said sullenly; but he was too famished to resist eating, and drank some beer eagerly. When he had cleared the plate the quick throbbing in his head ceased, and he could again see distinctly.

Mr. Cardew was sitting at the opposite side of the table reading a newspaper, which he put down at the same moment that the boy laid down his knife and fork.

"There is no fair speech between a full man and a hungry," said Jack. "Now, what were you doing at the till?"

The boy looked quickly round for a way of escape. The door was locked, and the key was in Cardew's pocket. He was silent.

"If you have anything to say for yourself, you had better say it now," Jack remarked. "Appearances are against you, you know, but appearances are sometimes against the innocent. Mind, I don't say that I will believe any cock-and-bull story that I am told, but I will listen." He paused a moment. That sharp glance round had pretty well convinced him that the lad was guilty. "Or if you like to make a clean breast of it," he said, "now is your best chance. I don't promise to let you go scot free, but I advise you to tell me the truth."

"Ain't going to be beholden to *you*," said the boy. Then he looked at his empty plate, and actually blushed.

"I couldn't help eating, but I wouldn't have touched your food if you had not put it where I could smell the bread and meat."

He spoke resentfully, and Cardew was more than a little surprised. The stress on the pronoun made him wonder. Was this some dismissed servant who had a grudge against him?

"*My* food? Does that mean that you have an especial grievance against me?" he asked. This was becoming interesting. On close inspection, Jack was sure that the lad did not belong to the habitual criminal class.

The blush had faded. The boy's thin hand was clenched hard on the edge of the table; he leaned forward, staring at Mr. Cardew again with the same fierce, half-fascinated stare that had surprised Jack before. "You—you killed my father, and every bad thing that has happened—is all because of you!" he cried.

He was incoherent, and desperate, and violently excited. It was as if he had flung his light weight against Mr. Cardew, who sat very still, and outwardly stolid.

"Whose son are you?" asked Jack at last. He knew what the answer would be, and it did not occur to him to doubt the truth of it.

"My father was Adam Henderson, and you killed him, and now you can send me to prison if you like," said the boy. His voice rose to a high, hysterical pitch. "Do! I don't care. I ain't a bit ashamed of stealing from you," he cried. "It is all your fault. We was all respectable while father was alive. If you had not killed him we should have kept straight all along. Mother wouldn't have got drunk, and I wouldn't have lost my place, and Jane wouldn't 'ave gone on the streets. You are rich, and I am starving, and it is your doing. But I've spoke my mind, anyway—all our minds, for mother she says the same—and I don't care if you hang me for it."

"Don't be such a fool," said Jack roughly. "Your neck is in no sort of danger, and you know that as well as I do."

Then he got up heavily, and unlocked the door, and flung it wide open. "There," he said briefly, "go! But don't try it on again. That I killed Henderson is no reason for your being a thief, and next time it won't save you."

The boy gave one sharp glance at him, and was off like a shot. Cardew sat down again, and fell into a train of thought that, to judge by his face, was gloomy enough. A clerk knocked at the door and looked in, but Mr. Cardew did not hear or see him, and the man withdrew again with lifted eyebrows.

"The boss looks fit to kill himself. You mark my words, he will one of these days. He is not himself when these fits of the blues are on him, and there is no knowing what will start them," he remarked when he returned to the office.

"He is a kind man," his companion replied gratefully; for Cardew had kept his place open for him during a very long spell of illness—"He is a kind man, though he is a bit queer-tempered. I daresay he is sorry for that boy."

"He has let him go," said the other, "and that is what he had no business to do. It ain't right nor just to let a thief loose on society, because you are soft about punishing him. We all know that Mr. Cardew has got especial reasons for disliking——"

He stopped short, for his fellow nudged him violently— Mr. Cardew had opened the office door.

Jack paused for a second on his way across the room. "Yes," he said, looking straight at the clerk, "I had especial reasons for fighting shy of sending that particular lad to goal. It is not a reason that applies to any other case. You are quite right, Mr. Smith, laxness *is* unfair to the community. There is too much talking here. Keep the discussion till after hours."

He walked home, striding along fast, with his head down, looking neither to the right nor to the left. Henderson's boy had made an impression on him that he did not even attempt to shake off. No man can sin to himself alone. Jack Cardew recognised that fact, with a realisation that was vivid because he was a man of vivid imagination, and morbid because circumstances had fostered in him a deep and ineradicable melancholy.

Gillian had a dinner-party that evening. Her dinners were usually successful, but on this occasion the host was so absent-minded and silent that for once she remonstrated.

"I know that these people bore you dreadfully," she said. "But I don't very often inflict any of the entertaining on you. You might have pretended not to hate them for one night. I was obliged to be civil to Lord Brancaster for baby's sake, and a dinner *à trois*, when two of the three won't talk is too appalling. Lord Brancaster always rubs you the wrong way, so I fancied that you would have objected more to having him by himself."

"So I should have," said Jack shortly.

The guests had all gone, and the husband and wife were alone together. Gillian rubbed the tip of her pretty foot along the fender rail. Her shining silken dress clung close to her figure and took golden and green lights when she moved, the diamonds on her neck sparkled. Jack put his hand before his eyes as if all this brilliancy jarred on him.

"I saw Henderson's son to-day," he said suddenly. "He was caught stealing money from the till. He is going to the devil as fast as he can go. His mother drinks, and his sister is on the streets. Henderson was an honest man. They were all right while he was alive."

"Were they?" queried Gill. She was rather startled by this bit of news, but her shrewdness was seldom caught napping. "Were they indeed? You don't know that, dear, unless Henderson confided his private and domestic affairs to you, which isn't likely. Well, I am sorry that you caught that boy. It was unlucky for you. I conclude "—and her voice sounded a trifle hard—"that you let him off."

Jack nodded. "I am not squeamish," he said, "but I could not—I could not have handed Henderson's son over to the police. He said that his ruin lay at my door, Gill, and I don't deny it."

"*I* deny it," cried Gillian, "and most emphatically. The boy lied, my dear, and if you were not morbid on this subject, you would say so too. It is absurd to put the sins of his family to your account. Sudden misfortune does not send people to moral ruin, unless they are already inclined that way. I suppose the boy implied that they were all patterns of virtue once?"

"I don't know. It wasn't what he said, it is what I feel," said Jack. "There is no use in arguing about it. I won't shirk facts." He stared gravely into the fire. "If it had not been for you and the child I'd have drowned the consciousness of them. As things are I must meet them. I won't pretend that they are not there."

Gill moved impatiently. "I wish you would be happy," she said. "You are a dreadful person to have to deal with, darling! You seem to fancy that you must either hang your self-respect and morality altogether, or else encourage your conscience to ride rough-shod and tyrannise over you. I've never met any one with less capability of striking a medium. Good gracious! it is close upon twelve, and the carriage has been waiting for ages. I suppose you will not come with me to Lady Braintree's?"

"I shall try to get hold of that chap. I wish that I had insisted on taking his address," said Jack.

"I hope you won't find him again. You will only make yourself more miserable than you are at present—if that is possible." She put her hands on his shoulders, and stood on tiptoe, with uplifted face. "Good-night. Do you know, Jack, that if you were any other man——"

"What then?" he said absently.

"Why, then you would not keep me waiting when I offer you a kiss," said Gill with a laugh. But when she was in the carriage the brightness faded from her face. Indeed, at heart she was a little sad, though she pulled herself together, and banished traces of care so soon as she entered the ball-room.

Mrs. Cardew would have considered it cowardly (as well as bad-mannered) to appear sad at a ball. "It is a point of honour to second one's hostess's efforts, and to play the game," she would have said. "If you cannot trust yourself enough for that, you've no business to accept an invitation." And in very truth a sometimes abused frivolous society teaches some most excellent lessons in self-control and unselfishness, and the children of light have perhaps in this respect something to learn from the so-called worldly. Mrs. Cardew did not enjoy that ball, but she successfully looked as if she did, and, as usual, she was surrounded by admirers.

One curious little incident that occurred, amused, though its comedy was not devoid of sting for her.

She had seized upon a momentarily vacant chair, while her partner plunged into the crowd round the supper-table. She turned with a laughing apology to the lady who was sitting next to her, and who was wedged almost into her pocket.

"I am afraid that I am crushing you," she said. "This is like 'chair-game' on a huge scale, isn't it?"

"Oh," said the lady with a gasp, "I have never before been to a London ball, and I do not think that I ever wish to go again. There are so many people that one cannot really see any one, and yet I know that there are all kinds of interesting celebrities present."

The keen disappointment in her voice amused, and at the same time struck Gillian as almost pathetic.

"That is Lord Salisbury there, with his back to the lady with the wonderful rope of pearls. That Chinaman is a member of the Chinese Embassy. The short girl on our left, in a green dress, is Miss Randedecken, the American heiress, and the tall lady with black hair is the wife of the Italian ambassador," Gillian said good-naturedly. "Let me see what more I can tell you."

"Oh, thank you," said the lady. "But the person I want to see is Mrs. Cardew. I suppose you must have met her, for you seem to know every one. Do you think that she is as beautiful as they say?"

"No," said Gillian. "I think that her beauty is over rated and that she is no better-looking than—I am."

"Are you a friend of hers?" the lady asked.

"I should not describe myself as Mrs. Cardew's friend, but I have some knowledge of her. Why are you so curious about her?"

"Why, hers is such an odd story," said the lady (who was a born gossip, and who had now thrown prudence to the winds). "It sounded so romantic! but they say now that she did not really care about Mr. Cardew. She married him for his immense fortune, you know, and she is so clever she has certainly helped him to live down disgrace. I have heard that the Insurance Company is sorry that it ever brought that action! It has lost more than it gained by it."

"Ah, I am delighted to hear that," said Gillian, with an emphasis that made the lady open her sharp little eyes.

"You like Mr. Cardew the better of the two?" she ventured.

Gillian's laugh was a little scornful. "Very much the better of the two! There is no comparison between them."

"I have heard that he hates society, but that he lets her spend his money and do what she likes. They are not so very happy together after all. I do not think it sounds as if she were quite nice, do you?"

"I daresay she isn't always 'quite nice,'" said Gillian. "She has had a hard fight for him, according to her lights. For my part, I wish her well."

"Oh," said the inquisitive lady, with a belated qualm of doubt as to the wisdom of her remarks, "I fancied that you did not like her."

"There are only two people in the world of whom I am fonder, and whose interests I should put before hers," said Gillian. "But here comes my ice at last."

She nodded and smiled with a mischievous twinkle in her eyes when she moved away. "How dismayed she will be when she prosecutes her inquiries a little farther! It will serve her perfectly right for being so dense and so rash," thought Mrs. Cardew, but her laugh was not quite mirthful. The strictures on her own conduct had not hurt her in the least. Any one was welcome to suppose that she had married Jack for his money, for none of us mind an arrow that flies quite wide of the mark; but one sentence stuck to her uncomfortably—"They are not so very happy together after all."

A light was still burning in the library when she got home. Gillian pushed the door open very gently and peeped in, but Jack was too intent on his work to see or hear her, and she stole away softly without disturbing him. She was glad that he had taken to writing again, that the old instincts were awake, yet it sometimes seemed to her that his books were nearer his heart than she was.

The fire in her room was cosy and cheerful, and the hardships she had once endured had given Gill an abiding pleasure in luxury. She took off her ball-dress, slipped on her dressing-gown, and ran lightly down the passage into the night-nursery. Her baby was sleeping soundly. She bent over the cradle, shading the light from him with one hand.

The boy lay with one arm thrown above his head. Gillian kissed his little pink palm gently, and listened to the sound of his soft breathing with a rapture with which no other music had ever filled her.

" You are growing very like him, my boy. I hope that you will have a happier life," she murmured.

She tucked the blanket round the child, and putting her candle down, knelt for a minute beside the cot. The yearning instinct to protect and guard, that should be in every woman, was strong in Gillian. While she knelt she shivered with a sudden fear of all the dangers that her love might not avert. Such a tender, easily-hurt wee body, such a precious little life, that might be so quickly blown out ! There are two powers that the strongest of us are apt to own our masters, and one is Death and the other is Love, but most women feel that the last will be the final victor. " And Jane is sure of it," Gillian said to herself, with the tenderly amused smile that the thought of Jane often brought to her lips. " But people like me, people who are naturally unspiritual, how on earth are we to know ? "

CHAPTER XII.

YOU ARE NO TRUE PRIEST.

THE new rector of Churton Regis stood at his garden gate and gazed rather gloomily at the smiling south country in which his lot had been cast.

Mr. Strode was a spare man, full of energy. He was nearer fifty than forty, but his black eyes were as bright and keen as they had been in his youth. His forehead was narrow and high, and his nose aquiline. He was olive-complexioned, but his character and manner were essentially English.

Mr. Strode might have sat for the picture of some Italian prelate, but he had none of the diplomatic tact that has characterised the magnates of the Church of Rome. Far from being " all things to all men," he was a trifle inclined to wave a red flag (metaphorically) whenever he encountered a bull.

He habitually wore his cassock—to the scandal and disgust of his parishioners, who looked upon him as a Papist in disguise—and a silver cross hung round his neck. He was, at present, the square peg in the round hole, whose position Gillian had once deprecated.

Mr. Strode did not like this fat and prosperous pasture. He was irritated by the ways of these slow, comfortable sheep ; they showed a most reprehensible tendency towards reversing the right order of things and attempting to lead their shepherd. He had become accustomed to dealing

with goats, and he was not sure that he did not after all
prefer them.   Yet he was by no means one of those men
who are born saviours, and to whom the seeking of the
lost is a sort of spiritual necessity.   During his ten years'
chaplaincy to one of Her Majesty's gaols he had, perforce,
seen a shady and somewhat hopeless side of human
nature, and the sight had hardened him.   Mr. Strode was
an honourable man, impelled by a sense of duty; therefore he had worked to the best of his ability in a cause
which he privately considered pretty hopeless.   He had
administered the law and the gospel (or at any rate his
version of them), undeterred by the certainty that the ground
he sowed was sterile.   His duty, in any case, was to scatter
the seed.

It was impossible for him to have faith in the efficacy
of his own preaching; but he had at first been more hopeful as to the possibility of doing useful work by helping
the men on their discharge.   Repeated failures had brought
home to him the truth of the proverb about sows' ears and
silk purses.   He did not succeed in his endeavours; possibly
because, in order to perform miracles, something is required
that he lacked.   Yet he went on with his endeavour un-
swervingly.   He was grimly loyal to the service in which
he had, perhaps mistakenly, enlisted.

Mr. Strode would have made a fine soldier.   He tried
to make a good priest, and gradually a deep and stubborn
affection grew and took possession of him.   One must love
something, and some men seem to be most fortunate,
perhaps because least exacting, when they expend their
devotion on an impersonal object.   A woman had once
played Mr. Strode false (that was in the days of his youth,
when he had taken her, as later in life he took his convicts,
in the wrong way), but Mother Church remained steadily
on her high pedestal.   He was a rich man nowadays,
unexpectedly rich through a legacy that might have pre-

vented him from taking orders, had it fallen to him in time, but he lavished the greater part of his income on his love. His study table was covered with plans for the rebuilding of the parish church ; his hot-houses were full of sweet white flowers that were destined to adorn the altar.

In enforcing the rules of the rubric, in fasting on fast days, and in strenuously asserting his right to dip unwilling babies bodily into the font, Mr. Strode was satisfying an instinct that might have found vent in a scrupulous exactness and smartness, had he held his commission in the Queen's service.

He was not verging towards Rome, though his shocked parishioners believed him to be so doing. He had seldom, to tell the truth, reflected deeply on the tenets of faith ; but he was a martinet by nature, and red tape of any kind was congenial to him. His living was in Lady Hammerton's gift, and the present mistress of Draycott was his godmother.

Mr. Strode strongly objected to the system of lay-patronage. He had thought fit to explain his attitude in a somewhat ungracious letter.

" I am bound to state that in the event of my accepting the living, I should hold myself in no way bound to defer to you in any matter pertaining to my office. I think, therefore, that you may very probably prefer to reconsider your offer," he had written.

His godmother had chuckled with amusement. She came of a family of honourable and crotchety gentlemen, and she understood Henry Strode much better than he understood her.

The view that the rector looked at was beautiful with the full, rich beauty of Devon. From where he stood he could see the woods of Draycott to the west. On the summit of the hill to the right was Oaklands Park, rebuilt within the last ten years by the rich soap-boiler, whose

charming wife was devoted to the service of the church.
Farther east again was a bit of heather-covered moor, the
nearest spur of Exmoor. Mr. Cardew had lately built a
hunting-box there, and the priest's face darkened when his
glance wandered in that direction. He hated Jack Cardew
with what he believed to be a purely impersonal and
righteous hatred. Here, he said, was a man who had been
proved a scoundrel by the law of his country, who lived
an openly irreligious life, but who was accepted in society,
not as a repentant sinner, but as a wealthy and prosperous
county magnate.

The hot anger that rose in Mr. Strode's heart when he
thought about these things sometimes warmed his usually
cold sermons into something approaching eloquence. He
was not addicted to making personal allusions in the
pulpit—he was neither of the school nor the type that does
that; but he did denounce the time-serving and mean
spirit that respects money more than honour, and which,
regardless of mud, licks the shoes of the rich man, with a
force that surprised and puzzled his congregation. It
puzzled, because the new parson was strictly conservative
in politics, and denunciations against wealth were usually
associated with expositions of so-called socialism in the
village tap-room.

His reflections on his parishioners were not on the whole
sympathetic, though he was full of plans for their benefit.
The last incumbent had been a King Log; but here was
a King Stork ready to stir up the pond to some purpose.

King Stork presently set out at a brisk pace for Draycott
Court. He was engaged to dine with Lady Hammerton,
and the prospect of a dinner-party added to his gloom.
He was not naturally sociable, and he was not at his ease
with women, but he had no excuse for refusing; unfortunately it was not a fast day.

He had determined to walk the ten miles, for he was

both fond of exercise and parsimonious in his personal expenditure.

Mr. Strode had more than one of the family characteristics strongly developed. Like his godmother, he was inclined to cut down pence and live abstemiously, that he might have the more pounds to lavish on his hobby. It was a fine trait; but a generosity that takes the form of meanness is not popular, nor perhaps easy to live with; he was not liked, even by those of his own household.

Unhappily for Mr. Strode, Devonshire lanes were never made for the man with a purpose, and his walk did not improve his humour. The sudden twist to the right that showed so enchanting a vista of green trees, the curve down into a hollow where the lords and ladies grew by a still pool, the twist back to the right that seemed to bring him almost to the point at which he had started, caused the priest to tighten his lips in a way which suggested an irritable temper ridden with a curb.

He had no love of scenery, and Devonshire lanes are made for their lovers. They are as full of sweet surprises as a maid in her teens; but they tease the unfortunate person who has no capability for loafing in him.

Mr. Strode prided himself on his punctuality, and he was late. Consequently his lean, close-shaven, face looked blacker than usual when he was shown into the drawing-room. His old cousin greeted him kindly, but with some perturbation of manner.

"My dear Henry, I thought that you were never behind time," said she.

"I started in excellent time, but your road through the wood misled me. I apologise," said Mr. Strode.

"And there ought to be a court-martial held on the road!" put in a voice behind Lady Hammerton.

The priest looked over the old lady's head, and his eyes met Gillian Cardew's. He was not a man at whom people often ventured to laugh. He had but small sense of humour, and he was apt to be morally overpowering. He felt, at that moment, as if he had crossed swords with an adversary.

Mrs. Cardew had spoken jestingly, but her expression was rather scornful than merry. Mr. Strode resented that expression indignantly. As a man he had given no woman reason to despise him. As a priest he was entitled to respect.

"Let me introduce you to Miss Haubert," said his godmother. She rested the tips of her mittened fingers on his arm, and led him across the room.

"I begged you to come early, for I wished to prepare you," she whispered. "But there is no opportunity now! You must just make the best of it. Luckily you are both gentlemen."

"What can you mean? What did you wish to prepare me for?" he asked in the clear, uncompromising tones that never sank to asides. "Why is it lucky that—ah!"

"'An' he might he would have sworn. The way in which he presses his lips together amounts to several big 'D's,'" Gillian remarked under her breath.

Jack Cardew, who had been standing with his back to the priest, turned round now and nodded curtly.

"I fancy that you and I have met before," said he.

"He was always a shameless reprobate. Any other man would have been abashed," the ex-chaplain reflected. He found it difficult after that unexpected meeting to bring his mind to bear on his social duties. Mr. Strode was not, as his hostess observed, "a good dinner-party man." He talked down to the supposed level of Miss Haubert's understanding, and his thoughts wandered constantly from her to Mr. Cardew.

How well he knew that bronzed, square-jawed face, and those bright blue eyes, that had once sought his in eager hope, but that had ever after regarded him with unconcealed insolence. Jack Cardew would never appeal to any one now. That was plainly to be seen. There was a force and dignity about him that surprised Mr. Strode. What right had such a man to dignity? Was it only the prison clothes that had made Cardew appear so different once? He tried to picture Jack once more in a convict's suit, but was interrupted by the sound of his neighbour's voice. He was vaguely aware that he had not attended to her last remark.

"I beg your pardon. What did you say?" he asked perfunctorily.

Enid Haubert's bright, sensitive face quivered with half-amused indignation. She was shy, but she was not wanting in spirit.

"I do not think that I need repeat my saying, for I have said it three times already," she remarked. "You were listening to your own thoughts all the while."

"I beg your pardon," said Mr. Strode shortly. Then something in the quaintness of her phrase made him smile.

"I *was* listening to my own thoughts," he owned. "But you would hardly wonder at my bad manners did you know what an extraordinary experience I have had to-night. I suppose that you have heard, for every one in the county has heard, Mr. Cardew's story. Well, I saw him last when I was chaplain of Dartmoor gaol." He spoke under cover of the general buzz of conversation, but Enid answered very softly, fearing lest Cardew should overhear.

"Oh, indeed; it is no wonder that you can think of nothing else," she said. "How glad you must have been that you were chaplain at that time."

"Must I? But why?"

"I meant that you must have been so glad that you had the opportunity to help, so far as it was possible for any one, in such an awful, incomprehensible misfortune."

Mr. Strode frowned. Enid had spoken in perfect good faith, but her words irritated him.

"I have no desire to be uncharitable," he said. "Indeed, as a priest my natural inclination must always be on the side of mercy, but I am bound to say that I consider that this modern sentimentalism about crime, this weak treating of sin as 'misfortune,' is leading the nation to the very hell in which it now professes disbelief. I see, of course, that you, in taking this view, are only carelessly repeating what hundreds of people are writing. Yet the youngest child, the most irresponsible woman among us, should be careful not to advocate these loose and pernicious principles."

Enid gasped, and Mr. Strode became conscious that he had been lecturing with some heat.

"I did not mean to speak harshly," he began.

"No, and it can hardly matter to me whether you do so or not," said Miss Haubert, rather unexpectedly. "But I did not at first understand what you meant. Do you really not believe in Mr. Cardew?" She glanced across the table at Jack. "If you were the youngest child, or the most irresponsible woman among us, you would know an honest man when you met him," said she, and after that she would speak no more to Mr. Strode, who, for his part, was quite untroubled by her bad opinion, having but slight respect for the intelligence of young ladies.

It was not a large dinner-party; there were but four men present besides Mr. Strode, and those four had all undoubting faith in Jack Cardew's honesty. Sir Edward Bevan took the bottom of the table, in right of his relationship to the hostess. The young squire of East Cheapham devoted himself to pretty Nina Tyrell (Gillian had used all her influence to persuade Lady Hammerton to invite Nina), and he wondered that he had never before met so strikingly handsome a girl. Colonel Hanson, a stout, middle-aged soldier sat beside Mrs. Cardew, and came to the conclusion

.12

that he was making himself unusually interesting, and that he had happened to hit on the very subject that Mrs. Cardew had most at heart. It was a conclusion that most men arrived at when Gillian took the trouble to please them.

Gillian's laugh was infectious, and so long as she was in the room the conversation never flagged, but the men had very little to say to each other when they were left alone. Sir Edward was never a genial host; Jack Cardew was in a silent mood; and the priest and the soldier agreed so heartily in their strictly conservative politics that there was nothing for them to discuss.

In the drawing-room the conversation was much brighter. Gillian was making her friends laugh over a story about an old woman who had told her that she wasn't "laying up any crowns of glory." Gillian's stories were always amusing, and they never lost in the telling. She had a quick eye for character, and her neighbours' weaknesses amused her. Life had taught her not to betray all she saw, and she preferred to turn the point of a tale against herself, because, since her marriage, she had aimed at popularity. Yet she was, even now, more liked by men than by women. Women suspected the keenness of her observation, and recognised her cleverness with some misgivings. Her present company was exceptionally fond of her. With Lady Hammerton Gillian was always at her best and gentlest, Nina Tyrell liked her (with reservations), Enid Haubert cordially loved and admired her.

Enid was engaged to decorate the new club-room for boys that had been built by Cardew. She was staying at the hunting-box, and was enjoying the moorland scenery with an intensity that seemed to her hostess almost pathetic. Enid was the only person who saw and understood an odd passage of arms that occurred during the course of the evening.

Nina was singing, in a strong, untrained voice. Jack and the colonel were standing by the piano. Lady Hammerton was talking brightly to her cousin, when the young squire crossed the drawing-room, followed by the black-visaged high churchman who had taken Miss Haubert in to dinner.

"Will you let me introduce Mr. Strode to you, Mrs. Cardew?" said the squire cheerfully. For his part he was glad to be rid of the priest, who had made him feel like a schoolboy, and with whom he had nothing in common. He retreated hastily to the piano, where Jack, with an almost imperceptible shrug of his broad shoulders, gave up the place by the music-stool.

Mrs. Cardew raised her head and looked steadily at Mr. Strode, and again he felt that her look was an insult.

"We hardly need an introduction," she said, and at the sound of her voice Enid glanced up, startled. "I have heard about you from my husband. You did a lasting piece of work in Dartmoor."

Mr. Strode's sallow cheek warmed as if some one had struck it. He felt challenged, and he had good fighting blood in his veins. He had never, since he was in his twenties, been so indignant with a woman.

"I will not pretend not to understand you," he replied. "You are resentful because I saw no reason to believe that, in one especial case, a jury had been mistaken in their verdict. I do not consider that I was in any degree blame-worthy. I feel it due to my profession to say this. As a man it can be of no vital interest to me"—he hesitated for one second, because Mrs. Cardew smiled contemptuously, and the smile angered him—"it can be of no vital interest to me to defend myself. As a priest I am bound to hold my office beyond reproach."

"I see. I congratulate you on the way in which you do so," said Gillian.

Enid moved her chair as if to break the tension of the situation. The concentrated bitterness in Gillian's low voice, the white anger expressed in the priest's face, made her heart beat fast. She would not have been the artist she was had she not been quickly susceptible to moral atmosphere; but all her sympathy was with the woman. Gillian's words were like knives; in a more primitive state of society Gillian would have tried to have killed the man who had sneered at Jack. And little Enid, whose life had been crossed by no such passionate love-story, who shrank from killing a fly, yet understood. "Was he unkind to Mr. Cardew in prison? Why, then, of course she must hate him," thought Enid.

"Lady Hammerton is making signs to you, Enid. I hope that she is going to ask you to show Sir Edward those designs for the new club-room," said Gillian.

She turned round with the frank interest that she always accorded to Enid Haubert.

"If he offers to give you a commission don't put too low a value on what you do," she whispered as Enid passed her. "Your work is worth double what it was before you had those lessons, and it never pays to be modest."

Enid smiled at the characteristic bit of advice, and crossed the room full of hope that more good luck was about to befall her. Mr. Strode sat down on the chair she had vacated. As he did so a rather fierce thrill of satisfaction ran through Gillian's veins. She, too, said to herself, "This is good luck"; but she would not forget that he was Lady Hammerton's guest yet.

Her nostrils dilated, and she put one hand over the other, and twisted her thick wedding-ring, not nervously— for Gillian had never known the fear of man—but with the determination to control her speech.

"Lady Hammerton, who is my very dear old friend, did not know that you and my husband had met before

until I told her so," said Mrs. Cardew. Her speech was
a trifle slower than usual, but the priest knew that she
was excited.

"Jack would not let her cancel the invitation on his
account, for he says that he does not in the least mind
with whom he eats."

(The convict's toleration afforded Mr. Strode a momentary
grim amusement.)

"And I," she went on, "I had no intention of being
uncivil to Lady Hammerton's guest. I had not supposed
that you would have wished to be introduced to me."

That you would have "ventured" was what she meant,
and the man mentally put in the word.

"Do you not think that, because you are her guest, you
had better let us end our conversation now?" she asked.

The priest rose to his feet with kindling eyes. "Shall
we look at the flowers in the conservatory?" he said; and
Mrs. Cardew smiled again, that scornful smile that was
a challenge.

"Oh, certainly, since you wish it, with the greatest
pleasure," she said.

She walked across the long drawing-room with the free,
stately gait that Lady Hammerton so approved. Her
husband raised his eyebrows when the folds of her satin
gown swept by him.

Was Gillian bent on captivating the parson? For his
part he hated meeting the fellow, though a dogged pride
had prevented him from sparing himself the ordeal, and
had carried him safely through it with apparent imper-
turbability. Gillian's spirits were equal to anything! But
then, Gill had not been in Dartmoor.

"We are going to look at the lilies, dear," said Gill.
"Mr. Strode covets them for his altar, I believe."

But when she and Mr. Strode stood alone together in
the conservatory, in which indeed there was no great show,

but only a pot or two of tiger-lilies, and a clambering mass of passion-flower, then she faced Jack's old enemy without any pretence of frivolity. A very intense emotion, whether it be of love or of hate, seems at times scarcely to need words in order to be made manifest. Gillian's indignant scorn burnt at white heat.

"What can *you* have to say to me ?" she asked.

"I have this to say," said the man. "You take upon yourself to congratulate me ironically on the way in which I did my duty as a priest. I conclude that you refer to something that Mr. Cardew has told you. You speak without justification." He held his head high but spoke with measured carefulness. He was fighting for the honour of his cloth. "I am not excusing myself," he said ; "neither do I wish for one moment to deny or retract anything I may once have said. Even had I held a most extraordinary opinion as to the innocence of one of the prisoners committed to my spiritual charge, I should yet not have had the right to ventilate it."

"Most people," said Gillian, "would have hesitated, under any circumstances, about kicking a man who was down. But I forget—you say you are not concerned to defend your conduct as a man. It is only in your official capacity that you are beyond reproach. I am not very clear about Church matters. I suppose that your priesthood lifts you above ordinary considerations."

"Pardon me, but you do not really suppose that," said the priest. "My office is to succour the helpless and to absolve the penitent. I have no commission to set myself in absurd opposition to the judgment of the law."

"It was no case of opposing the law," said Gillian quickly. She put her hands before her face for a moment. She would make this man see what he had done. She would *make* him ashamed. She was not crying. There were no tears in her eyes. She was but collecting all her force, in the effort to impress her view of his conduct on this antagonist, who had insulted Jack in the hour of sorest need. So long as he lived Mr. Strode never quite forgot that gesture, nor the thrill of passion in her voice.

"Listen," she said. "My husband was absolutely innocent. You do not believe that because you are no priest by nature. You are not of the kind who know when they touch the truth. I do not say that that is your fault. Every one cannot hold a divining rod. You were evidently not given one. Jack was sent to prison, but he was a very plucky boy, and he would not lose hope. He believed in several things that very few of us believe in now —in God, and in justice, and in the goodness of men. The hardships of the life broke his health, almost broke his spirit—but not quite. He was sent to the infirmary, and you visited him there. He turned to you, because you were a gentleman, and he wanted a word from one of his own sort. What had all that to do with the law? He did not ask you to agitate for his freedom, or to sign a petition, or to force the prison doors for him, did he? He felt himself on the verge of sinking, and you profess to help any one in spiritual need. Jack was never soft. He must have been pretty desperate when he told you that story. Do you happen to remember what you said to it?"

"I cannot, at this distance of time, recall the exact words that I used," said Mr. Strode. "But I am perfectly aware that I put no faith in his story."

"You heard him through to the end, and then you waved your hand," said Gillian. "'My good man,' you said, 'I've been chaplain here for three years. I can assure you that I have never yet come across any one who considers that he has been justly convicted. You all think that you have been ill-used, you know, every one of you!' Those were your very words. That you disbelieved was perhaps your misfortune. But I wonder why it was necessary to insult him?" Mrs. Cardew's face had turned rather white, and her eyes blazed. "Jack held out his hand to you when the waters were going over him, and you gave it a kick. You did your utmost to damn the soul that was—how do you put it?—that was committed to your spiritual charge. He did not drown—but that was not your fault. I hope—yes, I hope with all my strength, that on the day when the deep waters are going over you, you may call on the power that you trust in, and that it may kick you farther down."

"Gillian," said a voice behind her.

Gillian turned round and confronted Jack. "Oh, Jack dear," she cried lightly, "Mr. Strode and I have not found any white flowers. There are only flame-coloured lilies here, which I like better, but they are not so appropriate to a church, are they?"

She wondered whether Jack had overheard anything. It was impossible to guess, but she rather hoped that he had not. So long as she lived Jack was the one man in all the world to Gillian. Nevertheless, he and she had journeyed somewhat apart of late years. An impalpable barrier had thickened between them. Gillian had understood the recklessness that had possessed the returned convict. She had understood and sympathised with a tenderness and wisdom that had been unfailing and tireless. Now, as her husband's character righted and reasserted itself, she was dumbly aware that she was often at variance with him. Gillian was essentially practical, and Jack theoretical. His way was not her way, and his aims were often incomprehensible to her.

Jack paid no attention to the remark about the lilies. "John Saunders has ridden over to fetch us," he said gravely. "There has been an accident. The nursery curtains caught fire, and the house is burning."

"Stephen?" cried Gillian breathlessly.

"Stephen is at your step-father's house. The little chap was a bit hurt—not killed."

"Let us make haste to get to him," she said. "Are they putting the horse to? I saw the colonel drive up in a light dog-cart. His mare is very fast. Ask him to lend you his trap, Jack. We shall get there all the sooner. He can have ours."

Jack nodded. "That is a clever thought. Put on your cloak, Gill. I'll be ready by the time you are down."

She went at once. She had forgotten Mr. Strode. She did not even see him when he held the conservatory door open for her. She had no thought for anything but to get as soon as possible to her child.

In the passage she met Enid.

"Why, of course, you must come too," she said. "Borrow something warm to put over your head, Enid. We shall drive in an open trap."

Enid looked rather startled. "I hope that no one is hurt!" she cried.

"No one—except my boy," said Gillian.

Two minutes later the two women came down into the hall where the whole party had assembled to see them off.

"Jack is getting the mare in as quickly as ever he can. There is no use in fussing," said Mrs. Cardew. "Yes, please, Lady Hammerton, I will take that brandy-flask with me. Some one always faints or makes a fool of herself when there is an accident. It is quite likely to be useful. Oh dear, no, thank you, I don't want any. I have not got any nerves. I am not in the least upset."

Colonel Hanson was a little uneasy at having to trust his mare to Cardew's furious driving, but he valiantly rose to the occasion. Sir Edward kept making futile suggestions as to the cause of the fire. His first instinct was to find out who was to blame.

"An accident? How do we know that it was an accident?" he repeated.

Lady Hammerton trotted about with her arms full of warm wraps. Mr. Strode, somewhat out of it among all these staunch friends of the convict, watched the scene grimly. Mrs. Cardew's words were still ringing in his ears: "I hope that when the waters are going over you——"

Why, the woman had actually cursed him!

Mr. Strode was not superstitious, and he was angry, and anger is an antidote to fear, yet the force of Gillian's hate had made itself felt.

They were off at last, driving full tilt down the long avenue.

"So sorry to have given so much trouble," Gillian called out cheerfully, as they dashed away.

"Is the boy hurt? The mother does not seem at all anxious," the colonel said doubtfully.

The guests stood in the porch, watching for the last flash of the gig-lamp at the turn of the road.

"There! He is clear of the elms. He is driving like Jehu," said the colonel.

"Ah, look!" cried Nina Tyrell. "That must be it."

They all looked in the direction in which she pointed. There was a quivering red glow above the tree-tops. Now it died down, and then again shot up as the westerly wind fanned it.

"It's lucky he is so rich," said the squire. "Not like us poor beggars who depend on the land. Why, it will be nothing to Cardew to build another shooting-box."

"Sons cannot be bought," said Sir Edward snappishly.

"Jack is proud of his boy. I trust there is no great harm done," said Lady Hammerton. "You are quite right, Edward, one can't buy children." And she sighed, thinking of the unworthy heir who would come after her.

"It is just like Mr. Cardew's bad luck," said Nina.

And at that Sir Edward turned severely on her. He never lost an opportunity of preaching, and all times were in season to him.

"There is no such thing as luck, my dear young lady. There is Satan, who works mischief, and there is God, who chastises us for our good, but nothing is left to chance."

"Oh well, I did not think it sounded proper to say, 'It is the devil,'" Nina retorted.

She had really, for reasons of her own, intended to make friends with Sir Edward, but she could not stand being lectured. The least suspicion of a sermon always drove Nina to open revolt.

CHAPTER XIII.

CAN THE CREATURE FATHOM THE CREATURE?

> "'Thou hast gone astray,' quoth the preacher,
> 'In the gall of thy bitterness.'
> Thou hast taught me in vain, O teacher,
> I neither blame thee, nor bless.
>
> .   .   .   .   .   .
>
> Can the creature fathom the creature
> "Whose Creator is fathomless?"

SIR EDWARD stayed after the other guests. He was a lonely man, and his cousin's society was very pleasant to him.

The meeting with Cardew had excited him; he thought a great deal about Jack during the dull drive to Highfields.

The square, grey house, that was full of bitter memories, the house that his wife had fled from, and that Cyril, whom he had really loved, had deserted, seemed colder and gloomier than usual when he reached it. He seldom stayed long at Highfields, and when he was forced to go there, he lived in two rooms, so that there should be no need to uncover the main part of the furniture.

The pictures were protected from dust by newspapers. The chairs and sofas were shrouded in sheets. Draycott Court, which Gillian thought gloomy, was cheerful compared to Highfields.

The old butler tried to arrest his master in the hall, explaining nervously that some one had arrived, but Sir

Edward was getting deaf, and he was always impatient; he would not wait to hear what the man had to say, but went on to the library.

The room was unexpectedly light. Sir Edward was stingy over the consumption of gas and coal, but here was a fire blazing half up the chimney, the gas at full cock, and a reading lamp alight by the sofa.

"Why, what is the meaning of this?" Sir Edward cried wrathfully. "Why is my room lit up like a gin-palace? Who is responsible for this wicked extravagance?"

He stopped, and rubbed his eyes. A short, fair man rose from the sofa, where he had been making himself extremely comfortable, and came forward with an engaging smile. "Oh, father," he said, "it is ages since we have met, is not it? I have answered your letter in person, as you see."

He spoke lightly, with an assumption of ease. Only a very acute observer could have seen a suggestion of anxiety in his eyes that rather belied the frank smile on his lips.

Sir Edward shut the door carefully behind him (his family troubles were too big to be concealed, but he was proud, and he could not bear to think that the servants should overhear a quarrel) then—

"I long ago forbade you the house, sir," said he.

"Yes, yes, I know. That was most unfortunate," Cyril replied. He had the air of generously overlooking his father's peculiarities. "I had not forgotten that you did so, but it seemed really necessary that we should discuss this proposal of yours. It hardly strikes me as feasible, you know."

He put his head slightly on one side, and glanced up at his father. Then he shifted the lamp, and pushed forward an armchair.

"Won't you sit down comfortably, father?"

Sir Edward stared gloomily at his son. His silence

became oppressive. At last he spoke. "Three years ago I would have had you kicked out of the house," he said. "But to-night I will hear you, Cyril, for after to-night I do not think that we shall meet again." He sat down, leaning his head on his hand and gazing into the fire. "I do not know what I have done wrong," he said wearily. "I should have liked to have had an honest son—I should have been as proud as other fathers are. But God is not unjust, and I am punished. I must have been in fault."

Cyril Bevan moved hastily, and turned his head away. His conscience was of a singularly rudimentary kind; it had troubled him very little. He was naturally light, as his mother had been. Yet at that moment, and for the space of one moment, he was ashamed. The sensation was so displeasing that he hastened to be rid of it.

"Fault? Oh, it was nobody's fault, certainly not yours," he said cheerfully. "You lectured me, and you licked Cardew often enough, but we were both bound, from the start, to go to the bow-wows. That sort of thing is in the blood."

"Vessels chosen for perdition," the old man muttered.

His Calvinism chimed oddly in accord with the modern theory of hereditary taint.

"But Jack Cardew is honest," he added, after a pause.

"The jury were not of your opinion," said Cyril.

He did not, however, pursue the subject, which had no vital interest for him. He had not taken the trouble to come to this inhospitable house and to beard this unpleasant father for the sake of discussing Cardew's character. He had, in fact, come to see how his father was wearing. He noticed that the old man was shrivelled and yellow. It was a pity that it was so impossible to tell how much longer he would last.

Cyril Bevan was not young himself. He had, as he sometimes pathetically remarked, reached an age at which most men are fatherless, and Time, that patient teacher, had at last taught him some prudence. He was inclined to refuse to entertain the somewhat stern offer that Sir Edward had made once before, and had lately renewed.

If Cyril would join in cutting off the entail on the estate his father would pay £20,000 to be clear of him.

"The offer made in the spring of '91 still stands," Sir Edward had written, in reply to his son's last application.

He had written on a postcard. He would not waste a penny on his unworthy and unwelcome heir, when a half-penny would do.

"I received your kind communication," Cyril remarked with a smile, "but it grows late. Had we not better discuss this little business to-morrow?"

"No. I'll take your answer now," said the old man. "You'll have trouble in knocking them up at the Golden Lion if you do not go soon, and you will want a bed there."

"Oh, very well," said Cyril, and his momentary shame vanished.

His dealings had been crooked enough, as all the world knew; but he would not, under any circumstances, have refused a bed (that is, had he plenty of spare rooms) to any needy relative.

His father, he reflected, was about the meanest person he had ever stumbled across in the course of a pretty varied experience.

Cyril had no more conception of the moral indignation and horror that filled the old knight than had his collie, to whom this poor specimen of humanity was adorable.

He sat down again on the sofa and played with his dog's silky ears. He was kind to animals, and he felt supported by this faithful retainer's loyalty.

"So you want me to sell my birthright for a large mess of pottage," he said. "And of course you are aware that

I am hungry." He laughed softly. He had a pleasant and musical laugh. " It is such a quaint position for one's father to take up," he remarked by the way.

Sir Edward waited for the upshot of this preamble in melancholy silence. Once that casual comment would have roused him to an outburst of indignation. A quaint position, forsooth ! Why, it was terrible, heart-breaking. Did not this degenerate son know that his father would have died a hundred deaths rather than that such disgrace should have fallen on his house ?

But now the old knight said nothing—there was no use in more words.

" I allow that the proposal is very tempting to a man who is as hard up as I am. You have never wanted money, so you won't give me credit for the amount of resistance I am displaying. Twenty thousand is a flea-bite to you."

" Yes or no ? " said Sir Edward.

Cyril played with his dog and reflected. If by hook or by crook he could but hold on for a few more years then all this vast estate would be his. And it was not prudence alone that bade him wait. Nina's pretty lips had strongly given the same counsel, and Nina would not marry a poor man. On the other hand, creditors were pressing hard ; he literally had barely half a crown in his purse, and he felt weary, and disinclined for roughing it. The prospect of bodily discomfort had, as his father knew, great weight with this easy-going scamp. He would have sold his soul any day that his body might lie in soft linen. This, however, was a case of selling his patrimony, and the bargain was harder. After all, he had something of his father in him, and he waxed obstinate on any one's attempting to coerce him.

" I wish that you would give up playing Jacob," he said whimsically. " Give me twenty pounds without conditions, instead of twenty thousand with them, and I'll say thank you. And what is more," he added with a half-deprecating smile—"And what is more, I will do my best for the estate when it comes to me. You do not believe this, I know, but I am quite ready to be a pattern landlord. I will even marry, if you like. At one time you were very anxious that I should marry."

"At one time I still had hopes," said Sir Edward. "But I wish for no grandson now. It is better that the line should die out. Is it yes, or no?"

"No," said Cyril. And there was an unusual ring of decision in his voice.

He got up with a slight shrug of his shoulders. The lamplight showed the ignoble lines on his face; but for once his shifty eyes looked quite steadily at his father.

"You need not make that offer again," he said; "it wastes stamps. Come along, Gyp. You and I will go and ask Cousin Anne for a bed if we cannot get in at the inn. You won't shake hands. No; I thought you wouldn't. Good-bye, father."

He walked across the room jauntily enough, but paused when his hand was on the handle of the door.

"Gyp is lame. He is like his master, he is not so young as he was, and it is pouring with rain."

Sir Edward made no sign, and he went out.

Meantime, the three in the dogcart were exchanging but few words during that fast drive to Oaklands. Once Gill broke the silence with a question,—

"Can you not make the mare go faster? Give *me* the whip, Jack."

And Jack shook his head. "Stephen will not see you any the sooner if we are overturned into a ditch by the roadside. I am letting her go as fast as I dare. She isn't my horse. I say," after a pause, "very likely the chap's more scared than hurt."

"Very likely," Gillian assented, in a hard voice ; and Jack made no more futile attempts at crying peace.

They were eagerly watched for at the Park. The gates were wide open, and Mrs. Clovis met them in the hall and clung to Gillian with broken exclamations of sympathy and pity.

"My dearest love, how frightened you must have been ! What a shock for you, but, luckily, you have such iron nerves. To think of your pretty drawing-room being all spoilt, and the poor darling——"

"Where is he ?" cried Gillian. "Did you send for a doctor ? Oh, mammy, tell me quickly where you've put him ? Which room shall I go to ?"

"Why, Gillian, you actually bruise my poor arm when you grasp it in that rough way !" cried Mrs. Clovis, aggrieved. "The dear boy is in the room next to my own. I could not bear to——"

But Gillian was gone.

Jack followed her after a minute's hesitation. He had never set foot inside this house since the early days of his courtship. He knew that Gillian's step-father would have nothing to say to him, but there was no room for pride at this moment. He must find out how much Goliath was hurt.

The sound of the child's cries guided him to the right room. He pushed the door open, and looked in.

Gillian was walking up and down with her boy in her arms. She made a sign to Jack that he was not to disturb her. There was a bright spot of colour in either cheek, but she was singing in a very soothing, crooning fashion, and by degrees the screams subsided and the child drowsed in her arms.

"His left arm is scorched, but not at all badly," she whispered. "I shall get him to sleep if no one else comes in."

Jack heaved a mighty sigh of relief. "You can't walk up and down long with that rascal," he said. "He is a good weight. Hand him over here, Gill."

But the cessation of the song disturbed "Goliath," who began to roar afresh.

"Do go away," said Gillian, and Jack nodded, and went off to look at his remarkably large bonfire.

The house was still crackling gaily, in spite of the efforts of the firemen, who had arrived too late to save it. It had been panelled and raftered with old oak, and it burned like tinder. The stables had been caught by the flames, but the horses had been rescued. No life had been lost and all the refugees had been conveyed safely to Oaklands Park.

Jack elicited all the information he could while he stood in the midst of the crowd, and, with the greatest philosophy, watched his house burn.

"It is a bit of a waste, but it might have been worse," he said, in answer to some condolences.

He felt, in his secret soul, that that worse being escaped, he could hardly entertain any sense of injury.

The small figure with his night-shirt in a blaze in the night-nursery—the same little figure safe in Gillian's arms, with only his curls singed off, that was what the master saw. Goliath, though his inches only measured 37, managed to quite dwarf all else.

"You take it easy, sir," said the young groom to whom Jack had spoken; "but for my part, I could cry to think of those beautiful new stables—that haven't their equal in the county—being all so much charred tinder."

Jim's coat smelt of fire and one of his hands was bound up. He had, he explained, had a tough job to get the roan out, and had been obliged to bandage her eyes with his neckerchief. Excitement had loosened Jim's tongue (he was usually a shy youth), and he had momentarily forgotten his awe of Mr. Cardew. Jim had a great admiration for his master, and had, on one occasion, fought a bigger man than himself because the latter had declared that Cardew was no better than a thief.

"I would have got the harness out, too, if they had let me," he said regretfully. "They hung on to me when I was going into the stable the third time, but I believe I could have done it. I would have risked it, anyway."

"You would have been a fool for your pains, then," said Cardew curtly. "It's bad play to throw down trumps for the sake of trash."

"I don't take your meaning, sir," said the lad half sullenly, "but I was never one to mind a bit of risk." Mr. Cardew might, he thought, have shown more appreciation of his zeal.

"That's it," Cardew answered, with the smile that was so extraordinarily good to meet. "It is a good thing not to mind danger. There is never too much pluck in the world. Keep yours for something that is worth saving and having."

Even while Jack spoke he could have laughed at the commiseration that was offered to him on all sides. That illumination had made extraordinarily clear to him what was "worth having." When the fire was at last subdued, and he stood, in the grey dawn of the morning, surveying the water-drenched walls, his good spirits were not in the least assumed.

He treated the firemen and stablemen to a big breakfast at the Golden Lion. They all tramped down to the inn, and ate heartily after the night's unsuccessful work. Mr. Cardew's health was drunk with a good deal of shouting and with genuine enthusiasm. Jack never tried to be popular; but more than one of the men commented admiringly on the way in which the master took his misfortune.

Cardew engaged a room for himself at the Golden Lion. Mr. Clovis happened to be away on business, but Jack had no intention of quartering himself on the hospitality of Gillian's relatives. When he had had a tub and a sleep he intended to go to Oaklands to express his thanks to his mother-in-law for her kindness to Gillian and the boy. That he did not altogether like Mrs. Clovis was an additional reason for being punctilious in his behaviour to her.

He was just about to set out on this praiseworthy errand when he was delayed by the unexpected appearance of Sir Edward Bevan. The old man accepted his offer of lunch (rather to his surprise), and the two sat down to their meal in the best parlour of the little inn—Jack being filled with odd recollections that made him half inclined to laugh.

Cardew remembered that the last dinner he had partaken of in his guardian's house had been of bread and water! Regular prison fare. The knight's ideas of punishment had been stern and primitive. How very long ago that time was! Jack bore no malice now, for he felt as if that boy he remembered, that unlucky boy who had always been getting into scrapes, were quite another person; besides, when all was said and done, the boy had got the best of the last tussle—though possibly that was not a victory to be proud of.

"How is your son?" asked the old man.

"Oh, he is all right, I believe," Cardew answered carelessly. "His mother was a bit anxious about him till we got to Oaklands and saw that he was safe. Women are apt to get in a fuss, but of course he was all right."

"I am glad, for Mrs. Cardew's sake, that he is safe," said Sir Edward. He was a person of such slow perception that he really fancied Jack was indifferent to his child. Then he added gloomily, "I say that I am glad, but it may be no matter for sorrow when a child is taken away in a state of comparative innocence, and no cause for rejoicing when he lives."

Jack was amused at the characteristic suggestion. "You mean that if a chap's born to be hung, he'll escape burning, eh?" he said. "But the boy will do well, I think. He is his mother's son as well as mine. You are not eating anything, sir."

Sir Edward sighed, and pushed his plate away. "It is strange that we should meet again, Cardew. I have thought of late years—only quite of late years—that perhaps I made some mistakes when you were a boy. You were a stubborn lad, and unruly, and noisy, and very bad-tempered, and Cyril was far more docile. I fancied that Cyril had the better disposition of the two; yet Cyril——"

He stopped short, and put his hand before his eyes.

"I say," Jack said awkwardly, "it is all such ages ago. Why bring up old mistakes? Is that claret thick? You are not touching it. Oh, I forgot, you never touch wine."

"It does not seem so long ago to me. I shall not last much longer, and one's latter years fly fast. That is why I wish to make peace with you. 'Agree with thy adversary quickly, whiles thou art in the way with him; lest at any time the adversary deliver thee to the judge, and the judge deliver thee to the officer, and thou be cast into prison.'"

"Ah!" said Cardew, "but I am generally rather loth to do that to any one, sir. I have had enough of prisons myself."

He remembered that he used to be intensely irritated by Sir Edward's trick of quoting Scripture. It had once seemed to him that the Bible was a sort of armoury, from which such men as his guardian gathered weapons to throw at the ungodly majority.

"If you do not wish to be reconciled, say so," said the old man with sudden petulance.

Jack hesitated for a moment. Then he held out his hand. Were any man ever to treat "Goliath" as Sir Edward had once treated him, Jack felt that that scoundrel would deserve kicking; yet he was sorry for the old man, whose son had turned out such a mean sneak.

"You did make mistakes," he said gravely. "But I daresay I needed a good deal of licking—and you believed in me when most people did not. It's all right, sir."

It was certainly extraordinary and unexpected that after all these years he should meet his old guardian and make it up.

Sir Edward could never shake hands heartily. His fingers felt cold and limp. Neither could he ever have received an apology as frankly as Cardew did—he was not generous, but his conscientiousness was of heroic proportion.

"I hope that your own son will turn out well, and that you realise your responsibilities," he said. "You seem to be endeavouring to use your wealth as a means of doing good. I do not entirely sympathise with some of your schemes; to my mind you leave out the one thing needful, but I recognise" (there was a wonder in his tone that touched Jack's sense of humour)—"I recognise that you are trying to do good."

"Not at all. You are mistaken," said Jack.

Sir Edward waved aside the protest exactly as in the days of Jack's youth he had often waved aside the boy's denial of some unjust charge, and continued his oration in the high-pitched, dogmatic voice that awakened so many memories. Jack listened with mingled sensations.

"How the old fellow lays down the law still! He isn't so much altered, except that he has aged so. I daresay he never meant to do badly by me. Good heavens! what is all this he is saying? He means to cut off the entail on the estate and leave the old place to me?—but I don't want it! Why, he must be mad. Too much water drinking has turned his brain."

But there was no breaking into Sir Edward's speech. Jack had to sit it out. He listened to all the bitter reasons why this thing was necessary; why Cyril was unfit to bear rule after his father in the place where generations of Bevans had lived, and quarrelled, more or less, with their neighbours, and done their duty by their estate, and been finally buried in the family vault.

"He is bad—bad," said the old knight. "And it may be that I was in fault. I wish that my son had not been born."

"I say!" ejaculated Jack. He said no more for a minute. Then—"But it strikes me that one is bound to stick to one's own child whatever happens," he remarked. He had an absurd sensation of surprise at his own words. The moment after he had spoken it appeared to him singularly comical that he should have admonished Sir Edward. "Not that the way you treat your son is my affair," he added hastily, "only I do not want you to leave the estate to me. The idea is preposterous."

"Cyril's consent is necessary to the cutting off of the entail: he must be forced to give it," said Sir Edward. He had an irritating way of going on with his remarks without paying the slightest heed to protests. "I have cut off his allowance, and he has not the courage to starve."

"It is true that Cyril will never starve," Jack assented. He wondered, by the way, what that plausible rascal *would* do. "I'll have no part in this business," he said gravely. "Your son and I have never tolerated each other, but I have no desire to step into his shoes. I have enough on my hands."

"Your money will do the old place no harm," persisted Sir Edward. "And my will shall prove to the world that I, at least, have some respect for you. Your wife thinks that I was unfair to you. I do not know about that. You were not a serious-minded lad—but you may have repented now." He scanned Jack's countenance with an eagerness that was almost pathetic. "I trust that you have repented, and that you will do the best you can with your steward-ship. I have never allowed any alcoholic liquor to be sold on my property. I do not think I am asking too much, when I say that I beg you will respect my views, even though your own are unfortunately at variance with them."

"My good sir, in the event of your leaving Highfields to me, I shall build pot-houses, at intervals of ten yards, all down the avenue," said Cardew. "And if *that* won't knock this insanity on the head, I don't know what will," he reflected.

He had, at any rate, given Sir Edward food for con-sideration. The old man got up and put on his overcoat in depressed silence. He stumbled on the threshold as he was going out, and at that Jack's heart smote him.

"It was good of you to have lunch with me, sir," he said, "and I ought to be obliged to you for your kind intentions. I am afraid that I have not expressed my gratitude very prettily. I am much more grateful to you for an unexpected letter that I got in gaol."

They stood in the porch of the inn. Jack's old guardian lingered for a moment. Again he remembered that he had always fancied that Cardew was heartless and that Cyril was affectionate. But the time of his guardianship was over now. Nothing that he could do or say was any longer of much avail.

"Wherein I erred, may God in His mercy forgive," said he. Then with sudden sharpness, "But I hear that you are too clever to believe in Him. Eh?"

"Do you?" said Jack stolidly. "Well, what I believe seems to me to be rather my own private business, you know. Good-bye, sir."

CHAPTER XIV.

A WOMAN, AND A BEGGAR.

MRS. CLOVIS stood by the drawing-room window, watching Jack walk up the drive. Her pretty and delicate face wore a depressed expression, and it showed undoubted signs of age to-day. Little Stephen had wailed incessantly all night, and she wished now that she had not put the dear child in the room next to her own; she was not like Gillian, she could not stand sleepless nights. She wore lace ruffles at her throat and wrists, and her fair hair was becomingly puffed on her forehead, but she had just seen herself in the glass, and had observed how worn and thin she was growing.

In her husband's admiring eyes she was still beautiful, but even his admiration sometimes sharpened a secret pain that had of late taken alarming proportions. She suffered from a physical ache, too, at times; she felt vaguely as if the one had something to do with the other, but she tried to ignore both. She had been a *malade imaginaire* half her life, but now she shrank from doctors. She did not wish to talk about this strange uneasiness. She always felt ill when she had to encounter Jack Cardew. What had Gillian seen in this big, rough man, who was such an uncomfortable person at best, and at worst absolutely rude?

Mrs. Clovis had never liked Cardew, not even in the days when he had been young, and the fashion, and a literary lion! His birth had counted for something—she had been anxious that Gillian should marry into a "good family"—but she had never felt at ease with him. It had seemed strange to her that he should be popular; she had privately considered him an impracticable person, who either talked too vehemently on uninteresting and unconventional subjects, or was tiresomely and absolutely silent. But the distaste she had felt then was a very different emotion to the nervousness, almost amounting to terror, which she now experienced in his presence.

She flushed nervously when he came into the room. "Well, dear Jack, have you come to see after the darling boy?" she said. "Dr. Ferrol—such a charming young fellow, and so sympathetic—assures me that he will be quite his dear little self in a few days' time."

She had turned to meet Jack, and she looked up at him with a smile, though her lips quivered; she hoped that he did not notice the tremor in her voice.

"That is good," said Jack. He held her hand for a second longer than usual, and there was an unwonted kindliness in his tone. "Why, you are fagged out," he remarked. "The way in which we have taken possession of your house is too bad. I daresay that rascal kicked up no end of a hullabulloo last night. I should not be surprised to find out that he started the bonfire. He had always an unholy hankering after the match-box. Nothing will persuade Goliath to give up the thing on which he has set his affections. Takes after his mother, I suppose."

"He takes after some one else as well," said Mrs. Clovis with an attempt at playfulness. She was proud of her grandson, but she could not help wishing that he were not so like Jack.

"Shall I tell Gillian that you are here?"

"She saw me from the nursery window; she'll be

down in a minute," said Jack. " I wanted to see you alone
to thank you for your kindness."

" My darling girl is more than welcome to anything that
I can do for her," murmured Mrs. Clovis. Jack Cardew's
thanks embarrassed her.

Jack fancied that he understood her feeling. " You
think it is almost impertinent of me to thank you for
what you do for your own daughter, eh ? " he said.
" Well, I did not exactly mean to do that ! Of course I
know that Gillian is welcome—just as my own boy will
always be welcome to all that I can give him."

His rather stern face took its gentlest expression as he
spoke ; and Mrs. Clovis actually understood for one moment
why it was that some women liked Jack Cardew so much.

" But," he added, " it was good of you to ask me to
stay here. I cannot do it, you know ! I will not stay in
this house, because—to put it plainly—Mr. Clovis believes
me to be a rogue. He is quite justified," said Jack, with
his quick, whimsical smile, "and I rather respect him for
sticking to his own opinion, but it prevents me from
accepting your kind invitation, though it does not prevent
my recognition of your kindness."

He had never before made such a pretty speech to
Mrs. Clovis. It sounded a trifle stiff, perhaps ; that was
because he had rehearsed it beforehand, but he was
decidedly proud of it. Gillian sometimes told him that he
was tactless. It was a pity she had not heard that !

Yet oddly enough it seemed to have anything but a
pleasing effect on Mrs. Clovis.

"Oh," she cried plaintively, "you will fancy that
people still think dreadful things about you. But in reality
no one remembers about that unfortunate mistake. It is
put aside by the world. It is as if it had never been now."

Jack stared in some surprise. He said to himself that
he never could " make out " Gill's mother.

"There was not much fancy about the consequences of that little mistake," he replied drily. "As for its 'being as if it had never happened,' that is sheer nonsense. If it had not happened I should be a different man and Gillian a different woman."

"Oh, dear Jack, how you contradict me!" she cried; and to his immense amazement he saw that tears stood in her eyes.

Now, tears in a woman's eyes invariably filled this man with the deepest remorse and compassion. Indeed, his wife was apt to declare that a crying woman could get anything in the world out of Jack, and that she was convinced that it was a thousand pities that she herself was not of that species.

"I did not mean to say anything that could possibly vex you," he said gently. "You are quite right. The way in which people pretend to have forgotten is amazing. Gillian's cleverness has had something to do with their charitably bad memories, I fancy—only, you see, it is not possible that *I* should forget!" He threw back his head with the gesture that Gillian knew well. "Neither is there any reason why I should pretend to, for I was the injured person, as I hope yet to prove one day, for my son's sake. These excellent people who eat my dinners are very careful not to hurt my feelings—they only fail (some of them) to understand that I am not ashamed of that verdict."

There were things that he was ashamed of, but he would not talk of them to Mrs. Clovis. He was vaguely aware that every word he said jarred on her. He was glad when Gillian interrupted the *tête-à-tête*.

Gillian was paler than usual, but she would never own to being tired. Stephen was very cross, she said. He wailed if any one but herself held him, and she had been up all night.

"It is most fortunate that you are so strong, dear love. I am nearly worn out with weariness and anxiety, and Jack will not listen to my persuasions," said Mrs. Clovis.

The regret in her tone was forced, but Gillian looked eagerly at her husband.

"Goliath is not any worse? You are sure of that, Gill? Oh well, then, I can't stop," said he.

"I will leave you to coax him, dear one. He won't attend to poor me," said Mrs. Clovis as she left the room.

She had not tried very hard to persuade him, but then Jack was so obstinate that it would have been mere waste of breath to have argued the question.

"Dear Gillian has a will of her own, too, but she cannot always manage Jack; I do not think that he will give in," the mother reflected. "And, really, George would be so put out if he did by chance come back in time to find Jack here that it is just as well as it is. Gillian was anxious that I should invite her husband, but I need never tell George that I did so."

There were a good many little facts that Mrs. Clovis never told. She was fond of her husband, but she was one of the people who cannot be undeviatingly loyal to any one person—not even to the man whom they love best.

"Gillian," said Jack suddenly, "I can quite understand that it is natural enough that your mother should not like me, but why does she try to propitiate me? and what the dickens makes her afraid of me? Does she think that I may knock her down, or that I shall steal her spoons? If so, why does she take pains to be so polite to me?"

"Your imagination is too lively," said Gillian. "It is absurd to suppose that mammy has any reason to be afraid of you, but your downrightness is unpleasant to her. You are not the kind of man she gets on with. She makes a point of calling you 'dear Jack' because she dislikes family quarrels as much as a pussy-cat dislikes cold water."

" But I don't understand," he persisted.

" You never will, my dear," said Gillian, laughing.

There was a slight sharpness in her tone that was a sign that she was secretly anxious. Gill did not mean to entertain fear, but he is a guest who has no manners, who will force himself in, despite denial.

" I almost wish that you would stay, Jack," said she. " I hate to accept my step-father's hospitality without you, but the boy would not be so comfortable in a hotel. Moreover, it would really be an excellent move to make friends with Mr. Clovis."

" It was not I who refused to meet your step-father," said Jack.

" I know that he is as obstinate as an old mule," said Gill, " but he has been longing to relent for some time. When he hears that the roof has been burnt over our heads, he will feel that he has a valid excuse."

" If I was not an honest man before, I am no cleaner for the burning of my house, am I ? "

" You are not. But the majority of people are not logical," said Gillian shrewdly. " Pure reason is a stick that has precious little weight in the world. You and I may be reasonable, darling (especially I), but we are fools if we use that weapon as an every-day means of persuasion ! I gave it up long ago ! It is too fine."

" Anyhow, I cannot possibly accept favours from Mr. Clovis," said Jack, and Gillian dropped the contention.

She *was* reasonable, as she said, and knew when to hold her tongue. Nevertheless, she was half humorously and yet truly disconcerted when Cardew told her about his interview with Sir Edward Bevan.

" Dear me, if Sir Edward is pining to leave his estate to you, why not encourage him ? " cried she. " The public avowal of his belief in you would do good. After all, you are his cousin, and it is all in the family. I think you were very silly, Jack ! "

"Yes; I knew that you would think so," he said.

He always recognised Gillian's right to her own opinion, and Gillian sometimes felt as if the very recognition put her farther away from him. She had a contempt for sensitive women who are hurt by shades of expression, so she laughed and shrugged her shoulders.

"It is lucky you can afford to be quixotic! I must say that I should at least like you to have the credit of the refusal. May I tell mammy the story, in strictest confidence? It will soon be all over the place, then."

"No, you may not," said Jack shortly, for his wife's tone jarred on him. "But," he added after a moment's thought, "I do not think that your mother is one of the women who must blab."

"Nor do I," cried Gill, with mischief dancing in her eyes. "Mammy has plenty of discretion, she does not require nearly so many explanations as you. She understands which secrets to divulge and which to keep—as well as I do."

Jack laughed, but rather on the wrong side of his mouth. He found Gillian a bit too sharp, sometimes, and to-day she was in a hard humour. How was he to know that that was because Stephen's fretful wail was still ringing in her ears? He changed the subject, with an acceptance of their widely differing points of view that was again unwittingly galling.

"I have a letter from Mr. Molyneux," he said. "Do you gather from it that the old man is ill?"

Gill read the crabbed handwriting with some difficulty, and reflected silently for a minute.

"Yes, and I think that he wants very much to see you," she said at last. "I suppose that you had better go. Perhaps he wants to leave you his money, but that need not deter you! You can always fling it back in his face, you know."

"Shall I go? But I won't if Goliath is really bad," said Jack.

Gill hesitated for a second. The doctor had given a most excellent report. The child's arm had only been very slightly injured, though the shock had made him fractious. She did not wish to own, even to herself, that she was foolishly anxious. Neither would she cajole her husband into staying. Gillian had small scruple about what stick she used where the world was concerned, but she was scrupulously honest with Jack. Better women than she might have seen no shame in small wiles that she refrained from; but then, as she had once declared, her love for Jack was her religion, and perhaps the better women worshipped at another shrine.

"He wants you very much," she repeated. "Poor old Uncle Stephen, he never quite manages to like me! I am not his sort! I am too modern for him. But he was very kind to me—and I think that he loves you, Jack."

"Well, then, I will run up to London to-morrow, and I will look in again after dinner to hear the last news of the giant. Must you go now? I say, Gill, I am sorry you are vexed about what I said to Sir Edward. What shall I do to make up?" He caught her arm, as she was leaving the room, and held her for a moment. "Have you any wants left?"

Jack enjoyed buying presents for her.

Gillian twisted herself free. It was odd, but at that moment she felt as if the touch of his hand was more than her composure could bear.

"It is an extraordinary fact, but I do not want you to give me any more diamonds," she cried, with a laugh that did not ring quite true. "Your disinterestedness must be catching. One of these days we shall find ourselves setting forth on a wild-goose chase, clad in yellow dressing-gowns, with china bowls in our hands, and

14

leaving all our possession behind, like Prince what-was-his-name. There, I hear Stephen yelling! Good-bye!"

Jack went thoughtfully out of the house. Something was wrong between them, but he did not quite know what. It was part of the general wrongness of everything, he supposed. He did not attempt to analyse the situation. Gillian had stuck to him when no one else had; she had been his salvation. Therefore he would never throw any blame on her, even in his innermost thoughts. When their opinions clashed he took refuge in silence and went his own way—leaving to her a like liberty. It did not occur to him that liberty was not what Gillian wanted.

He took a letter from his pocket and read it while he walked across the flowery lawn and down the avenue of young trees. His correspondent was a London detective who fancied that he had found a clue to the identity of that mysterious person, who, according to Liza Pocock's confession, had gone into Mr. Cardew's room, and who had since inconveniently departed to that land to which no detective can follow.

Since the birth of his son Cardew had not ceased in his efforts to unravel that old mystery that Mrs. Clovis was so anxious to bury in oblivion. Once he had told Gill that he did not mean to waste time and substance in hopeless races after justice, but now his mind was changed. The instinct of care for his race had taken a strong hold on him. It is an instinct that is stronger in men than in women. A woman loves her own children, the babies she has born and suckled. The individual and personal touches her, but it is the man who is moved by the idea of glory or shame in ages to come. To both the child may be saviour—the child whose small hands are so mighty to compel sacrifice.

Jack frowned as he read. He entirely disbelieved in the widow woman of great respectability who swore that her brother (since killed in an Egyptian campaign) had been the lover of Liza Pocock. This was only one more of the many questionable specimens of humanity who were attracted by the hope of getting money out of him, and who were ready to swear anything with that end in view. At first he had been excited and keen on following up the least suspicion of scent. Now he was sick and disgusted with the whole dirty business. Only a dogged persistence for his boy's sake made him stick to it. His reading was violently interrupted by some one who ran full tilt against him; some one who was equally determined in pursuit of an object.

"Hallo! why don't you look where you are going to?" said Jack.

George Clovis, junior, whose bullet head had struck Jack, stopped perforce, and rubbed both hands through his short brown hair. "I *was* looking. I was going after that cat," he panted; "I was looking after her so hard that I did not see you. I hope"—as an after-thought—"I hope I did not hurt you much."

Cardew laughed. "You should hit your own size, sonnie. You might have knocked me down, you know."

George took the remark with matter-of-fact simplicity, and apologised with the utmost good temper. "I am awfully sorry," he declared.

"Such a big fellow should be careful," said Jack. "And my constitution is delicate, you see! Where has the cat got to now?"

The boy rested both his hands on his knees, and considered a high brick wall that divided the garden from the wood. "She went up over that," he said. "I believe I could get over it too, if—if you wouldn't mind giving me a lift." He blushed in making the request, and looked at the big stranger with deprecating friendliness. His mother would say that he was too bold, but he did so very much want to scale that wall.

"And how about getting down on the other side?" said Jack.

Master George was momentarily nonplussed; then he grinned cheerfully. "I can see about that when I am up. It ain't any use thinking about gettin' down from the bottom."

Jack laughed again, and swung the child suddenly up on to his shoulder, from whence with a shout of delight George scrambled on to the top of the wall and sat astride, with his short legs dangling.

"I have always, all my life—ever since I was quite little—wanted to be up here!" said George, in accents that were almost solemn.

"Then I hope that you like the situation as much as you expected to," returned Jack.

The boy comically resembled his father. Mr. Clovis, Jack remembered, combined some practical readiness with a sort of pompous simplicity.

"I like it more," said George, drawing a long breath. "It is the very beautifullest place to sit on that I ever saw. I should think"— with a proprietary wave of his hand— "that it was one of the beautifullest places in all the world. It does not matter about holding on to my boot, thank you. I am quite safe."

"Well, there is a gate ten yards farther on," said Cardew; "I think I will go through it—though I know that's an inglorious way of getting to the other side of a wall—if you will promise to sit steadily. You won't be giddy, will you?"

"I don't know what giddy is," said George convincingly, and Jack walked through the gate, little guessing, while he did so, that he was on the track of game more elusive than the yellow cat.

He liked this ugly, sturdy boy; boys had become interesting to him of late. He helped George down on the other side, and the two plunged together into the plantation.

"She must be wild, I think, don't you?" George said eagerly. "She is sandy with orange stripes, and she eats baby rabbits. Tame cats drink milk, you know. I don't believe this one looks at milk; she is much too fierce. She would bite your hand just as soon as not. I should not wonder if she were spitting at us from a tree now! Do you think that she will spring out like a tiger? Oh, I wish she would! Then I could shoot—that is, I could if I had a gun. I wish dad would let me have a gun. Do you think you could say to dad that it would be such a useful thing for the estate if I had a gun? You see there are wild cats and there are poachers, and—oh, I forgot!"

He stopped short, and his funny, freckled face became the picture of dismay. "That reminds me," he said, "my mother told me not to come in here to-day, because of traps for the poachers! I quite clean forgot! It is dreadful how things go out of one's mind when one has got business to do. I *had* to go after that cat. I suppose"—reluctantly—"I suppose I must go home and ask her if I mayn't go on with you. You could always unhook me out of a trap, couldn't you? Hallo! there is a man's hat bobbing about there, behind that fir-tree. Perhaps that is a poacher; anyhow, he is a trespasser—and dad is awfully angry about trespassers—so I must go on and speak to him."

Jack looked in the direction at which this small lord of the soil pointed with his grubby little brown thumb. Yes, undoubtedly there was some one in the plantation. George set off fussily, with evident intention of asserting his father's rights. Cardew followed to see the upshot of the interview. When they were both within a few yards of the firs George stopped, and looked round at his companion with a puzzled expression.

"Why, there is some one there who is talking in mother's headache voice," he said. "But I *know* that mother is in her bedroom."

Jack stood still—a rather high-pitched plaintive voice distinctly reached his ear.

"Oh, it is not the money that I grudge (though, indeed, you have already had an immense deal, Cyril), but it is that I cannot bear to deceive my dear husband. Besides, how do I know that it is for the last time? How am I to trust one word that you say? How am I to——"

"There goes the cat! I saw her tail up that tree!" shouted Jack. He pointed in the opposite direction to that from which "mother's headache voice" issued; then, as George darted off, he shoved his way through the firs and confronted Mrs. Clovis and Cyril Bevan.

His cousin smiled amicably. "Why, Jack, how are you? I hear you and the old governor have made up your differences," he said. "Poor old governor! I am glad of it."

Jack stared. He had not met Cyril since they were young, but he retained a contempt for him that he did not attempt to conceal, and that was perhaps the more galling because Jack was anything but Pharisaical.

Cyril was accustomed to being snubbed, but for once his philosophy failed him. He very heartily wished Cardew back in Dartmoor.

"Which is my shortest way back to the village, Mrs. Clovis? Will you show me?" he said.

Cardew turned to Mrs. Clovis with an absolutely stolid expression of countenance. "If you like," he said, in the level, expressionless voice that might hide anything or nothing, "I can easily show this—gentleman the way out of your wood."

Mrs. Clovis shrank from him with a nervous, involuntary movement. She had every reason to dislike Cyril Bevan, and Jack had never injured her, yet it seemed to her that there was brutality in the way in which he ignored his cousin's greeting.

"Oh no, dear Jack, there is really no occasion for you to trouble yourself at all," she answered quickly.

"All right. I don't want to interfere. I fancied I might have saved you some trouble, that's all," said Jack.

He saw them walk away together without further remark. His natural impulse had been to make his presence known at once. He hated eaves-dropping; he was sorry that he had unwittingly overheard so much. The very last thing he would have chosen was to be the discoverer of a woman's secret. He almost wished that he had gone away without speaking to Mrs. Clovis, but (little as she gave him credit for such a motive) he had been actuated by the simple desire to stand by her.

So Cyril Bevan was trying to get money out of Gillian's mother! Poor lady! Jack was sorry enough for her if she was in any degree in that dirty little sneak's power.

George came running back presently, shouting, "Mother, mother," with all his might, and was much disappointed to find that she had disappeared.

"Was it not mother after all?" he said. "It sounded just like her voice, didn't it? But I know"—with the importance of an only son—"I know that she would have waited till I came back. Who was it, if it wasn't mother?"

"Why, it was a woman and a beggar," said Jack. "Look here, George, I am sorry that we came into this wood, since it is against orders. Let us get out of it as quickly as we can!"

He strode along so fast that the little boy could hardly keep pace with him, and was filled with the idea that Mr. Cardew was troubled by conscience.

"I don't think it was your fault," George remarked consolingly. "I did not tell you that I might not go in the wood till after we were over the wall; and you could not possibly know, because always, till to-day, I have been allowed to come in here whenever I have wanted to. So you need not feel grave about it. I say, Mr. Cardew, what cheek of the beggars to trespass! I wish you had caught them! Mother will laugh when I tell her that the beggar-woman talked in her headache voice, won't she?"

"Do you always tell your mother everything?"

"Yes, I do. I tell her all my secrets, and she tells me all hers," said George. "She has told me an enormous big one this week that even dad does not know. It is about his birthday, and it is put away with a secret of mine in the right-hand drawer in the wardrobe in her room. It is in a little box, done up in cotton wool. It is partly gold, and it is partly off my head and partly off mother's head, and it will hang from a watch-chain—but I must not tell what it is, and dad can never guess, though he is always trying."

"Poor old Clovis!" muttered Jack.

They were out of the wood now, and he put his hand on the boy's shoulder as he bid him good-bye. "Look here, youngster," said he, "you are to tell your mother from me that I am sorry we went into that wood, but that I meant no harm. Tell her, too, that I strongly advise her to speak to Mr. Clovis about beggars, because I know that the beggar I saw to-day is a very bad one, who has done worse things than I could talk about to a woman. Will you remember all that?"

"Oh yes," said George. "And mother will be sure to tell dad, for she is awfully afraid of tramps. I am glad she was not in the wood if the beggar was such a dreadful bad one, though of course I should have taken care of her."

"Of course," said Jack.

CHAPTER XV.

BETWEEN MAN AND MAN.

MRS. CLOVIS hurried home by way of the village. She was nervously afraid to return by the wood; she felt that she had not the nerve to risk another encounter with her son-in-law. She was aware, when she considered the matter, that her fear was absolutely foolish. Jack had no right, and, in all probability, no inclination, to interfere with anything that she might choose to do; yet whenever her conscience distressed her with visions of judgment to come, she invariably saw this big, blue-eyed man as a merciless executor of justice.

Poor Mrs. Clovis was certainly not cut out to be the villain of any tale. Never was there a woman who more fully appreciated the advantages of respectability, or who shrank more sensitively from the least suspicion of blame. She had indeed been foolish when she was younger, but she felt that it was very hard that her foolishness should have had such extraordinarily grave results. It was doubly hard that because she had once, in what had seemed an insignificant matter, deceived Mr. Clovis, she should now be bound to go on deceiving him.

Her head ached violently after the excitement of her interview with Cyril Bevan, but when she heard the church bell ring she turned aside, weary as she was, to enter the parish church, and to form one of an exceedingly scanty congregation at the Friday evening service.

Two old women (they were pensioned by Mrs. Clovis, and were very anxious that she should notice them) were present, and Enid Haubert was sitting in a corner finishing a sketch of the west window. No one else attended the service, saving the clerk, who strongly objected to these innovations of the new parson, but who was forced willy-nilly to bear part in them.

Mr. Strode cast a quick glance round him when he entered the empty church. His clear resonant voice rang and echoed through the building as he read the "Dearly beloved brethren."

"He ought to have said 'brother,' for there is only one old man here," thought Enid.

It amused her that he should think it worth while to intone the service every Friday to nearly vacant pews. She observed that the altar was decorated with hot-house flowers. The flowers came out of the priest's own garden.

A bullet-riddled shred of an old flag (it was once carried on a desperate venture by a hand that is now dust before the desert wind) hung above Mr. Strode's head. It occurred to the little artist that here was a good and rather pathetic subject. She sharpened her charcoal and began to sketch vigorously. The prayers being read, Mr. Strode delivered a short address, to which no one paid much attention. The old clerk sniffed contemptuously, the two old women nodded, Mrs. Clovis leaned back with her hand pressed to her throbbing forehead. She had already done more than her duty in coming to church on a week-day evening. This was a work of supererogation which she felt ought to count very much to her credit, and enlist Heaven on her side.

It had seemed to her as if the devil himself were black-mailing her, and she longed to outwit him. It was not a time to be slack in religious observances—yet she could have spared the sermon. *Why* she believed that it would please Providence that she should sit with an aching head through a Friday service I cannot explain. Our poor brother the ass, as the most human of saints called his body, seems made to be arbitrarily punished for the sins that his driver commits. It must be allowed that, like most unfairly treated creatures, he is apt to bear malice and bide his time for revenge.

Mr. Strode was just about to cross the aisle on his way to the vestry, when an exclamation from the clerk made him look round. The grey-robed graceful lady, whose presence at these extra services had sometimes seemed to him like sweet incense, had fallen on the floor of the pew in a faint.

Enid Haubert ran to the rescue from her corner by the door, leaving her drawing block and crayons to be confiscated by the old clerk, but it was the priest who picked the poor lady up and carried her to the church porch, where the soft westerly wind blowing in revived her immediately.

Mr. Strode was invariably prompt. Having deposited his burden on the broad stone seat, he went in search of water, and the next minute returned with a tumblerful. He found Mrs. Clovis sitting upright, and apologising profusely in her pretty soft voice.

"I am so subject to fainting fits. I always faint in the hot weather, especially when I am over-tired ; but I cannot forgive myself for having given you so much trouble, Mr. Strode—and Miss Haubert too."

"I fancied that you were in bed with a headache," said Enid. "It must have been very bad for you to get up to come to church. I do not know what Mrs. Cardew would say."

"I cannot bear to miss this service, but dear Gillian is so different," said Mrs. Clovis gently.

The speech irritated Enid, perhaps because she greatly admired Gillian.

" Mrs. Cardew has been in the nursery all day. She cannot leave her little boy," she said.

" There is seldom much difficulty in finding reasons that prevent people from attending church," remarked Mr. Strode. " I wish that a few more among my parishioners would err on the side of over-much zeal."

Mrs. Clovis stood up at this juncture, a graceful swaying figure, and announced her intention of walking home. Her companions were still urging the advisability of sending for a conveyance when the discussion was ended by the advent of Mr. Clovis, who was driving from the station, and who on catching sight of his wife called to the footman to stop, and jumped out of the carriage with as much alacrity as if he had been a young lover, instead of an elderly husband of ten years' standing. He bustled up the churchyard path with a beaming face, which fell comically at sight of the cassocked priest at his wife's side. " Well, my dear, how lucky I came by this way," said he. " But to-day ain't Sunday, so why are you at church ? "

" It is Friday evensong, dear George," said Mrs. Clovis. " You have not been introduced to our new vicar, have you ? "

Mr. Clovis nodded grudgingly, but the new vicar was unfeignedly glad to see him. Mr. Strode had had enough of Mrs. Clovis, and was now eager to get her off his hands. He had no great liking for women.

" We have been trying to dissuade Mrs. Clovis from attempting to walk to the Park. The heat in church was was too much for her," he explained.

The concern and anxiety that were instantly painted on the face of Mr. Clovis seemed to the priest somewhat absurd.

" Why, what is the matter ? Now I come to look at you I see that you are as white as a lily." (Mr. Clovis never likened his wife to anything ungraceful, though where others were concerned his similes were apt to be homely in the extreme.) "What have they been doing to you while I have been away?"

"Nothing, dearest. I have only been anxious and tired. My poor darling little grandson was hurt, and there was so much to arrange."

Mr. Clovis drew her arm through his with a protecting tenderness that was very pleasant to her.

"You would think it was me who ought to be troubled with grandsons, wouldn't you?" he said jocularly to Mr. Strode, who did not respond. "I don't know why it is that the best people seem to want so much praying. It is like the clean ones who never do a thing to dirty their hands, but who wash after every meal."

He helped her into the carriage, with that almost exaggerated care which he enjoyed bestowing on this finest and most reverenced of all his possessions. Enid and Mr. Strode watched the carriage drive off. It appeared odd to Mr. Strode that so refined a woman should have married such a vulgar old shopkeeper. Almost unwittingly he gave expression to his thought.

"I had not happened to meet him before. I should hardly have guessed that he was the husband of that lady."

"I like him very much. I don't think he is in the least really vulgar," said Enid quickly.

Mr. Strode raised his black eyebrows. He now recognised that he had met Miss Haubert before. This was the second time that this slip of a girl had unexpectedly dissented from his opinion. He found his present parishioners so slow of comprehension (though it is possible that they occasionally understood more than their parson guessed) that he was out of the habit of expecting any one to grasp the meaning of a tone, and he was consequently annoyed that he had betrayed an opinion, which he was, however, too honest to retract.

He turned away silently, and was just about to lock the church door when Enid prevented him.

"Oh, please may I fetch my sketching block before you shut up? I left it by the font when I ran to help Mrs. Clovis."

"Then I imagine that Mr Jones has already pounced on it," said Mr. Strode. "He has my orders to confiscate any playthings that he finds in church. There are already three sticks of peppermint, one Robinson Crusoe, and two penny whistles in the collection. There was a dormouse, but I let that go."

"My sketching block isn't a plaything," said Enid. "It is a working woman's tool, and it helps me to earn bread and butter. I cannot afford to lose it."

"A working woman's tool." He looked at her with some surprise and a glimmer of interest. It had not occurred to him that a girl whom he had met at Draycott Court could be earning her own livelihood. Now he understood why she was slightly different to the majority of the young ladies he had come across at dinner-parties. She was more independent and less self-conscious. "Come along. I'll get it for you," he said, swinging back the big door.

Enid followed him anxiously to the vestry. "The sketch of that old window is for an art magazine," she said, when he had found the block. "One is obliged to make every line very clear and sharp for printing. It took me a long time to do."

"It seems to me excellent," said the priest, with some interest. "May I look at this loose sheet too? Is it a fancy picture? Ah!"

The exclamation, short and sharp, revealed that he had grasped the meaning of the artist.

It was a rough charcoal sketch of himself, in the act of preaching to two sleeping parishioners, and to a vista of empty pews. His spare, energetic figure was portrayed with some force. Above his head drooped the old flag. Above the flag was scribbled "Forlorn Hopes."

Enid coloured. "I am sorry you have seen that," she said.

"*You* at any rate have turned my sermon to some account," said Mr. Strode drily. "It is very clever. What magazine is it to appear in ?"

"In none. I only did it for my brother, and that is the same as for myself. Geoffrey likes to know all about everything, and it is easier to me to draw than to write what I see. But I will tear it up if you like."

She made the offer regretfully, moved thereto by his evident displeasure. Enid could not bear to hurt any one's feelings, but she knew that the sketch was good.

"I really did listen to your sermon," she added in extenuation, "I know just what it was all about ; and I did not draw while the prayers were going on, so I was not so very bad. It was the sight of that old flag that put the idea into my head. An old flag touches one so."

She smiled as she spoke, and the colour came into her little thin, wedge-shaped face. Mr. Strode was mollified.

"Yes, that flag preaches a sermon that even the sleepiest and densest member of my congregation understands," he said. "Do not tear up your sketch. May I—if you were not going to sell it—may I have it ? As a matter of fact, *I*, too, care about my commission ! "

"Why, of course you do," said Enid, who was puzzled by the defensive tone of the assertion, which had not been addressed to her, but to an invisible accuser.

In the intervals of his work Mr. Strode was constantly holding a silent argument with a voice which most unfairly and bitterly told him that he was no true priest ; that on the contrary he had done his best to damn a soul committed to his charge. He stoutly denied the accusation ; he triumphantly proved his accuser to be utterly in the wrong; he found excellent rejoinders that he had had no time to frame during that scene in the conservatory. Yet the voice was still persistent, perhaps because it was a woman's voice and unamenable to reason.

"Do have it, if you would like to," said Enid.

Mr. Strode looked at the sketch with kindling eyes. "One could hardly wish any one a much better fate than that he should be the successful leader of a forlorn hope," said he.

"Hardly," agreed the little artist. "There is one person for whom one feels more reverence."

"Who is that?" asked the priest.

"Oh, the unsuccessful leader," said the woman softly.

The shadows were lengthening when they stepped out through the vestry door into the churchyard.

"I wonder whether I shall have time to do an hour's work before dinner. My wall is nearly finished," Enid said.

But in spite of her ardour for work, she could not but pause for a minute to look at the soft, wooded landscape that lay below her, at the blue line of sea in the distance, at the pink roses that clambered over the graves at her feet. Beauty was truly to her "the vision of Him who reigns." Like Fra Angelica, she worshipped with her pencil; and if the apparent results of her labour were poorer, who knows, after all, how little apparent results matter in the spiritual world?

"Ah, you are decorating the club-room that Mr. Cardew has seen fit to build in my parish," said Mr. Strode.

He was not pleased at these doings that had been inaugurated during the reign of King Log. He had meditated starting a rival church club, but the lay influence was so strong that he was aware that his failure would be a foregone conclusion.

Enid promptly invited him to come and see her design. She was, she assured him, very lucky to get the chance. No one ever had kinder friends than the Cardews.

"I am aware that Mrs. Cardew is extremely popular," said Mr. Strode in a non-committal tone.

He walked down the hill and through the village street by Enid's side. It would have been petty to refuse to look at the inside of that new building, the sight of which fretted him every time he passed by. Mr. Strode was a person who tried his smallest action by a strict standard. His temper occasionally suffered from the strain; he took himself too seriously.

"I think," said Enid, who always quickly repented of anger—"I think that I was hasty at dinner the other night. You see one cannot help getting hot if any one implies things against one's friends. Afterwards I remembered that you could not know all that I knew."

"What do you know?" said Mr. Strode.

"I knew Mr. Cardew before all *that* happened," said Enid simply. "He was quite young then, and very high-spirited and very clever. We all thought a great deal of him. He was just the very last person in all the world to dream of going in for the sort of deliberate fraud that he was accused of. None of his friends ever could believe that he was in the wrong. It was an impossible thing to believe. I have been wanting very much to explain this to you. I daresay that you would be glad to believe that he is good, and of course it is difficult for you to be sure of that, because you were not his friend before. He has got into a way of looking like—like a blank wall, when he is with any one who does not trust him. I daresay that he put on that look when you met him in prison, and that it was no wonder that you could not get past it."

They had reached the club-room now, and stood in a very pleasant place. The walls were decorated with a design of tall hollyhocks, and the wooden floor smelt refreshingly of turpentine and bees-wax. Mr. Strode stared, with unseeing eyes, at the painting on the wall.

"Do you like it?" asked the little artist eagerly, "or do you think that there are too many pink flowers? Those grey buds come in well, but Mrs. Cardew does not like them. She cannot bear anything that is fading. Is not that curious? Still, one must paint a thing as one sees it oneself. It is not honest work if one considers one's patron too much. Do you like it?"

"No," said Mr. Strode sternly. "That is not an excuse that I should desire to urge; but no excuse is needed."

Enid started with surprise. She sometimes complained that people did not take art seriously enough, but here, indeed, was a critic who did not fail in that respect!

"I was not excusing it," she said faintly, then saw with momentary chagrin that it was not of flowers and buds that he was thinking.

"No excuse is needed," he repeated. "For I was and am convinced that the man was guilty. When he first spoke to me he was eager, and apparently almost boyishly expansive; an inexperienced person might have been deceived, but I had seen so many of them! Later he evinced a recklessly stubborn disposition that no discipline could subdue. Appealed to me? No, no, it was no genuine appeal. It was an attempt to deceive——"

"Hush!" Enid interrupted. "Whatever you may be unfortunate enough to imagine about Mr. Cardew, you must not say such things to me."

She took up her palette and paint-brushes, as a sign to him to go. She could not see to paint. She was vexed and disappointed.

"It was my fault for being so silly as to think that I could persuade you to believe in him. It would have been much wiser to have held my tongue," she said. After a moment's pause she added wistfully, "But I thought that perhaps you would have been glad to be persuaded."

Mr. Strode ceased to argue with that accusing voice. His gentlemanly feeling asserted itself.

"I beg your pardon. I was not thinking of you, but I certainly ought not to have spoken against Mr. Cardew before his guest," he said. "Of course I should be only too glad if——"

But he left the sentence unfinished, for his honesty choked him.

Then he stooped to pick up his hat and went out. He would have given a good deal to have been able to have completed that remark. As it was, the accusing voice pounced triumphantly on his failure.

"Ah, you cannot say it. You would not be glad to see Cardew cleared. In your heart you would be sorry. You are no true shepherd of souls."

Meanwhile Mrs. Clovis leaned back in the carriage and accepted her husband's attentions with a faint, weary smile. When they reached the house George rushed to welcome his father and was immensely surprised to see his mother.

"Why, mother, I ran up to your room and the door was locked. Gillian told me your head was still bad," he cried. "And, I say, I have got a lot of queer things to tell you, and Mr. Cardew sent you a message. He says the beggar we met in the plantation is an awful bad beggar, and that he advises you to tell dad about him. But of course you don't understand, because you weren't in the plantation. Oh, mother, isn't it awfully funny—do you know what I thought? I thought—just for a minute, you know—that the beggar-woman's voice was yours! Of course I did not see her, because just then the cat ran up the tree. But where have you been, mother, and is your head well?"

"Don't you pester her with so many questions," said Mr. Clovis. "She's been praying. That's what she's been after."

He spoke with the funniest mixture of admiration and irritation. His wife's piety always seemed to him to be a very touching crown to her womanliness, but he was jealous of the exactions of the Church.

"You ain't strong enough to be leaning up against hard wooden chairs. I sha'n't allow it now I am home," he said. "I'll be bound that long-faced gentleman don't pray till *he* is faint."

"I do not like to hear you speak against a clergyman," she said gently. "But, indeed, I have had a most weary time, and I am thankful to have you back."

And here at least she spoke the absolute truth. Mrs. Clovis missed her husband's petting when he was away; comfort and safety seemed to return with him. Her conscience had been playing bully all day, Jack had (unwittingly) terrified her, Cyril Bevan had meanly blackmailed her. She had felt herself a forlorn and tempest-tossed sinner, whose only refuge lay in penance and prayer. Now the very sound of her husband's hearty voice drove back these terrors. When he arranged her sofa cushions, and fussed over her, and scolded her for being "too much of a saint," it was as if she had stepped from a dark, cold waste into a cheerful, well-lighted room. She knew at the bottom of her heart that nothing was really changed; the howling wilderness might yet be her portion, but for the time she could forget it. In truth, she had managed to ignore uncomfortable facts during a good many years. She lay very cosily among the cushions, and her head ceased to ache. She enjoyed describing the thrilling event of the week, and all the worry and anxiety it had entailed on her.

Mr. Clovis was a person who liked to hear every detail,

and, like little George, he firmly believed that Eva told him " all her secrets."

" So Madam Gill is staying with us, after all ! " he said triumphantly. " She swore she would not till I asked her convict."

" I wish you would not call Jack by horrid names," said Mrs. Clovis. " Dear Gillian is wilful, I know. On this occasion she gave way for the boy's sake. The shock seems to have made him very nervous, and it was unwise to move him again."

Mr. Clovis drummed on the table—a symptom that he was perturbed. " She would do anything for her boy or her husband," he remarked. " I believe she would even swallow humble pie, which is a dish Miss Gill was never partial to. Look here, Eva—suppose she is right, and he never was in fault after all, eh ? "

" I always have said that I never believed him to be guilty of swindling," said Mrs. Clovis.

" Yes—-you said," he repeated doubtfully. " But you were dead against the marriage, my dear, so somehow I never thought you had much faith in him. There, don't look distressed. I tell you I am almost coming round. I've always seen that if you give a rogue rope enough he is safe to hang himself in time. Now Cardew's had plenty of rope since his marriage, and what's the result ? He has been gradually righting himself. Just at first I didn't think he would, but he has. I wish I knew the truth."

" Every one believes in him now," said Mrs. Clovis, shutting her eyes wearily. She wished that George had not hit on this subject.

" I have always vowed I would not have him here, just because Madam Gillian has managed to brazen it out and make the most of his money. I am honest myself. I draw the line before convicts. I don't think much of 'every one,'" said Mr. Clovis sturdily. "There is one whose real opinion I should like to get at, my dear."

"Whose? Gillian's?"

"No, not Gillian's—though I doubt if any one could keep the truth from his wife—not Gillian's, but Jack's." I should like to go up to him of a sudden, when he wasn't prepared. 'Look here, between man and man,' I would say, 'and in strictest confidence, just so as to know what to be at, did you do it, or did you not?' I can't but fancy I could tell by the first look of his face whether he did."

" But that is quite absurd, dear George, and I hope you will never do anything so very ridiculous. It is so much better to drop the whole matter and behave as if it had never happened."

Mr. Clovis shook his head regretfully. "I can't lump things like that. It ain't my nature," he said. " What's more, my idea isn't so ridiculous as it sounds. They say a criminal always gets possessed with a longing to confess. That's how lots of 'em come to the gallows. Why, what's wrong, my dear?"

"My head is throbbing again. I do not think I shall come down to dinner; but you ought to go to dress, dear, the bell has sounded."

"Well, you just stay quiet and take care of yourself, for good people are scarce," said he. "I'll tell you if I do ask the convict that question."

The fancy, perhaps by reason of its absurd simplicity, had taken hold of Mr. Clovis. All the while that he was dressing for dinner he kept wondering how it would be supposing that he were to present his naïve inquiry suddenly as if he were putting a pistol to the man's head. He chuckled to himself, and played with the thought. It seemed to him that he might jerk the truth to the surface.

He was preoccupied when he went down to dinner, and Gillian wondered why.

"So you've come to stay with us, for all you said you wouldn't," he said on meeting her.

"I did not reckon on our roof being burned over our heads, or on my boy being hurt. You have every right to your triumph," said Gill.

At that her step-father repented him of his speech, which indeed it would have been better to have left unsaid. Madam Gillian had a way of making a man feel small when she chose.

Nevertheless he recovered his spirits during dinner, and patronised Miss Haubert, with every intention of kindness, though with too much evident consciousness of the difference between the magnificence of his table and the sort of dinner she was accustomed to at home. Luckily, Enid had a bright and sympathetic nature, and was more easily amused than offended; moreover, she was upheld by the secret knowledge that she was not pitiable in reality, and that she would not have changed places with her host (had such a transformation been possible) for all the good things in the world.

Fancy having Mrs. Clovis to live with instead of Geoffrey! Fancy how dull to be quite old, with no visions of what one might live to do in the dim future! And oh, how sad to have so little colour in life that one's dinner became a source of interest, and one actually submitted to five courses, served by powdered footmen every night! That was all very well for a change, but how terribly tedious for a continuance! Poor rich man! She was very sorry for him.

George came in at dessert time, and stayed to chatter to his father when the ladies had left the dining-room. Mr. Clovis and George were excellent companions.

"There was an awfully bad set of poachers in our wood to-day," George informed his father, "but Mr. Cardew frightened them away."

"I did not wish you to have anything to do with Mr. Cardew, my lad."

"Why, he is an awfully nice chap," said George earnestly. "You would like him no end if you knew him as well as I do."

Mr. Clovis frowned. "As well as you do? What business had the fellow to be making friends with you?"

"Oh, he only talked to me to-day," George owned. "And that was because I nearly knocked him down. I was racing after the cat, you see. So then of course I had a conversation with him, and then he helped me over a wall."

"Humph! What did you converse about?"

"Wild cats and poachers," said George. "What makes you say 'humph,' father?"

Mr. Clovis rubbed the back of his head, as he always did when he was considering. "I don't see why I should not explain it to you," he said at last. "To tell you the truth, my boy, I don't know whether Mr. Cardew is a good chap or a downright bad one. There was a nasty thing happened to him once. He was convicted and sent to prison for trying to get money under false pretences—that means, by telling a heap of lies—but there are folks who have it that he never did the thing in spite of judge and jury, and there are others who will forget a deal if a man's got a mint of money, d'ye see? Now, you and I, we come of a clean family. We don't want no dealings with rogues—and that is a thing I want you to remember, though you won't be in the business— you come of a clean stock that has never had any call to be ashamed. When you are all among lords and ladies—as you will be—and thinking as likely as not of marrying a Lady Evelina de something or other, you can bear it in mind. 'My father was in trade, but I come of a clean stock, sir,' says you. And I should not wonder if that

won't be more than your lady's father will be able to trump;
for the Lord knows that half those grand families was
started the wrong side of the blanket."

Mr. Clovis was apt to wax eloquent on this topic, but
George was quite uninterested in his future proposal for
the hand of Lady Evelina.

"Was Gillian sent to prison too," he asked, "and did
they have planks beds and water gruel? I suppose that
they had to share one gruel between them as they were
married?"

Like his father, George had a great love of minute
practical detail.

"Your step-sister was not married then. She waited
till he came out of prison."

"Why, then of course he did not do it; besides, I know
he didn't, anyway," said George.

"Know? What do you know, Jackanapes?" said his
father, laughing.

Mr. Clovis had told the little boy the story in much the
same spirit as that in which his grandfather—who had been
uneducated—had occasionally consulted his Bible with a key,
thrust at random between the leaves; but the grandson
would not own that the oracle had weight.

"What do you know, Jackanapes?"

"He didn't tell lies, because he doesn't," said George
conclusively. "Dad, may I have a real gun to go about the
wood with, please, because there are so many fierce
poachers about?"

Mr. Clovis having refused this often preferred request,
which George brought out regularly at dessert time, always
with a fresh reason attached to it, sent his son and heir
to bed, and took counsel with his pipe in the garden.

"Because he doesn't." Well, was not that, after all,
the ground on which more than one honourable man built
his faith where Cardew was concerned? A liar can no

more keep his tongue from lying than a toper can keep his lips from the bottle. A man's character, like murder, will out. It was all very well to declare that Cardew's money and Gillian's cleverness bought golden opinions— to a certain extent, and with a certain class, no doubt they did—yet in his heart Mr. Clovis knew well that here in Cardew's own county there were men who trusted him now who had been inclined at first to hold back, and whose opinion could never have been bought. Moreover, these men were willing that their wives should meet the convict, and that was a very crucial proof of the genuineness of their trust. Then again, women believed in Jack, and that might perhaps count for something. Women, Mr. Clovis reflected, have a curious instinct for character. They have frequently been on the right side, even from the days when they followed the Galilean, weeping.

"I wish I knew," he muttered for the hundredth time, and at that moment he saw Jack coming up the drive; and impelled by a half-formed purpose, he walked up to the front door.

The two men met just under the hanging electric light that the soap-boiler had suspended from the roof of his Gothic porch. Jack lifted his hat rather stiffly.

" I should apologise for coming to your house," he said, " but I am bound to hear how the boy is before I finally decide to go up to town to-morrow."

Cardew was less embarrassed than Mr. Clovis; indeed, he was surprised to see that Gillian's step-father had some difficulty in speaking to him. He supposed, a little scornfully, that the old fellow was overcome by rage.

" There is no need for me to go inside your house," he said. " Gillian can talk to me here."

He was about to pull the bell, when, to his further astonishment, Mr. Clovis arrested the movement.

" No; don't ring. Wait a bit," said the master of the

house. "It ain't that I would prevent your going in to
speak to Madam Gill—for choose what a man may be, he
has a right to his wife—but there is a thing I would so
much like to ask you, that—well, 'pon my word, I can't
keep it back any more."

"I cannot guess what you can possibly have to ask me,"
said Jack.

The soap-boiler got redder still, and his protuberant
eyes seemed to start with eagerness. Jack noticed that the
diamond-ringed thick-fingered hand shook. He wondered
what "old Cloves" had in his head. Was it something to
do with money? He was not inclined to be encouraging.

"Well?" he said coldly.

"As man to man," Mr. Clovis blurted out suddenly,
"and before God, were you guilty of fraud or no?"

"*No,*" said Jack.

Then, almost as the emphatic denial crossed his lips, his
pride told him that he had been a fool to reply.

"I was not called on to answer you," he said, the next
moment. "It is a farce to ask me such a question. Had
I done the thing, do you suppose I should stick at swearing
I had not? You are just as wise as you were before."

Mr. Clovis drew himself up and held out his hand. "I
believe you, Cardew," he said simply. "And I wish I
had done that before. It seems childish—though, for that
matter, children ain't easily gulled by a bad person—but I
believe you, and I am glad I do! I wasn't sure that it
would convince me, but it has."

Cardew laughed outright. "The thing is manifestly
absurd," said he.

Mr. Clovis still stood perseveringly holding out his hand.
Jack's laughter ceased. Something seemed to have got
into his throat. It was absurd, of course, yet the obstinate
and kindly old soap-boiler's ridiculous proceeding made the
world the sounder to him.

He grasped Mr. Clovis by the hand with a force that made that gentleman exclaim, for the diamond ring had cut his finger.

"That will do, that will do," cried Mr. Clovis. "But I do not see that I am at all absurd!"

"All right," said Cardew, trying rather awkwardly to finish his laugh. "But if it is not you, why, then, it is the arrangement of everything that is mad, sir. No, I wasn't guilty. But I don't think we shall ever see that fact proved. Except for my son's sake I don't much care nowadays."

Mr. Clovis had opened the hall door and they were crossing the hall together. He shook his head over the last words. "You ought to care for your own sake. You are young yet," he said.

"I am close on the forties," said Jack. "Well, possibly one does not get much understanding in forty years, or in eighty either! One begins to have a rough guess at what is *not* worth having, that's all."

CHAPTER XVI.

"SINCE I HAVE HAD GOLIATH."

"Whate'er thou lovest, man, that too become thou must:
God, if thou lovest God; dust, if thou lovest dust."
Johannes Scheffer.

CARDEW found his old friend sitting up in bed, with his long legs drawn up to make a rest for a book.

"I am not done for this time, Jack," he said, "though I fancy that the next wrestle will about finish me."

He was gaunter than ever, but there was a good deal of vigour in the grasp of the long lean fingers, and the black eyes were not devoid of fire. He was unshaven, for he would not allow a nurse to shave him, and the bed-clothes were twisted uncomfortably. The room looked comfortless, even to the eyes of a man who seldom observed details.

"I do not see why it should finish you, if you take proper precautions," said Jack.

He had been waylaid by Elizabeth on the stairs, and had been entreated with tears to "speak reason to the master," whose curious and perverse methods of dealing with illness were driving her to despair.

"If you insist on bleeding yourself, and on sleeping with your window open, and on not seeing a doctor——"

"There, there, that's no matter," interrupted the old man. "What, Jack, are we a couple of crones that we

must converse together of pills and cossetings? I won't
have it. I have one disease that's bound to kill me anyhow,
and that's age. I thought I should have got the worst
of this year's round—and that is why I had a desire to see
you again—but no, I am too tough for the choker yet!"
He laughed with a queer twist of his big, humorous
mouth. "Too tough, though I am an old customer," he
repeated triumphantly. "But next time, Jack, Age will come
behind and strike me in the back when bronchitis has his
grip on my windpipe—and then this ugly body will be
done for, hey? And mind you bury it in the garden
in a basket, for I hate paraphernalia. I have made you
executor."

"But you may live another ten years if——"

"You may go if you can't talk sense," cried Mr. Molyneux.
"I am not so old that I can stand interference, sir. When
I feel that that period is approaching I shall certainly
give my flesh the slip."

And Jack was silenced.

"Not but what I am obliged to you for coming here,
and glad to see you, and I did not mean to seem the
contrary," the old man said restlessly, and after an uneasy
pause. He plucked at the counterpane with restless
fingers; he was a bad patient, and weakness made him
irritable, but he loved Jack Cardew. "Can't you sit
down and smoke? We've had a good many smokes
together. You will find a pipe and matches on the
mantelpiece. Lady Jane comes to see me, and she is
the only other visitor I care about, but of course she
can't smoke. You and I sat up half the night the first
time you dined with me. Do you remember? You were
full of ideas then. Lord! what wonders you were to do.
I was thinking last night that I should like to have you sit
and smoke by me again."

Cardew did as he was bid, and drew his chair up to the

bedside. The pipe set him at ease, yet he rather wished
that Mr. Molyneux had not suggested it. How kind the
old fellow had been to that eager youth who—save during
the moments when he was sure he was the veriest fool
alive—had expected to set the Thames on fire. Jack puffed
vigorously ; the smoke must have got into his eyes, for the
water stood in them.

" I am sure I don't know why you troubled yourself
about a conceited young ass," he said. " I suppose it was
because—as one gets on in years—boys have a sort of
interest for one."

" I don't know that I cared about 'em as a rule," said
Mr. Molyneux. " You've got more humanity in you than
ever I had. It told in your writings, it will tell again.
You're a much bigger chap than me, Cardew. I was born
a pedant and bookworm, but you were meant to help the
world to live."

" No, I made a hash of it," said Jack. He smoked
silently for a time, then broke out gloomily, ' You know
that I did, sir. You were ashamed of me when we met
in Gillian's room after I came back. Do you suppose I did
not see that ? Mind, I did not wonder. I am ashamed of
that time now. If she had been ashamed too, the devil
knows where I should be."

" That is true," said Mr. Molyneux. " And she was right,
and I was wrong ; but I was disappointed in you, Jack."

Jack laughed, but rather sadly. " You naturally expected me to be a hero after all the fine heroics that
I wrote," he said. " And I succumbed to the force of
circumstances, and the brute in me got loose "—his
forehead contracted as if with pain—" got loose and killed
a man. You would never have done that."

" No, I should not have done that," agreed the old man.
" And so I took upon myself to be disappointed. " Upon
myself ! " There was a certain fierce mockery in his tone.

Stephen Molyneux set no store by the opinion of the majority, but he was given at times to a bitter self-disparagement. It is perhaps as well for the sake of our sanity that we do not see ourselves too plainly—but Stephen had always been eccentric.

"And why not?" said Cardew shortly. "I've told you I wasn't surprised. Of course I knew that I had gone some way to the bad. Gill surprised me, not you. Of course I knew that I had fallen below your level. You couldn't help being the better man."

"Ay, but there's the mistake, said Mr. Molyneux. He relapsed into silence, watching Jack with a satisfaction that needed no outlet in words. The better man? No, no, only the smaller man. The man with fewer temptations and the less complete nature. He was glad he saw that now.

"I doubt he is not far off after all—he seems to have lent me glasses," he muttered dreamily.

When Jack asked "Who?" he repeated the question almost merrily, "Who? who? The one doctor who cures, lad."

Later his mind reverted again to the former subject. "See now, I should not have broken out in despair. No, for my blood was never so hot as yours. I should have frozen more likely. But it was because of the fire in you that I liked you—and then I was surprised because it flashed out and burned. Poor lad, poor lad! Why, you never took anything coldly in your life!"

"What I did, I did," said Cardew, looking straight before him. "And it is to God, if there is one—and since I've had Goliath I think that there is—it is to Him that I must answer. I don't want excuses made for me. That one is mad with rage and misery is no justification, when just the business of life, if one allows of a right and a wrong at all, is to keep that brute self in a leash. I knew what I was letting go."

"Well, well, you repent, like David," said the old man; and while he spoke the last remnants of disappointment and estrangement rolled away, and it seemed to him that he saw of a certainty that which should be.

"The old crank dies childless, and it is a natural law and right that it should be so," he said. "But your sons and grandsons are proud of the name you hand down to them, and you beget spiritual children too. Yes, yes—and I am glad that I have lived to see it."

Jack started, and took his pipe from his lips. Was Mr. Molyneux wandering?

"You are seeing a long way ahead, sir," he said.

"I have nearly done with time," said Mr. Molyneux. "But I have liked you above a little, Jack, and that I think I shall take with me," and a long silence fell between them.

So it happened for the third time within a week that a man Cardew respected, but from whom he had received hard measure, offered him expressions of renewed trust—his quondam guardian, Gillian's step-father, and now this old friend, whose disaffection he had accepted with secret bitterness, whose prophecy he heard with a strange sensation of awe. "I am glad that I have lived to see it"—but he had not seen it. Yet what is prophecy but the escape from the bond of time? and who could say what the the brave spirit even now beheld, as it neared its freedom?

Anyhow the illumination, or aberration, whichever it might be, was over. Mr. Molyneux spoke next in an irritable tone. "I hear you have come out in a new character, and are counted a good man of business in these days. You may as well give me your advice, then—though, mind you, I don't approve this money-grabbing phase.

"Of course I will help if I can," said Jack.

The accusation of money-grabbing only amused him, for whatever his faults might be they did not lie in that direction.

"Do you remember that print we talked of the last time we met? It is in the market now, and the British Museum is bidding for it. I fully think it genuine. Now if I buy it, I cannot afford to live more than another six months. There is only four hundred left now, besides what I have always put aside for Elizabeth—you'll see that she gets her legacy, won't you?—and that print will cost three hundred, I fancy. I wish that you would find out how far Mr. —— is prepared to go for the British?"

"Very well," said Jack. "What do you mean, sir, when you say you cannot afford to live for more than another six months?"

He asked in some trepidation, for Mr. Molyneux was apt to resent questions. He knew that Gillian was under the impression that her great-uncle was very rich, but rich men sometimes fancy themselves poor. On the other hand, he had had suspicions that old Stephen muddled his money matters.

Mr. Molyneux was momentarily inclined to snub the inquiry, but he relented. Jack might take some liberties that were not permitted to any one else.

"The fact is, I have lived on my capital for the last ten years," he said. "Why not? I have no son, and you have money enough. My father died at eighty-six, and so did my grandfather. I did not reckon on passing that period, and have not left a large margin. You might wire to me when you have spoken to Mr. ——."

"Do you mean to tell me that you have only four hundred pounds between you and destitution?" said Jack.

He turned round on his chair, and resting his arms on the back of it faced Mr. Molyneux. The old man smiled, a kindly, amused smile, such as a grown man vouchsafes to a child who is importunate over matters of no importance.

"Three from four leaves one, Jack," he said. "I must

certainly have that print. Luckily I spend little on other things. Oh, I daresay the hundred will last my time. There are one or two books that I should like Lady Jane to have. I picked them out before I took to bed. One must be careful what one gives to a lady. And there is an ornament or two that your wife might like. I know that she will send them to a shop to have the jewels reset, and that goes against me, rather; but all the same she shall have 'em, because I do not think that I did her justice. The colour of her hair reminded me of her mother, and that prejudiced me. But it was Gillian who stood by you, and I would make her my most humble apologies if I supposed that she ever cared about what an old fogey thought."

"Gill shall not have your stones reset, and she does not in the least resemble her mother," said Jack.

"That recalls to me that there is another thing I had a mind to tell you of. I have thought a good deal over it. I was fond of Gillian's father, but her mother is a lady who does not command my esteem."

Jack smiled involuntarily. It was unnecessary to have informed him of that fact, for Mr. Molyneux was no adept at dissembling, and the lady in question was fully aware of his sentiments.

"Gill has told me that you never hit it off with Mrs. Clovis; but that does not much matter, does it?" said he.

"She is not honest," said the old man. "I once sent her money for her daughter's education. I found out by chance years afterwards that she had never sent Gillian to school, and that she had paid her milliner with the sum I had given towards schooling. It was inexcusable. I did not of course press her on the subject, but the transaction proved her to be entirely unworthy of any trust."

Cardew sent the smoke up to the ceiling in rings, and said nothing. He inclined, in these days, to a large silence.

He did not trust Mrs. Clovis, but this irrevocable judgment struck him as "rough on her." Jack could be furiously angry and even implacable on occasion, but a woman pressed by duns would never get a stern sentence from him. Perhaps by reason of the "more blood in his veins" sex weighed the scales heavily when Cardew held them.

"Thus knowing her to be devoid of principle," Mr. Molyneux continued, "I observed with curiosity that she has some secret reason to fear you. I am not a tatler, therefore I have not mentioned this fact before, but I am persuaded that Mrs. Clovis burned your manuscript and is at the bottom of all your trouble."

"But that is quite impossible!" cried Jack.

While Mr. Molyneux spoke he had been rather impressed by the circumstance of some one else having noticed that Mrs. Clovis was afraid. He had occasionally refused admittance to the fancy that assailed him in his mother-in-law's presence. But the next minute he recognised plainly and sensibly enough that the old man was not quite himself to-day, that his prejudices, both for and against people were accentuated; they stood out, like the veins on a dying leaf, but reason was fading.

"Well, well, I fancied that you might be interested to know who did it, so I told you," Mr. Molyneux said. "But you are right to take no notice. The punishment of the unjust is not in our hands, neither does it consist, as the vulgar imagine, in stripes and death, but——" The sentence ended in a Greek quotation, and Cardew, whose Greek was somewhat rusty, shook his head.

"I was never philosophical," he said; "but I do not think that I have an enemy. It was fate—or something else. Here is Elizabeth with your gruel, sir."

"Throw it out of the window. I do not need it," said the patient. "Let me see, what were we saying?"

Elizabeth, with swollen eyelids, and with her usually

comely face puckered with grief, whispered pathetically to Jack, "The master won't listen to a woman. Do you make him swallow something, sir."

Jack, full of pity for her, and greatly oppressed by a sense of his own incapacity, took the tray, and sitting close to the bed coaxed and coerced with a rough tenderness that brought fresh tears to the woman's eyes.

It was terrible to her to see the awkwardness with which Jack fed the old master, and to feel how much more handily and comfortably she could have done it. There was tragedy to her faithful soul in the muddled bed-clothes (which she was not suffered to put straight) and in the way the smoke from Mr. Cardew's pipe curled over the food. But the feminine element that—so far as was known—had had no sway in the bachelor's life, was not allowed to smooth his death-bed.

"He is that scared of a woman meddling when he is ill, though as polite a gentleman as ever was when he is well, that I do believe there must once have been one who was too much for him," Elizabeth said to herself. "And his contrary ways now is all her fault."

Jack found her sitting on the stairs when he come out with the empty basin in his hand.

"I made him eat it, Elizabeth," said he. "But it was the toughest job I've ever been set to, and if it had not been that you were crying I should have given up. Now do for goodness' sake dry your eyes."

Elizabeth loved Jack Cardew, and in common with the rest of her sex had known better than to doubt him. She dried her eyes on her apron, and took the tray.

"God bless you, sir," said she. "You was always that kind-hearted. But what do you think about the master? He has not spoken a word of late till to-day; but since you come, I have heard his dear voice a-going and a-going whenever I've crept to the door to listen; and angry he would be if he knew how often I do that by night as well as by day."

"I have never heard him talk so fast before," said Jack.

"Did he speak quite sensible, sir?"

"Yes—I think so," said Jack doubtfully. "He is rather excited, and he said something I did not quite understand about a man who is walking in the garden and who can answer all the questions. Is any one in the garden?"

Jack unfastened the glass door that opened from the staircase on to the leads, and running down the grimy stone steps, stood among the flower-beds.

There was something pathetic in this smoky house-encircled oasis. A London garden is so surrounded by enemies. Cats and green blight lie in wait to destroy. The very petals of the flowers are touched with London black. Poor dainty little ladies blooming under sad difficulties! Since the master had been laid up the garden had been sadly ravaged. Mr. Molyneux had been in the habit of getting up at four o'clock every morning to dig.

"Dear me, sir, how pleased he was, the first time you offs with your coat and digs too!" said Elizabeth. "I remember it as if it was yesterday. 'Elizabeth,' says he, 'whenever Mr. Cardew comes, I am at home, mind. Not that it is likely he'll want to come again,' says he."

Elizabeth had followed Mr. Cardew wistfully, and again stood close behind him. Jack would fain have been alone, but he could not shake her off; she was terrified by her master's condition, and as restlessly uneasy as Mr. Molyneux's Persian cat, who had been wandering from room to room all day. She was no gossip as a rule, but anxiety had loosened her tongue.

"He seemed often a bit lonesome before you come, and a deal worse after you went," she said. "But oh! if he would but let me do for him——" and she began to sob afresh.

"Look here, I shall stay the night here, and if he should be any worse you shall fetch a doctor, whether he likes it or no, and I will take the responsibility," said Jack. "But for goodness' sake don't cry!"

Elizabeth made him a funny old-fashioned curtsey, and dried her eyes on her apron.

"Then I am to say it is by your orders, sir," she said. She had been a woman who had been jealous of interference, but in this trouble which she could not grapple with, Jack's masculine decision was of untold comfort to her. She retreated, a good deal cheered, but Mr. Cardew sat down on the garden bench in great depression of spirit. The place in itself saddened him, the place that was haunted by that hopeful and aspiring youth! The middle-aged man seemed to see the boy before him, and put the vision aside with an impatient "pshaw."

Presently he walked to the nearest post-office and cancelled all his engagements by telegram. Gillian would mock at this sudden change in his plans; she would say Elizabeth was too much for him. Indeed, the idea of the poor woman creeping at night to the door of her master's room had had something to do with his resolution; perhaps it was no wonder that her sex trusted Jack Cardew.

Dinner was a rather melancholy affair, but Jack ate and drank as best he could, having a thoroughly English horror of giving way to sentiment. Elizabeth brought out the best port, brushing the dust off each bottle as she plumped it down.

"I know that the master would wish you to drink it, for he always kept it for you," said she. "Indeed, sir, it was always called Mr. Cardew's port from the first evening you dined in this room, and he would not so much as look at it after you was gone."

Wouldn't he? "To the master's health," said Cardew with forced cheerfulness.

He raised the glass to his lips and sipped the wine with apparent gusto, and Elizabeth was satisfied.

It had been like the old man to pour out of his best for an impecunious youth who would have been equally pleased with a hot new brand, but, after all, that characteristic and unpractical generosity was not unappreciated. In truth, one learns to doubt whether any gift that has in it the element of our very best ever *is* wasted; it is perhaps rather the second-best, which is made up with just an alloy of calculation, that is exchanged for disappointment. Those who break their alabaster boxes and recklessly lavish all their sweet ointment are not the people who cry out on the ingratitude of the world.

Jack ate his dinner with outward stolidity, and a secret wish that all the old things in the room would not appeal to him. Imagination may be a gift of the gods, but there are moments when it makes its possessor miserable. Cardew would often have suffered and would perhaps have sinned less without it—but possibly the celestial gifts are not intended to conduce to our comfort.

When the meal was over Jack went upstairs again and entered the sick-room. Finding the old man asleep, he established himself in an armchair by the window with every intention of watching; but presently, as the night grew old, he nodded. Elizabeth had gone to bed with full confidence in Mr. Cardew, and in the silent house the hours slipped by on tip-toe.

It is odd to see how a person's expression may change in sleep, how the character that lies below the surface peeps out and shows itself unawares. One may feel ashamed to scrutinise a sleeping person, in the same way that one

would feel ashamed to surprise a secret. Cardew's face
was very sad when he was sleeping, but it was not ignoble.
Funnily enough the dream spirit had carried him to the
night-nursery in which he had been put to bed when he
was a small boy. His ambitious youth, his clouded and
tragic manhood were forgotten, but he admired again the
pattern of stiff pink flowers with violet centres that covered
the nursery wall, and he saw the black streaks on the rails
of the cot, where the paint had been scraped off by his
own mischievous thumb-nails while he was longing for the
time to get up. Some noise in the street outside
momentarily disturbed him, and the dream shook and
altered slightly, as the colours on a soap-bubble change at
a breath. The cot was still there, but the wall paper was
adorned with pictures from fairy tales. It was no longer
himself. It was his boy who was kicking restlessly, and
pulling with eager fingers at the brass knobs at the corners
of the crib.

"The chap is like what I was," Jack said to himself.
He was amused when the little lad scrambled over the
rails, and, after several unsuccessful attempts, set his
chubby bare feet on a cane-bottomed chair that stood by
the bedside, and then slid on to the floor. The sleeper
laughed with a fellow-feeling when the boy chuckled with
adventurous delight and advanced half-fearfully into the
shadowy room, making straight for the long coveted box
of matches that lay on the wash-hand stand. Goliath,
secured the matches, and then trotted back and sat down
on the floor in an ecstasy of somewhat guilty joy, with
his pink toes tucked under him. He struck match after
match, throwing each behind him when the flame got close
to his fingers. He had an air of intense earnestness and
importance.

"Little villain! somebody must certainly smack you
for this," Jack thought in his dream. The somebody

would probably be Gillian, for Goliath was too much for his father, who was exaggeratedly afraid of "hurting too much."

Then with a thrill of horror Jack became aware that the curtain behind the boy was on fire, and it seemed to him that the child jumped up suddenly, and rushed into the middle of the room screaming, with his night-shirt in a blaze. The next moment the nurse ran in, and enveloped the little figure in a rug, putting out the fire, then fled across the room with her burden. She tripped over a marble in her flight, and, instinctively stretching out her arms, let the boy, who was yelling lustily, fall on to his back on to the floor—and at that Jack woke.

"I must have jerked forward in my chair, and it was that that made me fancy Goliath had had a bad fall. What an old womanish dream!" Jack said to himself. But it had been so unpleasant that he was disinclined to shut his eyes again.

Towards three o'clock the patient woke, raised himself on his pillow and smiled kindly at Jack, evincing no surprise at sight of him.

"It is nearly morning, and he will soon be out walking in the garden, you know," he remarked confidentially. "A London garden is never up to much, as you see. I was half afraid he would not care to come. My flowers have not had so good a chance as some."

"I am going to make some tea for you," said Jack, in his most matter-of-fact tone; "how many lumps of sugar shall I put in? The spirit-lamp is blazing away like fun. The water will boil in a minute."

He feared that the old man was "queer" again, and made up his mind to fetch a doctor so soon as Elizabeth should relieve guard. In the meantime it seemed to him best to steadily ignore the "queerness."

Mr. Molyneux gulped down the tea eagerly. He was

thirsty, and his lips were dry. Then he flung his long legs out of bed. "Now I shall dig," he said; "I always dig before breakfast."

"No, no, sir, it is still dark," said Jack. "There will be no daylight for another three hours."

"What are you doing here? But there, there, you are always welcome, I hope you know that," said Mr. Molyneux. "Yes, you are very welcome, Cardew—but I must ask you to leave me for a few minutes, for I must dress myself. What is that you said to me about having no dress clothes? Nonsense, lad, I asked *you* to dine, I don't care about your clothes; but at this moment I must get up."

"I cannot dine with you to-night. If you'll get back into bed I'll explain why I cannot," said Jack; but Mr. Molyneux was not to be cajoled.

By degrees he became angry at his guest's unaccountable behaviour, and his excitement grew. Jack saw with dismay that he should have to use force to prevent him from wandering into the garden.

The necessity was painful to Cardew. He was miserable when he saw his friend's old-fashioned politeness struggling with a sense of outrage. He felt brutal when he used his strength, and he reddened with shame when Mr. Molyneux at last lay back panting on his pillow, and said reproachfully, "I could never have believed that you could have behaved so, Cardew."

It was ridiculous to take that to heart, and equally ridiculous to waste breath in trying to explain the situation, but Jack would have given a thousand pounds to have been sure that old Stephen Molyneux would not go out of the world angry and disappointed with him. Jack, as his wife often remarked, was not a very "reasonable person."

He was thankful when the old man shut his eyes and lay apparently exhausted by the struggle. He stole out and called softly to Elizabeth, who came down ready to relieve him.

"I am very certain now that you ought not to be left alone with him," said Jack. "But he has worn himself out for the present. He will be quiet enough for the next few hours, I fancy. I'll have a tub and some breakfast, and then I will look up the doctor myself."

"He'll be very angry with you, sir," said Elizabeth, but she was thankful that Mr. Cardew should take the responsibility on his own broad shoulders.

The morning was grey, as the previous evening had been. Cardew lingered in the garden when he had had his coffee, for it was barely six—the doctor would scarcely be up yet. He picked off the faded flowers in the heart-shaped border on the lawn, and pulled up a few weeds, wondering the while how Goliath was getting on.

Cardew's friendship was warm and genuine, but his own boy was much more to him than all the old men in the world. He was surprised at his own strength of affection for his son. Mr. Molyneux had been more unreserved than was his wont during the conversation of the previous day. Both men had possibly been touched by the knowledge that the time could not be far distant when they should neither listen nor talk to each other any more, but the prophecy about sons and grandsons was the point to which Jack's mind reverted.

"Your sons and grandsons will be proud of the name you hand down to them."

Well, if that were so, what did anything else matter? Life is hardly a merry business at best, but if a man's sons and grandsons hand down an honoured name through generations, why, then there seems some sort of satisfaction to be got out of the contemplation of it.

Jack stooped to tie up a straggling flower, and as he did so an understanding that was rather painful than otherwise came to him. He realised, as he had never quite realised before, how much store that old man had set by him, how bitter his disappointment must at one time have been, and how pathetic a childless man's fondness for a lad is.

"I am glad Gill insisted on his being godfather to my boy," thought Cardew. "I wonder why these lonely, oddly constituted lives——Hallo. His meditation was sharply cut short. The door that led from the steps on to the garden was opened. Mr. Molyneux came towards him, attired in a yellow dressing-gown, swinging a watering-pot in one hand, and with an eager, pleased smile on his lips. The old man's grey hair was dishevelled, and his step unsteady, but when Jack hurried to meet him he shook his head impatiently.

"What, what ? You mean well, Cardew, but you get in the way just now. Don't stop me, for I tell you that he is here." His tongue tripped a little, and his voice was thick. "I am late as it is," he said ; "I ought to have been out before, but he has waited on purpose to explain that passage. Ah, yes, you said your Greek was rusty— poor boy, no wonder ! but you must not interfere, Jack. Who are you to stop me ?"

He shook off Jack's hand with unexpected strength, but overbalanced himself in the effort and staggered forward.

Jack was just in time to catch the tall, swaying figure in his arms. He put it down on the gravel path and was about to shout to Elizabeth, when a sudden fear arrested him. Mr. Molyneux lay perfectly still, and the light had died out of his half-closed eyes. Cardew knelt down and put his hand to the old man's heart. There was no movement, but the lips smiled a peaceful, inscrutable smile.

In the smoky little garden a sparrow began to chirp, and the water from the overturned flower-pot trickled towards the dry borders. The flowers had missed the master's ministrations, but flowers and birds make no fuss about death.

Elizabeth came flying out of the house with terrified face and uplifted hands. "Oh, sir, the master has gone," she screamed. "He has clean gone! I left him fast asleep, and went to get him some broth ready for when he should wake, and when I—— But oh, my goodness me, what's this, sir?"

"Hush—don't make a row. You could not help it," said Jack. He rose from his knees and stood beside her. "Don't be frightened. We must carry him into the house—but there is nothing to be done. It is over," he said.

Elizabeth trembled and clutched Jack's arm, forgetting her manners, forgetting everything but the human need for support before the great mystery—which, after all, is perhaps less mysterious than life.

"He isn't—he can't be," she said.

Jack took off his hat, and stood bareheaded looking down. Perhaps he, too, had a vague idea that an unseen presence was still walking in the garden. "He has gone. I don't think we need pity him. He has found the answer," said Jack.

CHAPTER XVII.

OUR FATAL SHADOWS.

> "Our acts our angels are, or good or ill,
>   Our fatal shadows that walk by us still."
>
> *Beaumont and Fletcher.*

IT is curious to note how the shadow of ill-luck seems to hang over some families. Sir Edward was an unlucky man, Jack Cardew was unlucky, Henry Strode, who possessed—his godmother averred—all the family characteristics, was unlucky too, though he was only a distant cousin of the Bevans and Cardews. Probably, seeing that character is destiny, the ill-luck was in his very blood.

Mr. Strode was a singularly upright man, but he was also a singularly unpopular one. Every one at Churton Regis knew that the new parson was Lady Hammerton's cousin, and that it was by reason of his connection with her that he held the living; yet I do not think that any radical objection to lay patronage was at the root of the slow disfavour with which he was regarded.

These south country people were not violent in their expressions of dislike; they did not heave bricks at a stranger—not even when he wore a silver cross and walked about the village in a gown—but they presented to him an unbroken front of tolerably civil disapprobation. He made no way with them, and a depression that he tried manfully to shake off was riding him day in and day out.

Perhaps the soft climate of the valley, in which the rectory was situated, told on a constitution that had been fed on moorland air, and then, though he did not own this to himself, Mr. Strode was exceeding lonely. He was not a man who made friends easily, yet, like many reserved natures, he needed companionship; his very goodness was apt to become morbid; his immense fund of energy craved outlet. In default of a friend he would have been cheered could he only have found some enemy, such as starvation or drunkenness, with whom it would have been his sacred duty to wage war; but this comfortable and fortunate village was well looked after by the two rich families who had taken up their abode there. Mrs. Clovis was both charitable and pious, Mr. Cardew was a most generous landlord.

The parson could not complain because misery and destitution did not stalk the streets of his parish, but he would have been a happier man had he been thrust into rougher surroundings. Nothing frets more than a grievance of which the owner is ashamed. A grievance that can be openly worn is nothing in comparison. Mr. Strode was addicted to several private penances at this time: he fasted more than was good for him, and he mortified the flesh in other ways that were the concern of no one but himself. Yet I fancy that these penances partook rather of the nature of counter-irritants than of aids to holiness. They certainly did not increase the geniality of his temper, and they rather deepened the gulf, already too deep, between him and his fellows.

On one especial Sunday, however (it was the Sunday after Miss Haubert had gone home), Mr. Strode did, by a rare chance, hit on a theme that brought him in touch with his congregation. He preached on the flag that waved from the wall, and on the spirit which leads forlorn hopes and walks gaily to martyrdom. He would himself have made an unflinching martyr had he lived in the days when the Christians were thrown to the beasts. He never lacked courage, either moral or physical, therefore it was the harder on him when he lacked lions. He did not, as a rule, enjoy preaching; he was quite aware that he had no gift of eloquence, and an ineradicable honesty made him loth to coin sentences when he had nothing in special to say, but he waxed warm over the " Forlorn Hopes," and an unconscious fellow-feeling for men who strive companionless and alone lent pathos to his words.

Mrs. Clovis, her delicate, cameo-like face uplifted, listened with devoted admiration. Mr. Clovis nodded appreciatively more than once: he usually dozed during the sermon, and it was a triumph to have kept him awake. Old Lady Hammerton's brave eyes brightened, and Sir Edward—who had come to take notes of papistical practices—put off counting the number of candlesticks till the preacher should have finished.

Mr. Strode was not eager to catch the attention of the great people among his parishioners—indeed, like most of the High Church clergy, he felt that his work ought to lie more especially among the poor—but he was pleased to see that the farm hands and villagers were also, for once, listening to him. The little artist had given him a useful hint.

He was in better spirits than usual when he took off his surplice in the vestry, but as he walked through the churchyard a scrap of conversation that he inadvertently overheard brought back the cloud to his brow.

"You may say what you like, Jim, but I know the parson made your heart beat, by the way you snorted when he said that about the soldiers whose bones lie in nameless graves, but who won't be out of hearing when the roll-call is read."

17

It was Jim's sweetheart who spoke, and Jim was the young groom who had wished to plunge a second time into the burning stables to save Mr. Cardew's property.

" So he did—for the minute," Jim allowed. " But, bless you, a parson's sermon ain't got anything to do with what he is out of the pulpit. He talks as if he was the sort of chap to stand by any one who was down, but by all accounts that's the very thing he don't do. I was a bit taken by what he said about Christianity being the creed of the men who ain't afraid of pain, and of living and dying alone, and who ain't scared by what the world thinks, but when he is out of his surplice you don't find *him* backing the one against a hundred. ' No thank you, my man, I don't see myself consorting with such as you,' says he. ' The judge and bishops are all against you, and so you must be going to hell and I sha'n't believe a word you say.' "

" Oh, Jim, but did he ever say that ? "

" He did—to Mr. Cardew when he was in gaol for something I'll swear he never did. The butler at Draycott Court told me, and whenever I think of it I want to fight the parson," said Jim.

It was not what the parson *had* said, and the aspersion cast on him was most unfair, for Mr. Strode would never have turned his back on any man merely because he was in a minority. He had simply been incapable of distinguishing an extraordinary exception to a general rule, but those who give, pretty generally receive, hard measure.

Mr. Strode was not a person who greatly cared what people said of him, and he was the last to change his tactics for the sake of public opinion—in truth, an adverse criticism was apt to render him obstinate—but this was neither the first nor second time that his behaviour to Cardew had been held up to reprobation ; he had become aware that the stalwart figure of the ex-convict actually stood between him and any chance he might have had of successfully serving the cause of the Church in Churton Regis.

He strode quickly through the churchyard and slammed the gate in Lady Hammerton's face. He was sick to death of Jack Cardew. He was weary of that eternal argument which his mind could not dismiss. He was going over the same old ground again when he was forced to interrupt himself in order to apologise for his awkwardness.

"You need not tell me that you did not see who was behind you," said Lady Hammerton. "You were walking as if you had the family black dog sitting on your shoulders. But you preached a very well-written sermon. I congratulate you on it."

"I fear I cannot thank you for your congratulations," said the priest, with a severity that would have overawed any one but his intrepid little godmother. "The preacher has missed his mark when the listener thinks rather of the style than of the message."

"Dear me, dear me!" cried the old lady. "Something really *has* put you out. It is absurd to talk of me as 'the listener' when I held you in my arms the very first time you ever went to church. You live too much alone, Henry. Now I know you want to get rid of me, but I am going to ask you to let me have a look at your garden. There is a cutting I should very much like to beg from your gardener."

Mr. Strode's mouth did not relax its grimness. At that moment a very small excuse would have made him throw up his new living on the spot. He had indeed a good deal of provocation. A man should not expect to be a prophet in his own family, but it is especially trying to be met by some one who puts aside a serious speech with a reference to the time when the teacher was in long clothes. Lady Hammerton was not usually tactless, but she was perhaps not quite devoid of a spark of mischief, though she was sprightly rather than malicious, and her temper was of the kind that flashes and snaps, and is over in a moment, rather than of the more dangerous sort that smoulders in silence.

"I shall be delighted to give you a cutting from any plant in my garden," said her godson gravely.

He had plenty of self-control, and his godmother respected him despite that remark about his infancy.

She trotted along at his side, holding her well-darned silk skirt high up out of the mud. She had driven to church in a wicker chair, drawn by an old white pony, but the country people all bobbed to her as she passed, which was more than they did for Mrs. Clovis.

Mr. Strode's humour softened when they reached the garden and stood among the flower-beds, which were much better kept than the flower-beds at Draycott Court.

"What a number of white blossoms! The garden looks as if you were preparing for a wedding, Henry," said Lady Hammerton.

"Ah! I grow them for my church," he answered, with just that added touch of warmth in his tone that a woman —even an old woman—is quick to hear. It was as if he had said, "I grow them for my bride."

The old lady lingered among the flowers, and her godson unbent and thawed in her cheerful presence. He *had* been too much alone and he enjoyed her appreciation of his improvements.

"These two long borders down the whole length of the lawn, with the narrow strip of grass between, are copied from those at Draycott Court, as you see," he said. "I have no originality—even the sermon you admired was suggested by that little artist who sat next to me at dinner at your house."

The allusion to the sermon was a token of peace made ;

the scrupulous honesty ol the disavowal of originality was characteristic.

"Talking of that dinner, Henry," said his godmother, "I do sincerely wish that you could see your way to—well, to a civil understanding with Jack Cardew."

They were walking in single file, for there was not space for two to walk abreast down the avenue of tall white lilies. Lady Hammerton could not see his face, but she knew from the set of her cousin's shoulders that he resented that bit of interference. He was absolutely silent for a while; then he made a remark on the weather, but she was not to be so put aside.

"You heard what I said, Henry, and I have no doubt that you think I am trying to advise you on the strength of having given you a living. Yes, I remember quite well what you wrote to me. But this has nothing to do with your office. I would not touch anything appertaining to that for the world! It is simply as an old woman, and from the social point of view, that I speak. I am nearly seventy-five, you know, and I have kept my eyes open ever since I came of age and had to manage my own affairs. I have had to do with many men, good, bad, and indifferent, and I think that my opinion should count for something."

"My dear godmother," said the priest, turning round sharply, "I have no manner of doubt—in fact, I have the clearest proof—that your opinion counts for very much in this little corner of the world. So does Sir Edward Bevan's, and you and he have both voted openly for Mr. Cardew, and by so doing have given lesser people the excuse for following their inclinations and condoning a rich man's sins. As for me, my influence is of the slightest—there is hardly a place in England where the Church is less respected than she is here. For that very reason her servant is bound to lift again her high standard; she, at any rate, is no respecter of persons. I do not imagine that either you or Sir Edward are anything but disinterested," he added, with a swift turning of the tables that half-amused half-chagrined his would-be counsellor, "but I trust that you have fully realised your responsibility in this matter."

But an hour ago Mr. Strode had not been quite so certain of the justice of his own conclusions, but Lady Hammerton did not guess that. The man was a priest, and he was not going to allow her to reverse the right order of things and preach to him; whether on the score of old age, or on the more offensive score of patronage. Possibly she really liked him none the less for his independence; at any rate she gave up the attack with a good grace.

"I trust we have, Henry," she replied meekly, though with a twinkle in her eyes. "Sir Edward is obstinate too, but he has come round to Jack Cardew in a way I hardly dared to expect. I had more to say to you, but I see that there is no use in saying it. Yet, Henry, old people are sometimes right, and suppose—only suppose that one day it were absolutely proved that a terrible mistake had been made, that Cardew was honest after all—as his friends have always maintained—would not the Church's uncompromising attitude become a little awkward?"

"It is scarcely within the bounds of possibility that such a thing should happen. Mr. Cardew cannot in any case be tried over again," said he, frowning impatiently. "Unless an angel comes to convict me of error, I fear that I must continue to believe that the judge and jury knew what they were about."

"I do not think that you would receive that angel very warmly, Henry," the old lady murmured; but her cousin took no notice of that feminine last word, and the subject was dismissed.

Later in the day, long after his godmother and the white pony had jogged home, Mr. Strode received a note from Oaklands Park, but it did not occur to him that that effusive and delicately scented missive had anything to do with angelic messages.

He read the letter with some misgiving, for though Mrs. Clovis was the type of woman whom he admired in theory, in practice she occasionally wearied him. Mr. Strode preached on the advisability of confession to a priest, but his single convert sometimes made him repent his zeal. Whatever his failings he had no liking for spiritual gossip, and he was thoroughly manly. What was he to say to a lady who confessed that she slept too long in the morning, and that she had twice put sugar in her tea on a Friday? Mr. Strode had had very little to do with women. He supposed these trivial matters really did weigh on his penitent, though to his grosser mind they appeared slight. Yet surely once a week was often enough for any one to confess. Why did Mrs. Clovis so especially wish to see him now?

"Dear Mr. Strode,"—she wrote—"I am in great (spiritual) distress, and I most earnestly desire your help. Would it be asking too much of you to beg that you would come up to Oaklands Park this evening at about six o'clock? I have given orders that you may be shown into the boudoir, where I shall most confidently await you. I am sure (knowing your views on the subject of priestly counsel) that you will not fail me, and I rely entirely on you.

"I am sincerely and gratefully yours,

"Eva Clovis."

It was not easy to refuse this request, and yet it was with the greatest unwillingness that Mr. Strode complied with it. He had seldom bent his neck to any yoke save that of the Church, but the tyranny of the weak is curiously compelling and binding. That gentle despotism dragged him, much against the grain, up the hill to Oaklands, and forced him to present himself with a very stern air and bad grace at the door of Mrs. Clovis's boudoir just as the clock struck the hour she had appointed.

Mrs. Clovis rose from her sofa as he entered, and met him with a pretty air of deference. "This is so good of you; but I was sure that you would come," she said.

Somehow her soft voice, the luxury of the exquisitely furnished room, the effect of the lamp-light falling on the graceful, womanly figure, irritated Mr. Strode afresh. "You left me no choice, madam," he said. "I am bound to come when any parishioner—whether poor or rich—sends for me in my capacity of priest."

"Yes, yes, and that is such a comfort," she answered. "I never realised till quite lately what a real support and comfort the Church may be, and that she does truly hold out her hands to all who are in great distress."

"In great distress." The words struck oddly on Mr. Strode's ear, but he reflected that the lady was prone to exaggeration. "Great distress" sometimes meant gaunt starvation tearing at a door, ready to lay hold of the little ones; in this case it probably denoted a very refined and impalpable bogey. Mr. Strode had really more sympathy for material than he had for spiritual pain. Nature had not intended him for a confessor, and though he looked the part well enough, he was, at moments, dimly aware that his creed and his instincts were at war.

"Will you explain what it is that troubles you?" he said with a sigh, and he set himself to listen with a sort of grim patience.

Mrs. Clovis did not dare to offer him a cup of tea, though the little silver teapot, standing close at hand on a silver tray, and a plate of pink-sugared cakes were all ready for him. He would not take the armchair that was placed cosily for him, but stood by the mantelpiece and looked down on the penitent on the sofa.

"I hardly know how to explain," she sighed, "I have been so forced into such a terrible position." She paused, but he made no comment, and she was obliged to go on.

"Before I married Mr. Clovis we were poor, really pinchingly poor. In those days my heart often ached for my darling girl, and the only rich connection I had was so hard on me. Why are rich men so hard ? My husband indeed is an exception ; he is most liberal. But then some women have a very softening influence over men ; do you not think so ? I am always so sorry for any one who is poor, having known how constant worry wears one's soul out."

Mr. Strode glanced at the clock. "If there is any particular point on which you wish for spiritual guidance I am here to help you," he said.

"But if I do not tell you how I was situated how can you see how everything combined against me ? " she cried piteously. "Indeed, I do not think you will enter into my difficulty in any case, but I must speak of my trouble to some one, and no one but a priest is quite safe. You are bound to be secret, are you not ? "

She asked the question with sudden sharpness, and Mr. Strode was considerably surprised. Surely this gracious and liberal *dévote* had no secret crime on her conscience ? He had expected to be consulted on some such point as the necessity of fasting before taking the sacrament, or the advisability of going into a retreat (which Mr. Clovis objected to) during Lent ; but he could not fail to observe that this was an anxiety of very different colour to any that she had owned to before. Her lips twitched, and her eyes looked away from him. Nothing but that curious impulse that drives a criminal to unburden the mind to some one had made her send for him now.

"I should certainly hold myself bound not to betray a confession, though in the English Church we take no vow on the subject," he replied stiffly. "You had every opportunity of confessing in church last Friday. Has anything happened since then that has caused you to fall into serious temptation?"

"Last Friday? Oh yes, I remember I confessed all the little things I had done wrong since the Friday before—but this is a real difficulty that has been hanging over me for years. I could not have told you about it in church. One cannot explain a serious matter when one begins with a bit out of the prayer-book and talks into some one's ear. Besides that, I know that if any one were to sit in the front bench of the free seats in the left aisle they could hear what you say. Your voice is so very clear. It is not at all safe. I have heard that in the Romish Church——"

"What *have* you to say, madam?" said Mr. Strode, in that same uncompromisingly penetrating voice that she had complained of.

It seemed odd, even to himself, that he should have inspired her to confidence—a confidence greater than she had reposed in the most adoring of husbands; but perhaps his very want of sympathy made her trust him. Mr. Strode was not quite a man to Mrs. Clovis, but something sexless and symbolical; something on which one could fling the burden of responsibility without fear of betrayal; something that by imposing penances stood between her and a much more awful wrath, and that by sharing her secret seemed in some vague way to lessen her guilt.

"But if you hurry me I shall never be able to tell you," she cried tearfully; and again he curbed his impatience.

"We were poor," she repeated, "and I was never intended to rough it. I am not at all that kind of woman.

If I sometimes knew people in those days who were not in all respects all that could be desired, it was because when one is driven by necessity one cannot afford to be so very, very particular. There was one person of whom I saw a good deal, but you must not for a moment suppose that he was then what he is now. Oh, indeed, he was charming then, though Gillian never liked him; Gillian was wilful and had very decided opinions for her age. If it had not been that Mr. Clovis was, I may say, providentially thrown in my way just then, I might have married Mr. Bevan; but for the dear girl's sake it seemed my duty to——"

"To take the richer man," said Mr. Strode dryly.

"Not that I am mercenary," she said, blushing. (Mrs. Clovis could still blush as readily as a girl.) "No one loves to give more than I do. No one can truly say that I am greedy of money. Still, there was no doubt which man would make the best step-father to dearest Gillian, and, besides, one cannot be too careful about moral character. It seemed so clearly meant that I should marry Mr. Clovis. You believe in the leading of Providence, too; do you not, Mr. Strode?"

She paused for a moment as if expecting him to endorse her sentiment, and he smiled sardonically.

Mr. Strode was not a person who possessed much sense of humour, but he felt a certain grim irony in her question. The poor lady was quite guiltless of any satirical intention, but Fate has a way of giving us sly hits at times. Yes, he too believed in the direct leading of Providence. Good heavens, had he ever blasphemed to this extent? Had he ever worked for his private ends, persuaded himself that the voice of his inclinations was the voice of God?

"I? I believe in a very just God, and in a lying devil," said he sternly.

"Oh yes, of course; I never have agreed with the unorthodox people who do not think that there really is such a person as the last," she said eagerly. "If one once begins to doubt things there may be no end to it—I always say that. I believe in every single article that our dear Church teaches, for one had so much better be on the safe side, anyhow; and I am sure in these days when people have such strange ideas, it ought to count a little to my credit that I have never, never been anything but religious. I always insisted on Gillian's attending service when she was a girl; but Jack Cardew has the most extraordinary notions, he always had—— "

"Ah!" said the priest. "Now I believe that I can guess what sin is weighing on your conscience."

A more human and personal interest warmed his tone; his severity melted slightly. A light seemed to have broken on him.

"I saw something of your son-in-law when he was in gaol. I can understand that you have bitterly repented having allowed your daughter to marry him. No doubt his immense wealth was a temptation."

Mrs. Clovis laughed hysterically. The guess was wide enough of the mark.

"Allowed!" she cried. "Why, you don't know my daughter! If all the mothers and all the priests in the world had forbidden her, she would still have married Jack. She would not have given their objections so much as one thought. His wealth had nothing to do with it. Gillian likes good things—who doesn't?—but she would have taken him without a penny. No, no, that was no fault of mine. It is not that. Gillian would never forgive me if she knew, and I think that he would—would kill me. I wake up constantly in the night and see them both staring at me with knowledge in their eyes. It frightens me so! Do you really believe that every secret will be known one day, and that all the wrong things we have done will be

called from the housetops? But that would be so terribly
cruel! Who could bear it? One could never explain
then, and it would all sound so much worse than it really
was!" Her face was blanched, and she looked up at the
priest piteously. "I am not a bad woman. I could not
help myself, that is all. Indeed, I was never quite sure
that what he told me *was* so important, and to run the risk
of ruining my life—for dear George is so devoted to me and
I cannot live without affection—of ruining my life for a
scruple would have been foolish and—and almost wicked,
would it not?"

"If you could prevail on yourself to tell me what you
did, in the first place, I might understand why you did it
afterwards," said Mr. Strode.

Only a dogged tenacity that made him always determined
to carry out his purpose prevented him from taking curt
leave. The woman seemed to be incapable of telling a
story straight. Yet he had sometimes wondered at the
extreme tenderness of her conscience at the weekly con-
fessions.

A small, hard smile that made no pretensions to mirthful-
ness flickered on her white lips.

"Oh no, I do not think that you will," said she, "because,
you see, you are not of the kind who understand." And
the words, unexpected enough, pricked him. What was it
that they reminded him of?

"But I will tell you, because the thing has got on my
nerves and I shall go crazy over it if I keep it to myself."

She looked nervous, and her fragile hands clasped and
unclasped each other while she spoke, but the story was
still in the tone of a defence.

"Mr. Bevan often met me after I became dear George's
wife, but I need hardly say that I was never one of those
women who allow flirtations after marriage. I did
not wish, for many reasons which I need not enter into,

to make an enemy. It is always a mistake, and it is so unwomanly to do that. Mr. Bevan was staying in our house at the time when Jack Cardew was first engaged to my daughter. I did not quite like the engagement, but Gillian took her affairs into her own hands. Jack Cardew had just made a great literary success, and he was much run after, but I always thought that Gillian might have done better. For my part, I never could read his books, and he never took any trouble to make himself agreeable—in fact, he was rude to any one he did not like. I remember that I tried to patch up a reconciliation between him and Mr. Bevan, for I have always been a peacemaker, and I detest family dissensions. Mr. Bevan was quite inclined to be friendly, but Jack was almost brutal. 'I am not strait-laced, but I draw the line at shaking hands with him!' Jack said. It was most unpleasant, and very rude to me. I never could quite get over it. Well, it was after all our guests had left us that I renewed a correspondence with Mr. Bevan. I had not been accustomed to living in the depths of the country, and I felt *triste* just then. Dearest Gillian was away on a visit, and Mr. Bevan's letters amused me. Mr. Bevan can write charmingly, and I assure you that his letters were quite harmless; I should never have tolerated them had they contained the least suspicion of anything that my dear husband would have had reason to complain of. The reason that I did not tell George about them was simply that I cannot bear a fuss; and owing to something that Jack Cardew had told him, George had taken a violent dislike to Mr. Bevan. It has always seemed to me best to avoid any subject that may lead to dissension; I have a horror of harsh words. One morning—I think it came by the second post—I got the letter which—which has troubled me from the day I set eyes on it till now. I destroyed it long ago, but, unfortunately, I remember what was written in it, word for word."

Again she stopped for a minute; her breath came faster, and there was a spot of colour on either cheek. Mr. Strode was silent now from sheer perplexity; he knew not what to expect. Had Mr. Bevan, about whom he vaguely recollected having heard some unsavoury story, written insulting words which the poor lady could not dismiss from her mind, which, perchance, to a morbid sensitiveness, it had seemed a crime to have read, and an impossibility to forget? But no, she had just said that the letters were quite harmless.

"This is what he wrote, and I wish I had never read it," she said, speaking very quickly, and clasping her fingers tightly together as she reached the point at last :—' I have not seen your dear son-in-law lately; but yesterday I ran across a fellow who had just played a practical joke on him that had a bit of a sting in it. My cousin Jack, who is such a great man nowadays, had apparently squashed his brother-author's literary attempt with rather a heavy hand. Jack can be brutal on occasion. The injured genius, who is an acquaintance of mine, had just played the old trick of changing babies; he had put his own burnt child in the cradle of Jack's infant, and was in the act of carrying off *pro tem.* the prosperous heir to riches and fame.'" Mrs. Clovis heaved a long sigh, and leant back on the sofa as if a weight had been lifted from her. "I have never before mentioned that letter to any one, but it has haunted me. But indeed, my unfortunate silence has been my only—mistake. It is hardly quite a sin, is it? The rest is all sheer misfortune."

Mr. Strode put his hand before his eyes; his brain seemed in a whirl. When he at last spoke his voice sounded hoarse. "But what did it mean? 'The injured genius put his own child '—why, that must have been his book, the literary attempt that Jack Cardew had squashed —'in the cradle of Jack's infant' and he carried off Cardew's book? But it was Cardew's book that was supposed to have been fraudently destroyed for the sake of the insurance money, was it not? You do not mean that you knew of a fact that might have—— Good God, madam! You *can't* mean that you knew, that you actually knew something that might have proved that man's innocence and that you kept silence! You—you can't possibly mean that!"

His dismay was overwhelming; never in the course of his ministry had he been so utterly shocked and dumbfoundered; but Mrs. Clovis, having got over her confession, found it easy to pour out excuses, and defended herself almost brightly.

"Oh no, dear Mr. Strode, I do not mean that exactly," she said. "In fact, that is where circumstances were so hard on me. Of course I had not the least idea that I had been told anything of importance; neither had Mr. Bevan, when he wrote, the faintest suspicion that anything serious would result from the joke. The next thing that I heard was that Jack Cardew's book had been destroyed by an accident, and that the Insurance Company refused to pay up. My husband shook his head over that; he said that the refusal was most extraordinary, for that unless they thought that they had a very clear case they would never have ventured on such a step; he said, too, that Cardew was bound to bring an action against them. Then, indeed, it did occur to me that that letter had some bearing on the matter, but I did not at all wish to speak about it, because —well, because my dear husband was just a wee bit inclined to be jealous, and not having mentioned that he wrote to me—you understand—besides, it was hardly my business, was it? And I am sure that I have never approved of practical jokes. I must say, too, that I always have made a point of declaring on every occasion that, however extravagant Jack may have been, he never could have destroyed his own manuscript. I have said it over

and over again. Of course Jack was very extravagant;
disclosures were made at that trial that might have made
any tender mother—and I am devoted to Gillian—shy of
giving her consent to her daughter's marriage with him.
It appeared that he owed money to all sorts of dreadful
people with Old Testament names. He had backed some
friend's bill for an enormous sum, and the friend had left
him in the lurch, and there had been a bill of sale on his
furniture; he gambled too, as his father did before him.
There is no doubt that his misfortunes were largely due to
his own reckless carelessness, for the suspicions of the
company would never have been aroused if he had not
been so heavily involved. Of course I was terribly grieved
about the whole affair, but I felt convinced every morning
when I took up the *Times* that I should read that the
practical joker had turned up to give evidence, or else that
Mr. Bevan had at last come forward with a statement.
I read every word of the account of the trial, but neither
the man who perpetrated the joke, if it was a joke, or
Mr. Bevan, ever appeared in the court at all. Jack lost
the libel case and was arrested by the public prosecutor.
It was a fearful moment for me when I heard what had
happened. I would have given any sum of money that I
possessed, I would gladly have sold every ornament that
I had, if by so doing I could have ensured the poor fellow's
acquittal. Dear Gillian was not nearly so much alarmed
as I was. She was so convinced that Jack's innocence
must be proved. *I* suffered tortures, simply tortures."

"Why did you not insist on Mr. Bevan's making his
knowledge public?" said the priest.

"Insist? why, I did insist by every post," she cried,
"My husband was quite annoyed because I was always
writing letters, but I felt that it was my duty to use all
my influence."

"Then why did you not inform Mr. Bevan that you

would take the matter into your own hands, and tell your husband of all that you knew?"

"Oh, I wrote all that," she answered with a faint smile, "and a great deal more besides. He never answered a word; he was most careful not to commit himself, and I had no proof. I had torn up his letter; he knew that, too, for it has always been my habit to tear up letters. Of course I threatened to explain the whole situation to George, but—well, Mr. Bevan is clever in his way—though it is quite a different sort of cleverness to Jack Cardew's— and I suppose he guessed that I should not do it. You see, my dear husband has so high an opinion of me, and would have been so very surprised that I had not told him before, that his confidence in me might have been quite shaken. One should be very careful how one shakes any one's confidence, and a wife's first duty is to her husband, surely. I know you will agree with me there. Then, I often fancied that I must have misread that sentence. How could I suppose that Jack Cardew's friend would be so wickedly malicious? It seemed inconceivable! It was more likely that my eyes or my memory had played me false."

Again the man's voice broke in with a short, concise question that cut through the web of excuses. "Then what leads you to tell me all this now?"

"Mr. Bevan is getting all the money he can out of me," she said. "Oh, it always comes to a question of money in the end, with that kind of rogue! I ought to have known that! But, you see, I was really rather fond of him once, before I married George, who is so different and the best man I have ever met. George has such a respect for me, but Cyril Bevan has kept all my letters, and if he chooses he can sweep all the happiness of my life away."

There was real tragedy in those last words. Mrs. Clovis

spoke in a low, hard voice that had a ring of despair in it; her face seemed to have grown suddenly old and worn; it was as if she had dropped a mask. To some she would have been pitiable, in spite of, nay, rather by very reason of, her sins, but the confessor's moral indignation was stronger than his humanity. He was so angry that he could not trust himself to comment on the story, and before he had found words she went on.

"Cyril Bevan has no character to lose now, and no one could do anything to him, even if it were actually proved that he could have given evidence that might have made a difference to the verdict. As for Jack, his troubles are all over now, if he would but think so. All the burden and worry falls on me at present, and sometimes it seems more than I can bear. I used to turn to Gillian in any difficulty; she has such a strong nature and no nerves; she was a great stand-by; but I should be afraid to tell her what I have told you."

"I can imagine that you would be afraid to make such a confession to Mr. Cardew's wife."

"From the day she fell in love with Jack she seemed to think that no one's interests ought to weigh a feather-weight against his. She was cold as a girl—not like me in any way—but she is never cold about Jack. She must never, never guess. I must fight through my troubles alone, so far as my family is concerned, but I do feel that it would be a comfort to have the Church's absolution for what I may have done, or perhaps left undone, in the past; and I should like to have your advice, too. When one is very harassed one clings so to religion!"

Mr. Strode stifled an exclamation that would have been stronger had he not remembered his cloth.

"I cannot give you absolution," he said; "the Church I serve does not bless hypocrisy. The only counsel I have is that you should make what tardy reparation you can to the man on whom your culpable silence inflicted such bitter injustice. I can scarcely bear to contemplate the extent of the injury that was done to Mr. Cardew. Good heavens! I myself have added to—— You have much to answer for, much indeed, madam. I wish that, by any means, you could be brought to realise what he, an innocent man, must have suffered. I wish that——"

He pulled himself up with a jerk, and Mrs. Clovis laughed hysterically in a way which struck him as absolutely shameless.

"You were on the point of wishing me hard labour in a convict prison!" she cried. "And I would rather that than that George should know; I would much, much rather die than be lowered in his esteem. Ah, you do not understand, Mr. Strode; you would have to be a woman, and a woman who has been knocked about among horrid people, and who has had no money in her pocket, before you could sympathise with the intense relief a man's respect gives! I will not lose it, whatever happens. I will not——"

"Eva, Eva, where are you, my dear?" shouted a hearty voice on the stairs.

Mr. Strode made no movement; the whole course of events seemed beyond his control. Mrs. Clovis sprang up and ran to the looking-glass, with an instinct born, not of vanity, but of self-defence. She pressed her lace handkerchief to her eyes, and bit her pale lips, and rubbed her cheeks softly with the palms of her hands, and put the curls on her forehead in order. The priest smiled ironically, and his smile helped to restore her self-control.

"We are such vain and frivolous creatures, are we not?" she said, and then flung the door wide open and admitted Mr. Clovis.

"What on earth are you doing in here? Why are not you having tea in the drawing-room?" said he, eyeing the black-robed figure with evident and somewhat comical disfavour.

"Why, dear, because I did not wish to be interrupted," she replied, with that candour which is of all defences the most impregnable. "I was consulting Mr. Strode about something very important." She smiled brightly at her husband, whose momentary ill-humour melted when he met her glance. "I am glad that you have come in in time to join in the consultation! I was half afraid that some tiresome visitor would call. I am just going to show Mr. Strode the design for the new altar cloth that little Enid Haubert drew for me. You must both of you tell me exactly what you think of it. I always put more confidence in a man's taste than in a woman's."

She went to a cupboard and produced the design in question, spreading it out on the floor for both men to see.

"It is to be worked in gold thread on white satin," said she.

Mr. Strode glanced perfunctorily at the pattern of lilies, and then picked up his hat and took an exceedingly curt leave. He felt stifled; he could not stay in that pretty room, or listen to the gentle lady's soft voice a moment longer. Mr. Clovis shook his head with an air of worldly wisdom as the door closed.

"I know those fellows better than you do, Eva," said he. "He wasn't half pleased at my coming in just now! Oh, *you* are all right, my love—don't think I don't know that much! But these petticoated gentry, they ain't quite arch-angels for all their airs. I would be careful if I was you. Don't you be taken in by him."

"But, dear George, Mr. Strode does not even like me," said Mrs. Clovis, truly enough; "and he never looks at a woman—as a woman."

"Don't you believe that!" said the soap-boiler earnestly.

" If he says that, he tells lies, Eva. The man was clearly put out and couldn't meet my eye. You being the sort of woman you are, he would not dare say a word he shouldn't to you, but I don't trust his thoughts. Why couldn't he speak natural to me, eh ? "

"He has a most ungracious manner," said Mrs. Clovis, " but I do not believe that he has ever flirted with any one in his life. He would be simply horrified at your coarse ideas, George."

" Coarse ? bless me, I *am* coarse compared to you, and that is just why I warn you ! " said Mr. Clovis sturdily. " I declare, Eva, sometimes when I think what dangers you must have run when I wasn't by to take care of you, it gives me a cold shudder; it does, indeed. A good woman like you simply doesn't understand ; but as for that great, strapping chap, with his shaven chin and his monkish ways, he ain't so refined and innocent as all that comes to ! He was ashamed, my love, that's what he was. I saw it in his face ! "

CHAPTER XVIII.

"THE HEART KNOWETH HIS OWN BITTERNESS."

"The heart knoweth his own bitterness; and a stranger doth not intermeddle with his joy."

MR. MOLYNEUX was not buried in the garden, as he had desired, but in Kensal Green. Jack would willingly have carried out the old man's orders, but he found that there were obvious and insurmountable difficulties in the way; and, after all, it mattered but little where the worn-out shell was put.

Cardew and Lady Jane and Elizabeth were the only mourners at the grave. Elizabeth wept heartily and naturally. Jane's hands were full of flowers, and her small white face was sad, but its peaceful serenity was hardly disturbed. Jane's eyes had seen sadder things than death. Cardew's imagination was possessed by the memory of that last scene in the garden; his was not the type of mind which naturally inclines to materialism; it seemed to him impossible that the keen, eager soul, that had so scoffed at its ugly old body, should be buried with that which it had always over-ridden and despised. The sight of death brings to some—though not to all people—an inextinguishable belief in immortality. Cardew might have listened unmoved to a hundred pulpit discourses, and have turned away with a shrug of his shoulders and the remark that it was waste of breath to try to prove the unprovable; yet when the earth fell on the coffin of the old man who

279

had loved him, his heart said instinctively, as men's hearts have said again and again at the graveside, "He is not here."

Just before they left the churchyard Jane laid her flowers on the new-made mound. "I would not scatter them on his coffin," she said, "for he was so fond of flowers that he would not have liked them to have been buried, but I do not think he would mind my putting them here in this little pot full of water. He was so very, very kind to me. If one could bring all the kind deeds he has done and heap them on his grave, I think they would be piled up higher than the cemetery wall."

Jack nodded. The thought pleased him. Jane and Elizabeth gave a touch of womanly tenderness to that grim, last ceremony.

"He was a bit lonely, I am afraid," Jack said. "Well, I suppose most people are that; but he did more good than he knew, and I should think that no man had ever led a more innocent life. He was like the chap in the Bible, 'without guile.' He was an uncommonly good friend for a lad, I know that, and if ever any one's eyes were pure enough to see—— " He left the sentence unfinished, and Jane asked no question.

These two whom the old man had loved had spoken his funeral oration in those broken phrases. Both felt more than they expressed, and both were tenderly shy of saying more than the dead man would have approved.

"Shall I see you home?" asked Jack; but Jane shook her head.

"It is impossible not to be sad to-day, and, like Gillian, I prefer to do my sadness alone," she said.

"Gill is not often sad," said Jack, who had sometimes wondered at the friendship and understanding between his brilliant wife and this quakerish little lady.

"Oh, I hope not now," said Lady Jane, smiling.

They left the cemetery together, and parted company at the gate.

"You don't mind going home by yourself?" Jack asked.

"Why, no; I am usually by myself," she answered, with a faint surprise.

Jack stood still by the gate, and watched her small figure till it was lost in the everlasting stream of people. He had a trick, at which Gillian often laughed, of standing still in the street to follow out the thread of his thoughts. It seemed to him unnatural and altogether wrong that any woman should be usually alone; but he was glad that Jane had not needed his escort, for he was anxious to get through all the necessary business that had to be accomplished, and to go home to see "Goliath." He had missed two of Gillian s letters through having forgotten to let her know that he was sleeping in the old house in —— Street instead of Park Lane.

Mr. Molyneux had left everything in an inconceivable muddle. Jack had already spent weary hours in tearing up hoards of old letters, and in sorting a heterogeneous collection of prints, china, books, stones, and pictures. He had found one tiny sealed parcel with, "To be buried with me," written on it. *That* he had slipped into the coffin himself, unopened. He told no one of it, and he had no idea what it contained. Mr. Molyneux had chosen his executor well.

Elizabeth dried her eyes on the way home, and seemed to return to her every-day capable self. Cardew secretly hated having to lay sacrilegious hands on the old man's possessions; but Elizabeth was pleased that she might at last dust and tidy to her heart's content. Her very real and honest affection for her old master did not prevent her from finding speedy and natural comfort in work. She had wept genuine tears over his grave, but now it was time to draw up the blinds.

There was still one drawer full of papers to be looked through. Cardew returned to the uncongenial work with a sigh, while Elizabeth bustled off quite cheerfully to pack up the china. He had, however, hardly begun his task, when she came into the library with a yellow envelope in her hand.

"This has just been forwarded to you from Park Lane, sir," she said.

"*Come at once. Stephen dangerously ill. Dog-cart will meet night train.*"

Cardew read the message, and folded the telegram into a neat square, staring straight before him the while.

"I hope, if I may make so bold, that there is nothing wrong, sir?" said Elizabeth.

Jack was still staring at space, and he made no answer.

When she repeated the question he laughed oddly. "Wrong? The boy is dead, Elizabeth. That's all," he said.

He went to Devonshire that evening, leaving many things undone. What, after all, did anything matter? The absolute certainty that had seized him when he read Gillian's message never loosened its hold on him during the journey. The boy was dead; he was as sure of that fact as if he had seen the little life flicker out before his eyes. He read the *Daily Chronicle* during the journey to Devon, and between the sentences that his eyes followed he repeated to himself that it was over. There was no use in doing or feeling or saying anything, for it was over. He had come to the full stop, that dead wall against which love beats his wings in vain.

"It is impossible to foresee what will be the issue of the blunder which the Government has insisted on making," he read, and added to himself, as he turned the page, "The boy is dead."

In a vague way he was surprised that he did not

suffer more. He had fancied himself uncommonly fond of "Goliath," but he was not conscious of pain. Gill would feel it, he supposed, but as for himself—why, the thing was done.

There was an old gentleman who sat opposite to him and talked to him about politics; after a time the old gentleman got out at a country station, and then Jack was not quite sure whether he had had a companion in the carriage or no. Everything seemed shadowy and uncertain by the side of the one incontrovertible fact that the child was dead. When the train reached the south country it slackened speed, and stopped constantly. A High Church clergyman got in at the third station before Churton Regis; he was discomposed when he saw Jack.

"I rode out to see a sick woman at Simonsbath," he explained. "I was forced to accept a lift in the carrier's cart to Minehead, for my horse met with an accident. I barely caught the train. I did not see that you were in this carriage."

Jack burst into a loud laugh. "Why, man, do you take me for a girl? I am not afraid of being alone with you!"

Mr. Strode, for he it was, frowned and drew himself up. He thought that Mr. Cardew was purposely insulting, and that his ill-timed laughter sounded as if he were hardly sober. He did not guess that his companion was not drunk with wine, but with trouble. Mr. Strode had had a bad time of late. If he had shown small mercy to Mrs. Clovis, he had at least not spared himself. He would willingly have undergone any humiliation that would have helped to restore his self-respect. Now, in spite of the ex-convict's rough words, he plunged into that apology that he had sworn to himself that he would proffer on the first opportunity. He could not prevail on his soul to like Cardew any the better because of the revelation that had been made, but he could and would do his duty; and he did it, with a disregard of anything else that was characteristic of him.

"After all, it is fortunate that we have happened to meet," he said, speaking between his teeth, which was a trick he had when he was excited. "It is fortunate, because there is something that I feel I am bound to say to you. Circumstances have unexpectedly led me to acknowledge that I was utterly and culpably in the wrong in once refusing to believe your assertion of innocence. I do not in the least expect you to believe *me* now; but it is a fact that I would cut off my right hand, if by so doing I could undo the mistake I made, and the discredit that I brought, in your eyes, on the Church I serve!"

Cardew's blue eyes rested on him with an expression that he could not interpret.

"Eh? what? why, here is some one else coming round to me!" cried Jack. "And what on earth do I care what all the people in the world think? What does it matter? I would rather have the little chap! It is a bad bargain— I won't clinch it, I say. They are all coming round and I lose, 'Goliath.' No, no, I'll keep 'Goliath,' and let them all go to——"

Mr. Strode stared, with suddenly arrested attention. He had not expected, he possibly scarcely desired, Cardew to receive his apology kindly: the effort he had made had been for his own honour's sake, not for Jack Cardew's; but this reply shook him out of himself at last. He vaguely recollected having heard that the little boy at the Park was ill, but the news had not greatly impressed him. It dawned on him now that Mr. Cardew was in trouble. He seemed fated to misjudge this man.

Jack put his hand to his forehead and pulled himself together.

"Why, it is the chaplain," he said. "I did not notice who you were. Very sorry I can't attend to what you've got to say just now. We are nearly at the station, and I am in the deuce of a hurry."

The train slackened speed while he was speaking; he sprang out of the carriage before it quite stopped. Mr. Strode followed. A dog-cart was waiting; Jack sprang up and took the reins, leaving the groom behind. Mr. Strode went up to the young fellow—whose conversation he had once unluckily overheard—and asked him what news there was of the child.

Jim, whose face was very red, and whose temper was apparently very short, muttered something that sounded like, " What's that to you ? " but, on the priest's repeating the question sharply and authoritatively, replied "that the little boy was dead, worse luck." Then—"But I lied to him," he added, turning from the priest to the station master, and pointing in the direction in which Jack had driven off. " I couldn't for the life of me shape the words to the master ! Not that it made a bit of difference, for he knew."

The blaze of light made Jack blink as he stepped into the warm hall. Mr. Clovis met him, and grasped his hand with a pressure that was partly nervous.

" I do not know how to tell you, Cardew," he said, " Eva should not have left me to break the news. Women understand how to—to say these sad things, but, upon my soul, I——"

" When did the little chap die ? " said Jack.

" Four o'clock this morning. There ! I have done it very badly."

" There is no use in talking about it—it's done," said Jack heavily. " Where is my wife ? "

" She will not leave the child. Her mother cannot get her away; you must do something with her, Jack; you must exert your authority. She is in the nursery."

Jack went up the stairs slowly and heavily, and opened the nursery door. Gillian sat in the rocking-chair, with the little white body across her knee. Her face was colourless, and her eyes were full of pain. Jack shut the door, walked across the room, and put his hands on her shoulders. When she did not stir he knelt down by her and touched the child's waxen cheek with the back of his hand. Then she spoke.

"It is of no use." (The words were like the echo of his own.) "You can do nothing, and I cannot give my child life again. We have lost this time, Jack, though I tried my hardest. It—it wasn't my fault."

"I know, I know. Poor Gill, poor mother!" he said, under his breath.

Gillian shivered, and her expression changed. "I would not let any one take him out of my arms till you should come."

Jack put his hands under the child's body and lifted it.

"This is not the little chap," he said brokenly. "Why it is not in the very least him, you know, Gill."

"No, but it is all there is left of him," said Gillian, with white lips. She was quite tearless, and her voice sounded hard.

"I don't believe he isn't somewhere," cried Jack.

It was the protest of his nature, sudden and illogical and passionate ; but when Gillian shook her head he felt helpless to comfort her. No words could still that hungry yearning.

"It's part of me that has been torn away—but there is no use in crying out," she said. "Jack, I will be sensible presently, but you won't let them come near me—yet—will you ?" Some one knocked at the door. "Oh, I can't bear them !" Gill cried.

Jack, with an instinct of protection, stood in front of her. He felt that it was not fair that any one should spy on

Gillian in her hour of grief—on Gillian who was so strong as a rule.

"Don't come in. I'll come," he shouted.

He kissed the small peaceful face on his arm, and laid the little figure down on the bed, holding Gillian back when she would have taken it again. She yielded with a hopeless gesture that went to his heart, and sat down with empty hands dropping idly on her lap. Jack went to the door, and found Mrs. Clovis crying in the passage.

"Oh, Jack, it is not right that my dearest Gillian should not allow her own mother to comfort her, and you must not let her sit in there all day and night," the poor lady cried.

"I don't know that there is much comfort," Jack said, in a dull voice. "But you had better let her alone. Gill is sure to be reasonable—she'll come round after a bit."

He shut the door again, and Gillian looked up at him with a wintry smile. "Mammy will think that was brutal of you, my dear," she said. "But I *will* come round if you'll give me time. Just now the pain of it makes me—fierce."

She rocked to and fro in the rocking-chair, and Jack sat down by the table with his head resting on his hands.

That awful anguish of bereaved motherhood was more than he could bear to watch. It might have been better had he taken her in his arms, but he was always shy of endearments.

Presently she stopped rocking, and began to tell him all that there was to tell. She had been dissatisfied, and had at last sent for a London doctor. The child's arm had healed, but he had a pain in his head, and was constantly sick. She had written to Jack, and had expressed her anxiety strongly in her last letter, which had been sent to Park Lane, and had, through some mistake of the servant's, never reached him.

" I wish I had not gone up to London," he said at this point.

" I ought not to have let you go," she answered; " I was anxious even then."

" You told me that you were not," said Jack.

" Yes, I remember that I said I was not. I was a coward. I did not dare own to myself that I was afraid— and he seemed a little better that day. Mammy and the doctor were both sure that he was better, and I did so want to believe them—but it was cowardliness. You ought to be angry with me, Jack! I almost wish you would be. It would hurt in a new place."

" It is all bad enough without that," said Jack. "And, Gill, I couldn't be angry here."

He spoke under his breath, and nodded towards the bed.

" Go on—tell me the rest now." And Gillian told the short, pitiable story very quietly.

The child had been seized with convulsions, and had died just before the London doctor had arrived.

" He could not have prevented it though. No one could have prevented it. Fate is too strong, and it is very cruel," she said.

Jack stood again by the bedside, and a long silence fell on them.

" It is something that we do not understand, Gill," he said at last slowly.

" Ah," cried she, " I do not want to understand any more. My baby who was alive is dead—that is enough for me, Jack."

She shed no tears, and she could not eat that day, nor sleep that night. Jack wondered whether she too would fall ill, but her excellent physical health seemed to stand the strain, and by the next morning she had recovered her composure.

She insisted on attending the funeral, and bore herself very composedly, though she turned white when the little coffin was lowered into its last resting-place.   She defended herself, on her return, from any allusions to her loss.

Jack went for long, solitary walks, and was more silent than ever.   Stern necessity had once taught him to meet his troubles alone.   It is very difficult for any one who has thoroughly learnt that lesson to admit companionship in any crisis of life.   There are veiled mysteries which meet each of us as we go on our way ; strange figures that rise before us in the path, as in the old Jewish story, the "angel of the Lord" barred the path of the prophet.   Jack was by nature susceptible to spiritual impressions, though the monotony and misery of his life had at one time driven him to do his best, or his worst, to kill his soul.   Moreover, he was chivalrous, and the weakness of childhood had laid tight hold on his affections.   Well, the child was dead—but behold, after all, that was *not* "all," for the father's love was still painfully alive.   This mystery filled him with a grief which, after the first shock, was not wholly bitter.   He met it again and again, and perhaps arrived at some sort of conclusion as to its meaning ; at any rate he took the blow that had shattered a good many hopes with some dignity.   It was his interference alone which prevented Gillian from sending away the nurse without a character.

"The doctor hinted that the child had had some fall that we do not know about," Gill said.   "If that is so some one ought to be punished.   I hope that the woman —if she dropped my boy—will never get another place. I hope that she will starve."

Jack frowned thoughtfully.   He remembered that odd dream, but he was too manly to let such stuff carry practical weight.   ·

"We have no actual proof against the nurse," he said,

" and the boy was fond of her. We cannot stain the little chap's memory by cruelty."

"Why should we be the only people to suffer ?" said Gillian ; and Jack made no reply.

Their points of view had diverged widely of late, and both were conscious of that fact ; Jack in a puzzled, vague way, Gillian sorely, and almost angrily.

Gill's seemingly equable temper had always been one of her strong points, but it was distinctly strained at present, and she was easily jarred and irritated.

Poor Mrs. Clovis, who was really grieved at her grandson's death, was shocked at the manner in which Gill accepted the inevitable. Gillian burnt all the letters of condolence that were sent to her—unread, and resisted, nay, laughed at attempts at consolation. Mrs. Clovis, who thoroughly enjoyed expressions of sympathy, could not in the least understand her daughter's shrinking from them. Cardew, on coming into the drawing-room one evening, found her in the lowest possible spirits over Gillian's behaviour.

"Dearest Gillian is so hard," she complained, "and she really does say the most shocking things ! I suppose she loved the poor little darling, but she behaves as if she had no feeling whatever. Dear Mrs. Lacy has just been here ; she is a charming woman, and I thought it might cheer Gillian to talk to her. Mrs. Lacy lost a child last year of whooping-cough, and she was most anxious to meet Gill. She said, so touchingly, that she liked to think that her own dear little one, and Gillian's boy are now at play together in the golden streets of heaven, and oh, Jack, Gillian actually laughed quite loud. 'I have no imagination, Mrs. Lacy,' she said, 'but my baby always wanted to fight with other children, and a golden street sounds to me a dangerous place for a tumble!' Mrs. Lacy was most dreadfully hurt, and so am I ! How can dear Gillian bear to jest on such a subject ? "

"Gillian is too sore to stand sentiment," said Jack, tugging at his moustache. "I don't suppose that she feels particularly merry."

He was not feeling particularly merry himself, but he noticed, as he had noticed once before, that Mrs. Clovis was looking unusually ill and frail and worn, and the observation made his tone gentler than it would otherwise have been.

"I am sorry that we have brought you so much trouble," he said, and the kindliness of his voice seemed to affect his mother-in-law strangely.

"Oh, Jack, if you only knew!" she cried brokenly.

Cardew was just about to leave the room in search of Gillian, but at that he came back to the sofa.

"I say," said he, "I do know that something is wrong."

She looked up at him with frightened, resentful eyes, and he hastened to reassure her. "Do not be alarmed. I am not the sort of brute to harry a woman, whatever my sins may be. I never meant to say anything to you about what I overheard; but I cannot help seeing that you are distressed, and I cannot help guessing that that dirty little beggar who was blackmailing you in the wood may still be at it. You had much better tell Mr. Clovis, but if you can't do that, why, here am I at your service. I think I can promise to tackle Cyril Bevan. Of course, anything you choose to tell me shall go out at the other ear when I have done helping you." He smiled the sudden, frank smile that seemed to some people to throw an odd, unexpected light on his character. "I do not mean to be impertinent," he said, "but somehow I fancy it may be easier to speak of a—mistake to a fellow for whom you have no especial affection, and who has stumbled into pretty bad holes himself, than to speak of it to the man who worships you. But mind, you'll be wiser if you tell him."

Mrs. Clovis listened to this speech with a surprise that was unfeigned. That Cardew should have come to so clear a conclusion, yet never before have said a word about it, that he should show so unexpected a tenderness for her, and so intuitive an understanding, set all her preconceived notions about him upside down. Gillian always said that Jack was soft about women. Perhaps, after all, it was no such great wonder that Gillian was so fond of him. For the space of one moment confession all but trembled on her lips; then she recovered her self-control, and looked back with horror at the wild impulse that had assailed her.

"Why, you ridiculous Jack," she cried lightly, "there really is nothing to make a fuss about!"

"All right," said Jack. "I am going to find Gill now."

"I gave poor Mr. Bevan a—a little assistance for the sake of old times. There was no harm in that, was there? But still I hope you will not mention what you may have happened to hear," she said, putting a detaining hand on his arm.

Jack freed himself a trifle roughly. "I am not a cad!" said he, and thereby unwittingly effaced the excellent impression that he had equally unwittingly made.

He found Gillian in the nursery; she was busy putting away sundry small garments in a cedar-wood box. Her capable, finely formed hands folded and smoothed unfalteringly, and there were no tears in her eyes. The sight of those wee bits of things and of his wife's occupation gave Cardew a lump in his throat. He stood fiddling with a pair of black buttoned shoes, till Gillian, with a touch of sharpness, asked him whether he wanted her for anything, and begged him not to fidget. He put the little shoes down silently, and she repented of her impatience.

"I am just as cross as a bear with a sore head," she cried. "Why don't you say so, Jack? I am getting as full of nerves as mammy!"

"Your mother seems to be very unhappy about you!" said Jack.

"Yes, mammy is more than I can bear just now," said Gillian. "I can put up with anything but condolence—but that is too much for me! You don't know what it is, my dear, for men are exempt from that form of torture. No one would dare to condole with you. Can't we go away from this place, Jack?"

"We will go to-morrow if you like," said he. "But the house is being painted, and I fancied you would hardly be up to the bustle of a hotel."

"Not 'up to it.' Why not? I am perfectly well, and I should like a bustle; it would do me all the good in the world. This quietness is awful, Jack. I can't sit opposite grief with my hands folded. I must do something, or I shall go mad."

The restless misery in her voice was not lost on Jack, but the next minute she laughed. "How shocked poor mammy will be!"

"Of course I know that Mrs. Clovis does not like me, but you and she always seemed to get on. Why is she no comfort to you now?" said he.

"Oh, we get on beautifully in smooth water," said Gill, "but at bottom I am a coarse person with no pretty sentiment about me! Mammy hates coarseness." Some old memory made her smile, though rather bitterly. "She never could understand why I stuck to you, but still we never actually quarrelled, not even when I was most unhappy. Really, you know, mammy and I have some traits in common, and her advice is often excellent. She helped me arrange my first dinner-party splendidly, though she has worried me to distraction lately. I ought, in justice, to remember that."

"I don't know whether you are speaking seriously or not," said Jack, who indeed found Gill's way of being unhappy somewhat hard to grapple with, "but I see you hate that any one should try to comfort you."

Gillian looked at him wistfully. "They talk such nonsense!" she said. "When one is starving one ceases to be amused at the nice, polished little stones that are commonly offered for bread. What is the use of telling me that I shall meet my baby again in heaven? It is so silly! I know that I am not a good woman, Jack, but even *I* would not have my poor little darling remain a baby always in order that I might have the satisfaction of seeing him again. A childhood that never could grow into youth and manhood would not be beautiful; it would be sad and hopeless. I think my boy is dead—altogether dead—but that is better than their ridiculous theories! 'Always a little innocent child in heaven,' they say. My poor Goliath—who was stretching out his little round limbs and laying hold of life with his growing mind every hour of the day—who never stood still for a second, always a child? Indeed, I should hope not."

"You don't believe it, so why mind what foolishness they talk?" said Jack.

"Oh, because——" she cried, and then swallowed something that seemed to rise in her throat and dropped the subject.

Because she was a woman, and her whole soul, and her body, too, were crying out for her child. Because she wanted him, though her reason told her that she should never see or feel him again.

"Jack, dear, I am ashamed of being such a fool," she said after a pause, "but the fact is I can't trust myself to be civil just at present. Acquaintances are not nearly so trying as near relatives on these occasions, because they do not 'console' one. Let us go to-morrow, and I will promise to be myself again!"

"We will," said Jack.

He did not venture on any attempts at consolation after that bitter little comment of hers, though he was dumbly sorry for Gill. It was a pity! for he could have accomplished what no one else could. One word or touch of his might have loosed the tears that would not flow, and to have broken down would have done Gillian good. Comfort is no matter of words, and reason is singularly incompetent in the place where fierce misery reigns ; but Jack had had but little experience in women, and had not yet learned that it does not in the least matter what a man says, so long as he is the right person to say it.

Part III.

297

CHAPTER XIX

ANOTHER FAITHFUL FAILURE.

"Give him a march with his old bones; there, out of the glorious
sun-coloured earth, out of the clay and the dust and the ecstasy—
there goes another Faithful Failure."

SIR EDWARD BEVAN sat resting from his labours
in the great hall at Highfields. He had been busily
engaged in dusting his ancestors, whose long-chinned,
narrow faces looked down on him from the walls; a large
silk handkerchief was spread over his knees.

Sir Edward had a fancy for doing odd jobs with his
own hands. An irritable restlessness was perhaps partly
answerable for these freaks; but he always declared and
believed that he did such things in order to set an example
of economy to his servants. It was a form of economy
that did not conduce to popularity. After his death Sir
Edward was recognised as a public benefactor, and the
Spartan simplicity of his life received some meed of
approbation, but during his lifetime his virtues wore a
peculiarly irritating garb.

Sir Edward sat in a high-backed oak chair by the
carved stone mantelpiece. He had climbed the ladder in
order to dust his namesake, who had ridden by Cromwell
at Marston Moor and had prayed with the men of his
own household before the storming of Dartmouth, and had
finally been killed in battle. Sudden death was a fate

which had overtaken a large proportion of Bevans. It was said, indeed, that no firstborn son of the elder line ever died in his bed.

Sir Edward thought of that superstition while he smoothed and folded the silk handkerchief. He thought of it and sighed enviously. To have been killed while fighting the Lord's battles was a death that any man might count most fortunate; but as for him, his lines had fallen in evil and inglorious times! Moreover, he was ashamed because of the mean scamp who, alas! called him father.

His meditations had just reached this melancholy point—at which they invariably arrived, no matter what started them—when an imperious ring at the bell surprised him.

"I suppose I am to say 'not at home,' sir?" asked the old butler, with a disgusted glance at the ladder and the silk handkerchief.

Sir Edward had been about to deny himself to the intruder, but the question rubbed him the wrong way.

"You will do nothing of the sort," he said. "I do not engage you to suppose or tell lies, but to open the hall door for me."

So it came about that the visitor was admitted and that she stepped into the dreary hall, where both the Sir Edwards seemed to be regarding her beauty with the gravest suspicion.

She was quite young, and her cheeks were glowing and her eyes shining. She wore a dark-green fur-lined cloak that set off her pure and brilliant colour as green leaves set off the petals of a pink flower. When she caught sight of Sir Edward, she walked straight up to him without more ado.

The old man stood up to receive her, but did not put out his hand. "I cannot remember that I have had the honour of meeting you before. May I ask what is your business with me?" he said.

"Don't you remember me, Sir Edward? We met last at Draycott Court," said the girl.

Her heart was beating fast, but excitement always became her; and, fortunately for her, she was aware of that fact, and the knowledge inspired her with a kind of desperate courage. She knew that her beauty always fought for her.

At the mention of Draycott Court Sir Edward *did* remember her. "To be sure, to be sure. You are Miss Tyrell," said he.

"No, I am not not Miss Tyrell," said Nina.

Something seemed to catch at her breath, and she pressed both hands to her heart, with a gesture that was quite natural and unstudied. She was impatient with her own folly; she was in the habit of fancying herself a bolder and worse woman than she actually was.

"You are nervous," said the old man, not unkindly. "Sit down, and take your time."

"No, no, I hate waiting! I'll tell you at once—that's what I have come for. I am not Miss Tyrell any longer; Sir Edward, I am Nina Bevan—I am your son's wife."

She expected an outburst, perhaps of astonishment, perhaps of rage. Cyril frequently made fun of the "governor's abominable temper," and Nina, who had unfortunately found it impossible to respect her own father, was unprepared to respect her husband's. She was ready to cajole or to defy. She had rehearsed the interview many times. It had always been dramatic in rehearsal, and she had always played the leading part. It was, as usual, the unexpected that occurred.

In small matters Sir Edward Bevan was often petulant and ludicrous; his son, being a person of small soul and quick humour, had seen the ridiculous side of him; but where the question was of large issues the old knight's absolute sincerity rang true and gave him dignity.

"My son's wife!" he repeated gravely. Then his querulous, deeply-lined face shone with an expression of deepest pity.

"You poor girl! Now God help you!" he said. "For I fear that if you are Cyril's wife you have fallen into sore straits."

Nina stood and stared at him, with just such a look as a very naughty child may wear who in the midst of her naughtiness is seized with misgivings. The green fur cloak slipped from her shoulders to the ground. She blushed, and stooped blindly to lift it from the floor. Shame and a desire to run away suddenly possessed her.

Sir Edward took the cloak and hung it over the back of the chair which he offered her. He had no idea of the impression he had made on this little reprobate. Sir Edward was always eager to convert sinners, but he would have been surprised had he known that he had never before so nearly realised his ambition. No thought of preaching was in his mind; he was simply filled with horror because so young a girl had been beguiled into matrimony with such a man as Cyril.

"Sit down and tell me whether my son sent you here," said he.

"Oh no, I just came on my own account," she answered, and the reply was partly true and partly false.

This move had been of Nina's devising, but she and Cyril had thoroughly discussed it. A bold strategy always commended itself to this girl, who had certainly a spice of the born adventuress in her.

"The governor is so stingy that he *may* refuse to have anything to do with you," Cyril had remarked. "If that happens you must just wire to me and join me in London. On the other hand, it is possible that he may look on you as a brand to be saved from burning; and in that case you might come round him and eventually patch up a peace

between us. I am tired of being tabooed. I'm getting
old, Nina ! You may truly assure my father that my mouth
waters for a slice of fatted calf—but he's a precious long
time about killing and cooking it !"

Nina thought of that conversation while she sat in the
high-backed chair, and endeavoured to collect her wits.
She was fond of Cyril, and, strange as such a fact may
appear, it was not unaccountable, for the slippery, elderly
scamp had very companionable qualities. She had been
ready to play her husband's game and out-general the
enemy. She was puzzled by the moral shock that Cyril's
father had given her ; she made an effort to overcome it.

"We were married in Liverpool, where I was staying
with a great-aunt, who is very old and childish. We have
been married six months. Would you like to look at
this ? " she said.

She held out a copy of the marriage certificate.

The old knight put on his spectacles and read the
document aloud, very slowly and carefully. His eyesight
was beginning to fail, and he interrupted himself to carp
at the faintness of the ink and to rub his glasses. Nina
fought with an almost hysterical desire to snatch the paper
from his hand and read it for him.

The situation tried her nerves more than she fancied
that it would, though it was not, after all, in the least
degree melodramatic.

Sir Edward, having at last finished reading, returned
the document to her with a stiff little bow, and pushed
his spectacles on to his forehead.

"It is probably correct," he said. "I conclude that you
married without your father's consent ? Obedience to the
fifth commandment has gone out of fashion."

A very bitter expression crossed Nina's face.

"I did not ask my father's consent, and I believe that
he does not wish to have anything more to do with me."

"That's bad, very bad," said Sir Edward. "You were exceedingly wrong. You have given great provocation; yet children have done worse things and been forgiven."

He sighed so heavily that the sigh was almost a groan. "If that were all——" he muttered. Ah, if he could but wake to find that bad record a dream, and that the extent of his child's misdoings had been a rash marriage, how gladly *he* could have forgiven!

"But he is without conscience and without natural affection. A nature thoroughly depraved," he said sternly.

Nina, full of her own schemes, did not understand. "I thought it best to come straight to you," she said appealingly, and at that the man's heart smote him.

If Cyril had no conscience, Sir Edward had a singularly exacting one, and his sense of responsibility was keen and vigorous. This girl had flung herself on his hands because—to his bitter grief—he was Cyril's father. He accepted the situation.

"I shall go to see Captain Tyrell," he said. "I will do what I can to appease his just anger. In the meantime you must remain here."

"There is no use in your going to see my father," said Nina calmly, "and his anger is not just. My father"—she hesitated a moment, for a certain pathetic pride had always hitherto restrained her from making family revelations—"has never had any fatherly feeling for me! He grossly ill-treated me when I was a small girl, but Polly—who is now my step-mother—protected me. Polly will tell you some very odd stories if you go to my home and ask her whether I have spoken the truth. Perhaps you will understand then why it is that *I* am not so shocked at poor Cyril. Cyril is kind, anyhow! I don't think he would try to hurt a child. The fifth commandment sounds like a satire to me! But I hope you won't let all Churton Regis know about what you may hear from Polly ! I don't mind its bad opinion, but I *won't* have its pity."

She hid her face against the back of the chair in a way that was almost childish.

"Oh ! don't look at me like *that*," she cried. "I never guessed that you would be so horribly shocked ! I fancied that you were never sorry for people."

Sir Edward opened his lips to speak, but restrained himself and turned away from her.

No good man—and he *was* good—could have heard such words and not burnt with righteous indignation against Nina's father; but he was also suspicious, and he seldom trusted either his own or other people's impulses. It was always possible that the young woman might be telling lies.

He took up his hat and stick and put on his coat. Was this thing true ? Well, he would know whether she spoke truth before the sun set.

Sir Edward went out of the house without another word to the distressed lady who had flung herself on his protection. He was not going to commit himself, or to take sides against parental authority without just cause ; yet on his plain face there was a look such as his ancestor might have worn when he was going to fight the "curled, blaspheming courtiers" of the Stewarts. It was a look that boded the captain no good.

"If the man is what she describes, it is time that some one should tell him that he is a blackguard," Sir Edward said to himself, and he forgot that his years numbered nigh on eighty. It was a fine forgetfulness, which I think must have counted in his favour when the last hours of strenuous, if somewhat injudicious, service were accomplished and his sword was delivered to the Master, who judges not as men judge.

As for Nina, she was left to that which she most dreaded

—to solitary reflection. She got off the high-backed chair after a time, for it wearied her and made her back ache. She spread her cloak—it was a present of Gillian's—on the stone floor and sat down on it, nestling close to the fire for warmth. The hall was cold, for Sir Edward was chary of coal. She looked very pretty and pathetic as she sat all alone in that great gloomy place, yet she did not conceal from herself that she was in reality no high-minded heroine. An odd touch of self-scorn often coloured Nina's meditations.

She presently pulled a pencil and a pocket-book out of her pocket and began to scribble a letter to her fellow-conspirator. How amused Cyril would be! Cyril always saw the funny side of everything! On the whole she fancied that she had been successful, though she had felt much more uncomfortable than she had expected to feel— and Sir Edward had not been funny!

Nina's pencil paused in the middle of a sentence, and the tears rushed into her eyes. " I'm a bad sort—I always was—but I will never laugh at Cyril's father again. Never, so long as I live! " she promised herself.

At that moment the butler came into the hall and looked curiously at her. " Sir Edward said you was going to wait here till he came back, miss, and that that wouldn't be for some hours," said Miller. " Shall I fetch you a cup of tea ? "

Miller would have been more than human had he not experienced some curiosity about this sudden appearance of Miss Tyrell; but he was kind as well as inquisitive. He had a wife and daughters of his own, and he was convinced that whatever misfortunes the poor lady was in, a cup of tea could not come amiss.

Nina accepted the suggestion with gratitude, and Miller took her into the library where Cyril had had his last interview with his father. There was a picture of Cyril on the wall. It represented him as a very angelic little boy, with long golden curls, and a sweet smile, and a pink-and-white complexion.

"That was Mr. Cyril at the age of seven, miss," said Miller; "I remember when it was taken."

He brought in the tray with bread and butter and tea, and he dragged Sir Edward's writing-table up to the fireplace and lit the fire. It was strange to see this beautiful lady sitting in Sir Edward's leathern arm-chair. Miller could not but wonder what would come of it.

Nina's spirits began to revive. Anything was better than waiting alone. She suddenly confided in Miller. "*I* am Mr. Cyril's wife," said she, and this time she enjoyed the sensation that the announcement caused.

The old butler, who perhaps knew more about the ways of gentlefolk than did Nina, was indeed aware that it was very odd of her to take him into her confidence, and as for the startling news, he was perhaps not *quite* so surprised as he appeared—he had gathered something from his master's face—but he was a good old fellow and he was thankful that he had been wise enough to bring up the tray with his own hands.

The family honour was safe with him, but the footman might have presumed on the lady's incautiousness. For the rest, Miller considered that poor Mr. Cyril might have done worse than this.

"He was always an affable gentleman, miss—ma'am, I should say," Miller said, when he had regained his breath, "and he was clever with dumb animals. He sat up the whole of one night with an old bull-dog that was dying. I always said after that that Mr. Cyril had a deal of kindness in him, though he had been so unfortunate,"

"Oh, tell me some more nice things that he did," cried Nina, with unconscious pathos.

She had heard so many bad things that it pleased her to hear some good of Cyril.

Miller was pleased, too. Miller did not think of Mr. Cyril with the horrified loathing with which most decent men who knew his story regarded him. Perhaps the butler judged the family he had served from boyhood by a different standard to that which is applied to ordinary mortals; or perhaps the elderly scamp was still in his eyes but a *young* gentleman after all. He searched his memory diligently for some more creditable tales.

"He once brought back a prize; I think it was for proficiency in arithmetic, ma'am. Sir Edward did not appear to take any pleasure in it, and I can call to mind that Master Cyril was a bit disappointed. He gave the prize to me—I was under footman then, and I was fond of books—and though I could not read it, seeing it was in a foreign tongue, I took it very kindly of Master Cyril. I have it by me still, and the binding is beautiful!"

That was the extent of Miller's evidence in Master Cyril's favour. Perhaps it hardly counted for much! Cyril had been kind to animals and quite ready to give away that which cost him nothing. Nina, however, made the very most of it.

"Thank you, Miller, I have enjoyed hearing all that," she said. "What you have told me quite proves how harshly people judge him. There has never been any one to put things in a right light."

"No, ma'am, nor there has, ma'am," said old Miller with comfortable acquiescence. "And Mr. Cyril had a heavy cold on him last time he come; it did seem a pity he couldn't have stayed the night peaceful and natural! But, as you say, ma'am, there never *was* no one here to put things in the right light."

"If only there had been he might have been just as good as other people," said Nina wistfully.

Mr. Bevan would certainly have been amused could he have heard that conversation! Perhaps he would have been touched. No one is utterly bad, and, after a fashion of his own, he was fond of Nina; indeed, he was actually fond enough of her to put himself to some inconvenience for her sake. At the very moment when she was standing up for him in his father's house he was on his way to Devonshire.

Cyril had a good deal of confidence in Nina's powers of fascination; but he had also great belief in Sir Edward's capability for being disagreeable. The possibility that Nina might be turned away from the door at Highfields, or that his father might take it on himself to lecture her, made Nina's husband distinctly uncomfortable. Cyril was seldom angry, and he was still seldomer uncomfortable on some one else's behalf. The sensation greatly surprised him!

He had told Nina to wire to him should her scheme fail; yet, on consideration, he felt that he should prefer to be at hand to help her. Hence his sudden journey. It may safely be averred that he had never before taken so much trouble for an unselfish motive; but the miracles that love works are happily unlimited. Like the sun, it shines on the just and the unjust, and brings manifestations of life out of ugly places.

Mr. Bevan travelled in a first-class carriage; for, however hard up he might be, he usually managed to secure to himself creature comforts. The little middle-aged gentleman in the fur-lined coat was treated with respect by the guards and porters. In spite of his insignificant height he could look as if he were "Somebody," and his pleasant manner won for him an easy popularity. Cyril had more than one manner; he was a born actor, and could play almost any *rôle* he chose, but the grand gentleman pose came quite naturally to him. Despite all his shady and disreputable experiences he cherished the belief that he should one day turn over a new leaf and be the master of Highfields and a county magnate.

He owed his father a double grudge for having lived too long and for trying to baulk him of his reformation.

It was nine o'clock when the train reached Churton Regis. Cyril strolled, in a leisurely manner, towards Captain Tyrell's house. Polly would tell him the news, and he should hear from her whether Nina had really had the audacity to carry out her plan.

"She has 'cheek' enough for anything," he said to himself with a smile.

It was lucky that the evening was dark. Even in this apparently peaceful corner of England there were unpleasant people who would dun him if they got the chance. He limped slightly, and his lameness annoyed him; he put that, too, to his father's account. He had been very ill with rheumatic fever after his last interview with Sir Edward. He had got wet through and through on his way to the inn, and during his illness he had been entirely dependent on the kindness of the inn-keeper, to whom he, at present, owed money.

Sir Edward would not pay a penny of the bill! Sir Edward was still trying to force his son to consent to the cutting off of the entail.

It was a curious fact that that son, who had never before showed any interest in the old place, or any tenacity of purpose, should now evince an obstinacy that equalled his father's. It perhaps proved that Cyril was, after all, no changeling; he had, at any rate, one family characteristic!

"It is only a question of holding out; but ' holding out ' is deucedly unpleasant," Cyril said to himself. "There's a terrible amount of vitality in the old man. I believe his health's a good deal better than mine, in spite of his liver! He'll never give up the ghost while he can possibly hang on to it. Hullo! what's that?"

He had just reached the cross-roads. To the right lay the road that led to Captain Tyrell's house, to the left the way to Draycott, and straight ahead was the village of Churton Regis. A sign-post pointed in each direction; under the sign-post Cyril saw something—a something that appeared monstrous and grotesque in the half-light. He was near-sighted, and the thing seemed like a black, shapeless body with a man's head protruding from its middle. When he got close up to it, he saw that a horse had fallen on its rider and had broken its knees; it turned agonised eyes to him; it was injured past recovery. Cyril was sorry for the creature; he was always much more pitiful to animal than he was to human pain.

He lit a match in order that he might see whether the rider were alive, but his first thought had been for the horse.

"You must be a fool, or you must have been drunk, to have let the poor beast down on this hill," he said coolly. But he dropped the match with an exclamation of dismay when the light fell on the dead man's face.

He scrambled hastily to his feet and shouted lustily, then set off at full speed for the village. He was not a good runner, he was inclined, like Hamlet, to be "fat and scant of breath," but he ran with all his might. Horror pursued him—sheer, unreasoning horror. It was Sir Edward who lay at the cross-roads.

Had Cyril Bevan received the news of the old man's death by letter he would not even have pretended grief. All the world knew that he and his father had been at daggers drawn for years. He had openly wished Sir Edward dead time and again. He did not grieve now, but he shuddered.

It was appalling! That grim, silent meeting had been too much for his nerves.

Cyril, who had been so hopelessly unimpressionable, who had been amused by all the knight's sermons, was actually impressed at last!

CHAPTER XX.

"LIFE'S NOT LONG ENOUGH FOR HONEST MEN TO QUARREL IN."

LONG mournings are out of fashion at present, but the shortness of Mrs. Cardew's retirement rather scandalised even the set in which she lived.

Gillian was absolutely greedy for enjoyment during the winter that followed the child's death. She was livelier than ever, though her high spirits were less catching than they had been, and the healthiness of mind and body that had characterised her seemed lacking.

Gillian had always been energetic. She had liked to be "doing," because she was a capable woman to whom action was joy. An underlying originality and breadth of thought had been as salt in the baking of the pies into which she had dipped her clever fingers. A kindliness, often unconscious, but growing out of her tenderness for her child, had sweetened and inspired much of her work.

The kindliness was missing when Gillian emerged from her seclusion, her sallies inclined to be more caustic than merry; and while her reputation for brilliancy and the multitude of her engagements grew, her popularity decreased.

Cardew saw little of his wife during that winter. He too was fully occupied, and their ways diverged more widely than ever. He was uneasy about Gillian, but it seemed that there was neither time nor opportunity to express sympathy. She had buried her grief fathoms deep, and apparently feared nothing so much as its resurrection.

One morning, when he came down to breakfast, he found Gillian sighing over a long and highly perfumed letter.

" Mammy's letters are so terribly voluminous," she said, " and her pretty pointed handwriting is not so legible as it appears at first sight. I wish she would not write to me so often."

Jack laughed. " You are the only woman I know who does not like letters, Gill ! "

" I don't like mammy's—they bore me, because they are full of her feelings," said Gillian. " Do you want to hear the news ? Mr. Clovis wishes to send George to school, but mammy 'cannot but fear that her dearest boy's peculiarly original character will not be properly under-stood at Eton.' Dear me ! what fools mothers are ! There are two sheets on the Eton question. Let's see what else she says ? Mr. Clovis is 'foolishly anxious about her health, and wants her to consult a London doctor '— I suppose that I had better invite them to our house !— 'A most shocking event occurred yesterday. Sir Edward Bevan was picked up at the cross-roads. His horse had fallen on him, and he was '—oh, Jack, but this *is* news—'he was quite dead, when his son, who was walking from the station, discovered him !'"

Jack looked considerably startled. " Dead ! " he repeated blankly. Then after a pause, " Poor old chap ! I wish I had behaved better to him ! "

" It is for Mr. Bevan to say that, not *you*, Jack; but probably Mr. Bevan has no qualms ! Why, here is more startling intelligence. ' You will be surprised to learn that it has transpired that Cyril Bevan was privately married to Nina Tyrell some months ago.' Good gracious ! that was a bold stroke on Nina's part ! ' So far as any one knows at present Sir Edward has left no will.' If there is no will the money as well as the estate will fall to his son, won't it? Ninon is lucky!"

Jack looked up with an expression of disgust. "Lucky? It's horrible!" he said. "If that girl had been my daughter I'd rather have strangled her with my own hands than have seen her the wife of that little brute."

"But you know you've got some very high-flown notions about women, dear!" said Gillian. "Nina does not expect too much of Mr. Bevan, and, really, he is a very good-tempered person. He won't beat her, or bully her. Probably he'll be respectable now that he has come in for the property you despised. I daresay they'll get on as well as most couples. Every one will eventually call on Nina. You see if they don't!"

Jack reddened. "I'm not over-nice," he said; "I'm the last fellow in the world who has any right to be Pharisaical, but I won't have *you* go inside Cyril Bevan's house. You don't understand——"

Gillian laughed, a hard little laugh. "My dear Jack, one would fancy I was seventeen!" she said. "That's how Mr. Cloves talks to mammy! Mammy thoroughly enjoys it, but *I* don't go in for such immaculate innocence. I quite understood what you once told me, so did Nina —and this is the result."

Jack got up quickly. He had a strong dislike to the discussion and to Gillian's tone. When he got to the door he turned round.

"I say, Gill, I wish you wouldn't talk in that sort of way; women are not meant to!" he said.

Gillian laughed again, more bitterly than ever, but her laughter ceased abruptly when the door closed. His rebuke touched her because she loved him, but the pain that she tried to stifle was making her reckless. Sorrow and loss seem to leave some natures unchanged, but Gillian took them hard.

" Perhaps they were not meant to be so unhappy. I am sure our affections have got too largely developed ! " she said to herself. " I wonder whether Nina will be happy ? She can't possibly care for Mr. Bevan much. Will she care for her babies if she has any ? Poor Ninon ! I hoped I had succeeded in saving her from that marriage. I *did* save her for a time, but in the end I have failed." Her face grew thoughtful. " That seems to be my usual fate. I get what I want, but the upshot is failure ! "

The sense of failure was heavy on Jack too during the whole of that foggy winter's day. Some few things that he had striven hard to do he had done ; but he was too sad to feel the satisfaction that he ought to have felt in an accomplished task.

That very morning " Henderson's boy " took passage for Australia, and started on what Cardew hoped would be a new life. Jack had perseveringly and doggedly insisted on that lad's reclamation. He had been absolutely determined to save him. He had struggled as he would have struggled for his own son. He had taken no oath, but he had held himself bound to do his utmost. He considered himself in debt to poor Henderson's ghost. Jack thought at times that if ever Henderson and he were to meet in that next world (where one cannot but hope that a good many crooked things may be made straight) then the man he had killed might, after all, be not unwilling to shake hands with him. Henderson had been a straightforward, manly fellow—perhaps he would recognise that the convict had done his best for those children.

The fact of becoming a father had increased Jack's sense of responsibility ; it had, as he himself was dimly aware, made another man of him.

The boy was dead ; but Jack could never again be as if " Goliath " had not been born.

" God sends to every man a prophet in his own tongue."

Cardew held most sermons in abomination, but nevertheless a stammering little tongue, that had learnt but few
words, had taught him a new name for that strong eternal
power which we call as best we can—knowing always
that behind and beyond our feeble best is yet a better.
To find a new name for one's Deity is to find a new way
of looking at the whole of life. It is a discovery that
reaches backwards and forwards and causes a good deal
of revision. It is a discovery that is apt to seal a man's
lips—at least for a time.

Later in the day Cardew intended to make his way to
the Middlesex Buildings. He had long ago fulfilled his
promise to "look Geoff up." He was fond of Geoff now,
and he liked to sit rather silently in that queer attic and
listen to the brother and sister's chatter.

Geoff was quite at home with Cardew, but Enid was
sometimes oppressed by memories. The young genius
who had been "Bertie's friend" had appeared to be not
so *very* much her senior ; but this grave, undemonstrative
man, who looked ten years older than his actual age,
seemed to belong to another generation, to be old enough
to be her father. Moreover, though Enid liked and
admired the Cardews—would, indeed, have gone through
fire and water for them, had there been a chance of so
showing her gratitude—she could never forget that she
had once begged of Jack. It had been for Geoff's sake,
but it was not the less a painful recollection.

The Hauberts had been singularly fortunate of late.
Enid's designs for wall-papers were becoming quite fashionable, and every one of the sketches she had made in
Devonshire had been sold. They were now preparing
to move into better quarters, where Enid would have a
studio and Geoffrey a room in which there should be
space for a big table with drawers for his microscopic
specimens. Geoff had lately had professional lessons in

the art of mounting; but he had needed but little teaching. His fingers were as delicate in touch as it is possible for fingers to be, and he was keenly interested in his work. Rather to Enid's amused surprise, he had lately found a patron and a kindred spirit in Mr. Strode.

Geoff was at present busy in mounting specimens for Mr. Strode's microscope, and the attic was sweet with flowers that had been grown in the priest's hot-house. It was *too* sweet, Enid declared. The scent made her head ache; and she cried impatiently that the poor things looked out of place in a garret.

There must certainly have been something especially depressing in the air, for even Enid was decidedly cross. After having vainly endeavoured to paint in a room reeking with fog and hot with gas she flung down her palette and brushes in despair and went out into the raw atmosphere of the streets.

Enid was a born Londoner, and fog did not, as a rule, dismay her, but this was certainly an exceptionally thick one. When she first ventured into it it was yellow, and the gaunt pile of the Middlesex Buildings could be dimly seen like a ghost from the other side of the road. Quite suddenly the yellow turned to a deep orange, and the Buildings entirely disappeared. A dog ran against Enid's knees and she was rather frightened, not because she feared dogs, but because she could not *see* it! She turned round intending to go home; she turned twice and then lost her bearings. She fancied she had only turned once, and that she was walking in the opposite direction.

She gave a boy, who carried a torch, a penny, in order that he might escort her over the crossing. The boy shouted lustily, and she held on to his arm, thinking the while that this adventure would amuse Geoff in the re-counting. She dismissed the boy when he had pioneered her across.

"The street seems broader than usual, but of course that must be the effect of the darkness. Here is your penny. I know that I must be close to the Middlesex Buildings now," she said.

The boy shouted something in reply, but the sound of his voice was muffled. He grabbed at the penny and was swallowed up by the fog. Enid laughed at the hobgoblinish effect of the sudden disappearance of torch-bearer and torch; then she turned to look for the buildings, and behold, they too had vanished.

Her hand struck against some area railings—she was in a street of squalid private houses, though she could not discern so much as that—and she held tight on to them and groped her way along, with her face still set in the wrong direction.

It seemed to her that she walked for hours, that she became quite dazed with fatigue and hunger, that she was in a bad dream, and that nothing about her was real. Sometimes she heard shouts, and once or twice torches flashed by her. Once a very thin, dirty hand caught her dress and she shrieked and tore her skirt away and ran a few steps—then she went on and on and on.

As a matter of sober fact, but ten minutes elapsed between the moment when she parted with the boy at the crossing and the moment when she met a friend, but to the end of her days Enid could never believe that! The fog scare had caught her, and fear, like ecstasy, effaces time.

If she momentarily lost her hold on the rails she was in terror, and would creep back a step or two to find them again. At last her trembling fingers closed on some one else's fingers, and the some one said, " I beg your pardon," curtly, but in the unmistakable accents of a gentleman.

"Oh, can you tell me where I am?" cried Enid.

Something that was familiar to her in the man's voice

gave her confidence, but caused her no surprise. In a bad
dream one is never surprised.

"I believe that we are in the neighbourhood of King's
Cross," said the voice.

" But I've wandered for miles, and I started from that
neighbourhood ! " Enid cried.

She peered up anxiously at the stranger, trying in a
dazed way to remember who his voice and manner
reminded her of. He was tall and she could not distinguish his features till he stooped to look at her. Then
the little silver cross that he wore caught her eye, and she
clutched him with both hands and gasped with relief.

"You are Mr. Strode," she said. "Oh, I am so glad to
see any one I know, because I have quite lost my way and
Geoff will be getting dreadfully alarmed, for I've been out
for hours and hours. But I *can't* be near King's Cross
still."

Almost while she spoke the fog changed colour and
became a shade lighter. The outline of shabby, dingy
houses was just visible, and the twinkle of a gas jet
glimmered in a window a few yards farther on.

"I am absolutely convinced that we *are* near King's
Cross," said the priest ; "I think that we are in a side
street leading oft the Pentonville Road. It's not a very
sweet part for you to be alone in"—an odour of rags and
poverty assailed his nostrils as he spoke. "Come, Miss
Haubert, where were you going ?"

" I was trying to go home," said Enid meekly ; " the
Middlesex Buildings are quite close to the Pentonville
Road, but I fancied that I was very far away. I don't mind
what street I am in so long as I know where it is," she
added confusedly. " I mean I'm not a bit afraid of being
in a poor street—I'm poor myself, no one could expect to
get anything from me ! I was frightened because I felt
lost and couldn't see my own hands, and thought I should

never get back to Geoff.   But it's better now—I can almost distinguish your face !"

She smiled, though it was not yet light enough for any one to see *that*, Mr. Strode struck a match on the friendly railing, and made a futile attempt to look at his watch.

"I do not believe that it is at all late in the afternoon," he said.   "In a fog people frequently imagine that they have wandered for a long time.   I will see you to your own door if you will allow me."

Enid made a funny little grimace and then accepted his offer.   She was piqued that he should fancy she had "imagined things"; but on the other hand the fog scare had shaken her nerve, and her pride was not strong enough to support her alone.   That bad dream still hovered too near !

"If it is not troubling you too much," she said ; "but you were on your way to the station, were you not ?"

"Oh, my parish can survive without me," he said, with a laugh that was not intended to be sad, but which at once awakened Enid's quick and sympathetic attention.   "Take hold of my arm, please, and keep close.   We will make for the main road ; the shops there will give more light. Yes, I shall miss my train, but that does not matter.   I can put up at an hotel for to-night.   I have resigned the living of Churton Regis.   I came to town to-day to see an old college friend who is working in the East End.   He is over-taxed, and I have offered to give him a hand.   I am not—so far as money goes—a poor man ; I can afford the luxury of giving my work—such as it is.   But I am bound to own that the gift is of no great value.   Hitherto I have been worse than useless."

It was still so dark, and Enid was so much shorter than her companion, that she could not actually *see* the expression of his face when he had pronounced that sentence on himself.   Yet she knew how his lips closed and tightened.

Under ordinary circumstances he would not have spoken
of his own affairs to her.

" Don't you think that you are rather hard on—on Mr.
Strode ? " she ventured in a low voice.

" On whom ?   I don't catch your meaning."

" On yourself."

" Certainly not.   There is never room for doubt about
plain facts," he answered sternly.   " A man does his work
well or he does it ill.   *I* have done ill, or have made
culpable mistakes.   Ah ! now we have hit on the Pentonville Road.   Do you know at which end of the street stand
the buildings ? "

" Oh yes—even I can tell you that," Enid cried, laughing.
" Will you come in with me and see Geoffrey ?   How long
poor Geoff must have been waiting ! "

She repeated the invitation some minutes later when
they stood in the courtyard of the buildings.   She had, at
first, hoped that Mr. Strode would decline, for she was
longing to recount her adventures at ease ; but when she
saw his face, by the light of the gas jet that lit the public
entry, its troubled weariness gave her a positive ache.
Any suffering always touched the little artist; her vivid
imagination realised it at once.

" Oh, *do* come in," she cried impulsively.

" Thanks ; but I must be going on," said the priest, and
then some impulse made him for once change his mind.
" Yet, after all, I do not believe that there is a ' must,' for
no one waits for me," he said, and followed her up the long,
dreary flights of stone steps.

Up and up and up they went, only pausing when their
ascent was impeded by families of babies who made the
public stairs their playground.   The children grinned at
Enid and stared at the priest.   They did not stare medi-
tatively like Devonshire children, but inquisitively and
cheerfully ; they hardly troubled themselves to move, but

glanced pertly up from between his feet, just as the London
sparrow glances up at the passer-by.   Much has been
written about the sadness of childhood in our great and
beloved city, but our street urchins are not always doleful
—not even when they are at their dirtiest!

"Our room is a long way up," said Enid apologetically,
"and we are very 'muddly' to-day, because we are just
about to move into a new home.   I hope you do not mind
a muddle.   We mind it too little!   We are an untidy
family."

Mr. Strode smiled stiffly, as people smile whose muscles
are unaccustomed to the exercise.   He had found life no
joke of late.

To a man of the priest's temperament nothing perhaps is
more strange and painful than uncertainty.   Mr. Strode
seldom debated long about anything; yet during the last
month he had been troubled by two questions.

On finding it beyond his power to persuade or to coerce
Mrs. Clovis to a full confession ought he to betray her
confidence and to make public what she had told him?
Seeing that the woman, who had once said to him, "You
are no priest by nature," was proved right, and being convinced that he was a bad and incompetent shepherd, ought
he to resign his charge?

He had arrived at a conclusion on both points, but he
had suffered much and slept little while he was making up
his mind.   It was a positive relief to be forced to talk and
think on a new subject.   He felt that he should enjoy seeing
the lad who wrote such intelligent letters on botanical
subjects, and for whom Miss Haubert had made sketches of
the parson during the sermon.   He was amused by the odd
place in which Enid lived.   He looked round with kindly
interest when the girl opened the door and ushered him
in.   Then his expression grew suddenly grave and tense.
Apparently, forgetfulness was never to be allowed him!

Geoffrey was talking merrily, his snub-nosed, comical face bright with pleasure. A broad-shouldered man sat next the sofa, with his back to the door. On hearing Enid's exclamation—which was not devoid of dismay—the man turned to smile at his little hostess ; on seeing the tall figure behind her he rose to his feet.

"Well, I'll look in to-morrow, Geoff. You may count on me to do porter. Good-bye for the present," he said.

"But—oh, I say—you promised that you would stay to tea, and you've only just come !" cried Geoffrey.

Mr. Strode stood still, with his hand on the door-handle. "There is no occasion for Mr. Cardew to cut his visit short," he said. "Now that I have seen Miss Haubert safely home I will take my leave."

"Oh, please, please don't," cried Enid. "Why, you have just climbed up a hundred steps, and you mustn't, either of you, go away like that !"

Her distress was so real that, as she stood between them, both men hesitated.

The Hauberts, like many poor people, were sensitively hospitable.

Then Mr. Strode metaphorically drew out that private scourge, which he was inclined to wield rather relentlessly. "Mr. Cardew has not only the prior right to be here, but he has also a right to object to my presence," he said. "I have no legitimate reason to object to his. I have been in the wrong."

Cardew raised his eyebrows. He vaguely recollected that this old enemy of his had said something to the same effect before in the train, but the words had then left no clear impression on him. He did not like Mr. Strode ; he had once heartily disliked him ; but he was keen enough reader of character to guess how much that recantation must have cost, and to respect its honesty. He sat down again, to Enid's relief.

"On the whole, I am glad that you give me the opportunity of speaking with you," he said. "There is a question that I should like to ask—that is, if Miss Haubert will not mind my talking of my own affairs."

Mr. Strode crossed the room and seated himself by the table. He was painfully conscious that this man had once before had something to say to him; but Jack had at that moment no thought of the interview in the prison infirmary. He was fast out-growing the bitterness that had once possessed him. Enid perched herself on the foot of Geoff's sofa. The brother and sister were very interested spectators of this scene. How they would discuss it when their visitors should have gone!

"So long as you will both stay and have tea comfortably you may talk about what you like," said she. "You were right about the time, Mr. Strode, it is only 4.30, after all."

She felt that it was as well that Mr. Strode should be proved right about something. When he had stood by the door and stated, through his teeth, that he had been in the wrong she had blushed hotly. She had a healthy horror of scourges.

"You see," said Jack, who was very capable of going straight to his point—"You see, I can't flatter myself that my personality has ever inspired you with confidence; but I understand, from what you have lately said, that you have changed your opinion of me. I believe that you told me as much when we travelled together. I am sorry, by the way, that I hardly took in the gist of your remarks then; but I was a bit bothered about something. I conclude you had a cogent reason for changing your mind. I have never been able to find tangible proof that I'm not a blackguard. What is your reason? I think that I have the right to ask."

"No doubt," said Mr. Strode; "but I have not the right to answer."

There was no hesitation about him now. At that moment his instinct, both as a man and as a priest, revolted from the idea of betrayal!

"Then you are in possession of some knowledge that nearly concerns me, and you deliberately withhold it."

"That is so," said the priest, nodding grimly.

Jack shrugged his shoulders and was eloquently silent. Had he remonstrated Mr. Strode would have spent a happier half-minute. Neither of these men had ever shirked or dreaded an encounter with any antagonist in the flesh; but in the silence Mr. Strode's own conscience accused him. He could have argued stoutly with Cardew, but, as it was, the strained expression returned to his eyes.

Enid broke the spell. "When I have any awful crime to confess, I will confess it to you, for, after this, I shall know that you will never tell!"

"Oh, ho—then it was a confession, eh?" said Jack.

Mr. Strode got up and pushed back his chair. "Miss Haubert is too clever," he said. "I do not wish her to find out more, so I will go. Yes, it was a confession. Naturally you consider that I am acting unfairly by you, but what you or any one may think is not my business. I must do what seems right. I am trying hard to induce the person who put me in possession of certain facts to make her—his—*its* disclosure public. I will swear, if you like, never to rest till I have succeeded in that endeavour!"

He looked pale and worn and stern. Enid was again sorry for him; but Cardew was moved in another and quite unexpected way.

"Oh, swear nothing of the sort on my account!" he cried. "The poor unfortunate devil! What a time he or she or *it* must be having!"

And at that Geoffrey suddenly broke into a peal of laughter, and the tensity of the situation relaxed. Mr.

Strode sat down and drank his tea, and no one asked any more questions. Cardew looked steadily at him once or twice, and on getting up to go held out his hand. " I say, I suppose we may as well shake hands—that is, if you'd like to," he said somewhat unexpectedly.

" I have certainly every reason to wish to shake hands with you," said the priest; and the extreme severity of his tone made Geoff smile again.

His long-fingered, nervous hand met Jack's unwillingly. *This* perhaps was part of the penance. One can force oneself to an avowal of past injustice, to reparation, to anything in the world except to honest liking. There, the strongest will is powerless. Love may be killed, but he can never be coerced; and no argument has ever yet prevailed with him.

Cardew smiled too. He suddenly understood this man. Jack was occasionally visited by flashes of inspiration.

" Life's not long enough for honest men to quarrel in," said he; " they may as well stand together against the rogues—that's reason enough for me. I don't want any other."

And at that the priest's long dislike melted all at once, his sombre eyes lit up, and he returned Jack's grasp firmly and warmly.

" But I wouldn't be too down on the black sheep if I were a parson," Cardew added, and so went on his way; glad, on the whole, that that old feud was done away with. He had never thought to have made friends with the fellow, but it was not in his nature to meet an apology coldly, and it is easy for the victor to be generous.

CHAPTER XXI.

"*I WILL HAVE NO MORE TO DO WITH HER.*"

MR. STRODE paid a long visit. He had spent a bad quarter of an hour, but now he was happier than he had been for weeks. A sense of relaxation crept over him; his somewhat morbid conscience was for once at rest, and his stiffness vanished in Geoffrey's cheerful and wholesome company.

Enid had no scientific knowledge of flowers, although she loved them; Latin names conveyed nothing to her. Finding the conversation slightly tedious, she presently slipped out of the room and betook herself to the packing of her few possessions. She was almost sorry to bid farewell to the attics in which she and Geoff had fought so hard a fight, but it was always the person, not the place, that constituted home to her, and she was thankful that it was a move for the better.

The howl of the gaunt wolf was very far away now : tears were in her eyes when she considered how rich she was. She presently began to overhaul the old play-box that held her relics. They were all sacred to her dead brother's memory, for this little artist had never been in love, though she had loved much. Father and brothers had filled her heart, and her work had been her romance. Yes, there was poor Bertie's cigar-case, and the portrait of the ballet-dancer, and the studs that a mysterious "some one" had given him. These things could not be left behind.

There, too, was that brown-paper parcel whose constant return from publishers had caused so much heart-burning. The very sight of it was painful to Enid, and yet she had never had the courage to destroy it. She and Bertie had once nearly quarrelled over that manuscript. She had copied out the whole of his novel for him, and had certainly not grudged the labour, though she had been obliged to rise early to accomplish the task ; but she had been moved to impatience when her brother had declared that her babyish handwriting was the cause of its rejection by publishers. Poor Enid had never owned to any one, not even to Geoff, that her last words to Bertie had been words of anger. Geoff would have said, " But you know it was quite Bertie's fault, Judy !" and she could never stand hearing Bertie blamed.

She dragged the parcel from the bottom of the box and sat pensively looking at it. She was a very loyal and tender little soul, and I do not think she confessed to herself that Geoff was more to her now than Bertie, with his shallower and vainer nature, could ever have been. She devoutly believed that had her elder brother lived he would have been a great writer. Death had made her faith secure, had carried poor Bertie beyond the reach of unkind test or adverse criticism. Perhaps, on the whole, death had not dealt harshly with Enid !

We sometimes hear of so-called "strange" presentiments, but it has always seemed to me that it is the absence of intuitive foreknowledge that is really strange. Our bodies give warning of coming illness, our ears catch the sound of the footstep of any one we love afar off ; but our souls may be within but a moment's distance of a great joy or a great grief, and we may be utterly unconscious of what is coming ; or we may touch the clue of a mystery and, except in rare cases, no instinctive apprehension will thrill us.

"I wonder if my handwriting has altered much since I copied for Bertie! I will just peep at it," thought Enid.

*　　*　　*　　*　　*

Some minutes later Mr. Strode, looking up from the minute fragment that he was examining on a glass slide, exclaimed in astonishment,—"Why, Miss Haubert, what has happened? Are you ill?" he cried.

"My goodness, Judy, what's up?" said Geoff.

Enid stood before them with a blanched face, holding a huge pile of manuscript in her hands.

"Oh, Geoff, this—this, is Mr. Cardew's book!" she gasped. "And all those years, those dreadful years that he was in prison, it has simply been lying at the bottom of the old play-box under my bed! It is *his*. It is signed with his name, 'Jack Cardew,' quite large and clear. *I* copied Bertie's novel; this is not in the least like my writing. This never was Bertie's; but I took it from the policeman that dreadful morning when he was brought home, and I put it away and could not bear to look at it. It was done up in the brown paper that belonged to Bertie's parcel. I am sure of that. See, the address on the outside is in Bertie's writing, and I remember the bit of pink and green twist. How could I know? It pretended to be Bertie's!" poor Enid cried in despair; and then flung the manuscript on the table, and buried her face in her hands. "Oh, Geoff, just think of all those years! all those years!" she sobbed.

Geoff whistled, and, leaning across the table, dragged the pile of paper towards him, turned the pages over and examined them with puckered lips and troubled frown.

"Don't, Judy," he said at last, "don't be an idiot. There is no use in going on like that. We must tell Mr. Cardew, that's all. I should think that he'll be glad that it is found anyhow, though how the dickens his story could possibly have got inside Bertie's parcel beats me. It seems to be a sort of conjuring trick. I suppose that it really is the manuscript that there was the row about?"

"He couldn't have lost two!" said Enid, laughing hysterically. "Oh, Geoff, he will think that it was poor dear Bertie's fault, and I am sure that it wasn't."

"He won't; he isn't that sort," said Geoff gruffly, "Bertie was his friend. Mr. Cardew won't fancy beastly things about his friend. He would be the last person in the world to do that. I wonder you don't know him better, Judy! You don't understand him a bit if you think Bertie's memory isn't safe with him."

Jack would have laughed had he heard that proud, boyish declaration of faith; but it stood for a good deal. It is not every one who can inspire hero-worship.

Mr. Strode, who was watching this scene with mingled feelings, marvelled at the lad's confidence.

It had never occurred to the priest that the manuscript might be still in existence. His mind had been so full of the ethical view of the situation that practical possibilities had not suggested themselves to him. He took up his hat and bade the brother and sister good-bye; they evidently wished to be left together, and, for his part, he desired to be alone in order to think over what had happened.

They are happy who face life hand-in-hand, and the close friendship of a brother or sister is a singularly good gift to have received from the gods; but Mr. Strode felt an unaccountable irritation when he saw how Enid turned at once to Geoffrey for counsel and support.

"It is high time for me to go. I am sorry that you are distressed, Miss Haubert," he said.

"Why, it is awfully silly of Judy to take things so," said Geoffrey with brotherly candour; "I can't think what she is fussing about. Mr. Cardew will be able to prove now that he was all right. No one worth caring about ever believed he wasn't, but—— What are you frowning at me for, Judy?"

Enid smiled with wet eyes, and made an eager endeavour to cover that last remark.

"We have not half thanked you, but I should never have found my way without you. And we have said nothing about all the beautiful hot-house flowers you have sent Geoffrey."

"There is no occasion for your brother to thank me," said Mr. Strode, "but I should strongly advise you to avoid getting lost in back streets for the future."

He lingered yet a moment; Enid wondered why. He opened the door, then turned as he crossed the threshold.

"If you have no objection I will come to see you in your new quarters," he said, with that extreme decision of tone that was, perhaps, a form of shyness.

Geoff chuckled when the door had closed on the tall, spare figure. "*I* should strongly advise you not to have too much to do with that parson for the future," he remarked. "He might order you to marry him one day, and where would you be then?"

"How can you laugh and talk nonsense?" cried Enid. "I feel as if I should never be merry again, when I think about the awful, cruel thing that happened, and all by chance!"

She was pale still; the shock of the discovery had unnerved her. Her imagination was more vivid than Geoff's, and her childlike, trustful spirit seemed to be suddenly confronted with the blank horror of a world without a ruler.

"It was all a silly mistake, and that is what makes it so awful," she cried piteously. "Why had Bertie got Mr. Cardew's papers? He never could have meant to do any harm—and yet the harm was done. It is as if some merciless, malicious fate were guiding—no, not guiding, playing—with our lives. If an enemy had destroyed the novel, one would say, 'How fearfully wicked!' but one would know that in the end wickedness must be found out and punished. That was what I always thought would happen—some one would be found out and punished. But after all it was no enemy. At the worst it could only have been a practical joke on Bertie's part, and then just by accident the joke was turned to bitter, bitter earnest. Bertie was killed before he could tell me what he had done. Nothing put it into my head to open the parcel! No, I just put it away without cutting the string, without dreaming what finding those papers would have meant. Mr. Cardew has been kind, very, very kind to us, and we let him be sent to years of misery when one look would have saved him. But it wasn't our fault. It was blind chance! It makes me shiver. Anything may happen, I suppose—nothing really interferes. Oh no, I don't mean it," she added, with a swift recoil from her own words, "but it seems so, Geoff."

Geoff fought for a moment with a boyish disinclination to speak on so serious a subject. "He is a much bigger sort of chap than either of us, Judy," he said at last. "And he has gone through a lot more. Yet *he* does not think that now. I know he doesn't, because once—when I was feeling rather bad about something I couldn't do—he told me so. He thinks it's not chance. I expect, somehow, that he knows."

The next morning Jack told his wife of the incident of the parson. Gillian was anything but pleased.

"I can't rise to these heights," she said; "I can hate, and I believe that I can love well, but I can't do first one and then t'other. I do not understand blowing hot and cold. You are growing much too angelic for me, Jack!"

Jack was silent; and after a moment Gillian asked sharply, "Was that all? Do you mean to say that

you did not even insist on Mr. Strode telling you what
he knew? Oh, I wish my spirit might inhabit your big
body, my dear, if only for a day."

Jack laughed. "My big body would probably be hanged
for slaughtering a parson, or it might get the worst of
the encounter. In either case it would be in an undignified
predicament. But I tell you one thing, Gill, I firmly
believe now, that before we are many hours older we
shall know the truth about that old mystery."

"Why do you believe that?"

"The secret is forcing its way out at last. It is struggling to get free!" said Jack. "But it has been a long
time in the dark—too long a time! Even a year ago I
should have been more eager."

They looked at each other with a world of sadness in
their eyes. Then Gillian turned away with a hard little
smile.

"Yes, it will be too late!" she said. "Well, for my
part, I do not believe in presentiments. I think that the
truth will emerge in time to dance over our graves. On
the day on which we are buried an 'Extraordinary Confession of a Thief' will be published."

"Gill, it is you who are bitter now," he said.

"Mammy and Mr. Cloves will reach Paddington by the
3.45," said Gillian, with a hasty change of subject.
"Mammy is sure to be knocked up by the journey, so I
fear that we must be a family party to-night. I suppose
you won't turn up till dinner-time? Very well, I won't
expect you before then, unless your presentiment comes
true. Will you bet five pounds on hearing some startling
piece of intelligence to-day? You won't? Oh, then I
don't think much of your prophecy, Jack. You lack the
first requisite of a prophet, you are not cock-sure."

The lightness of her tone jarred on Jack. It was impossible to make Gillian take any subject seriously at

present. Yet he knew that at heart she was anything but gay. She irritated him at times, but the irritation was only on the surface. He thought of her tenderly, though with some perplexity.

When Jack had gone Gillian wrote dozens of business letters; then she lunched out, and went to a scientific meeting. She preferred to fill every moment of her day as full as possible. Happy people can afford to rest, but Gillian hated to possess her soul in quietness.

Then Mrs. Clovis arrived and Gillian welcomed and made much of her. Gill was an excellent hostess, and she really enjoyed surrounding her guests with luxuries.

Mrs. Clovis was finally settled on the sofa in the sitting-room leading out of the bedroom that Gillian had arranged for her. She glanced appreciatively at the many pretty things round her.

"You are a most fortunate woman, dear love," she said, with a gentle sigh. "It seems to me that you have everything: health—which is so much greater a blessing than money—and such an exquisite home. Why, what makes you lift your eyebrows? Oh, dearest, of course I had not forgotten your sad loss, but you see you do not even wear crape now, so really——"

"Really what?" said Gill brusquely. "I don't know what you mean, mammy. Yes, of course I am very lucky. I bought those roses in Regent's Street to counteract the depressing effect of the fog. Are not they lovely? I think I will put them by your sofa and leave you to dream that it is summer. You ought to have a good sleep before dinner."

She escaped from the room with a sense of relief that she was half ashamed of. It was absurd after all these months to be still so sore that she could not bear a casual allusion to her "sad loss."

"I won't, no, I *won't* be such a fool!" poor Gill said

angrily to herself. "Good heavens, one would think that I was the only woman who had ever seen her baby die, and the thing is as common as the eating of eggs!"

The butler met her at the foot of the stairs, and interrupted the scolding.

"What? A visitor so late as this? Why, it is nearly time to dress for dinner!" said she.

Gillian had no intimate friend save Lady Jane. She expected to see that little lady's grey bonnet and quakerish dress when she entered the drawing-room; but it was a very different figure that advanced to meet her, and the tone that greeted her was half shy, half defiant—as unlike Jane's as any voice could be.

"Oh, Mrs. Cardew, I hope that you are pleased to see me, even though I did not follow your advice," it said. "I suppose that you have heard that I have married Cyril Bevan after all."

"Nina!" exclaimed Gillian. She was actually taken aback for once. The remembrance of Jack's very strongly-expressed opinion flashed across her mind.

"Oh, you are not at all pleased," said Nina. "Then I will go. Good-bye."

"No—stay," said Gillian.

Somehow some quality in this badly-behaved and rash young woman always appealed to her.

"I will not pretend that I am glad that you are Mr. Bevan's wife," she said frankly, "but you need not go on that account, need you? We have spoken rather freely to each other before now. I am glad to see you again, Ninon. I am glad you cared to come to see me. I will ring for some fresh tea. Sit down, won't you?"

"I do not want any tea, for I have something to tell you that takes away my appetite," said Nina.

She sat down with a nervous laugh, and Gillian waited wonderingly.

"I was in two minds about whether I would come," Nina proceeded. "If you had not been so kind to me once nothing would have induced me to tell. It was a toss up, you know, for I nearly walked off just now. But you are much nicer than most women. I usually hate them. Mrs. Cardew, will you promise faithfully that if I tell you something to my husband's discredit he shall never suffer by my confidence?"

"No," said Gillian; "for I think it would be most foolish of you to do any such thing. Keep your own counsel, Ninon. If a woman once begins to confide, the desire to go on doing so grows on her. The desire for sympathy is like the craving for drink; it had better be suppressed at once."

"Oh, my goodness!" ejaculated Nina.

She was not offended, but she stared hard at Mrs. Cardew, and she arrived at a decided conclusion. She concluded that Gillian was unhappy.

Gillian turned on the electric light and sat down on the sofa; she was quite unconscious of her visitor's penetration. Nina, with her flashes of cleverness, her occasional unscrupulousness, her odd, persistent loyalty to her rough step-mother, had always been interesting. Behold her again, handsomer, more of a woman and more of an enigma than ever! Nina always brought the whiff of violets with her; their clinging, fresh scent was associated in Gillian's mind with that strange, elusive personality.

"Was I ever too much given to confiding in other women? I should not have said so, but then we are told that we do not know ourselves," Gill's visitor remarked demurely. After a pause she added in a casual tone, but with mischief peeping betwixt her eyelashes, "I fancied that a piece of information I acquired lately would interest you, because it concerns something that once, long, long ago, happened to Mr. Cardew; but I will not tell you now."

Gillian started and changed colour. "If it is anything that concerns Jack, tell me quickly," she said.

Nina laughed triumphantly, and stretching out her slender foot, pushed a ball of knitting-silk that lay on the floor, and set it rolling.

"But certainly not, Mrs. Cardew. I have suppressed the inclination to confidence now; it might have led me to delirium tremens, you know. I do not at all wish to become a confirmed drunkard."

Mrs. Cardew clenched her fingers together and resisted the temptation to shake her visitor. She was perfectly aware that to betray anger would be fatal, but her self-command had been over-strained of late, and it was neither so easy nor so perfect as it had once been.

"The retort is yours, Ninon," she said. "I promise what you like. What have you heard that concerns my husband?"

"I have suppressed the inclination," Nina repeated, with demure mischief. Then a half-melancholy expression shifted like a shadow across her beautiful face. "Ah, how very much you care! But you have always believed implicitly in Mr. Cardew, have you not?"

"Yes," said Gillian shortly.

"That is so odd. Now I only believe with reservations. For example, I believe that Cyril usually tells me the truth, for we are really very good chums and we stand by each other. But if any one proved to me that in some particular instance Cyril had thought fit to lie, I should not be surprised; dear me, no, not in the least! I should not be shocked, either, though I should think it very silly of him."

"I think you are wise there," said Gillian. "And I hope that you are enjoying your good luck and the envy of Churton Regis!"

"Oh yes, thank you. But I do not want to stay long at Highfields. The place makes me dull. It has an even

more extraordinary effect on Cyril—it gives *him* the creeps.
You would hardly credit it, but he has grown frightfully
nervous. Do you know that there is a saying that no head
of the family ever dies in his bed ? "

" Why, yes, Lady Hammerton firmly believes in it, and
also in a family ghost; but surely Mr. Bevan, of all people,
does not pay heed to a superstition ? "

" But he does," said Nina. " Do you know, I do not
believe that Cyril ever realised till quite lately how much
of his father's blood is in him. He had no family feeling
at all, he often said so. He was proud of being cosmo-
politan. While the old man was alive he did nothing but
laugh at him. But now "—Nina paused dramatically—
" now we actually have prayers in the chapel every
morning, and they get longer and longer! Yes, you may
well look surprised. I thought Cyril was joking when he
proposed that we should do such a thing! It is really
very funny, isn't it? but it is also very cold and rather
gruesome."

" Do you mean to say that Mr. Bevan—Cyril, I mean—
reads prayers himself?" asked Gillian, whose imagination
was vainly endeavouring to picture that cheerfully callous
rascal engaged in such an incongruous occupation.

" No, that would be more than I could stand," said
Cyril's wife quickly. " Mr. Strode reads. It was his
idea. He has been staying with us. He is a very odd
person, but I think he is good, and Cyril has a respect for
religion."

Gillian put her hands to her head. " My dear Ninon, I
feel as if the world were turning somersaults. An ultra
High-Church parson staying at Highfields, and Mr. Bevan
filled with respect for religion ! "

" Yes, I know it is startling. I laughed a great deal at
first. Of course it is absurd. But one ceases to laugh
when one is third in a trio and the other two are in deadly

earnest. You cannot fancy Cyril in earnest? No more
could I unless I had seen him so. You see he got a scare
on the night when he found his father dead by the cross-
roads; added to that, he is out of health. He had an
attack of rheumatic fever last autumn, and he caught a
fresh chill at the funeral. He is terribly afraid of death."
Nina's upper lip curled disdainfully; whatever her faults,
she, at least, was seldom afraid.

"I do not understand such nonsense," she said, "but
Cyril half believes in all sorts of bogies. He pretends that
he doesn't; he is ashamed of his fears. But then, I find
him doing queer things in order to propitiate—— Something; and I know that the creeping, secret terror is there
all the time. It is strange."

Gillian said nothing and thought a great deal. It certainly
was a strange tale. The family ghost most surely entered
into it. There was evidently a spirit that haunted even
this outcast son of the house—a half-religious, half-
superstitious instinct, that had ruled his forbears, that had
been trodden down by Cyril, but that now returned to
assail him.

The honest, fanatical father had rejoiced with a whole
heart in a somewhat narrow creed; the son half believed,
against his will, and trembled. Cyril's first idea had
always been to cheat, and his second to compound with a
creditor. At present he was endeavouring to cheat the
devil. A good, honest repentance was beyond his reach,
but if possible he would evade penalties.

Nina's manner grew graver as she proceeded with the
story. "Cyril had to go to bed after he got back from the
funeral. Mr. Strode helped him home. He was in violent
pain, and he was shivering and shaking so that he could
hardly speak intelligibly. I sent for the doctor, and for
poor dear old Polly, who is a good nurse when she is
sober. Old Dr. Macnaughty was very kind—doctors are

much kinder than other people; I suppose, because they are in the habit of thinking ‘What is to be done?’ instead of ‘Who is to blame?’—but he had to go to look after a tiresome woman in the village that night. Cyril was in a high fever and delirious, and I could not keep him in bed, and Polly had not come. Then Mr. Strode offered to stay, and I was thankful that he did. It was an awful night; I do not care to remember it.”

She shuddered at some recollection and then smiled again. “It was dreadful—and yet I laughed, once, to think how funny it was that Mr. Strode and I should be nursing Cyril together. He was so decided, and rather cross, but I do not know what I should have done without him. The odd part of it all is that Cyril is grateful to him too. Cyril begged him to stay with us when it was discovered that the rectory drains were all wrong. To my surprise, he came.”

“I do not see that that was surprising,” said Gillian; “parsons have an excellent way of dropping into comfortable quarters.”

Nina shrugged her pretty shoulders. “You don’t like him! You hardly ever say clap-trappy things, but that remark was not a bit up to your style. It was wanting in penetration. Mr. Strode is not the fat and comfortable kind; he is a most uncomfortable person. He fasts and drinks nothing but water. I suspect he wears a hair shirt, and a cross with sharp edges. I believe that he came with the hope of converting Cyril. He has certainly managed to frighten him! Cyril is unnerved and utterly unlike himself; he told me a great many things that I would rather not have heard about, simply because his conscience was bullying him. Among other stories he told me about your mother and Mr. Cardew.”

Nina paused, on the very brink of revelation, deterred by a momentary qualm of doubt. “You are not very

devoted to your mother, are you? It would not break
your heart to hear something rather bad of her, would
it?"

"It would not break my heart to hear anything bad
about any one. Hearts don't break," said Gillian.

Nina looked dubious. She guessed that Mrs. Cardew
was still fretting about that child. For her own part she
did not understand why any one should care so much about
a baby. Nina's views on the subject of babies were
heterodox. Yet among all Gillian's acquaintances this un-
principled little lady was the one who was sorriest for her
and who did her the most justice.

"Well, I will tell you. It will give you something
fresh to think about," said she. "My husband and your
mother knew what happened to that manuscript. They
knew before the trial took place. Cyril and your husband
seem always to have had a strong antipathy to each other;
I suppose that was why Cyril held his tongue. A friend of
Mr. Cardew's—I think the name was Halbert, or Hubbard,
or something like that—carried off that unlucky book and
left a heap of ashes in its place. He met Cyril just outside
Mr. Cardew's door, and told him what he had done. They
laughed together over the joke. Cyril says that it struck
him as a slightly dangerous game, and that he remarked at
the time, that Jack Cardew was a queer-tempered chap to
play tricks on. When he next wrote to Mrs. Clovis—they
seem to have written to each other pretty often—he told
her what had happened. He knew that she did not much
like his cousin, and he thought the story would amuse her.
He had not the faintest notion of what would eventually
come of it. It seems that the hansom that Mr. Hubbard—
no, Haubert, that is the man's name—took, ran into a 'bus;
Mr. Haubert was thrown against a lamp-post and killed on
the spot. Cyril heard what had become of him months
later, but while the trial was going on he wondered that

the practical joker did not come forward to explain matters. He says that Bertie Haubert was only a young ass, and that he meant no harm—but only to give Jack Cardew a bit of a fright."

Gillian sat with her fingers tightly locked. Her brain seemed working unnaturally fast. Already she had pieced the puzzle together. What was it that Liza Pocock had said? Surely that all fitted in. "I did not mean to do Mr. Cardew any harm; but now I think that I did injure him without wishing to. I fancied that I might get him "—why, that must have been Bertie Haubert—"into trouble, if I let on that he had gone into Mr. Cardew's room. He told me not to tell of it. I did not know then that he was dead. No one guessed that he was anything to me. How should they?"

"The housemaid swore at the trial that she let no one into Jack's rooms during his absence; she, too, 'meant no particular harm,'" said Gillian bitterly. "All these people, with the exception of Mr. Bevan, had no reason to be malicious, and 'meant no harm.' They only played tricks, stealing by way of a joke, perjuring themselves lest their lovers should be blamed, suppressing evidence lest—— But why did mammy suppress that letter?" She rose suddenly and rang the bell. "I will send up to her room to ask her to come down. We will have the truth out—at last."

Nina jumped up; she was actually a little frightened, and it took a good deal to alarm her.

"Are you going in for a family row on the strength of this information?" said she. "Because if you are I will go. You see, Mrs. Cardew, I have had a surfeit of family rows!"

"Mammy and I have never had anything so vulgar as a row in our lives!" said Gillian. "We separated amicably for some years while Jack was in prison, that was all."

She made an effort to speak as usual, but her eyes were very bright. Nina felt as if there were thunder in the air. When the servant had gone with a message to Mrs. Clovis, Gillian again prevented her guest's departure.

"No, Nina, I will not keep you more than five minutes, but it is only fair that my mother should hear and refute such a serious accusation. If you bring such a charge as that against a woman you must be prepared to stand by it or to retract it."

"Must? I don't see any must!" cried Nina petulantly.

"But I do," said Mrs. Cardew. "It is a pretty big one, and it stands in front of the door."

She smiled with her lips, but her eyes were unsmiling. Nina flushed with anger, but the next moment forgot defiance in curiosity. Mrs. Clovis entered the room.

"Well, dear Gillian, you see I have managed to come downstairs. Dear George is so foolish! he never can enjoy his dinner without me, so I determined to make the effort. Why did you send for me, my love? Is it very late?"

She walked across the room with slow, graceful gait and bowed coldly to Lady Bevan. Mrs. Clovis considered that Gillian was by no means so careful as she should be. There were very extraordinary tales afloat about Nina's marriage. It was a preposterous hour for any one to be calling who was not on most intimate terms. She glanced meaningly at the clock.

"Yes, it is late," said Gillian, "but Lady Bevan and I have been having a very interesting conversation. One moment, Nina, and then I won't delay you any more. I do not want to make any mistake. Did you state that you were told by Cyril that my mother knew—" she stopped suddenly, because Mrs. Clovis had changed colour and gave a suppressed cry, but the pause only meant that she had observed, not that she pitied. At that moment she had no pity—"that my mother knew that which might have saved my husband? Did you state that?"

"Do you know, I thought that you were a sensible person who never made scenes!" said Nina, hastily putting on her veil. "How awfully mistaken I was! But one lives and learns. I simply must go now."

"Yes or no? Did you mean me to understand that, or have I entirely misunderstood you?" said Gillian.

Nina looked from daughter to mother. She had never liked Mrs. Clovis, but her sympathy was nearly always on the side of the culprit. She was half inclined to eat her own words out of a curious and perverse desire to thwart justice.

"It surprises me that you should listen to this—lady's gossip, Gillian," said Mrs. Clovis; and that speech decided Nina.

"You understood rightly," she said, "and I believe that I could prove my words. That was what I said. I think I've said about enough for one day."

Gillian hesitated a moment and looked at her mother. Then she opened the door. "Thank you, Nina. I won't keep you any longer."

"Oh!" said Nina with a gasp, "you are much angrier than I expected. I think you are angrier than any one I have seen in my life," and she ran down the stairs quickly and out of the house.

Gillian turned and faced her mother.

"It—it is not true," said Mrs. Clovis faintly. "That is, it is not true in the way you imagine."

She gripped the back of a chair to save herself from falling. This horrible bodily weakness that was always playing her false made it impossible for her to concentrate her energies on a losing game. "I do not understand why you take her word against mine, Gillian," she said. "It is very unnatural of you to accuse your own mother—but you were always unnatural."

"Turn round and look at yourself in the glass, mother. I have not accused you."

Gillian stood very still and upright. Mrs. Clovis sank on to the sofa and covered her face with her hands as if she were warding off a blow.

"Don't, don't, dear Gillian," she cried, with a touch of plaintive fretfulness. "You stand there and allow yourself to think the most dreadful thoughts of me; and all the time you have no conception of how I suffered or how it happened."

"Do not trouble yourself to explain," said Gillian, "for I feel that I am much too stupid to understand. If you were to explain from now till Doomsday I should be no nearer comprehending how a mother could let the man her daughter loved suffer as my Jack suffered when she might have prevented it. I would have died to help him. For seven long years I was thankful when each day was over, and all the day long his misery was heavy at my heart. I hardly dared think what he was feeling, but I never forgot it; never once. Yet you had no mercy on him, or me—though you must once have carried me as I carried my baby. It is beyond my comprehension. Am I really your flesh and blood ?"

"Hush! hush! Gillian. You must not say such things to your mother."

"I am sorry that you are my mother," said Gillian.

She spoke gravely and simply, as one who states an incontrovertible fact. Gillian was not self-conscious. Her words were terrible, because they represented absolute truth.

"It was Cyril Bevan's fault," said Mrs. Clovis eagerly, "and, indeed, I always wished to tell. I was miserable. The worry of it made me quite ill. But you see, my dear,

George would have been so surprised and so shocked if I *had* told. Surely you do see that, Gillian? I never could bear family disturbances—of course, I know that that is my weakness. I never was one of those women who do not mind quarrels. Indeed, indeed, dearest, I did not mean any harm to poor Jack. It was only that circumstances were too strong for me. My heart is beating so fast that I cannot explain properly, but if I could make you see how it all was you would forgive."

"I think not," said Gillian slowly. "I do not doubt that you have a hundred excuses for what you left undone. They do not interest me; keep them for your own comfort. Only one fact concerns me. You let Jack be condemned, knowing that he was innocent. I shall not forget that so long as I live. If I wished to forget it I could not—but I do not wish to."

"Now you are cruel! and you are certainly very un-reasonable," said Mrs. Clovis. "Every one ought to be allowed to explain. Whatever my faults may have been, I have never refused to listen to any one. The poorest beggar——"

"Ah, we know that you are so soft-hearted that you will empty your purse for the beggar in the street rather than refuse him alms, and you are also so soft-hearted that you let my Jack be driven near to madness," cried Gillian, with sudden passion. "Cruel? What is cruelty? Is it to wish to give pain? I am helpless; I can't make you realise what you left him to bear. If I could make you bear it now I think I would."

"Hush! hush! You are talking wickedly," cried Mrs. Clovis, "and your wild words positively horrify me. Don't stare at me like that, my dear; you almost frighten me."

"I was only thinking," said Gill, in an odd, impersonal tone; "I was thinking over the cruelty question. It had not occurred to me before that the cruellest people are those with such delicate nerves that they cannot suffer a pin-prick or a rough word. We poor sinners, who are not so finely made, are not 'in it' with them. I could not have been silent as you were; but then I was never sensitive. My skin is not so thin. It would never have occurred to me that it was possible to evade a prick at the sacrifice of my child's happiness and by embittering a man's life. You are a curious study. If you were not my, mother I should be interested—as it is, it's not amusing."

She put her hand to her throat. Anger, and something else that was not anger, seemed to choke her for a moment. She had not been an admiring daughter, but she had once had a protecting affection for Mrs. Clovis.

"As it is, I only hope that I shall never see you any more," said she. And then, as so often happens, bathos came tumbling in on the very heels of tragedy.

George Clovis junior burst into the room and dashed up to his mother, talking very loud—his voice was like his father's—and brimful of jollity. Behind him stood Cardew, his face wearing that peculiarly stolid expression that his wife knew was a sign that he was secretly excited.

"Oh, mother, the circus was splendid! Listen! it was such an awfully splendid joke! The clown comes up to the bobby like this, you know, and stares into the bobby's face, and the bobby looks at him *so*—trying to be grand and all that. And 'what do you say, sir?' says he. 'What is the colour of my eye?' says the clown. 'D'ye see any green in it?' 'Why,' says the bobby—— But, mother, you are not listening a bit." George's good-tempered face clouded momentarily; then he turned with unabated eagerness to Gillian. "How do you do, Gillian? Isn't it jolly that we have come to London to stay with you? Look here, do let me tell you what the clown did. It really was awfully funny. How far had I got? Oh, I know. 'Why green?' says the bobby, and at that the clown——"

"I am sure it is awfully funny, George," said Gillian, "but I have just been hearing such an awfully funny story that I do not feel equal to another."

Jack looked inquiringly at her over George's head. Something in her tone arrested his attention. George stared open-mouthed; he had been sure of his step-sister's sympathy! Gillian liked boys and was generally very ready to laugh either at, or with, him.

"You do not ask me what my story is," said she. "But you shall hear it, Jack, and so shall Mr. Clovis. It has been kept secret quite long enough. It is this——"

Mrs. Clovis sprang to her feet with a sharp cry, looked wildly round her, and then almost threw herself upon Jack Cardew.

"Stop her! Don't let her go on, Jack! Oh, Jack, not before my boy," she cried.

It was no thought-out plan, but simply unerring instinct that prompted that appeal. Mrs. Clovis knew at that moment that of the two the man was the most inclined to mercy, and that he alone could make Gillian pause. She clung to him with hands that trembled, and her voice broke with sobs.

Jack flushed to the roots of his hair.

Mr. Clovis's cheerful voice sounded from the staircase; he had a way of shouting a greeting before he entered the room. "Hallo, hallo? You all there. How is Madam Gillian? George and I have got back from the circus."

"Oh, Jack—not now, not just now," Mrs. Clovis gasped in an agonised whisper. Her face was drawn, as if with mortal pain.

Gillian's lip curled scornfully; she did not hold out her hand to her step-father. She was as merciless as fate itself. "You have come just in time to hear," she said.

But Jack stepped forward. "If it is something that the boy ought *not* to hear, then wait," he said.

At his sudden movement Mrs. Clovis's fingers relaxed their hold on his arm; almost before the words had passed his lips she slipped in a faint on to the floor.

Mr. Clovis rushed forward with an exclamation of dismay. "Why, what have you all been about?" he cried indignantly. "It don't seem to me that you take the least care of Eva when I am not by! Can't you even help me, Gillian?"

He was on his knees beside his wife, with red, anxious face, fussy and perturbed. Gillian, who was usually the most practical and helpful of women in an emergency, stood like a statue, tacitly refusing to move a finger in aid. George dashed upstairs to fetch his mother's maid. Jack, after a moment's hesitation, lifted the poor lady in his arms and carried her to the open window and flung up the sash. The cold air revived Mrs. Clovis, and she was presently escorted to her room by her devoted husband and son, and by the maid, who had arrived on the scene with smelling-salts.

When they were left alone together Jack turned to his wife with wondering inquiry. "I have something to tell you, Gill. But it seems to be a day of sudden revelations. My dear girl, you looked like an embodiment of ruthless vengeance just now. What on earth has your mother done?"

"You and Mr. Clovis would both have heard what she has done if you had not stopped me," said Gillian.

"I stopped you because she was in an agony of terror and because she said, 'Not before my boy.' But what the dickens were you about to say?"

"Oh, only this," Gillian answered bitterly, "only that it seems that my mother knew, actually *knew* what had become of your manuscript. She did not mention that little fact. She let you go to penal servitude instead. But, poor dear, she cannot bear to hear me tell the tale. No, that is too much for her delicate nerves! When it comes to *that* she appeals successfully to the mercy of the man she injured! To your mercy, darling!" She wrung her hands together, and threw them out with a gesture that was unconsciously dramatic and full of passion. "I will have no more to do with her! I *hate* my mother, Jack. When I think of what she let you endure I hate her, but most of all when I think that she dared— she dared appeal to *you* to shield her."

CHAPTER XXII.

"OUR WAYS ARE BOUND TO DIVERGE."

"Greed, cruelty, injustice, crave (we hold)
Due punishment from somebody, no doubt."

JACK and Gillian dined together that night. There was no family party after all. The maid presently came down with a message from Mr. Clovis to the effect that his wife was better, but not equal to coming into the dining-room, and that he and George would prefer to stay with her. She was apparently seized with a nervous dread of solitude, and could not bear to let her husband or son out of her sight.

Mr. Clovis was accustomed to humour his wife's whims; indeed, he was proud of them. The way in which she clung to him satisfied both his heart and his vanity. He had been doubly tender and doubly fussy over her since her illness.

"She ain't one of your great bouncing independent women who can stand up for themselves," he would say. "She is full of her little fancies, bless her! She would break her heart if I wasn't kind to her. *I* understand Eva, but there isn't one in a hundred who would make her so happy. Not that I am taking any praise to myself, mind you. But I saw from the very first moment I set eyes on her that she ought to be taken care of. 'She ain't the sort to rough it,' says I to myself, 'she is a deal too delicate, *inside and out,*' and I was about right."

Mrs. Clovis was not so good a woman as her husband imagined. It is to be feared that the inside of the platter left something to be desired; yet I do not think that his affection was therefore wasted. It is by giving that we attain salvation. Her small soul added something to its stature because she loved her kindly, admiring soap-boiler, as she had not loved the more critical and keen-witted husband of her youth.

Gillian's father had been too clever for the pretty lady. He had turned her small pretences and affectations upside down. He had waxed bitter and satirical over little every-day insincerities. He had been a far abler man than Mr. Clovis, but he had not made his wife happy, and he had not made her a whit more honest! Never yet, alas! has a soul been saved by adverse criticism.

"She is afraid," Gillian said contemptuously, when she received the message.

After dinner Jack told his story. Enid had come to his office that afternoon and had brought him the ill-fated manuscript that had wrecked his youth. He made few comments on what had been discovered, but when he had finished the tale he said gravely, "I was sure that the truth was struggling to get free. It is very extraordinary."

Gillian listened eagerly. She was still white and unlike herself. She talked fast and excitedly. She made Jack recount every detail that he could remember of Bertie Haubert's visit to him. She laughed when Jack narrated how ruthlessly he had crushed the young man's literary attempts.

"You were rashly candid in those days," said she; "but I think that Mr. Haubert had more than his fair revenge."

"The poor chap did not in the least mean to hurt me," said Jack quickly.

"Oh dear no! he only did it," said Gillian. "No doubt

his intentions were excellent. 'They were all—all honourable men.'"

Jack raised his head as if to protest further in defence of that friend of his boyhood, but the words did not come. The habit of silence is hard to break, and he reflected instead. He reflected that the curve of Gillian's cheek was much less round than it had been, and that the vertical line between her eyebrows, which he had first noticed the week after her boy's death, had deepened. He also reflected that he had never seen her look handsomer than she had looked that evening when she had stood stern and immovable while Mr. Clovis and George flew to her mother's assistance. He said to himself that it was hard on Gillian that her mother should have been the one to keep so culpable and injurious a silence. He wished he knew how to say to her that she had a hundred times made up for anything that her mother might have done or left undone. But he did not speak, and while he was still pondering, the opportunity for speaking slid away.

George came into the room, and walked straight up to him, with a somewhat defiant air.

" My mother sent me with a message to you," said the boy. " She said I was to say, ' Please will you come upstairs to say good-night ? ' and I was to give you this."

This was a tiny folded slip of a note. Jack opened it, and read the contents. His face wore its most stolid expression the while.

" My DEAR JACK,—I entreat you—not for my own sake, but for the sake of my boy—to hear me—only to hear me, before you tell my husband, or let Gillian tell him. Think what it is to spoil a child's faith ; and, besides, I never meant to injure you. I am very, very miserable, and quite upset about this sad affair. Surely you cannot be so hard as not to listen to me. You must remember that I am your wife's mother."

23

Gillian came behind her husband's chair, and read this missive over his shoulder. She bit her lip when she got to the last sentence.

"Unfortunately for your wife," she said in a low voice.

Jack put up his hand and caught hers as it rested on the back of his chair.

"Why, your hand is burning, Gill!" he said. "I say, this is a pretty business, isn't it? And what on earth am *I* to say? If it were a man I should know well enough what to do; but one simply can't pitch into a woman."

"That is exactly what she knows so remarkably well," said Gillian. "It is a shame to her sex that she makes it her refuge."

Jack frowned warningly, with a sudden recollection of George's presence. "Cut away, old chap; you are not wanted just now," he said.

George opened his eyes very wide, and his round face grew very red. "I don't know what you and Gillian are saying about my mother, but if you are saying horrid things—and I believe you are—they are all horrid lies, so there!" he declared, with unexpected force and spluttering with eagerness.

George and Mr. Clovis were both apt to turn scarlet and to splutter, on the few occasions when they lost their tempers.

Jack patted the lad's shoulder. "I beg your pardon. You are quite right, my boy," he said. "We forgot you. Now do make yourself scarce."

"I ain't going till you tell me what message I am to take back," said George obstinately. "Mother told me to be sure to bring back a message."

"Say that you will not go, Jack," said Gillian.

But he shook his head. "It is not fair to refuse to listen to her. I suppose that I must go. I would a hundred times rather not. All right, George; you may say that I will come."

"Dad and I think that it is awfully good of my mother to want to say good-night to you," said George, glaring at his step-sister defiantly; and so departed, banging the door after him.

Gillian laughed. "What it is to have such a devoted son! How much did he understand?"

"He understood the tone of your voice and the expression of our faces," said Jack. "And I wish that he had not. He is a very fine little chap!"

"Oh, I daresay, for he takes after his father," said Gillian. "But at this moment I can't like her child."

Jack got up ruefully, and walked up and down. "Well, I must face it," he said.

"Oh, do be angry, Jack! Do not look as if *you* were ashamed!" his wife cried.

Jack shrugged his shoulders. "But I am. That is the queer part of it. I am angry too, of course. It was a pretty mean trick to play. I cannot for the life of me understand about it. But one can't see a woman covered with confusion and not feel awfully ashamed."

"Oh, don't! don't!" she cried passionately. "It maddens me to hear you say that! Don't pity her, Jack; she is not worth your pity. She has made profit out of her 'sensibilities.' She has flung her fine feelings down on the counter till there is nothing honest about her; till she hasn't a sentiment that rings true."

Jack looked at her wonderingly. This was that other Gillian, whose very existence was known to so few.

"But you and I must go through with this dirty business as best we can, my dear," he said gravely; and so left her.

Mrs. Clovis lay on the sofa in her sitting-room. She was almost as white as the filmy white gown that she wore. Jack, on entering the room, was shocked to see how ghastly she looked. He cordially hated a scene, and

the righteous indignation, which would have blazed hotly
had a man been the transgressor, did not break out now.
He had every right to be wrathful, but he did not feel
particularly inclined to vent anger on Mrs. Clovis. It was
so difficult for him to realise that a woman could have
behaved as, to all appearance, she had.

He sat down in an armchair a little way off from her,
and played with the knick-knacks on an ornamental table.
"You sent a message to me, so I have come," he said;
"but I do not know that there is any use in listening.
Of course you must have had some sort of reason for your
silence, but I do not care much to hear what it was."
He looked at her for a second with, so at least she fancied,
the expression she had dreaded in her dreams. "I think
excuses are better let alone."

Then, to his immense surprise, she began to laugh
hysterically.

"My dear Jack, I was not going to offer excuses," she
cried. "I could explain—but I will not trouble you. Let
it be supposed, if you please, that I am the wickedest
woman and the most unnatural mother in the world.
Imagine, if you like, that I rejoice in cruelty, that I was
glad when you were sent to prison. Ah, if you only knew
what tortures—— But no matter—Gillian says that I am
cruel. Let my own daughter be my judge. She judged
me unheard; but I am too weak and far too unhappy to
care to spend my breath in pleading for myself."

She paused, and pressed her wasted hands to her side.
Cardew shifted his chair uneasily and stared at the fire.
He was not a fool, and he knew that the woman was trying
to make capital out of his manliness. Yet there was no
doubt that she was frightfully ill; she appeared to be almost
at death's door.

"It is not for myself that I am speaking," the faint voice
went on, "but—and, whether you believe me or not, this

is true—I have always, always done my utmost for my dear husband and for my boy. It is for their sakes, for their sakes entirely, that I bring myself to entreat you to keep silence about this miserable mistake. Do not tell them, Jack! Oh, surely, surely it can be no great deprivation to you to forego hunting a poor unfortunate—for I have been most unfortunate—woman to death!"

"Hold hard!" said Jack.

He twisted round in his chair and addressed her with an effort. He hated this interview more every moment; yet there was a dignity in his tone that overawed her. "No one has any reason to imagine that I take a pleasure in bullying women; but you have no right to ask for my silence. I will not promise it. If that is all that you wish to say to me I will go."

"Jack, dear Jack," she cried weakly; and dragging herself up by the back of the sofa, she leant forward and stretched out her hand to bar his way.

Jack paused, because, much as he longed to go, it would have been sheer brutality to have thrust so weak an arm aside. "I wish you wouldn't do this," he said awkwardly. "See, Mrs. Clovis, I hate to come down hard on a woman; yet, after all, there is such a thing as justice. One does not like, for the sake of one's own self-respect, to hit any one who is down; therefore I have not enlarged on what injury you did to me, though, God knows, it was not a light one, or on what you made Gillian suffer—besides, *that* is too sacred to chatter over. But those facts are and will always be. In the face of them, isn't it a little— indecent, that you should say to me, 'Keep silence, Jack, lest now *I* suffer a little too'?"

"Ah, not a little!" she cried.

Jack straightened his shoulders and drew back out of reach. "The world shall not know," he said; "at least, not through me. Mr. Clovis can do as he chooses. It is not probable that he will choose to publish such a story. I have found the manuscript, or rather "—a touch of awe unwittingly crept into his voice—" or rather, I did not find it; but it was brought back to me this very day. There is, fortunately, no need that your name should appear in the affair."

"Then why tell my husband anything?" she cried with painful insistence. "Jack, I do not believe that you will tell him. I cannot believe it. But Gillian—Gillian is so hard to me. She never has cared for any one in the world but you. You can prevail with her; you can persuade her. She is like a stone to her poor mother! She seems to forget——"

"That is enough," said Jack sternly, and with a sinking heart Mrs. Clovis realised that she had made a mistake. "My wife requires no defence. It is simply absurd that *you* should call her cruel. It is a little too much." And so he left her.

Possibly his chivalry would have overcome his indignation had she not played that false note. But the limitations of her character frustrated her design. Mrs. Clovis had never been able to understand loyalty. It had not occurred to her that to say one word against Jack's wife was to compass her own undoing.

Jack found Mr. Clovis waiting for him outside the door. "What is all this about?" that honest gentleman asked impatiently. "I can't make head or tail of it! Here's my wife fainting, and taking on, and declaring she must speak to you alone. And there was Madam Gill staring like a stuck pig, instead of helping her mother. And here are you looking as solemn as if you were going to be hanged —and what's it all about? That's what I want to know! I have had enough to knock me down for one day without coming home to fresh worries. It was all I could do to put a bold face on and keep the corners of my mouth up at that blessed circus; but I wasn't going to disappoint the boy. And now here's more trouble; and I can't even put a name to it! What's it all about, eh?"

"Let us have a smoke," said Jack, "I can't tell you on the stairs."

But when Mr. Clovis was established with a pipe in the smoking-room, Jack still found himself in no hurry to begin the tale. It was an uncommonly awkward story to have to narrate. Why, after all, should he be at the pains of telling it? Jack had a warm respect for "old Cloves"; he did not wish to quarrel with him. Yet you can hardly tell a devoted husband that his wife is a deceiver and not quarrel. Of course the accusation was provable; but the more Jack thought about it the less he liked the job of driving the truth home. Mr. Clovis was so simple where his wife was concerned; so proud of her refinement, so unselfishly devoted. It is only a mean nature that enjoys the actual process of opening a good man's eyes to some one's badness. In theory, and beforehand, one may indeed strongly desire that the good man should be undeceived, but when it comes to practice the operation is apt to turn one sick. Jack began to forget the sinner's iniquities in his sympathy for the husband. He suddenly made up his mind that it was not his business to play executioner; though of course Gillian might do as she chose.

"You ain't throwing much light on the subject, Cardew," said Mr. Clovis anxiously; "I wish you would out with it, if you have any bad news for me." He laughed nervously. "But there, why should it be bad news? The fact is, I am a bit upset to-day, and I don't seem able to get a grasp of things rightly. I have heard something that is rather hard to digest. I shall have to get a night's sleep before I'm my own man again."

"I am sorry that you have heard something bad," said Jack; "I hope that that smash up of Robson's hasn't touched you?"

"Bless you! It's a deal worse than that. It ain't money at all. It's about my wife."

"What?"

"Yes, it's about Eva—that's where the damage is. I went to her doctor this morning, to ask him privately what he thought of her state of health. He is a great fool! I don't believe him, mind you. No, I don't believe him at all. He didn't give me the impression of a sharp man; he hummed and hawed too much. 'There is one thing I want to know,' says I, speaking quite cool and collectedly, as I am speaking to you now, 'will—will she live or die?'" Mr. Clovis choked over the words, and Cardew examined the sole of his boot and puffed vigorously. "Now you would think I should get a direct answer out of him, would not you? Not a bit of it. 'We may be wrong in our diagnosis,' says he, 'but if it is what I fear, she has only a few months left.' 'I don't want any ifs,' says I. 'It's impossible for me to say more than that,' says he. 'Then what the deuce is the use of you?' says I. 'If you can't so much as give a straight answer to a simple question, and if you can't cure her, what *can* you do? What are you paid for?' Well, I daresay I ought not to have said that. It seemed to put my gentleman's back up. But a man might make allowances when the other chap's wife is dying of cancer. Not that I believe it. It ain't likely, you know. Well, the doctor just rang the bell. 'Good-day to you,' says he, as grand as you please. 'Good-day, sir,' says I, as cheerful as possible, for I wasn't going to let on that it had been any blow to me; and out I walked. I haven't told a soul expect you, Cardew, nor don't mean to. If it is true—but it isn't—why, even then I think I am right. Such as she don't need extra preparations for death. Women ain't like us—I mean the good women ain't. Their sins are sponged out when they say their prayers every night at their bed-sides. But Eva is nervous,

you know, and I won't have her worried. I shall just keep
a stiff lip, and I know you are safe—but you don't think it
is true, eh?"

"If I were in your place I should have another opinion,"
said Jack.

"Why, this is the second opinion. I didn't make much
by that move," said Mr. Clovis gloomily. "But there, it
is not to be expected that one big gun would say the other
big gun was wrong. Why, of course I know that! I am
not so simple as to suppose they would contradict each
other. These doctors are as thick together as thieves.
Your pipe has gone out, Cardew."

"Oh, d——n it all, it won't draw!" said Jack.

Mr. Clovis struck a light and held it out. He was
cheered by something in the expression of Jack's face and
tone. Cardew was genuinely sorry; "old Cloves" quite
understood that.

"You're a good chap, Jack," he said. "Now you may
as well tell me what else has gone crooked."

"Oh, nothing much," said Jack. He smoked silently
for a minute, and considered the situation. "We have
been having an exciting afternoon. I have made an odd
discovery, and women's nerves cannot stand excitement.
My wife and her mother had a bit of a row. I am sure
that my wife was entirely in the right, but you may tell
Mrs. Clovis that I have changed my mind—I'll do what
she wishes now. She wished me to speak to Gill for her,
and I refused—that's all."

"Good Lord!" said Mr. Clovis. "You don't mean to
say that all that fuss was about nothing but a tiff? Well,
I take it very unkindly of Madam Gillian that she should
say a word to hurt her poor mother just now."

"Gillian is not unkind. She was justly angry on my
account," said Jack. "But there is nothing to be gained
by reviving the discussion now. It is dead; so let us

bury it. Talking of burying "—he went on with a hurried and transparent attempt to change the subject—" Talking of burying, reminds me that I have not yet told you of a most wonderful resurrection. I am pretty well cleared at last, I fancy."

He plunged into the story about the manuscript, and partially succeeded in arresting the attention of his guest. At any other time Mr. Clovis would have been immensely and jubilantly excited. As it was, the thought of Eva's illness pressed on him, so that his effort to listen to Jack was pathetic. He rose at last, with a smile which he vainly tried to make cheerful. "I am truly glad that you will be cleared. Eva will be very glad too," he said. "It seems to me that somebody ought to be well whipped for the mistake. It ain't fair that an honest man should suffer like that and no one smart for it. You say it was pure accident? Well, I am dull to-night. I don't seem to take it all in. Look here, I don't believe what that doctor said. I don't believe either of 'em. They were in collusion, and they were backing each other up. I shall try an outsider; but don't you say a word about it to my wife. Good-night, Cardew. I'm not surprised that the murder's out. I knew you were an honest man that time asked you the question, and as for George, why, he didn't need to ask. Well, you may laugh, sir, but I declare that little chap is as knowing as possible! You never managed to deceive *him* into thinking you a rogue."

"Oh, George and I are capital friends," said Jack.

"He stood by you finely," said the proud father.

"And perhaps some day I will stand by him," said Jack Cardew.

When Mr. Clovis had gone, he sat with his head on his hands and thought of his own boy, of George, of George's father, and in his heart was a great pity, and the strong sense of fellowship.

Presently Gillian entered the room. "Jack, have you told him?" she asked.

She was still white and stern. She mistrusted Jack's mood. It is easier—for a woman at any rate—to forgive an injury to herself than an injury to her dearest. That last, to some of us, trenches on the impossible. Gillian had never taken count of small injustices, she had never been spiteful; yet at that moment she would have seen her mother in the dock without a pang of pity. Had she not once seen Jack in gaol?

"I have not told him, and I do not mean to," said Jack.

"Then I will," said Gillian.

Jack shook his head. "No. You will keep the secret, Gill."

Gill was silent; but the silence meant resistance.

Jack sighed. "Sit down, and let us talk about it," he said. "We must thresh this matter out and have done with it."

"There is no need to talk," his wife answered. "My dear Jack, I foresaw that my mother would get the better of you. I can imagine the whole scene. She wept profusely, and you relented. Tears always disarm you! Well, I know how much they are worth, and I am not melted by them. There is nothing to discuss."

Jack kept his temper with an effort. "I am not a fool," he said shortly. "As it happens, I was not overcome by your mother's tears. I refused to make any promise of silence to her. She should have been ashamed to have asked it of me."

"She should indeed," said Gillian. "Yes, dear, I know that I am unchristian, and I daresay I am undaughterly, but I do not pretend to goodness."

"I wasn't going to preach," said Jack. "We will leave Christianity out of the argument just now. I have promised to persuade you to be silent; but it was not for her sake that I gave way. It was for the boy, and for old Cloves. But I think that it was most of all for the boy."

Gillian's lips pressed harder together. "For the boy," he said. She knew well enough that it was not of George only that he was thinking. She was dimly aware that the baby hands, for whose touch she yearned, had led her husband a long way on a strange road. Yet the knowledge seemed to make her heart the harder against Mrs. Clovis. That a woman should deliberately and in cold blood sin against her own child, for the sake merely of her own comfort, seems, to the ordinary and normal woman, a fact that is monstrous and quite incomprehensible. The natural instinct of womanhood was very strong in Gillian. She had nothing but scorn for the mother who lacked the first impulse of maternity.

"It is a pity for a little chap to hear bad things about a parent. I know that by my own experience," Jack went on.

"The pity lies in the parent's doing the bad things," she retorted.

"The sin lies in the doing," Jack said gravely, "but the shame falls on the children. That is a queer arrangement, isn't it? One is forced to make rough guesses at its meaning, because one can't disbelieve in justice and yet keep one's sanity. But that is not at all what I meant to talk about. Under ordinary circumstances I should not attempt to prevent you from telling Mr. Clovis anything that you chose. The reason that makes me interfere is very simple. Mr. Clovis has just told me that the doctor believes your mother to be hopelessly ill—in fact, dying. It seems that she has not many more months to live. In that case we may as well stand aside, I think. We need not add bitterness to her husband's grief, nor blacken her boy's remembrance of her."

Gillian remained inscrutable and unmoved. At that

moment Jack realised that his wife had drifted a long way
from him : he could no longer guess what she felt, nor
what she would say or do. She seemed indeed to feel
nothing but a certain annoyed perplexity. This piece of
intelligence, that had so startled him, left her cold.

"My mother has an extraordinary facility for shirking
consequences," she said at last, "and she cannot bear
to be thought ill of. If she sees no other door of escape,
perhaps she will die."

Jack was silent; he was possibly shocked. Gillian
presently forced a yawn, though she was not in the least
sleepy.

"I think that I may as well change my dress and go to
Mrs. Speake's 'At Home' now," she said. "It is late,
but her parties are late affairs."

Jack caught her dress as she would have left the room,
and detained her.

"But you will not tell Mr. Clovis. The poor old chap
was not a bad step-father to you, Gill—and he is a good sort."

"It is not my fault that his wife is not good," said
Gillian. He should have chosen better, dear. As for me,
I had no choice in mothers." She tried to speak lightly,
but the intensity of her indignation broke through the
forced lightness. "She should not sleep under this roof
to-night if this were my house, Jack."

"It is lucky for you it is mine," he said gravely.

"For *her*, you mean."

"No, for you," he repeated. "Look here, Gill, you
shall not tell Mr. Clovis that story with my consent."

She looked at him, with some surprise at the unwonted
tone.

"I don't often interfere with you, do I ? ' he said.

"No, not often," Gilian owned. Some thought made
her frown, and then smile a trifle bitterly. "Not too
often, for you and I have grown so thoroughly sensible."

He wondered a moment what she meant; but he let her go. Then the vague uneasiness that had often stirred in him of late took form, and he wished that he had begged her to stay.

It was not right that Gillian should be always going out alone. It was strange that she should care to go, when her boy—but no, he would not do her an injustice; he knew well enough that she mourned her boy sorely, day in and day out, though she could never wear her heart on her sleeve. Cardew had no glibness of expression. He could indeed write with a certain force—but he never wrote about himself, and his pen was readier than his tongue. He felt before he thought; he had felt for a long time that there was some shadow between him and Gill; but he had not cared to put the feeling into words. There are people who are reserved even with themselves, and who are loyal to their very core. They arrive at their conclusions slowly in matters where their affections are concerned, though they may be prompt in action. They inspire the one or two who love them with a great trust. They may have the most glaring and obvious faults, but one is very sure of their virtues.

Jack could not sleep that night, and the morning brought him no counsel. It brought him Gillian instead. She came into the room, in morning dress, with her hat and cloak on.

Jack sat up and rubbed his eyes. "Did you go to an 'At Home' in that gown?" said he.

"No, dear. I am not quite a lunatic," said Gillian, laughing. "It was three o'clock when I got home, and it was not worth while to go to bed. I changed my dress in the dressing-room and went for a walk. It was much more like you than like me to go in for such an erratic proceeding, wasn't it? Well, I have been thinking over our conversation of last night. It seems to me that on the whole it is too silly of us to dispute over whether my mother shall be punished or not. You prefer to leave vengeance alone. Very well, I daresay that you are right; and anyhow, I hate a fuss. Have it your own way, Jack, only do not expect me to tolerate her, for I am not cold-blooded enough. I am a pagan, you know. You see, Jack, I am quite willing—no, I am not willing—I am quite ready to allow that you have a right to be as good as you choose; but I can't and won't be good too; consequently, there is only one way out of the difficulty."

"And what is that?" he said.

"It is for me to go away," said Gillian cheerfully. "I have arranged it very neatly. I have wired a message to myself. It will be here at breakfast time. My friend is very ill and begs me to come at once. That is for the benefit of Mr. Clovis and the servants. When my mother has the grace to depart—I should think even she must feel ashamed to stay long—I will come back to you. Dear me! you need not look grave. It is really a most excellent plan. You may bless your lucky stars, dear, that your wife does not fly out of your house in a rage, and leave an enigmatical note pinned on to your pin-cushion! I declare I nearly did that, Jack; but my sense of the ridiculous saved me. I am not young enough to enjoy emotional exits. Now mind that you remember to be surprised when the telegram comes. You are very bad at plots."

"But, I say! I don't like this arrangement," said Jack.

"Neither do I like yours," said Gillian calmly. "If I had my way Mr. Clovis should know everything at once. Why should my mother be allowed to pose as a saint? Well, I won't enter into that argument again. We are not children. We can agree to differ. I will not fly against your commands, because it is very silly to make scenes; and you will not force me to meet my mother for the same reason. I hope that you won't make your cold worse; your voice sounds as if it were on your chest. And, please, don't forget my address. I will write it in your pocket-book. See? I am going to Lady Jane. She is such a safe and respectable hostess."

"What, now?" said Jack.

His voice sounded so rueful and puzzled that Gillian laughed.

"Oh no. Not this moment. My mother never comes down to breakfast. I shall have time to pour out your coffee just as usual; and then I shall interview the house-keeper and tell her all about my sick friend, and arrange about your dinners. Mrs. Brown is devoted to you; she will make you very comfortable. We won't have any melodrama. I am afraid I was rather melodramatic yesterday, Jack. I have an uncomfortable suspicion that I behaved like a tragedy queen—I, who so despise volcanic women! I am sorry. I will not do that kind of thing again, dear. I have got a box of cough lozenges, and I have put it on the top of your razors. Do be sure to take it in your pocket when you go out."

"Bother the cough lozenges! Look here, I have not agreed to this," said Jack.

Gillian turned round and faced him. "Then will you tell my step-father the truth, and clear the house of my mother?"

"No. You know that I will not do that," he said slowly.

"And you know that I will not meet her," Gillian returned.

She played with the things on the toilet-table, and tried to master the tendency towards again becoming tragic. In very truth she was startled at the intensity of her own anger against Mrs. Clovis; just as she had once been startled at the intensity of her own love for Jack.

"I really cannot play a game of hide-and-seek in my

own home. It would be so tiresome," she said. "It is
a great pity that you do not like my little scheme; but
you are so appallingly magnanimous that our ways are
bound to diverge! It is better to diverge than to quarrel."

She left the room with a nod and a smile. Jack turned
the matter over and over in his mind while he was dressing. Of course it would neither be fair nor possible to
insist on his wife's remaining. Mrs. Clovis's conduct had
been indefensible; Gillian had every right to be angry.
Jack had never coerced his wife in any manner. That was
not his way. He owned to himself, with a smile, that the
man who attempted such a thing would have a precious
stiff job.

Yet one remark of hers stuck in his mind. "It is better
to diverge than to quarrel." Was that indeed true?

Jack held his temper with a very strong curb, never,
alas! forgetting, that it had once killed a man. Gill had
a hearty contempt for the kind of woman who raises a
storm in a teacup. They never quarrelled. Yet the
question haunted Jack.

"The fact of the matter is that we have diverged such
a remarkably long way already," he said to himself, with
some pain, and a good deal of surprised realisation.

On the day when he had come home bitter and reckless,
a man whose life was, in his own estimation, spoilt, Gillian
had flung her soul at his feet—now it was often hidden
from him. Yet he loved her more now than he had loved
her then, and he was an infinitely better man.

Gillian came down to breakfast looking exactly as if
nothing had happened. When the telegram was handed
to her, she read it aloud with every appearance of surprise.

"I have received a message: 'Do come at once. You
are much wanted. Jane ill. No one else available.' What
am I to do? But of course there is but one thing to do,
I must go."

24

"Why, you are not surely going away with your poor mother so ill and all?" said Mr. Clovis indignantly.

"Is Mrs. Clovis worse this morning?" Jack inquired with an effort.

"Yes, she is. She did not sleep a wink all night. But her daughter don't seem to think it worth while to ask after her," said Mr. Clovis in a hurt tone.

"I am very sorry to appear unkind to you, Mr. Clovis," said Gill.

"Well, well," he grunted, but half mollified, "it is not to be expected that you should be as anxious as I am. Still, I do think you might at least have been to your mother's door to see how she was."

Gillian gave the telegram to Jack with a twinkle of mischief in her eyes. "You see, Jack," she said, "I have no choice. It is impossible for me not to go."

CHAPTER XXIII.

INVISIBLE BONDS.

"For man is a spirit, and bound to all men by invisible bonds."
—CARLYLE.

GILLIAN sat in Lady Jane's peaceful room, and waited for her friend to come in. She had not been near Jane for a long time, but she had no doubt about the welcome she would receive.

The quietness of that small, daintily clean home seemed to Gillian like the quietness of a church after the rush of a great thoroughfare. She was apt to mock at "sentimental fancies"; but, though she would not have owned to the folly, she was haunted by the idea that the very atmosphere was made sweet by prayers, and was full of a grave and gentle peace. She leant back in Jane's chair with a look of unwonted relaxation and weariness.

It was now nearly six o'clock, and Gill had been rushing about all day. She had had lunch at the stores, and had shopped all the afternoon in Regent Street. She had taken a most matter-of-fact and cheerful leave of Jack. Her last words to him had been an injunction to remember a business appointment that he had made for that afternoon. Jack was careless about engagements.

No woman had ever left her husband's house in a more unemotional and sensible manner. Yet she felt strangely exhausted, and as if she had undergone a pretty severe moral strain. This rather surprised her; but the woman who is capable of loving and hating as Gillian loved and hated does not often analyse her emotions.

Presently Jane came in, and exclaimed in genuine delight at sight of Gillian. "It is very long since I have seen you, my friend."

"Very long," said Gillian, kissing her. "I did not feel inclined to come near you before. I lost my boy, you know."

"Of course I know," said Jane.

"And I did not want to talk about it," Gillian added quickly. "And yet to you I could not talk nonsense. I am supposed not to mind much, you know. I had rather people thought I did not mind much. Now we will change the subject. Jane, I have a great deal to tell you about Jack's affairs; but before I begin I must ask if you will let me sleep in your guest-room? or is it at present occupied by a repentant Magdalene?"

"It will be the greatest treat I have had for years to have you to stay with me!" Jane said truthfully. "It is very fortunate that I have no other guest. Come and put away your hat and cloak. Have you any luggage?"

"Only a bag which holds my night things. You are supposed to be very ill, and you wired to me. Now I wonder whether you really would have done anything so sensible? I have quarrelled with my mother—this is true, Jane—and I have left her in possession of the house. It is a first and a last quarrel. We shall not make it up. Jack understands the situation; but I do not wish to enter into particulars."

"I will not ask questions," said Lady Jane. "But I am sorry that you said that I was ill, because that is not in the least true."

"Dear saint, I took your name terribly in vain! But it could not be helped. Are you not shocked that I have deserted my mother?"

"No, for I am perfectly sure," said Jane with quiet decision, "that Mrs. Clovis must have been entirely to blame."

"That is right!" cried Gillian. "You know nothing whatever about it, my dearest saint! But I always feel that the strength of your prejudices is refreshingly human! All the more so because you are under the impression that you are unbiassed."

"I am not prejudiced," said Jane, colouring. "I simply speak from knowledge of your and her characters."

They stood in the tiny guest-room, and Gillian glanced round it. It was very small, and the walls were blue and white. The bed had a white coverlet with a blue design embroidered on it. The design was of a tree with spreading branches; that 'tree of life' that is to be found in much of the old English needlework. A scroll wound among the branches, bearing the words, "No wind killeth the tree that God planteth."

Gillian shrugged her shoulders. "And how about the trees He does not plant, eh, Jane?"

"They do not exist," said Jane placidly.

Opposite the bed hung a print of Albert Dürer's picture of the knight who rode through the valley of death. There was a wooden cross above the door.

"Why, the room looks as if you had expected me," said Gillian. "The bed is made, and there are clean towels put out."

"The room is always ready," said Lady Jane. "And it is never long empty. One never knows how suddenly it may be wanted, and I could not bear to be unprepared for those that are sent to me. But you, Gillian, you are my very own friend! When you come it is a holiday and a festival."

Later in the evening, when they had had tea together, Gillian told Jane of the finding of the manuscript and of the steps that Jack was going to take to make the truth known. Of her mother's guilt she said nothing. She smiled a little sadly in response to Lady Jane's congratulations.

"Yes, he is cleared," she said. "The oddest part of it all is that we have lost the power of rejoicing. Jack and I have been as solemn as two owls over the discovery! Once I should have been wild with triumph. Jane, I have done all I told you that I would do. I have made friends with the world and the etceteras for his sake—a little bit for my own too—every one has come round to him, and now a crowning proof lies in our hands. Why am I not more glad?"

"You have been over-working yourself," said Jane tenderly.

"Over-playing is what you mean," said Gillian. "But I tried to be quiet, and quietness nearly drove me into Bedlam. I can't rest. I think that I must have eaten witches' apples, and their juice has got into my blood."

"Then do not eat them any more," said Jane softly.

"One must eat something, and I am not pious," said Gillian.

Jane sewed after tea. She worked exquisitely, and she found great enjoyment in putting fine stitches into linen.

Gill watched her rather enviously. "Do you ever get restless?" she asked.

"I was unhappy once," said Jane; "I am not now. The world is sad, I think; but underneath the sadness one finds—God."

She spoke the last word in so low a whisper that Gillian rather guessed than heard it. She sighed impatiently. "My dear Jane, you possess a mysteriously spiritual nature. I do not. Spiritual food is indigestible to me. I never understand what sermons mean, even when I believe them to be genuine. As a rule, I believe them to be nothing of the sort. The worst of it is, that Jack has developed a spiritual nature too, and he is getting beyond me. He is struggling to altitudes that I can't breathe in. I could help him when he was in despair, but he is the sort who must either be very very good, or very reckless. He never did anything by halves. You see, I can't be very good. I don't even wish to be—so there is nothing for it but more apples."

Jane opened her lips to speak, but thought better of it and was silent. She was a woman of strong prejudices, as Gillian had remarked, but she had also a certain discretion that had been learnt in the school where experience teaches. Not that that stern dame manages to impart the higher wisdom to the majority of her scholars. Jane loved Gillian, as she loved no other woman, with a strong and equal friendship. Yet she knew that she was not the right person to help her. There was only one who held the key to Gillian's heart.

"But men are often singularly dense," said Lady Jane with much apparent irrelevance. "They have all the best chances, and they frequently let them slip. We stand by and see the pity of it, and can do nothing at all."

"My dear Jane, why this unprovoked diatribe?" asked Gillian, laughing.

"I was answering my own thoughts. It is a bad habit that one falls into when one lives much alone," said Jane.

Gillian did not sleep that night, but that was no new experience. She had suffered from insomnia ever since her child's death. She lay wide awake, and wished that she were among a crowd of people. When morning dawned she stared at the picture of the knight. His mouth, and something in the set of his shoulders, reminded her of Jack. The gruesome phantoms that surround that most excellent warrior made Gill feverishly angry and impatient. One's emotions are often unruly after an unwilling vigil.

Few painters have portrayed silent conflict more vividly than has Albert Dürer in that curious picture of the man riding through mopping and mowing shadows, with teeth clenched, and a strong grip on the rein of his frightened horse.

"You won't condescend to notice them. Well done! They are not worth looking at," Gill murmured. "But *I* ought to be there to scare them away."

Gillian was not artistic, but she understood very well what that old artist had meant. One learns more through one's heart than through ne's brain, after all.

She stayed with Lady Jane for four days, and they were among the most miserable days of her life. The restless bitterness that possessed her was more or less apparent in her conversation; but she made herself very amusing, and, at times, very useful to her hostess. She alluded no more to "witches' apples," and Jane never forced a confidence.

One day she remarked casually that her mother was still too ill to be moved. "It must be a great bore for Jack," she said. "But, of course, if people will go in for being so preternaturally generous, they must expect to be bored."

On the fourth day Jack made his appearance. He was too large for the tiny room, and Lady Jane, who had grown old-maidish, felt that he was somewhat out of place. He stood in front of the fireplace, and fidgeted with the clock on the mantelpiece. His shoulder brushed against Jane's carefully trimmed lamp.

"Please, will you sit down?" said Lady Jane in her soft, even voice. "I fear that you will inadvertently break that globe."

"How is Gill?" asked Jack abruptly.

"She is doing a great deal; she never tires," said Jane; and at that moment Gillian came in.

"Dear me! Have you come to call upon me, Jack? How very amusing!" said she. "Or," and there was an involuntary eagerness in her tone—"Or has my mother at last seen fit to depart?"

"I wish that you would come back," said Jack. "No, Mrs. Clovis has not gone yet. But if you could see how unhappy Mr. Clovis is about her, you would not care to add to his troubles."

"I do not wish to add to his troubles," said Gillian coldly. "You don't understand, Jack. If I went back I should have to pretend that I was on my usual terms with my mother. There are limits to my powers of pretence, dear. I will not do it. No, Jane, you need not go; we have nothing to discuss." But Jane went.

"She is the most gently obstinate person in the world!" Gillian remarked with a smile. "She does credit to my nursing, does she not? But I think she isn't quite out of danger yet."

"You are making a mistake," said Jack.

"I can't help it!" she answered. It seemed to her, for a whimsical moment, as if two demons were fighting for and in her. "I cannot get outside my own character. I don't want to forgive her."

"Then you will not come? Well, you are wrong," Jack repeated. But he did not contest the point.

When he got to the hall door he found Jane waiting for him.

"I want to speak to you," she said. "It is about somethin for Gillian. I do not wish her to hear."

To her surprise Jack frowned and reddened. His own mind was so full of this perplexing estrangement that he fancied that Lady Jane was about to intrude advice on him. The next moment he was ashamed of his suspicion.

"To-morrow is her birthday," said Jane. "I have been

working a screen for her room; it is being made up at a shop in the Strand. The shopman promised me that it should be sent home last week, but it has not yet come. The shop is not far from the office of your Diamond Company, and Gillian tells me that you are often in that direction. I was intending to ask you if you would be so very kind as to inquire about my work for me, should you happen to be near the shop; but I see that it would be a trouble to you."

"Why, of course I will do that," said Jack. "I thought you were going to say something quite different."

The little lady drew herself up, and looked at him with such surprised dignity that he had the grace to be ashamed of his suspicion.

"I beg your pardon. The fact of the matter is that I have a guilty conscience," said he. "I know that I have a genius for making a hash of things." He smiled ruefully. "I am sure you must think so, don't you?"

"Since you ask me—yes," said Jane.

"Gill is wearing herself out. I daresay it is just as well that she should stay with you for a bit." He swung the door to and fro and lingered. Seeing that Lady Jane had *not* offered to interfere, he was half inclined to desire her counsel; at the same time nothing would have induced him to tell her, or any woman, that anything was wrong between himself and his wife. "She misses the—the little chap rather, I suspect."

"Why, of course," said Jane.

"You can't reason about that sort of thing, can you?"

"Reason?" cried Jane with unexpected warmth. "Does reason ever help any one who is unhappy?"

"No," he answered bluntly. "Nothing helps an unhappy person except—— Well, good-night, Lady Jane."

It was freezing out of doors. A few small flakes were

falling, but it was too cold to snow heavily.   Cardew turned
his steps riverwards, and presently walked along the
Embankment.   He stopped, in spite of the cold, to watch
the gulls skimming over the water and perching on the
floating lumps of ice.   The yellow and dun snow-clouds
hung low, and the current ran black between the ice-blocks.
But a few miles out of town yesterday's snow was white
as a christening robe on the sleeping country; here the
coating on the stone balustrade was already thickly crusted
with smuts, and salt and cinders had been thrown down in
the roadway.   London never sleeps; she knows nothing
of the muffled stillness that reigns after a snowstorm in the
country.   Yet her winter, too, has a penetrating beauty of
its own.   Cardew was poet enough to feel the spell of the
city, which, once felt, seems to enter into the very blood.

There is a dancing woman who wears a black veil, and
who jigs to strange tunes, barefooted, on the pavement—
and she is London.   There is a tragic woman who cries
aloud to Heaven; we shiver when we hear her voice, she
haunts us when we feast—and she is London.   There is
a strong woman whose breasts have suckled great men,
who is the mother of a hundred inventions; whose children struggle and attain, and give place to others in a
ceaseless stream—and she is London too.   Once in a while
this woman lifts her veil, and her eyes meet yours.   Then
you have seen something that you will not forget, however
far you may wander; something that will remain with you
till the last silence falls.

Cardew was about to cross over to Norfolk Street, on
his way to the Strand, when a noisy procession of Salva-
tionists forced him to wait.   The sight of them recalled
to his mind the recollection of the consumptive man who
had once accosted him on the bridge.

"Poor chap! he was spitting blood then.   By this time
he must be dead," thought Jack.

The remembrance of the little "captain" momentarily amused him. The "naturally shy man," driven to aggression by his aggressive form of religion, had seemed to him both funny and pathetic. Jack wondered if the poor chap was now reaping some reward of his ill-advised efforts. Want of gumption is sorely punished in this world. Jack thought of the hollow-cheeked, round-shouldered little apostle with a smile and a sigh. Then all at once it occurred to him that nowadays he often practically recognised that the question which had nonplussed the injudicious preacher might after all be answered.

"What earthly right has any one to interfere? Why have not I as good a right to go to Hell, if I choose, as you have to go to Heaven?" he had asked.

And even while he put the riddle the reply to it was given in the fierce outraged sympathy that he himself felt for all who were going down, who were dogged by ill-luck, and driven by despair; who, humanly speaking, had no chance, and had never had a chance. No man is himself alone. The "invisible bonds" that bind him to his kind are as real as the flesh and blood that grew in his mother's womb. He has a right to interfere, because the life of every other man is, in a sense, his own. In his childhood he knows this well enough; injustice dismays and hurts him with a sense of personal injury and perplexity; possibly as he grows up the primitive instincts weaken, but some among us keep their childlike outlook through all the length of days. Perhaps he must be something of a thinker who apprehends the fact of unity with his brain, but the illiterate enthusiast who cannot fit two thoughts logically together grasps it practically.

"At the same time there is no denying that the illiterate brother is a great nuisance, when he takes to blaring trumpets and to going into religious hysterics," thought Jack as he made his way up the Strand.

He had an antipathy to most religious forms, noisy or otherwise. It was an antipathy that lasted his life.

He did Lady Jane's commission, and found that the shop was actually under the very rooms in which Gillian had been living when he came home from Africa. He was possessed with the desire to see them, and he found, on enquiry, that they were to let. They were seldom long empty, but the last tenant had died suddenly. He mounted the long flight of stairs very thoughtfully, and presently stood in the very room to which he had come to meet the woman who had waited for him.

The sitting-room was cheerless and cold. The small bedroom that Gillian had slept in had no fireplace. Cardew, who was aware how keenly Gill appreciated luxury, wondered how she had put up with such discomfort. He looked round him with a grave face; then, sitting down by the window, he scribbled a few words in his pocket-book, tore out the leaf, and asked for an envelope. He enclosed his note, and directed it to Mrs. Cardew.

" I will take these rooms from to-morrow," he said.

He had not had the faintest intention of writing a letter or of entering that room when he went into the shop; he acted on one of the sudden impulses that occasionally impelled him. His grave and somewhat impassive manner impressed the landlady; but Gillian, had she been present, would have laughed at the suddenness of his determination.

On his return home, Jack found Mr. Clovis in a state of mingled exultation and misgiving. The exultation was openly paraded, the misgiving lurked in the background.

It appeared that the new physician's opinion was absolutely at variance with the opinion of both the other doctors.

" He is the only sensible one of the lot!" Mr. Clovis cried. " I could see that with half an eye. He is a sharp chap, if you like! He has got his wits about him. 'In my opinion,' says he 'there is no malignant growth.' 'You mean,' says I, 'that I was frightened with a pack of lies?' But at that he drew in a bit. 'I meant nothing of the sort. I should not dream of using such an offensive term,' says he. All the same that was what he *did* mean, Jack. That was the long and short of it."

Cardew smiled grimly. He was glad, for Mr. Clovis's sake, that there was new hope. Moreover, he hated to think of any woman suffering tortures. Yet there was a certain irony in the situation that did not escape him. He had nearly quarrelled with Gillian, who was worth a hundred such selfish sentimentalists as her mother, because he had been moved by the belief that the woman who had injured him was dying. Now that she had his promise of silence, she was perhaps after all *not* dying.

"Eva will get better yet. You think she will get better, don't you?" Mr. Clovis cried, with an appeal that was almost child-like in its simplicity.

"Upon my word, I should not wonder a bit if she did!" said Jack; and rather to Mr. Clovis's astonishment, he laughed outright.

CHAPTER XXIV.

THE SALVATION OF TWO.

"Love's not Time's fool, though rosy lips and cheeks
  Within his bending sickle's compass come.
Love alters not with his brief hours and weeks
  But bears it on, e'en to the edge of doom—
If this be folly and upon me proved
I never writ and no man ever loved."

"SO you have come. I am glad of that," said Jack.

He stood in the bare little room in the Strand, and he turned to greet Gillian with a half-deprecatory smile.

"Of course I know that you think that this is a very foolish arrangement, Gill," he said. "But I was so possessed with the desire to talk to you here. Do you remember that it was on your birthday that I came home?"

Gillian did remember very well. "Oh, was it?" she said carelessly. "My dear Jack, how badly this room needs dusting!"

She was beautifully dressed, but as her velvet cloak brushed against the table it became marked with a line of dust.

"Your note amused me, Jack—and surprised me. It was very funny of you to give me these rooms for a birthday present. I ought to appreciate the sentiment, but I could wish that you had had them cleaned. Look at that!"

She walked to the window, and as she spoke she rubbed her finger along the window ledge, and held it up, coated with black.

"Yes, it was in better order, and it was full of flowers on the day when you waited for me," said Jack.

"Twopenny bunches of berries, and red chrysanthemums from the basket at the corner of the Strand," said she. "I did not know that you noticed them. I am glad that you did not try to renew that effect to-day! Don't sit on that chair. I can see that its left leg is going to give way under you. I never thought much of the furniture here, and it is in worse condition now than it was in my time. Besides, you don't grow lighter with advancing years, and neither for the matter of that do I—and after all there is no particular reason why we should be here at all, is there?"

Jack kicked the chair aside, and seated himself on the table. "Never mind the dust. I'll buy you a new gown," he said. "Sit on the window seat. That's safe. Well, yes, I have a sort of reason. It seemed to me I should get at you better in this room. I daresay it appears absurd, but I don't know that what a thing appears ever matters in the least. You cannot say you hear some one ringing at the bell here. Thank goodness no one knows where we are. Gillian, have you and I quarrelled?"

He saw the colour come into her face, but she answered lightly, "Good gracious, I trust not! That would be such a highly unoriginal thing for a husband and wife to do." Then a rather odd expression came into her eyes. "Of course it might be interesting to find out which of us is really the strongest. But no; quarrels are too vulgar and brutal. We will have none of them. We have agreed to differ, and that is all. You shield my mother because she is a woman; and I, because *I* am a woman, my dear, hate her. I have come to the conclusion that men can't hate as women can. What do you say?"

"I don't know, or care," he answered. "You are not 'Woman' in the abstract. You are *the* woman who was fool enough to fall in love with me when we were young and walked in a Fool's Paradise, and who—I suppose that was more foolish still, eh?—who stuck to me when there wasn't much Paradise left, and the view had ceased to be pretty. And I am not 'Man' in the abstract, but the man who is your husband. We have agreed to differ too much. It is a bad plan. Look here, Gill, in theory it is all right, but in practice it is—I beg your pardon—it is damnation. It is freezing the life out of us."

"I thought that people were generally damned in a very hot place; but no doubt you know best, dear," said Gillian.

She laughed nervously. She could not, for the life of her, meet Jack's words simply. The trick of covering her emotions with a jest had grown on her, and she was strangely nervous. She did not wish to make an idiot of herself; yet she felt helpless for once. Her attempts at fencing were futile. Was she glad or sorry?

"You thought wrong, then," said he. "Fire never killed a soul yet, let the priests say what they will. It has saved some, I think."

"Have you turned preacher?" she cried. "Because, if you have, I will agree to all your arguments in advance, and save the discussion. You can consider me converted, dear! Now don't you think that we had better be going? We have sacrificed enough to memories, I am sure! It is the sort of thing I, personally, hate doing, my dear. It is so much simpler to take each day as it comes and not remember! I only came because I am such an amenable wife—except when you try to make me overlook mammy's little peccadilloes—and because, fond as I am of Jane, the undiluted society of my own sex does bore me after a—rather short—time. Do not you think that is horrid of me?"

"Gill," he said, "you are holding me back with all your strength. Why?"

Gillian stared out of the window, and a mist floated before her eyes. "Don't, Jack," she said, in a low voice.

He got off the table and came nearer. "But why, Gill?"

She was physically tired, and she was sick at heart. She could not bear to feel that she was not mistress of herself and of the situation. She had meant, at any rate, to have avoided anything approaching to a scene—and yet the traitor within the gates was glad because Jack was too strong for the citadel. The traitor within the gates is such an extraordinary, unaccountable person!

"I have not had much need to do that. I have known for some time that you and I are miles apart," said she.

"By my fault, eh?"

But at that her loyalty protested. "No, no; not by your fault. I do not think exactly by my fault, either. I suppose by the natural order of life. A woman falls in love, and then she marries and bears children, and then she begins to die. Do not look startled, dear. I am remarkably strong and well. I am not going to tell you that I have an incurable disease gnawing at my vitals, like the Spartan boy's fox. But all the same I am beginning to die. Every one is who has passed youth. That is why everything seems on a dull level. That is why I do not enjoy anything, or care for any one as I did once. Once I was happy if you were in the same room with me. Now we have grown older and more sensible. That is quite right; and when we get yet a little farther on it will not any longer seem so dull. It is all perfectly natural, and it is no one's fault."

Jack smiled in spite of himself. "That was a clever answer, but it was not the truth, Gill," he said. "It did not strike me that your emotions were wanting in vigour when you heard what your mother had left undone. We were not boy and girl when we were married, and we are not growing younger—but it hardly seems to me that we have no vitality left. It does not seem so to you either."

"Perhaps not," said she. "But, my dear Jack, life would become impossible, and barely decent, if one habitually trotted out the whole naked truth."

Cardew glanced round the room, and then looked at Gillian again. It was difficult to him to speak; he was making such an effort as he had never made before. Unadorned truth is indeed a somewhat awful guest to entertain. One can never forget her words. They mark a crisis, and they have everlasting life in them. One hears them through all succeeding years, and through the babel of tongues.

"You spoke the very truth once—in this room," Cardew said; "and it saved me. It was the only thing that could have saved me then. Nothing but your love for me stood between me and the devil, Gillian. If you had not been waiting that day——"

"Oh, do you suppose I don't know? I know, and I knew. You need not tell me that," cried she. She held up her hand to stop him, and the colour flooded her face and the tears filled her eyes. "I made violent love to you, Jack—but it was not the time to hesitate; it was the only thing to be done just then. You need not remind me of that day. Do you think that—that one ever forgets? But now it is different. Whatever might happen to you, you would never 'go to the devil' now. You have found your footing, and, what is more, you are climbing to heights that are far beyond me."

"Why, Gill," he interrupted, with sudden illumination—"Why, Gill, I am a stupid, blundering fool, but of course I want you! Did you think I didn't? I have let you go, but I have wanted you all the time, and I believe that you want me. Heights that are beyond you? Nonsense, we must stick together, my dear. Look here, I have been idiotic enough to suppose that it was but fair to let you follow your own way, but I had much better have made you come mine, eh? Gill, I am trying to get at the meaning of all sorts of things—I can't understand them alone. I *won't* understand them alone."

She stared at him silently, with the unshed tears standing in her eyes. She saw that he flushed to the roots of his hair—that was turning grey now—with the endeavour to force himself to speak of those deeper things that underlie life and that make its reality, but which he could never talk glibly about.

"I won't understand them alone," he repeated. "My God must be your God. My dear, if He is to be found we must find Him together."

She half turned from him, because she was afraid that the tears would fall, and he put his hand on her arm.

"I could not say this to any one else in all the world," he said simply, "and it is the sort of thing that it is difficult to say—even to you. But you—why won't you be yourself to me? Gill, do look at me!"

Gillian turned with quivering lips. "I wish you wouldn't," she said. "The fact is, I don't dare be myself, because——" And then, without any warning, she broke down, and slipping away from his grasp, sat down on the chair by the table, and leaning her forehead on the wood, sobbed and sobbed, with long, choking sobs that frightened him.

The barriers were swept away at last.

"Oh, Jack, I could not help myself!" she gasped at last. "It was most dreadfully silly of me! But I—I am so awfully miserable about my boy still, and you seemed to have got so far off. You are getting so—so good, you see. But I—I long for my baby. I try not to give in.

Other people lose their children and get over it. It is so cowardly to make a great fuss when one is hurt. I don't mean to. I did not mean to—but I do want my little boy so much, so much."

And at that he took her in his arms and comforted her, with words that were quite illogical—broken phrases whispered for her only, that shall not be written here, being sacred—but that, after all, held consolation.

And later Gillian dried her eyes and went home with him.

They walked together through the crowded street, and talked but little by the way. When they got to their own door Gillian remembered about her mother, and smiled.

"You are quite wrong," she said. "It is altogether preposterous that mammy should be let off like this; and I am going in for an entirely immoral course of action in supporting you. Mind, I do not forgive her now."

"All right," he said, "I daresay it is immoral, Gillian. We must hang morality for once. You see, I can't round on her now. After all, your mother is very unimportant. What really matters is that you and I are going to keep together."

And a laugh that was quite genuinely happy broke from Gill's lips. It was a long while since he had heard her laugh naturally, and the sound pleased him.

"That is all very well, darling," cried she. "But do you know that you walk with very long strides occasionally, and it is *I* who will have to keep in step?"

She was ashamed when she went up to her room to see how swollen and red her eyes were. "I have never, never—but once before—been such a goose!" she said to herself. "And it was Jack's doing then."

The recollection reminded her of Jane. She had left that little lady without a word; she must write to her at once. She hesitated for a second with her pen in her hand, and then wrote very fast.

"MY DEAREST SAINT,—I have given in very absurdly, and have gone home. If you were any one else I should invent a hundred reasons for your edification, but I do not mind owning to you that the whole proceeding is *un*-reasonable! Mammy is still here, but Jack has over-persuaded me. He is determined to drag me up mountains. It seems an unwise enterprise on his part, does it not? Yet I think on the whole that you will be glad, and so, do you know, am I. Dear Jane, I am very grateful to you. There was so much that you might have said, and so many questions that any other woman would inevitably have asked! I am most grateful to you for your silence. You gave me time and space to breathe in. That trio about whom we have talked have not helped me to forget my boy; I doubt if they cure heart-ache, and they charge heavily—and Jack has set his face against them. I mean to throw away the witches' apples if I can. Of course that is an odd thing for me to do; but one is bound to do odd things if one likes such an odd person as Jack. I will send a man with this letter at once, and he can bring back my box. I will come to see you very soon. I should like you to burn this if you please—but you may keep my love, dear saint.

> 'Yours,
> "GILLIAN CARDEW."

Her head was aching so that she could hardly see to sign her name. She despatched the note, and then threw herself down on the bed and shut her hot eyelids. The walk had been long, and she was tired, but the restlessness that had so possessed her was gone. Jack had apparently exorcised that unquiet spirit. She slept soundly, and Cardew, when he came up to dress for dinner, found her still in a deep, dreamless slumber.

He stood by her side with a great thankfulness in his

heart. There would not have been much satisfaction in seeing his good name wholly restored if the woman who had clung to him through shame and ill-report had been alienated.

Gillian would probably never have done anything very outrageous; her common-sense and her pride would have prevented that. Yet there are more ways than one of going down hill, and there are paths that have no danger-signals that yet wind to the bottom.

Jack was conscious that he had "done a good day's work" and that he held his wife's hand firmly in his own again.

This hotly-loving and passionately-hating woman, with her horror of mock sentiment, with her half-mocking out-look on the world, of whose good things she was so willing to make the most, with her surface frankness and her real reserve, was bound to him by bonds that could only be broken at the cost of all that was finest in her nature. Gillian had challenged grief and found him strong; but she was not the woman to give in. Had she not met love, too, there is little doubt that she would have hardened her heart, and have ultimately won one of those victories that cost more dearly than defeat.

Jack was glad that he and Gillian stood together once more; yet I doubt if he ever quite understood, that even more surely than her love had once saved him, his had that day saved her.

As for Mrs. Clovis, she hardly knew whether to be glad or sorry when she was told that Gillian had returned. The scene with her daughter had thoroughly unnerved her. She was anxious to leave the house as soon as was compatible with appearances; yet from the bottom of her heart she was desirous of departing in peace. She hoped that Gillian had been brought to see things in a more becoming and softer light, but was aware that she could seldom be cajoled into seeing through other people's spectacles! It was terrible that "the dear girl" should be "so hard on her own mother," Mrs. Clovis repeated sadly to herself. In spite of Gillian's plain speaking, she did not grasp the fact that it was the desecration of mother-hood that had fairly shocked Gillian. Neither did it occur to her, while she speculated tremblingly on her daughter's probable behaviour, that Gillian had simply flung reason aside, and had come back because love is, after all, much stronger than hate, and Jack wanted her.

"Your mother is very unimportant," Jack had said; but that was from his point of view. The majority of us are important to ourselves.

Gillian came down late for dinner, but took her place with no apparent embarrassment. "Lady Jane is out of danger," she said to her step-father, "and so, of course, I was able to come home."

The old soap-boiler glared at her in silent indignation. He had always before liked "Madam Gill." Yes, even when she had defied his authority and stuck to her convict; but he could not get over her desertion of her mother.

He shook his head and turned to Jack. "She ain't fit for the move yet," he said, pointing overhead with his thumb; "but so soon as she is we will be off."

The situation certainly was awkward, as Gill had known it would be, but she cared very little about that. There is a certain amount of danger in being one of the people who care for a few things very much. So far as happiness goes, one had perhaps better bring offerings to a row of little minor deities; but the other nature has its compen-sations—sometimes.

During the following day, Gillian solved difficulties by sticking close to Jack's side. There was a good deal to be arranged, and she was in her element when she was advising him on matters of business. It was at her suggestion that Geoffrey Haubert wrote a letter to the *Times*, in which he stated where and how Mr. Cardew's manuscript had been discovered. In the same edition appeared a letter from Cardew's publisher. This gentleman was ready to vouch for the fact of the recovered work being identical with that which was to have run through the —— *Magazine* in 1883. He had read the manuscript himself in the first instance; it had then been returned to Cardew, on the latter's wishing to make some alteration in the concluding chapters. This was followed by a short letter from Cardew himself.

"It seems to me that it is my business to see that no imputation rests on the name of my dead friend," Jack wrote. "I am absolutely certain that the purloining of my papers was an idle joke. The joke had somewhat grim results, but it was a result that could not have been foreseen by Mr. Haubert, and had he not been killed in an accident on the afternoon of July 6th, 1882 (that is the day on which he took the manuscript), no harm would have resulted from the trick, and the parcel would certainly have been returned to me."

"Is that your business?" said Gillian. "Your friend cost you pretty dear. I wonder why on earth it all happened? Probably there is no 'reason why,' though; and there is nothing gained by puzzling over it."

"I think that there is a reason why," said Cardew. "But I doubt if you and I shall hit on it on this side of the grave, my dear. The circle may be a bit too big for us to see."

"Then we had better not trouble ourselves about it," said she.

They were sitting in the library, with the letter before them. Jack pushed it aside, and looked at Gillian with the sudden smile that so transfigured his face.

"Oh, of course, there are lots of people who never do trouble themselves about the why and wherefore," he said. "But I must, Gill. I don't know *why* that is; but I do know that I must either sink, or else swim with the whole of my strength. The reason of the pain and injustice that one sees? Good heavens! it must be a precious big reason, to justify the torture and hopelessness of half creation!"

"I was not worrying myself about 'half creation,' you know," said Gillian calmly. "It is you that I care about; and if we come to why and wherefore, I am sure I can't think why I was ever so silly as to start doing that!"

Then she laughed contentedly. "Jack," she said, "after all, I do know why. It is because I always felt that you were bigger than most of us. You are meant to do big things. You will help the world to live. Already weak people are stretching out their hands to you."

He shook his head; but he felt that it was curious that she should use the very words that old Mr. Molyneux had once said to him. Then the melancholy that had become part of his nature, that in a weaker man would have paralysed action, asserted itself.

"To me? But they don't know—there are things that never wear out, Gill."

Gillian sighed impatiently. "Jack, it is because of that," she said. "Look here, I think that it is a shame that you should have suffered. To me, other people's good does not in the least make up for it; because, as you know, your little finger is worth more to me than all the other people in the world. And yet—though I grudge it— I see that that suffering has given you a sort of power which not every one possesses. Somehow I have heard before that going down into hell is a preliminary to saving others. You can't, as a rule, help a person to get out of a place without having been in it yourself. Mind, this

sort of transcendental theory isn't in my line ! I daresay
I am talking arrant bosh. I only think about these things
because you do. You'll never turn me into a Lady Jane,
my dear."

"I don't want to," said he, laughing. "I have the very
deepest reverence for Lady Jane ; she is goodness itself ;
but I should think she would be slightly chilling as a wife.
It is queer that you should be so fond of her."

"She is the only woman in whom I have ever had the
least inclination to confide," said Gillian. "Because you
see she too has been—but never mind ! Jane's affairs are
not our business. You have not dated that letter correctly,
dear. Shall I make a copy of it ? "

They plunged into business again, and talked no more
of those hard nuts on which mankind seem bound to cut
their wisdom teeth—whether they crack the shell or no.
Yet those few words had brought them into closer touch.
Sometimes on our way through the world we join hands
with those who are like ourselves, who are spiritual
brothers or sisters ; but the deeper and wider revelation
comes to the man or woman who learns to understand a
nature *un*like his own.

Gillian had just left the library, when she was confronted by Mr. Clovis.

"If I am not giving you too much trouble, I should
like to have a word with you before we leave this house,"
said he, with something that sounded like the snort of an
angry bull.

"Oh, certainly," said Gillian.

She was rather sorry that her step-father was annoyed ;
but, whatever her failings, she was never in the least afraid
of any one's wrath.

" What have I done ? " she asked. "Are you going to
scold me ? You never did that when I was a little girl.
Mammy always said that you spoilt me. Will you not

come into the dining-room? We cannot talk comfortably here."

Mr. Clovis followed her into the dining-room, and Gillian pushed an armchair and a footstool up to the fire for him. Gillian had always looked after her step-father's creature comforts. She instinctively liked to make people comfortable. Mr. Clovis refused the armchair. It was a little absurd of him, but he knew of old that "Madam Gill" could, as he expressed it, come round him, and he did not wish to be beguiled into amiability. He stood on the hearth-rug and glowered at Gillian, who suppressed an inclination to laugh.

"Dear me! What is the matter?" she asked.

"I ain't responsible for you now, Gillian," said her step-father. "If your own conscience don't teach you what is the matter, I don't know who is to. All I say is that I hope you will be ashamed some day."

"I will not wait for some day. I will be sorry now, if I have offended you," said Gillian, who had not the least desire to quarrel with Mr. Clovis.

"Me? It wouldn't so much matter how you behaved to me. I ain't complaining on my own account, nor haven't any cause to. It is your behaviour to your mother that——"

"Oh, it is that, is it?" interrupted Gillian. Her tone changed and she drew herself up. "My conduct appears extraordinary and indefensible," she said. "I do not any longer go near my mother. I do not press her to stay with me. That is perfectly true. I admit it; and I do not choose to offer any excuses. You have known me since I was twelve years old, Mr. Clovis. I do not think that I was a bad-tempered or sullen girl. I leave you to draw what conclusion you like."

Now this was not a soft answer, and yet it stemmed the torrent of the soap-boiler's indignation and made him reflect.

He was not in the least a stupid man, and he saw the force of Gillian's allusion to her childhood and girlhood. It was true that he had often remarked admiringly that "Miss Gill" had an uncommon lot of good sense. Gill had never been jealou or irritable. Most girls would have been at least a little sore at seeing themselves superseded, but she had made the best of things and fallen into place without a sigh. She had always been ready to yield in small matters, for the sake of peace. She had never shown a trace of that most common feminine propensity for making mountains out of mole-hills.

Mr. Clovis sighed heavily and shook his head.

" What is the use of setting me conundrums to guess ? " said he ; " I don't understand it. I am sick and tired of a business I can't make head or tail of ! that's what I am ! But there is one thing I do see plain enough, and that is that we ain't welcome here. I have ordered a carriage to take us to the Metropole this afternoon, for my wife seems a bit better to-day, and it will be round in half an hour. Your mother seems to wish to say good-bye to you, but I won't have her worried and upset. For my part, I think if you cannot behave as a daughter should you had best keep away."

" I quite agree with you," said Gillian gravely.

She was heartily sorry to hurt Mr. Clovis, but she felt that the break between herself and her mother was final. She had said that which could never be unsaid. She could scarcely even understand how it was that Mrs. Clovis could desire to patch up a semblance of peace.

" Then I will take my leave of you now, if you please," said her step-father, fuming again at her cold reply. " I am sorry we have troubled you ; but, to speak my mind plainly for once, Gillian, I must say that—— " But she held up her hand to stop him.

" No, no, Mr. Cloves," she said. " You have only heard

one side of this case, and you will never hear the other. You are not in a position to deliver judgment."

She spoke with some warmth, and possibly the nickname that she had always called him by, when she lived under his roof, recalled memories that softened him. He was silent for a minute, and stared at her with an odd mixture of shrewdness and kindliness. No one with the least knowledge of character could look at this woman's face and imagine her to be cold-hearted.

"Madam Gill," he said at last, "I am a great many years older than you, and as you have just been sayin', you were partly under my charge when you were a girl. I have often and often thought as I did wrong when I let you go and live all alone in London, because you stuck to Cardew. I was riled at the way in which you set aside our authority; but I own now that there is an authority higher than ours that makes it natural for a woman to leave father and mother—let alone step-father—for the sake of the man she is promised to. Now I say I was wrong, and I don't want to wrong you twice. That's why I will try to believe that your behaviour ain't quite so bad as it seems, though, mind you, it is hard to swallow."

"I think that that is very good of you—but you are good," said Gillian. For a moment the tears stood in her eyes. She would have shaken hands with him, but seeing that he was unwilling, she desisted.

"It is all beyond me; but anyhow I am very fond of my wife, and I don't believe she is in any way to blame— and you know, choose what the reason is, you are not an affectionate daughter to her; and so——"

"Oh, I understand," said Gillian half laughing. "I understand quite well why you can't shake hands, for I am very fond of some one too! That is where it is! You and I are dreadfully human, Mr. Clovis!"

So Mr. and Mrs. Clovis departed, and Gillian did not say

good-bye to her mother; but neither did she tell her
husband of her interview with her step-father. The
displeasure of "Mr. Cloves," was unavoidable, but it had
given her some pain, and she possessed a sturdy pride that
made her unwilling to fuss over small bruises. Jack
would have been indignant on her behalf had she told him,
and she wished to save him from minor troubles. Gillian's
comradeship would always carry with it practical use; if
Jack insisted on making for the stars she, at least, would
not add to the number of stones in his path. He had also
insisted on her companionship, and therein lay cause for
content.

And here I feel as if the story should be left.

The man and woman whose twisted lives I have tried to
follow must soon be lost again in the crowd. That great
crowd that is always moving on to God knows what
mysterious goal. That great crowd that is made of individual characters, whose limitations are set by the same
hand that set the boundaries of the salt waves, and that
yet seems at times to have one common life beating
through it.

I am loth to lose sight of Jack and Gillian, but they are
entering on a new phase, and the witches' apples are dropping from her hands. There is perhaps no such thing as
an end to any life, but my pen shall soon write "finis."

Let them go, having saved each other? Ay, but by
reason of that saving power, that I believe was before all
the worlds began, before men shaped creeds, or women
cried, "Nay, but greater than creed is love."

Yet, because some who have read this story may like
to know what happened next, I must own that Gillian has
not yet forgiven her mother. Indeed, of late years Mrs.
Clovis has begun to feel herself the injured person. It is,
as she plaintively remarks, so extraordinary that she should
have a daughter so unlike herself. "Dearest Gillian was

never demonstrative, but nowadays one would imagine that she had no heart at all." This, however, is only of late years, for months after she left her daughter's house the impression made by Gillian's indignation, and by that interview with Jack—which she never likes to remember —lasted, even painfully. Moreover, Mr. Strode gave her no peace on the subject of full confession; and the fear of death added point to his adjurations. Moved, or rather driven by him, she did at last write a very lengthy statement of her "mistake," which she gave to her husband, begging him to read it when she was not in the room.

Mr. Clovis took the paper from her reluctantly. "I don't believe that you ever did anything very bad, my dear," he said. "But I can see that you are making yourself miserable, and that the man in petticoats has been bullying you. Do you really *want* me to read this?"

"No—o, George. But I feel I—I ought to," she said with white lips.

Mr. Clovis put the closely written document in the fire, and she gave a little cry of surprise—perhaps of relief.

"Very well. Now you have done as you ought," he said. "And whatever was in it has gone up the chimney. But mind, Eva, there is one thing I don't like, and that is priests about."

"Dear George, there was never anybody so good as you are!" she cried gratefully. "And I am sure that I never wish to see Mr. Strode again, for the weight is off my mind now."

"Then just you set yourself to getting well," he rejoined with cheerful tenderness; and from that moment, as he always averred, she did begin to recover.

The third doctor was right. Mrs. Clovis bids fair to live to a ripe old age, and she is still adored by her husband and son. The church at Churton Regis owes much to her munificence. It has never again been allowed to fall into the neglected condition from which that unpopular vicar, Mr. Strode, first rescued it.

Lady Hammerton asserts that her godson was worth a baker's dozen of his successor; but Lady Hammerton is in a minority.

"Henry Strode has all the family failings," she says. "He always reminds me of my dear old friend, Sir Edward. He is as obstinate as my white pony, and he was born with blinkers on. He can only see one view of a case— but at least he never squints at the loaves and fishes. He is a man—not to say a gentleman—and there are not too many of that sort left in the Church."

But Lady Hammerton is getting to the stage when the light begins to fail, and her brave old eyes to see the world in shadow.

Cyril has shut up Highfields and has gone abroad. He is an unexpectedly jealous husband, but no one knows whether Nina repents of her bargain.

Enid and Geoffrey Haubert moved successfully into bigger rooms, and they are happier than most people. Mr. Strode goes to see them sometimes, but he will not go too often. That peaceful home atmosphere disturbs him, for he holds himself pledged to a life in which there is no room for a woman. His conclusions may be just, or they may be mistaken. Even the wisest among us are bound to make so many blunders, that one learns to suspect it is not so much what a man does, as why he does it, which matters in the long run. Mr. Strode does what he thinks right, even though it be to his own disadvantage; and his single-mindedness tells a good deal more than he guesses. It is a comforting fact that, though the dust raised by the clash of conflicting opinions is somewhat perplexing, we are pretty much of one mind as to ethical qualities. The wrong-headedness of my brother may be extremely apparent to me, and the error of my

26

opinions may shock him at every turn, but we both of us lift our hats to integrity and self-devotion, whenever we are obliged to recognise them.

One painful memory Mr. Strode will carry with him always ; but, because he remembers, many a black sheep has found him unexpectedly helpful, and curiously slow to judge. Had he never met Jack Cardew in prison, he would never have been haunted by a bitter recollection— and he would have been a harder man. So inextricably woven are the threads that bind us to each other, so unfathomable and far-reaching is the answer to Cain's question.

Even as I write these last words, I know that the thousands of stories that are never told, that no man puts into words, are being lived out all around me, in the streets and squares and alleys of this great London. Binding us each to each is an invisible bond—for an injury done to the weakest is done to us all, as our deepest instinct tells us— and yet between us is that invisible wall that cannot be passed ; for no one knows the whole of his brother's or his sister's life. It is a mighty paradox, and hard to understand ; but the children and the simple solve the problems that the learned state. The man and the woman and the child have wandered far, since Eve, with Eden behind her, and her first-born in her arms, cried, "I have gotten a man from the Lord" ; yet, I think that when they find their way, they will still find it together.

THE END.

Printed by Hazell, Watson, & Viney, Ld., London and Aylesbury.